SONG OF LYRAN

Song of Lyran

KRISTI CASEY

Truly Kristi

SONG OF LYRAN may be purchased for educational, business, reading group, or sales promotional use. Kristi Casey is available for select readings and speaking engagements. Address inquiries and requests to kristi@kristicasey.com or Truly Kristi, c/o PO Box 746, Sautee Nacoochee, GA 30571.

To learn more about Kristi Casey, visit the author's website at www.kristicasey.com or follow her on social @trulykristi.

Original cover art by Lex Sanders
Cover concept by Jenny Schisler Hinely
Design by Alix Po

First Printing, 2022

CONTENTS

Part Two

Part Three

Epilogue

To Lex, my rainbow Stxrlight child. May you always find the light, no matter how dark things get around you. I hope it won't be long before you appreciate how brightly you shine. You will always be the best part of me.

Part One

~ 1 ~

HONEY

Nights test Honey's endurance. If she doesn't time going to bed right, her husband Chad keeps her up with choking and snorting sounds. She elbows him. He snores louder.

No use in staying here, being mad at not being able to sleep, she thinks. *Or at him for not being able to control himself.*

With a heavy sigh, she pulls herself up and out of bed. She moves easily through the dark now. When she first lost her sight, she often stubbed her toe or ran into the door jam. But now, she moves easily through the darkness.

Without thinking, she flips on the bathroom light. She laughs. It's been seven years since the veil drew itself over her vision. She forgets she's blind sometimes. A part of her still expects to one day turn on the light and see it. Even though that is impossible.

Seven years blind—just a fraction of my life. One day I'll realize darkness has claimed half of it. Then it will own three-quarters. If I live long enough, the part of my life spent in light will shrink to nothing. The girls will have to remind me that a world without darkness exists.

Honey tastes salt in her mouth and realizes she is crying. She remembers a story about widows in Africa. They wash their faces with tears.

She imagines her face encased in salt.

Would it crack open in the heat of the day?

She washes her face and imagines it cracking open like an egg.

If I had a chance to be reborn, who would I become?

She reaches for the towel, but the bar comes loose in her hand. She stumbles, cracking her head against the wall.

Shoot!

Pain blossoms into a hungry flower. It takes root in her forehead and digs its claws into her jaw.

She straightens up and freezes. Her mouth works in disbelief.

Am I . . . seeing?

From time to time, she sees silhouettes or patterns of light. But this isn't that.

This is different.

Honey leans closer to the mirror. Something like a mist passes between her and it. She's not imagining it.

Something is happening. Is that really my face?

Her breath catches in her throat. Her rational mind knows she will never regain her sight.

Maybe she's dreaming?

But this feels real.

The last time she saw her eyes, milky growths had nearly eclipsed her irises. But she is looking in the mirror now and she sees the green-gold eyes of her unblemished youth.

My eyes!

These are the eyes that first beheld her husband Chad. They welcomed Emily to this world and wept at her parents' graveside.

She wants to run into her children's rooms and look at them. Drink them in. She's never seen Amy's face. She lost her vision when Emily was a toddler. The hunger to know what they look like now is intense.

But Honey fears if she looks away from the mirror, she'll lose this small window of sight. And after such a long time in darkness, she does not want to stop seeing, even though her vision isn't clear. Mist is swirling between her and her image in the glass.

What is it?

It almost feels alive. It wraps around her, sharpening and then blurring her vision. She blinks and becomes caught in her own gaze.

Now Honey cannot look away. Her arms are frozen to the edges of the sink. She cannot move.

As she focuses on her eyes, the rest of her face flickers. Like a slideshow, the shape and color morphs into different people. But her eyes do not shift at all.

There are hundreds of faces, moving so fast Honey can barely see them. Then they begin to repeat. Some linger longer than the others. Some of them don't even look human. She sees a warrior with a lion's head, a girl with no mouth, a broad flame-haired woman, a nun . . . they are so different from one another.

But they all have my eyes.

Honey's green-gold eyes.

~ 2 ~

SEKHMET

She gives the man one warning. He deserves no more than that. When the guard prods Sekhmet to move a second time, she rips his arm from its socket. It makes a soft popping sound as it pulls free.

Heads turn to watch the man scream. Sekhmet notes she is not the only Lyran in captivity. She saw many lion-Aspect Lyran warriors among the Brotherhood of the Snake's slave cargo. Other Lyran soul families from the Many Worlds, are here, too. She knows the Sirians by their feathered wings and the Pleiadeans by their ebony skins and horns. They stand out like angels next to the human Essene and Christos Templar captives.

Our allies no longer look like children of the garden, she thinks mournfully. *They are starved and scared. Where were they taken?*

The Brotherhood ambushed her off the shore of Lemuria, during the evacuation. She wonders if an island can have a shore if it's sunk.

At least we destroyed their Atlantis base. Now neither of us have a proper earthly home.

She realizes she's still holding the guard's arm in her grip. It reminds her of a turkey leg. Her stomach growls. Saliva fills her mouth.

How long has it been since I've eaten?

She can't remember. She lifts the man's arm to her mouth.

Food is food, isn't it?

The smell of it assaults her. She can't bring herself to bite down. She drops the limb and turns away. She will not indulge her appetite in front of her captors.

Besides, to feast on such cowardly flesh . . .

She shudders.

I will not become a monster. I will remember who I am. I am Sekhmet: first of her line, Aspect of the One, lion-hearted Lyran warrior, lover of the Source, and defender of its light.

She turns her face toward the sea. The waves smash themselves against the rocks without losing hope or strength. The darkness of the cliffs makes the blue of the water shine brighter than the sky.

How long would it take to swim back to my people?

It doesn't matter. Swimming is not one of her talents.

I wish I had wings, like Mikha'el.

Something warm licks her foot. The guard, it seems, was full of blood. Now her patch of ground is thick with it. She steps closer to the ship.

Rough voices herald the approach of new guards.

Oh, good, reinforcements.

The guards yell at her.

She focuses instead on a point beyond the horizon. If she closes her eyes, she can feel the Source vibrating, connecting her to her scattered people. She wants to go home, reunite with the others and become One. But it's not time.

Not yet. I don't have the Answer yet. I have just begun to fight.

A sharp sting shakes her shoulders. Now Sekhmet is on the ground, twitching like a fish.

Damn them.

She forgot about the guards' coiled machines, gifts of the Brotherhood.

What cowards are they who make these children do their dirty work?

The pain is intense, and she cannot control her limbs.

Try this again. You will not catch me with a turned back. I will rip your faces off.

The tips of the guards' boots come into view. She bares her fangs and extends her claws, but the Brotherhood's lackeys stay out of reach.

When I finally catch you, she thinks wildly, *I'll kill you. Kill you all.*

~ 3 ~

FILOMÉLA

The tips of Filoméla's fingers burn. As does the area between her palm and thumb. She's worked on making this tapestry every day for months. Every joint and patch of skin employed in working the shuttle and loom aches. Her shoulders are so tight, they might never relax. But this pain is nothing compared to the shame she feels when she looks at her body.

Just a few more passes. Then you can rest.

Filoméla pulls the thread across the weave three more times, presses the pedals down, and pulls the shuttle tight to bind it. She sighs with relief.

Done.

She leans back to admire the tapestry. It bears no resemblance to the artistic work her teachers trained her to create. Its message is blunt, stark, and plain. The images bruise her eyes.

Art is child's play, and I am a woman now, she thinks bitterly. *Besides, truth is more important than beauty.*

The weave is tight and strong. Every strand of thread declares her pain. She runs her finger across the violent images, admiring the colors.

Purple, for Tereus's abuse of royalty. White, for the pure light he darkened. Red, for her virgin blood spilled. Yellow, for his cowardice, mutilating her to keep her silent.

No one could see this and not weep.

An icy finger of dread creeps up her spine.

How will I fill my days now that I've finished?

Her hand flits to her swollen belly. She shudders.

The monster inside her is quickening. It kicks. She pulls her hand away, repulsed.

She draws a blade. For a moment, she considers plunging it into the monster. But she does not want to die with it. She wants to live and claim her revenge.

I can kill the monster after it's born, she consoles herself.

She uses the knife to cut her work free of the loom.

"Filoméla?"

It is the servant boy, her only friend. Barely out of childhood, he is skinny as a spider. Like most of the slaves in this foreign land, his hair is flame-red. His eyes are pale as moonstones and flecked with amber. He doesn't wait for an answer before coming in.

Why would he?

Her fingers touch the network of scars on her throat. They are a souvenir from the night her sister's husband, her tormentor, King Tereus ripped out her tongue. She lives in silence now.

The boy smiles shyly as he places her breakfast on the table. He gathers her dinner dishes, chastising her for eating so little.

She raps on the loom to get his attention and holds up the tapestry. It is the size of a merchant's prayer rug.

Easy to conceal.

She looks at the boy and shakes it at him.

His smile lights up his whole face. "You're done?"

She nods.

He limps over and tucks it under his shirt. "I'll get it to your sister, Queen Prōknē, I promise." He leaves her to her thoughts.

Filoméla rises from the loom to stretch and gazes out the window at the wild wood beneath her. She watches the servant boy hobble through the woods towards the clearing, where she imagines he'll find a road to the castle.

How long will it take him?

Her heart skips. Her breath is shallow. Something panicky claws its way through her chest. The work drove her for so long, she worked on it so consistently, she feels unmoored without it.

How will I fill these miserable days?

Memories wash over her. She remembers when Prōknē wed Tereus. Filoméla cried for weeks. Her father's house was so empty without Prōknē's laughter and mischief.

How happy she was to see Tereus visit.

"Your sister is so lonely without you," he said. "Please join us as our guest to bring joy to my sweet queen."

How Filoméla's heart leapt at the thought of seeing her sister again. And how could her father deny his request? Who wouldn't want to make Prōknē happy?

We were fools to trust him. Did his beauty blind us to his ugly nature?

King Tereus marriage to her sister marriage brought a long-desired peace to their twin kingdoms. But Prōknē married for more than duty. She loved him, with his startling violet eyes and dark, black hair. Tereus was so young, handsome, and charming, Prōknē felt blessed by the gods.

He spoke well, too. When Tereus came for Filoméla, he swore to protect her. He promised her father that he would keep her safe on the long journey back to his kingdom in Thrace.

"Allow me to escort your youngest and no harm shall befall her," Tereus said. "I swear to you, on my life, she'll be reunited with her sister as healthy as she stands before you now."

Instead of reunion, all I found was ruin. Tereus lies about everything. I wonder if he told Prōknē I'm dead?

The monster kicks again, reminding Filoméla of how deep Tereus's corruption wounds her still. Since she can no longer scream, Filoméla opens her mouth and lets a ghost of a howl spool out of her like hot, venomous, vapor. In her mind, it fills the room, setting it ablaze.

Would that fire be purifying or poisoning?

She imagines poisoning *him.*

No, that's too good a death. Too quick.

The fates, she hopes, have something much worse in store for King Tereus.

What a child I was not to see . . .

Her cheeks burn thinking of how easily the snake had fooled her and her father. Her sister, too.

Does Prōknē know that she's married to a monster? Will she weep and tear her hair when she finds out?

Filoméla remembers when she used to weep. That river dried up months ago.

A beast, deep in the woods, howls in pain. Filoméla's soul answers it.

I know how you feel. I hope one day we may both be free.

She wanders to the table and takes a bite of bread. She doesn't need much to stay alive. The monster, though . . . the monster is ravenous. It always needs feeding. She resists it as much as she can. She washes the dry bread down with wine. Wine is good. She can't taste it, but she enjoys its numbing effect.

She opens the door and walks through the halls, avoiding the servants' eyes.

I'm sure they are glad that I can't cry and scream anymore. Not that it ever moved them to help me.

She hates them as much as Tereus.

None of them ever tried to stop him from hurting me. Did it please them to see a noble person laid low? Did they enjoy the way he treated me like his property?

Did they think I enjoyed it? Did it make them feel better about themselves?

Or were they too afraid to stand up to him?

All of them are worthless. Except for the boy.

The servant boy tried to help her once. He heard her screaming and tried to pull the King away. But Tereus hurled the boy against the wall and shattered his leg. He was young enough that it knit up well. But he'll always limp.

She pictures him delivering her message. She imagines her sister unspooling the tapestry and seeing its truth. She hopes her work is clear enough to communicate her pain and spur action.

For the first time in months, Filoméla smiles.

Prōknē . . . avenge me.

~ 4 ~

FORACH

The child clings to her legs. Forach laughs, pries Aoife's fingers loose, and pats the child's bottom. "Go play. Mind you don't drown while I do the washing."

The children leap like trout among the rocky stream of the Sionna River. Forach watches Aoife run along the bank to join them.

Oh, to be that light and free again.

She places her basket down. As she does, a long lock of bright, shining hair tumbles out of its braid and leaps into the water. She straightens up to tuck it back, thinking nothing of how her back has arched. Until she notices the young boys have stopped their splashing to gape at her full figure.

Forach warns them, "Let your head get turned by every pretty girl and one day, someone will cut it clear off."

All men ever want is beauty. But what happens to the beauty herself? Misery and suffering under the burden of their attention.

She should know. If she looked as common as clover, would Prince Conn had fancied her?

No. My beauty cost our tribe so much blood. And the price the prince paid for his lust was death. Was any of that worth it?

Conn's father, the High King Cormac mac Airt, would not say so. He lost an eye defending his rapacious son when Forach's people came to free her.

Now none of us Déisi can live in Tara.

It's small comfort that the High King's deformity now keeps him from sitting on the throne there.

We are the true exiles. He's still the High King.

She shakes water off the dress, and her misery with it.

What's past is behind me. And before me is a promise. Why curse my fate when it brought me Aoife?

Forach beckons to the child. She sweeps the giggling babe into an embrace and showers her with kisses.

"You are a blessing to the cursed," Forach laughs into Aoife's neck. She inhales her daughter's scent. It is fresh like the breeze and as deep as the dark earth beneath their feet.

Forach sighs happily.

It is a kind of magic to be bound to a child.

A horn sounds, calling the women and children back to camp.

Forach curses.

She's barely started, and she has a half-a-day's work. But you can't keep the council waiting. She lifts Aoife to one hip and the basket to the other. She follows behind the dripping, joking boys as they all make their way to the gathering place.

At the center of a ring of elders, under the Chieftain Tree, stands young Ethniu. Barely past her girlhood and not yet a woman, the strange child is draped in pelts, like a thing of the forest. Her strange dark hair and glittering purple eyes unsettle Forach.

The others assume that Ethniu possesses magic. But Forach suspects she is more than a *ban-cumachtach.* She wouldn't be surprised if Ethniu is part sidhe, or a full-blood child of the fairy folk. Strange and dark as a nut, she certainly doesn't look like one of them. Forach's people have hair like flames and skin so light it glows. That sets them apart from the other tribes in this pale valley.

There is nothing golden about Ethniu. But she is fiery.

Forach had the unpleasant opportunity to cross her once or twice. She does not wish for it again.

You can't cut across Ethnui's path without bleeding a little.

The king steps forward. Forach's breath catches.

Why does Da look so old? He didn't look like that this morning.

A wild panic seizes at her heart. She wants to run to her father, ask him what is wrong. But that was why the horn had sounded, had it not? She'd know soon enough. Along with the rest of the Déisi.

Ethniu lends the old king her arm and nods to someone over her shoulder.

The brawny warriors of the king's guard carry in a sack of meat. They lay it on the cleared ground by the king's foot. At Ethnui's signal, the men pull back the sackcloth.

A hundred mouths moan. Two hundred eyes begin to weep.

This is no sack of meat.

It is a butchered man.

No. Not just a man.

Forach's heart shatters.

Cian.

It is the king's son, her brother Cian.

Oh Cian!

Not that she can tell by his face. Someone has flayed most of his features away.

It is the shock of flaming hair that still flies from the skull.

It is the old scar on his forearm from when her pony kicked him into the river.

It is the one pale eye flecked with gold sparks that the High King's men left in his head.

Oh Cian! What did you do?

The air is thick with sorrow.

It takes Forach a minute to realize that the howling sound on the wind is coming from her own throat.

She is not alone.

A hundred hearts cry together. They fill the sky over the Déisi campsite.

Forach surrenders to the keening. She is nothing but an open wound and wanting. Her tears flow like the Sionna River over the body of her brother. They join the tears of her people and turn the ground beneath them to mud.

The sea air wails with them. Its salt will scour their hearts and wash him clean.

~ 5 ~

JUANA

"Do you think you will stay? I heard you were with the Carmelitas, but only for a brief time."

Sor Juana turns towards the Jerónima nun assigned to welcome her. "Sor Tamzin, I expect I shall be very happy here."

She likes the way Tamzin's face glows. Juana knew many luminaries in her old life as a lady in waiting. But no one shone like this at court. Sor Tamzin doesn't need rouge to look in bloom. The love of God lights her from within. Juana wants that illumination, too.

"Plus," Juana says with a smile, "the Carmelitas didn't have a particularly good library. I crave time alone to study, reflect, and learn. I could live two lifetimes and not work my way through all the books you have in this convent. "

"And you brought so many of your own!" Tamzin marvels at the crates of books littering the floor of Juana's cramped cell. "You'll have to store some of them in our locutorio. You know, they say San Jerónimo always enjoyed the company of learned women. You must be in the right place." She blushes and lowers her eyes. "I wish I was one of them."

"It's never too late to learn," Juana tells her.

"If God wills it. But I don't think I received the talent or inclination." Tamzin beams, and the shadows vanish from her brow.

"Welcome to San Jerónimo y Santa Paula, Sor Juana. I hope you will be incredibly happy here." She leaves Juana in solitude.

Juana surveys the spartan room.

It is not opulent, but it holds more promise than any chamber I had at court.

She unlaces her outer and inner bracings, steps out of her corset, and takes a deep breath.

This is the first day of my free life. I am free from society.

An old Nahuatl word, *tlazohtlalōcā*, springs to her mind. It is hard to translate into Spanish. The closest Juana can come is, '*the love with which one is loved.*' She feels that love now, and she is blessed to know it.

Nothing stretches before her but days without distractions. She is finally free to commit herself to study and purifying work.

No one will pressure me to wed. No one will force me to bear children. This is a heaven on Earth.

Feelings of love and gratitude overwhelm her.

Her arms outstretched and body unencumbered, Juana offers herself to God.

I promise to develop what is divine in me to become nearer to thee, to bathe in your divine light, Great One.

She stands there for a moment, imagining light flowing in, out, and around her. Then, she dons the heavy, plain habit of itchy wool that Tamzin left on her bed. Even in that rough dress, Juana feels whole, wrapped in protective love.

She tries on her chosen name. "Sor Juana." The edges of her mouth lift. She adores the meaning of Juana, '*God is gracious.*' It is her birth name. She didn't want to choose a different one.

I am the same person, merely a different aspect of myself here than I have been allowed to be in the outside world.

She also likes how the name Juana ties her to her favorite saint, Juan el Bautista.

Like him, she often feels as if she is crying out into the wilderness. She dips quill into ink and writes her convent name on the top of the page. The letters shimmer.

God is gracious, indeed.

~ 6 ~

HONEY

It's a relief to be out of the house. In its cloistered space, last night's dream itches at Honey like a wool sweater. It's good to feel the ground beneath her feet and the sun on her cheeks.

Thank God. Something solid. Something real. Not like that creepy dream last night.

Honey shivers and grips Chad's arm tighter. The wind tugs at her hair. She imagines it blowing away all the green-eyed strangers and mist from the mirror.

Amy and Emily laugh as they run ahead of their parents. "Don't get too far ahead!" Honey warns.

Chad's hand grips her elbow, radiating strength. He guides her around the obstacles on this rare family outing.

She squeezes his hand and smiles. "Why don't we hike as a family more often? The girls love it. I do, too."

Chad's laugh sounds nervous.

"Why is that a silly question? We used to hike all the time!"

She feels the mood shift between them like a living thing.

"Honey," Chad begins. "No one went anywhere during the pandemic. That took years from us. And besides, we used to hike a lot when you could *see*."

"Ah, well, I'm not an invalid," she protests. "My feet work fine. We've gone, what, two miles already? I'm not winded."

As if to humble her, a root entangles her foot, and she stumbles, falling into Chad.

She recovers, but nature has proved her husband's point. He leaps at the proof. "See? This is dangerous. We shouldn't have come."

Honey's cheeks burn with the possibility that he is right. Her anger flares at her own dreaming. "I'm not a child. It's okay if I fall and scrape a knee. I won't break like an egg."

She instantly regrets taking out her frustration on him. "I'm sorry."

He's good to me. I'm lucky he stayed after I lost my sight. He's not trying to hold me back. He even let me have a second child.

Of course, she had to wear him down first.

What really chafes her is what he doesn't have the courage to say aloud. The fear that lurks under everything he does. It rears up whenever she wants to try something new or go back to things she loved doing when she could see.

It is risky, he'll say, or dangerous. But she knows what he's really saying is: *You have enough. Why ask for more? Why can't you stop fighting the reality of your situation? Just surrender already.*

Because I can't, she thinks. *Surrender means death.*

Little feet run towards them. She can tell by the pattern of them, that it is Amy, her youngest, the lightest, and most carefree. Emily, the cautious one, follows close behind.

"We found it! We found it!" Amy cries.

Emily clarifies, "The waterfall. It's close to here."

"Well, lead me to it!" Honey frees herself of Chad's guiding hands and gives an arm to each of her girls.

Before he can stop them, they begin to run.

Chad yells at their backs, but he cannot reach them now. "Slow down. Your mother can't run!"

"Watch me!" Honey flings back.

Oh, sweet freedom!

She forgot how fast she can run. She used to be one of the fastest girls in school. She drops all caution and pumps her legs until the girls must keep up with *her.*

Honey's ears fill with the sound of whipping wind and laughter. Feet pound dirt, leap roots, and crush dry leaves. She trusts her instincts to guide her.

This is what I want. What I've always wanted. This feeling. Who needs eyes when the body has so many other precious treasures to give?

She feels an overwhelming joy spread like wings over her and the girls. She imagines this love of life is what's keeping them from falling. For a moment, Honey forgets her fear of everything she can't see. She no longer cares about what waits for her in the darkness, wanting to pull her down and humble her.

Amy tugs her sharply to the right. Honey stumbles. For a second, she fears going down, but Emily helps her stay up and make the turn. They emerge from the well-worn forest path. Feet slap weather-beaten wood instead of dirt.

Oh, the rushing!

The sound of the waterfall is deafening, like a lion's roar.

"Oh, girls! We made it!" She kisses their heads in gratitude, inhaling their scent: sweat mixed with strawberries.

Emily now, at her sleeve, "Isn't it beautiful, Mommy?"

She doesn't need to see to know. She feels the truth of every curve and edge of it with her soul.

"Yes. Yes, oh, yes, it is!"

~ 7 ~

SEKHMET

The lead collar bites into her neck, but Sekhmet doesn't give her captors the pleasure of seeing that it pains her. She strides toward the slave ship unbowed, unbroken.

The Brotherhood of the Snake's lackeys give her a wide berth. They feel the danger radiating off her. But it's her leonine form that they fear. It is too alien for them. Anything different is bad. That's what the Brotherhood of the Snake teaches them.

Cowards in every way. She spits at the lackeys. It scatters them like acid. *If you knew the true faces of your fathers, you'd shit yourselves.*

She knows what they don't: the Brotherhood hide behind human faces, but their forms are monstrous. But these stupid humans will not see. They will not open their minds to know the truth. They are content to live in dark ignorance and condemn what they don't understand.

Dummies.

A chain connects the collar at her neck to manacles at her wrists and feet. From her ankles, other chains bind her—to the Essene in front and the Christos Templar behind. The guards are dumb, but smart enough to keep the Lyrans separated.

Division is what they do. But we will unite . . . and then . . .

The guards prod, and her line shuffles up the gangplank like cattle. Sekhmet burrows inside, into a place of calm within herself, and tests the metal.

She sighs. *It's nonconductive.*

She's seen no snakes, but their fingerprints are all over this slave transport. They must know her talent. She can't find anything near her that's magnetic or conductive. Her green-gold eyes probe the body of the ship. Nothing of use there, either.

I'll bet it's made of another dead metal. Bastards.

Sekhmet knows she's on her own, but it still surprises her that there have been no rescue attempts.

Is it possible no one knows where I am?

Pity licks at her heart. She smothers it.

I'm not alone. We are all Aspects of the One. And we will triumph.

A whip zings past her cheek. She flinches. The next lash bites into the Essene's bare shoulder. Blood blooms and spills across his bare back.

I'm sorry. Are we moving too slow?

She glares at the guard, trying to provoke him. He lashes out at her. She catches his knotted whip in her teeth, ignoring the sting on her tongue, and yanks. The guard hurtles forward. She lets go of the whip and buries her fangs into his neck. She brings up the manacles to pin him there and gnashes down harder.

For a moment, there is silence. Then, horrified shouts and sandaled feet pound toward her. She shakes her head and ratchets her jaw tighter, and tighter still, until her teeth meet.

With a satisfying crunch, she severs the neck bones and last piece of gristle in the guard's neck. The man's head bounces off her stomach and knees, landing on her foot. She kicks it out of her way and roars, daring them to come closer.

~ 8 ~

FILOMÉLA

The moon is in a provocative mood. It is fat and low, spreading a veil of dusky rose light that menaces the darkness, driving it back.

In Thebes, this is a holy night. Or, if you're not initiated into the mysteries of Dyonysos, a 'cursed night.' The male servants went home hours ago to barricade themselves in their homes. They have barred their windows to keep out Semele's light for fear of going mad if they gaze too long upon the moon goddess.

Fools. You can't keep wickedness out any more than you can keep wickedness in.

The monster kicks. Filoméla feeds it more wine. For some reason, it won't sleep. Not content to rest in its mother-prison, the monster kicks again. She attempts to drown the monster by draining her goblet. Wine stains her cheeks and chin. It dribbles down the front of her nightdress. She shrugs.

No one's here to see.

It's been days since she's changed her clothes. She doesn't bother to clean herself, either.

My whole life is a stain. Why shouldn't my outer state reflect the one within?

She thinks about the village girls celebrating tonight. She imagines them dressing up, stripping down, and running wild through the woods. This is the one night they don't have to worry about any consequences for acting as they wish.

Should I dance naked in the moonlight, too? See if the gods will take me? It would be nice to feel ecstasy. Although, I'd settle for joy.

She pours herself another glass of wine.

Would the maenads let me join them? I'm not schooled in the mysteries.

Dyonysos Eleutherios is the great liberator. Yet the maenads, in their ecstasy, might end your life. Like everything else in this place, celebration mixes with terror. You never know where you'll be safe.

Oh, Thrace. How I hate you. Why is everything about you brutal and strange?

Filoméla gazes at the twisted landscape outside her window. In the woods, the tree canopy is weak, and the trees themselves are stunted.

Figs, olives, and grapevines—things born to be low and twisted—that's all that grows well.

They say the twice-born Dyonysos is from here. His cults are certainly stronger in Thrace than her homeland. Filoméla wonders if it's true that maenads offer him blood sacrifices. She wonders if she could get them to rid her of the monster in her belly.

Music is playing. The pipes and drums disengage from the melody. They reel into something darker, more primal. Laughter, shouting, and screaming follows.

Filoméla's skin prickles. Whatever is happening in the wood sounds horrible.

It also sounds fun.

On this night, anything is possible.

She closes her eyes and pretends she is a maenad. She bursts into Tereus's bed-chamber and mutilates *him*. Only she doesn't cut off his tongue. No. She takes something far more precious.

She laughs and drains the wine from her cup.

Thank you for your wine, Dyonysos. It certainly eases suffering. And, oh, how I've suffered.

Filoméla chokes back a sob. She opens her throat to voice her anguish. But without a tongue, there is no ululation. The sound she makes is deep and wretched.

She remembers the wounded beast in the forest. It hasn't cried out today.

It must be dead. Lucky thing. Won't someone put me out of my misery?

She sits upright.

That's it!

She isn't brave enough to end her life, but if the maenads catch her, surely they'll kill her, won't they?

She leaps to her feet, knocking over her chair, and banging her knee against the table. She spills what's left of the wine, staining her bare feet as purple as her mouth. She waddles down the hall, lifting her long skirts so as not to trip. She wants to run, but she cannot with the monster taking up so much of her midsection. Finally, she throws back the latch, flings open the door, and lets in the night air.

Only the doorway isn't empty. A wild creature of the forest, with blue-black eyes and sticks for hair, stands there.

Filoméla is rooted to the spot. Terror deadens her limbs. She begins to tremble.

This is what she wanted but she no longer wants it. She cannot even call for help. If they take her and tear her to pieces, no one will ever know what happened.

A foolish girl meets a foolish end. That would serve you right.

The wild thing crosses the threshold.

Filoméla skitters back from the doorway. She doesn't want them in the house. But there are twenty or more women as wild and dirty as the first pouring in. They surround her.

She smells their animal musk, and above that, the sticky odor of spilled wine.

Please, Dyonysos, be merciful. Let this be over quickly.

~ 9 ~

FORACH

Forach wrings out the rag and watches trails of her brother's blood slide down the walls of the clay bowl. She dips the rag into a basin of fresh water to rinse it.

There is a rhythm to the washing. Although it pains her to see Cian's body this way, there is a healing power to the work that allows her to make peace with his passing.

Someone blows into the cave like a frigid wind. Dread prickles up and down the back of Forach's neck. She doesn't need to turn around to know who must be behind her.

Ethnui.

Forach doesn't stop working, merely says, "Say what you want to say and be done with it. I'm in no mood for more."

Ethnui's voice, deeper and raspier than any of the tribe's other girls, responds. "Maybe I'm admiring your work. Or I could be here to lend a hand."

Forach snorts. She picks up the bowl and shifts position, so she can see the girl. "What is it you be wanting, Ethnui?"

"To pay my respects."

The way Ethnui rasps, reminds Forach of a viper in tall grass. She lowers the rag and raises her eyes. "Why are you really here?"

Ethnui smiles, revealing a mouth of pointed teeth. "A truce."

Forach shivers at the sight. People whisper that Ethnui feeds on blood. Forach thinks the teeth are for show, meant to scare rather than use, but they still make her uneasy. “We’re not at war.”

“Aren’t we?” Ethnui raises her eyebrows and takes a rag off Forach’s pile. She leans across Cian’s torso to dip it in the water. She wipes blood and dirt from the caved-in part of Cian’s skull, the part Forach hasn’t had the courage to touch yet. Ethnui frowns. “This looks like war.”

Forach is grateful Ethnui is willing to clean Cian’s broken skull. She knows she’s not strong enough to face it.

They work in silence. Finally, the body is ready for the shroud.

Ethnui drops her rag in the bowl. “Shall I place the coins?”

“No, I can do it,” Forach says, fetching them. She lays a coin upon the eye on the right but hesitates over the other. There’s no lid on the left, not even an eye. Just a dark, wet gash running from jaw to hairline. Forach isn’t sure where to lay the ferryman’s piece.

A bony hand tightens around her wrist. Ethnui hisses, “You see what they do to us. Say the word, Forach, and we can take our revenge. Your father looks to you. He won’t act unless you say so.”

The shock of Ethnui’s touch and words shakes Forach out of her confusion. “Isn’t it enough to be in exile, to wander over the land with no home? You’d have us all killed, too? No. I’ll not be speaking for revenge. There’s nothing in that but more death. And I’ve had enough, haven’t you?”

Ethnui snatches the coin from Forach’s fingers and drops it into the gaping eyesocket in Cian’s skull. “You’re already as dead as your brother, you just don’t realize it yet. Only when you die for good, you’ll go it alone. And only the ravens will mourn the loss of you.”

~ 10 ~

JUANA

Juana lets the words well up and simmer inside her. It is a luxury to live in solitude and prayer. To have this blessed space to be alone with her thoughts.

She's taken a voluntary vow of silence. She's been observing the other sisters, thankful they do not expect her to engage with them. This slow entry to her new life is blissful as a warm bath. She takes pen and ink and paints her thoughts across the page.

Sisters vow poverty
yet bring slaves up from sugarcane fields.
Remnants of their plantation before-lives,
this luxury means they're only poor in spirit.
The original sin
was not that woman sought knowledge,
but that she's so easily discouraged
from seeking it now.
If only men were made truly
in God's image,
then they would let
women rule them,
rather than their impulses.

Juana sighs happily as she cleans the nib of her pen.

That's all that needs to come out tonight.

Thoughts are like weeds. You can pull out the bad ones three times a day and still have more work to do in the morning.

Best to let the pretty ones grow and find a use for them. There is always time to come back and tend to the deeper ones, help them grow to nurture the soul.

The bells ring, calling her to supper. She sits with Tamzin and her friends.

Juana feels someone's eyes on her. It is Madre Abadesa, the mother superior. She is not smiling. She never smiles. Juana wonders if she's exhausted by the job of ministering to their souls.

Heavy is the head that wears the crown!

That is the wrong thing to think. Now she imagines Madre Abadesa wearing a ludicrous golden crown. Before she can stop herself, Juana laughs at the absurd image.

"Oh my!" Tamzin exclaims.

Juana covers her mouth with her hands and reddens. Horrified that she's broken her vow of silence in such an undignified manner, she rises to leave.

A stern voice stops her. "Sor Juana."

Oh no. Madre Abadesa.

Juana drops a small curtsey to show respect.

Madre Abadesa turns. "Walk with me."

Juana follows her out of the communal dining hall.

"You know, there was another Sor Juana de la Cruz," Madre Abadesa says. "About a hundred years or so ago?" She glances at Juana.

Juana nods. The learned woman was another reason she took this holy name.

"She was one of the few women approved to preach in public. An extraordinary permission to extract from the Church."

Madre looks hard at Juana. "Is that one of your aspirations, too?"

Juana shakes her head. She hungers to learn. Not to teach.

"Good." The Madre walks away briskly.

Is that it?

Juana wants to laugh again. She resists the urge and examines her thoughts instead.

No, I don't want to stand in front of crowds and talk. I want to move people with my words.

She wants to write. Put down her thoughts and ink them into history.

When you speak, the wind carries your words away. Actions are remembered only for as long as the people who know you live. But write, and your ideas will find homes in the hearts of generations to come.

So many things are wrong with the way the world is, the way people treat each other. There is so much Juana cannot do because she does not have the power to change anything.

But one day, my words might inspire people to think and act differently.

That is why she writes: for the children who will heal the world and set things right.

Too bad neither she nor Leo will be alive to see that day. She smiles thinking of her dead friend, the countess. Leo hated the idea of Juana becoming a nun. But they both knew that Juana would have to marry eventually if she stayed in society. Juana wanted none of the burdens of marriage.

By marrying Jesus, the only children I'll have are my books. That's the life I want.

Leo could not argue with that reasoning. They both knew too many bright women who'd met their end on a bloody birthing bed. Or frittered away their talents at court. To her credit, Leo acknowledged Juana deserved more, and gave her the freedom to pursue it.

Juana remembers Leo kissing her forehead. She mourns the loss of that great woman, but she will never forget her. Her memory is a blessing. And it continues to inspire her.

I will leave my mark on the world, Leo. I shall do it with my thoughts and my pen.

~ 11 ~

HONEY

Honey climbs out of bed quietly, afraid to wake Chad. But she needn't bother. He blithely rumbles away, like a lawnmower. The girls always ask how she can sleep through that noise. They can hear him through the floor upstairs.

"I barely hear it anymore," she tells them.

It isn't a lie. If she's already asleep when he climbs into bed, then she can sleep through it. But if she tries to go to bed after him . . . or if she feels restless, like she does tonight . . .

She pads to the front door and hesitates.

What am I doing?

Before she lost her sight, she once found a bear nosing around their flower garden, looking for food. Sometimes, in winter, she thinks she hears wolves howling at the moon.

A little, lilting voice within her responds, *What treat is a middle-aged woman in her nightgown? You're hardly a snack. Too much fat and gristle on you. Go on, out with you.*

Honey chuckles and unbolts the door. She steps, barefoot, onto the wooden deck and edges closer to the woods. She can feel branches crowding the spaces around and above the porch.

She remembers there is a little square deck, a step down from the main porch flanked by two sets of short stairs. The one to the right goes down the path to the driveway. The one on the left leads to the woods.

She used to stand here and look at the moon when she could still see. She's long since stopped. But now she needs to know if she can still feel the moon, the way she can feel the sun on her skin. She knows tonight it's full. That feels like the best time to test what she can sense or not.

Honey shuffles to the edge of the porch and carefully steps down onto the wooden platform. She tilts her head back and raises her face to the sky.

No warmth.

But she feels something all the same.

A lightness?

Not as strong as the sun's embrace.

A caress?

Yes. That's more like it.

She smiles and leans into the feeling. A line of poetry comes to her.

Moonlight against my cheek, gentle as a lover . . .

A sigh escapes her lips.

She feels such joy, she wants to sing.

She remembers something a vocal teacher once told her about music. "Life squeezes you, and that's the sound that comes out."

Life has squeezed me.

She wonders what sounds will come out of her.

Honey discards the layers of her life. She wants to strip down to her essence.

She peels off the burden of adult-onset blindness.

She discards the husband snoring noisily inside.

She loosens her bonds to the two small girls sleeping above her.

She becomes a bird of the forest.

A nightingale.

Free and lovely. Full of song and power.

She spreads her wings and begins to sing.

There are no words at first, just melody.

When the words come, they flow from her like water.

They soar over the leaves of the trees and embrace the moon.

She feels connected to everything that is—a source within her that runs deep and clear.

Song after song, Honey pours more of herself into the music of her making.

Violent shouts from her family erupt from the house, urging her away from the moonlight.

Honey is reluctant. But eventually, she lets them drag her back to the dark, sleepy house.

~ 12 ~

SEKHMET

No one knows where the ship travels. But it doesn't matter. The misery of seasickness only lasts for the first week. Now the waves are a metronome, keeping time of captivity that is without end.

Sekhmet feels the wet boards beneath her, counting scratches she's made in the soft wood.

Twelve days.

The hold smells like shit and despair. On her left, the Essene makes soft, sobbing sounds. From time to time, the Christos Templar moans, reminding them all that he hasn't yet died of his wounds.

If I could reach you, I'd put you out of your misery.

But the chain that binds her to the wall only stretches so far.

The humans will die soon. Am I horrible for not taking the time to know them or smart for not bothering? Now there's nothing but my own misfortune to mourn.

She must focus on her mission.

Everything else is a distraction.

Besides, what good are alliances with people who wield no power?

Powerless.

Does that apply to her, too? She sits in her own filth, like them. Her neck is chained to the wall, bound from head to hands, hands to ankles. And her ankles connect her to the future corpses of others.

She snorts. Yes, she is weak, dirty, hungry, and bruised.

But powerless?

She will never, ever, relinquish her power.

No one gives you power. You're born with it.

A tender, little voice whispers, *You can lose it. You can give it away.*

Sekhmet bangs her head against the hard wall to knock the traitorous thought loose.

She stretches her legs and begins to massage the cramps out of them.

I haven't lost any of my power.

But thc doubt has shaken her.

She tosses her head. This isn't really her inner voice.

It's the snake of darkness sowing his seeds of doubt.

She tenses the muscles in her arms and legs, holding them firm for a few seconds before releasing them. She hates not being able to walk free. She longs to breathe clean air and see the sun.

But she refuses to weaken or die here.

She tenses her muscles again, focusing now on a different group. She may not be able to move freely, but she doesn't need to roam to keep in condition. She has no sparring partner. But no one can stop her from mentally running through battle scenarios.

They can't defeat her until she gives in or gives up.

And she doesn't intend to do either.

Eventually, they must land.

And when they do, she'll be ready.

~ 13 ~

FILOMÉLA

The stench of wild things fills the hallway. Forty eyes and twenty thundering hearts overwhelm Filoméla. She falls to her knees, hands leaping to her belly. Immediately, the protective posture feels ridiculous.

Don't I want them to rid me of this burden?

The maenad queen hisses, "Sister, we've come to liberate you!"

Filoméla trembles. If the stories are true, maenads tore Orpheus's head from his body with their bare hands. And he was the son of a god. She's a mere mortal. Surely, they'll rip her as easily as sack-cloth. She prays her death will be swift.

Perhaps I'll see my father and sister again in death.

Filoméla doesn't know if the servant boy has yet delivered her message. She hopes its truth will transform her sister into a living Fury.

Avenge me, Prōknē.

Filoméla feels pressure her back. She holds her breath and braces for pain.

Instead, several hands gently lift her to her feet and embrace her. The wild mass of women holds her.

There is tenderness in this embrace. Love has been withheld from Filoméla for so long, that something breaks inside of her. All the tears she's held back rumble in her chest, fighting to come out.

A door is opening. Her heart is thawing. The women begin to keen. And the sound of their collective sorrow washes over Filoméla. The last thread of her control snaps. The tears erupt, volcanic in their rage.

Filoméla opens her mouth and breathes along with the women's lamentations. Her sorrow heaves and breaks in waves.

Carry my shame to the gods.

The women hold her tighter. She does not know where she ends, and they begin. The grief they express together is endless and all-encompassing. They mourn their loss of innocence. They rage over trust betrayed. They demand vengeance for violence men enacted against women. They grieve over dashed hopes.

And even this does not scratch the surface of their outrage. There is so much injustice in the world.

Filoméla feels salt hardening on her cheeks. She imagines a river of tears, absolving her of the blood guilt she feels. She never asked to be her sister's rival in the marriage bed. She does not want to be a lover or a mother. She would gladly trade anything to be innocent of this darker side of love.

Tereus submerged me in this frozen place for months. Is this the end of that bondage? What kind of life will I be fit to live outside these walls?

The wild creatures stop crying. For Filoméla, it is a patch of sunlight poking through rain. They part to make room for the queen of the maenads to approach.

Tears have cleared two paths down the wild one's dusty, blood-streaked cheeks. Through the grime, Filoméla sees the black sky of her eyes have flecks of blue lightning in them.

No . . . it can't be.

These are eyes she recognizes. They belong to someone she loves and has longed to see.

Filoméla cannot make a sound, but her mouth moves, trying to communicate her relief. Something electric pulses between them.

"Sister," Queen Prōknē says, "we've come to liberate you."

~ 14 ~

FORACH

The wind tears at Cian's funeral shroud as if it wants to wake him from death. Forach and her father hold the ragged piece down over the naked corpse.

Aoife twirls, her ragged dress transmuting the wind's fury into a kind of joy. It's too much. Forach places a hand on the girl's shoulder. "Pay respects and mind yourself."

There are so many weeping women. Cian had been fair, and many girls fancied him. Forach wonders how many of these women's legs he managed to spread.

Spring will bring many flame-haired blossoms.

She shakes her head.

Don't disparage the dead. Or fault the young for their youth. At their age, I felt the hunger myself and how it can drag you under.

She thinks of Conn bearing down on her. She banishes the shock and pain of that ugly memory.

The dirty prince doesn't deserve any more of my time.

Aoife grins up at her with Conn's smile.

I already think of him more than he deserves. But she'll make that smile her own. She'll grow up strong outside of his shadow and make her own light.

Aoife wraps her arms around Forach's leg and bounces her head against it. Forach places a hand on the wild bopping curls. She does her best to silently communicate, *Be still.*

The child looks up at her with questioning green eyes, mirrors of her own.

"Not long now," Forach whispers. "They'll be setting your uncle Cian to rest and then you can run and play all you like. All night if you want. We'll be too drunk to stop you."

The child beams and peppers her leg with grateful kisses. Forach's heart swells. She kisses Aoife's head. Her heart swells with love and thanks for this miraculous gift.

Even beauty emerges from dark times. And joy.

Forach scans the crowd again. This time, she's looking for someone specific. She reddens when they lock eyes.

Óengus.

A shiver of anticipation warms her belly.

It's amazing how one name can belong to two such different men.

Her uncle, Óengus the Dread Spear, is their tribe's champion. Uncle Óengus is brutal, bawdy, and often drunk. If he isn't, he's brawling to avenge some wrong, real or imagined. When aroused, terrifying blue flames shoot from the black pits of his eyes.

Conn abducted her and refused to return her to the Déisi. It took him a year to come for her, but eventually, Dread Spear brought the Déisi to Tara. They nearly ripped down the tower to free her.

Would he have come at all if people hadn't started questioning his manhood for tarrying?

She is grateful that Óengus and his men breached the stronghold. She saw the blow with which Dread Spear struck Conn dead. With that same thrust, the spear's spiked chains maimed the High King Cormac mac Airt and killed a royal steward. It was the most beautiful thing Forach had ever seen.

Until Aoife . . .

But it was gorgeous to see one man strike down three wicked ones with his spear.

Even though it was the first and last time our people won at anything, she thinks grimly.

The High King attacked them several times since then. After the last brutal defeat, he sent them into exile from Tara. Every time Forach's father forges an alliance the High King pressures their ally to break it.

It isn't enough to defeat us. He wants to destroy us.

Forach tucks a flapping piece of linen under Cian's hand. She grips it and squeezes.

I know how desperate our situation made you. With no place to call our own, we all feel helpless. But I could have told you it's useless to fight. We must make our homes in each other's hearts. I wish you were still with us.

There is a hole left by Cian's death. Forach's heart rattles around it like a dried-up seed. Breathing in hurts. Breathing out brings no relief. She feels pinched all over by present and past. She can feel her kinspeople looking at her. The weight of their stares adds to her burden.

I know they blame me for our misfortune. But I didn't ask to be taken.

After that trauma, she wanted no man. Until her sweet Óengus . . . it's a relief knowing that she can still feel. Enjoying his company is one of her only pleasures, when they can find the time to be alone.

My Óengus.

Her Óengus is gentle, sober, and thoughtful. He is a leader of men in a way Dread Spear will never achieve.

How odd the same name can sit so different on each of them.

Forach treats her Óengus to a flicker of her smile. He winks, accepting the invitation to find her after the burial.

Looking away, her eye snags on Ethnui. The pale weirdling nods her respect, yet even that gesture feels profoundly disrespectful.

Hair prickles the back of her neck. Forach smooths it down and nods.

This is Cian's day, and I'll keep the peace.

It's time for the burial. Dread Spear approaches to take her place by Cian's corpse. She tucks the shroud around the body in the wagon, so it won't catch on the wheels, and steps aside. Dread Spear and her father yoke themselves to the wagon and pull the cart toward the cliffside caves. Forach joins the parade of people trailing them.

Forach takes Aiofe's hand. It's a slow slog uphill to the burial cave. They push the wagon so the whole burden won't be on her father and uncle's shoulders.

In the cave, there are no more words. Only weeping as her kinsmen lay treasures and tokens to keep Cian company on his journey to the other side. They seal up the mouth of the cave with stones.

Someone takes up a drum, and a fife joins in. The little ones dance after the piper, twirling back down the hill towards the center of the camp. There, they'll play and run wild while the adults drink, lie, and laugh.

Forach watches them go. She will join them, but she needs a moment alone with her brother first. She knows he's no longer attached to what lies in the cave, so she turns her eyes to the sea. The water has always called to them.

She and Cian used to play in the Sionna as children. Until Conn found her bathing there, it had been her favorite place in the world. Following the Sionna River to the sea had been one of the bright parts of their exile. Many times, she and Cian had shared a skin of whiskey sitting here or a place like it, watching the sun sink into the water. They would laugh into the wind, daring each other to do better. Forach smiles, remembering how they played like puppies on the edge of the world.

The waves beat a rhythm to rival the funeral drums. Forach feels dizzy looking over the edge, but it is the right way to say goodbye. She places a hand on the rocky cliff to steady herself and looks to the beach below. Wild horses run along the sand: a white mare chased by a red stallion.

She laughs at the irony.

Oh, Cian. Even in death, you'll be chasing the fair ones to bed.

She feels better thinking he's finding new ways to show his lust for life in the Otherworld.

An arm slips around her waist. She tenses.

But the voice is one she welcomes. "Gentle, my sweet. I don't want to lose you to the sea."

My Óengus.

Forach relaxes. She leans her head back against his chest. He smells mossy and warm, and his thick arms prevent the wicked wind from reaching her.

His rising excitement presses against her. She will not waste it. She twists in his arms and seals her lips to his. A shiver runs through them. It lights her up from tongue to toes and every point in-between.

He stumbles back and she presses him against the damp stone wall. She smiles and hitches up her shift. "There's no point in being on time for a wake, is there?"

Being alive is the best way to honor the dead.

~ 15 ~

JUANA

A knock at the door startles Juana from her writing. She wipes the nib of the quill against a rag and lays it to dry. She lifts the large oval amulet up off her bed, pulling the *escudo de monja* over her head. All the sisters have their shield as part of their formal habit. Juana chose one of brass. It is her armor against the outside world. But not all the sisters observe their vow of poverty as strictly. Juana's seen nun's shields with pure gold leaf, pearls, even precious stones inlaid on ivory.

Who are you to judge? You took your slaves with you to the Carmelitas. We don't become worthy all at once. As we know better, we do better, taking tiny steps towards God.

The knocking becomes insistent. Juana opens the door. Sor Bridget, Sor Paola, and Sor Tamzin stand there, looking festive.

"We came to welcome you back to the world of the chatty," Sor Bridget says. She pushes her way into the room without an invitation. She clears a space on Juana's small desk. There, she deposits a jug of wine, a hunk of cheese, and a loaf of bread that she's smuggled out of the larder. "Congratulations on completing your vow of silence!"

Juana laughs. The sound grinds its way up from her belly. Her voice sounds rough and strange. "What is this?"

Sor Paola and Sor Tamzin clap their hands and close the door.

"We haven't had a chance to get to know you properly," Paola explains. She kisses Juana's cheeks in greeting.

Paola's innocent kiss stirs something sleeping. Something Juana thought was dead. For a moment, Juana feels Leo's hands on her face. She tries not to blush.

Juana forces her mind around cold, hard things, like icicles and metal rods, until her urge to cry passes. It is too painful to remember Leo, knowing that she no longer walks the Earth.

Tamzin pulls four small cups from her habit. "I hope you don't mind. It's our little way of greeting you."

Juana is relieved to have a distraction. "How could I mind? I haven't spoken a word to anyone for six months." Juana takes a glass of wine from Bridget and sits beside Tamzin on the floor. Her throat is burning.

"Good, because if you did, we'd have to drink and eat in Tamzin's room, and it stinks in there," Bridget roars.

Tamzin sighs and turns her moonlike face to Juana. "I have pets," she says by way of explanation.

Bridget squeals in outrage. "Rats are not pets!" She hands cups of wine to Tamzin and Paola, then sits heavily on the desk. Juana says a quick prayer it will not shatter.

"Sisters," Paola breaks in. "We didn't come here to talk about rats! Let's have a toast! To our newest sister: Juana."

Bridget perches on the desk and sips her wine. A wide grin spreads across her ruddy face. Her eyes twinkle with mischief. "Now that we've plied you with wine, we'd like to know what kind of sinner you were before you darkened our door. So, start your tale, and don't leave out any of the sexy or dirty bits, if you please."

Juana freezes. *What can I tell them?* She certainly knows what she doesn't want to say: I loved a woman who died. I did not want to, but I bore her husband's child. I ran away so I wouldn't have to marry him. I don't want to be a wife and mother.

Paola teases Juana. "Ooooo . . . you're so quiet. It must be something good."

Tamzin reddens. “If it puts our souls in peril, then maybe we shouldn’t talk about it!”

Bridget laughs. “As if we won’t be confessing and getting our souls washed clean in the morning.” She prods Juana. “Go on then. Speak.”

~ 16 ~

HONEY

Honey rises before dawn, prepping the girls for school. How disorienting the darkness used to feel. Now that the sun no longer rises for her, there is no point in staying up all night or sleeping in. It's either time to rise or time to sleep, which simplifies things.

Mornings before school are so busy. The family schedule will veer into chaos if she forgets to complete a single task. There is so little time.

She places bowls and boxes of cereal on the table and calls the girls to come down. Amy requests cuddles and a dispensation of more time. Emily pads down the stairs with vigor. Honey kisses Emily's head and makes her way up the stairs to Amy's room.

"It's your fault I'm so tired," Amy crabs. "You woke me up howling at the moon."

Honey curls her body around Amy's and kisses the back of her head. "I wasn't howling, I was singing."

"It sounded horrible."

Honey can feel Amy slipping back to sleep. She shakes her gently. "C'mon. Breakfast is downstairs, you need to get up. I don't want you to miss the bus."

She keeps insisting until Amy finally sits up, freeing Honey to go.

Chad is in the kitchen. He hands Honey a cup of coffee. "What the hell got into you last night?"

Honey laughs, though his words wound her. “What do you mean?”

He sighs and sits down. “That awful caterwauling.”

Caterwauling?

“I’m a trained singer. That was art.”

Emily chimes in, speaking through a mouth full of cereal. “Your art is bad.”

Honey ignores them, yelling up the landing, “Amy, you’re going to be late! Are you getting dressed?” The grunts sound promising. She touches the clock, and it tells her that it’s already six-thirty. Honey yells again, “You’ve got ten minutes before we must leave! Hurry up!”

Emily clears her throat. “I’m done with my cereal, Mommy.” Emily is always looking for praise. Honey kisses her, takes her dish, rinses it lightly, and puts it in the dishwasher.

Amy finally pounds down the stairs and plops into her seat at the table. “Where’s my cereal?”

“You get a banana,” Honey says, thrusting one at her. “No time for cereal now. Eat quick and brush your teeth.”

Chad pushes his chair back. She waves a hand to get his attention. “No, no, I’ll walk them.”

“Don’t be ridiculous,” he says.

“I’m not,” Honey replies firmly. “I’d like to walk them to the bus stop. I used to do it all the time.”

“But . . .”

“Humor me.”

He remains silent. In that silence, Honey can feel his disapproval coming at her in waves.

What has gotten into me? How will I get back without the girls?

As if he can hear her thoughts, Chad says, “I’ll follow you to help you back.”

“I don’t need your help,” she lies. Honey can’t put into words why she wants to stumble back by herself, but it feels important. She must do it alone.

"Don't be ridiculous." Chad sounds angry now.

She imagines twin lines of frustration carving deep grooves into his forehead. She knows she should feel guilty. Instead, his resistance infuriates her. "Don't call me ridiculous, or you'll be in the market for another wife."

The girls *oooooooooooo* at their father.

Emily snaps a finger, "That'll show *you.*"

Honey zips her coat and claps to get the girls' attention. "Stop taunting your father and grab your coats."

As she touches the doorknob, she doubts she's up to this.

What am I doing?

But the girls rush past, and their enthusiasm carries her out the door.

"Wait!" Chad stops her on the porch and thrusts a walking stick in her hands. Honey protests. But he insists. "You'll need it on the way back."

The woods feel different than they did last night. Still strange and dangerous, but beckoning. Honey shoves the walking stick under an arm. The girls each take a hand and pull her down the steep driveway. They laugh, happy to be the ones in charge. "C'mon, we don't want to miss the bus!"

At the end of the driveway, they travel a narrow patch of gravel until they reach a path through the woods. They emerge by the neighborhood's back gate, where the bus will pull up to fetch them.

Honey tries to count the steps, memorize the turns, and remember the roots that trip her as they walk. But the harder she concentrates, the more difficult it is to remember any of it.

The girls board the school bus and shout, "I love you!"

As the bus door squeezes shut, an icy panic grips Honey's heart.

She takes a deep breath and slowly turns around.

I just need to turn around and go back.

She feels the edge of the road with the walking stick. It doesn't feel that simple.

Just walk up this road until you reach the woods.

She marvels at how calm her inner voice sounds. As if she walked blind through the woods every day.

Still, she starts to move, cautiously.

She moves so slowly that it takes five minutes to take her first five steps. Impatient with herself, she erupts. "Oh, for Chrissakes! You'll never get home walking like an old woman."

There must be a better way.

She remembers hearing a story on NPR about a blind man. He made clicking sounds with his tongue. The echoes helped him ride horses and move through the world blind.

Echolocation. Worth a try.

She clicks her tongue and waits for the sound to roll back to her. She keeps clicking. But the sound conjures no magically mapped landscape. She fights the urge to sit down and cry.

Why did I insist on doing this to myself? What am I trying to prove? Should I wait for Chad to come and find me?

The calm, lilting voice returns. *Don't be such a baby*, it chastises, *this is your street, your wood, your yard. You know this place. Let your feet carry you home.*

Before losing her sight, she did walk this path daily. Theoretically, muscle memory should be able to help.

Anything is better than crying like a baby.

She tells the inner voice to be more supportive. Then, she takes a step. She takes another and stumbles, scraping her knee. She curses.

I don't want Chad to be right. I can do this.

She uses the stick to stand upright. After a few taps to define the path, she begins again.

One step at a time.

Finally, she feels tree canopy closing around her. She takes a grateful breath.

This must be the mouth of the path parallel to the road.

If she continues, it will take her back to her driveway.

I'm going in the right direction!

It is slow going, but the further she gets, the more familiar it all feels. She notices that her feet are better at finding the path's edges. They tell her when to fork right. She hears cars passing.

That means I'm close to my driveway!

When she emerges on her driveway's gravel tip, she lets herself cry tears of joy and relief. She turns left up the driveway and begins the long walk up its curving slope. She mounts the porch steps easily and finds the door. She throws it open, triumphant.

The conqueror returns!

Beaming ear to ear, she shouts, "I'm home!"

Silence greets her.

She doesn't care.

I don't need a crowd to know I've done something amazing.

She pours a cup of coffee and sits on the porch. Windchimes tinkle in the breeze. She feels strong and brave.

A car door slams. Chad storms up the steps. "Where the hell have you been?"

Honey laughs. "What do you mean? The bus came and then I walked home. Did you go looking for me?"

"You were taking forever. Of course, I did." There's an edge of hysteria in his voice. "I drove around the whole neighborhood looking for you."

"I was right here." Honey means to sound comforting, consoling, but his hurt is stirring her up, making her angry. She wants him to be proud of her. She's proud of herself. "Can you believe I did it? All by myself?"

He says nothing. But the slam of the door warns she'll need to work harder to get back in his good graces.

~ 17 ~

SEKHMET

Her fingers probe the gashed wood beneath her cheek. She counts the days of her captivity and stops. She has no idea how many days she's been sick or unconscious and unable to leave a mark.

Useless.

She rolls onto her back. Then, as vomit rises, to her side.

I've survived this long. Pity if I choked on vomit now.

The nausea is no longer from the motion of the ocean. Now, it's the simple act of putting anything on her stomach that upsets it.

Her throat burns for a moment. The warm liquid pools under her neck. She doesn't have the energy to wipe it away.

Oh well. There are worse things in my hair. What's a little more spit and bile?

She can tell by the stink on her right that the Christos Templar finally died.

The guards removed the Essene's body a few days ago. But the rats it attracted remain.

Sekhmet shudders remembering how they scrambled over her to feed on his corpse. She doesn't enjoy eating carrion, but she will do anything to stay alive. Even if it comes back up, there must be some nourishment her body can capture.

Maybe I can snag a rat or two before they remove the Christos?

Her mouth waters. Her laughter comes out hard, sad, and guttural.

I used to be so proud and here I am fantasizing about eating rats.

Sekhmet wonders if hate alone can keep her alive.

If the guards get slack, I'll drink their blood, too.

Above her, on what she imagines is the deck, voices shout. There is the sound of metal grinding, people grunting, and a splash. The scraping metal sound travels like a snake through the bowels of the ship. It reminds Sekhmet of something.

The chain. The splash.

Is that the anchor?

She turns to the Christos Templar. "Too bad you didn't hang on, old boy. Looks like we've arrived."

~ 18 ~

FILOMÉLA

The clutch of wild women closes around them. Filoméla hangs onto Prōknē like a drowning woman. She buries her head in her sister's neck.

Reunited.

The gods have a sense of humor to reunite them in this way. The queen stands bedraggled and wild. The recent virgin is grossly pregnant.

We are both lost and found on this night of liberation. Are all the gods as drunk as Dyonysos?

"I got your message, the tapestry." Prōknē takes Filoméla's face in her hands and kisses her cheeks. "That is what you endured?"

Filoméla nods, tears burning the skin of her cheeks. She flushes and looks away.

Her sister's hands stroke Filoméla's swollen belly. "How long?"

Filoméla looks up, confused.

"How long until the baby comes?"

Filoméla opens her mouth. She wants to say, "It's not a child. It's a monster." But ugly sounds catch in her throat, bump up her neck, and out her mouth in a series of hisses and grunts.

Prōknē's face cracks open and sorrow pours out. "Oh, what else has he done to you, sweet sister?" She peers inside Filoméla's mouth. She grips her little sister tightly, shaking them both with her sobs. "He cut out your tongue so you couldn't tell me the truth?"

"My queen," says one of the maenad handmaidens, "if we don't leave soon, daybreak will catch us on the road."

Prōknē pulls back and addresses Filoméla, "Is there anything wrong with your legs?"

Filoméla shakes her head. Tereus's absence has given her time to heal down there. If there's been any benefit to the monster, it's that it scared its father from her bed.

"Good," Prōknē says, "because I'm taking you home."

The cautious handmaiden extracts a disguise of skins and vines. The women strip Filoméla.

Prōknē draws a sharp breath as she takes in the story Filoméla's scars tell. Her voice shakes. "There are so many ways he's hurt you . . ."

Filoméla looks down at her naked body. The bruises have faded, but the scars on her wrists and ankles stand out pale and pink against her deep olive skin.

Prōknē snarls, "That bastard."

Prōknē's words tug at Filoméla. Filoméla spent such a long time covering all her soft parts. She's been so deliberately hard, protecting what she could preserve from his abuse. Giving in to tenderness now hurts. But at least she can see a future. She has hope. There is the promise of freedom. That wasn't the case this morning.

My sister is here. She is here. The gods heard and answered my prayers.

Prōknē has always been wise, but Filoméla has a new admiration for her clever sister. It is the perfect night to liberate her. Women are not free to travel without male escorts except for this one celebration. And people are so terrified of maenads, they will be able to travel unmolested.

The women transform Filoméla into a maenad. Prōknē takes Filoméla's hand. "We're going to punish him for what he did to you."

Prōknē takes a wine skin, swigs from it, then spills a dollop of wine on the floor. "Dionysus Eleutherios, twice-born god, he who intoxicates and liberates, hear my plea. By the light of your mother Semele, this will be the last night my husband will sleep peacefully in our wedding bed." She looks around the circle of women. "Witness with me." She passes the wineskin.

As the women drink, Prōknē draws a blade swiftly across her palm. The knife follows the wineskin around the circle. Now they are all full of wine and blood. Filoméla begins to feel light-headed.

Prōknē raises her arms. "Dyonysos Zagreus, horned god of the doors between death and life. Open your mysteries to us this night of all sacred nights. Fill us with the strength of your sisters, the Blessed Ones. Bring us justice and help us punish this wicked man."

The queen lowers her arms. "Come, my sister. We will find our answers on the road home."

A door is opening.

A barrier is falling away.

They run out into the night.

~ 19 ~

FORACH

Óengus kisses the base of her neck, working his way up to her ear. Forach tilts her head to taste his lips, not knowing if the salt is from her tears or the sea air.

His breath grows ragged as he crests the wave of his passion. It breaks over them both. Her own rush of hunger and relief meets it.

As he recedes, he brushes a strand of loose hair from her face. He kisses her and dreamily murmurs, “Marry me.”

She pushes him away, laughing, ignoring the hurt look on his face. “You’re drunk on passion. Besides, I’m a ruined woman. You can’t marry me.”

He protests, but she stands firm.

“It’s dangerous enough for you to take a Déisi to wife, but one whose bairn could lay claim to the High King’s seat? I love you alive, Óengus. What good are you to me dead?” She grips his naked ass for emphasis, to remind him of the sweetness of what they have. “The High King will kill you if you marry me.”

He breaks her hold. The way his muscles ripple under his skin makes Forach hungry again. She tries to pull him into another round of lovemaking.

But he holds her off. “Cormac mac Airt and his kin have taken enough from you and your people. He doesn’t have as many friends as you think.”

"Doesn't he?" Forach's frustration curdles into anger.

This is my fight. Why does everyone keep jumping into it?

She knows it isn't fair to rage at Óengus, but she doesn't know why he won't let go. "Seven battles have we fought," she hisses. "How many people have to die before we let it be?" Her green-gold eyes spark with anger. "It doesn't matter how many of us perish," she says. "The High King will never be able to punish us enough. We took his son and gauged out his eye. And by disfiguring him, stole his right to sit on the throne of Tara. We're going to be paying for those trespasses the rest of our lives."

Óengus tries to interrupt.

She stills him with a cold hand. "I'm not saying I regret anything. He's a rotten man, and I'm glad Dread Spear crippled him. He doesn't deserve to sit upon the throne in Tara. Exile suits him."

She spits on the memory of the High King *and* Prince Conn.

"Does it suit you?" Óengus's voice is gentle, gentler than she deserves. His hand around her waist pulls tight.

She wants to spend the night under the stars with him, touching souls and making light out of the darkness. But thunder clouds are gathering. "If we don't dress and get back to camp soon, we'll get caught in the storm."

He presses against her until she looks at him. "Does exile suit you or your people?" He catches her arm beneath his and holds her face so she cannot look away. "Marry me and I'll give the Déisi a home. You and your people can stay and farm these lands forever. Isn't that what you want? To cease your wandering and make a home for yourself and Aoife?"

Home.

Forach's eyes burn.

"I could be a father to her. And give you more children of our own to raise up. This could be your home."

Home.

The word burns a hole in her stomach and sucks the breath out of her chest. "Óengus mac Nad Froích, you be asking me if I want a home?"

The tears are flowing, but she will not let him see her cry. She does not want him to misunderstand. She rolls off him and faces the sea. "More than anything in this world, that's what I want. But while the High King lives, anyone who tries to help us will be wiped from the face of the Earth. I'll not bring that destruction down on you, or your kin. None of you asked for my trouble and I will not share it."

She rises and pulls her dress over her head. "We better hurry if we want to stay ahead of the storm. Besides, they'll be missing us at the wake."

"I'm not afraid of him," Óengus says, kneeling before her. His hands squeeze the warm handles of her hips. They turn everything below her waist to water. "My people are strong. They'll fight for anything I say is just. And with Dread Spear leading your people, we can resist Cormac and defeat him. Just say the word. I will make this happen. For you. I'd do anything for you."

Anything for me?

She looks down at the beautiful man on his knees. A flash of lightning flickers, bringing his lovely bones into sharp relief. She loves him. Not that it matters.

Maybe it's best I be gone. So, he can live a full, long life.

She kisses his forehead and tries not to think about how near to death his love might bring him. "We need to hurry. Get dressed."

She watches the sea beat the sand into bits. No sign of Cian's fiery soul chasing the white horse of death along the shore.

Brother, I hope you've found happiness and a place to rest. And, I hope one day, we can all join you in peace.

Something moves in the bushes. A pair of gem-like eyes meet Forach's. Their violet light vanishes almost immediately into a thatch of leafy green. It's too tall to be a hare, too short to be a full-grown human.

The blood in Forach's veins chills. She feels sick.

Only one person enjoys skulking in the shadows: the amethyst-eyed witch.

Forach's mind races.

How much did Ethnui hear?

~ 20 ~

JUANA

Juana isn't sure where to begin her tale. There's a thin line between being accepted and shunned.

How much is too much to share?

Tamzin must sense her fear. The moon-faced nun gently prods, "Why don't you start with why you're here."

Juana relaxes. There's a safe enough answer to give to that. "I need to be in a place where I can devote myself to my studies."

Bridget roars with laughter. "You entered the convent to read books?"

Juana flushes. Spoken aloud her ambition sounds tiny. But she's worked so hard to get here. Fought so hard to have the library she has.

It's no small thing to have the courage to know. To fight for the right to have an education.

She feels the blood rising in her cheeks.

Did I choose wrong? Am I surrounded by people who prefer to remain ignorant?

Tamzin inserts herself, a shield between Bridget's derision and Juana's embarrassment. "Did you want to go to the university?"

"I begged my mother to let me go," Juana confesses. "She refused."

Paola leans forward. "They wouldn't let you in anyway. They don't admit women."

Juana's juts her chin out. "I would have dressed like a man."

Paola and Bridget laugh as Tamzin sucks in a scandalized breath.

Bridget wags a finger. "You've got balls. I like you."

Tamzin clutches her rosary. "You'd have to cut your hair."

Juana rolls her eyes. "It's hair. And I've cut it before."

"You have?"

The other women laugh at Tamzin's expense.

Paola's eyes have a curious weight as they settle on Juana. "That's a very daring act."

"It's just hair," Juana insists, trying not to flinch under Paola's attention. "It doesn't have any magical power."

Tamzin swallows hard. "It's what makes us beautiful."

"Nonsense," Juana says. "I can't see any of your hair under your habit, but your soul shines out so purely, Tamzin. I swear, you are one of the most beautiful women I've ever seen."

A red flush creeps up from the high neck of Tamzin's habit, spreading over her face like poison ivy.

A smile tugs at the corner of Paola's mouth. "Have you always been such a connoisseur of women's beauty?"

Now it is Juana's turn to blush.

Is she flirting with me?

Bridget's curiosity saves her from purgatory. "Why did you cut your hair?"

Relieved, Juana switches to that topic. "I was learning Latin. But so slowly. So, I made a bargain with myself: if I could master grammar by a certain time, I'd be able to keep my mane. But if I failed, it would have to come off."

"You didn't!" Tamzin is still scandalized, but Juana can feel that the shock is now tinged with admiration.

"I did!" Juana laughs. "And I had to cut my hair off . . . twice! But I learned my lessons."

"That was very brave of you." Paola's gaze is intense. It makes Juana feel hot and prickly. It repels and attracts her.

Juana forces herself to meet Paola's dark, blue-flecked eyes. A current of electricity passes between them. With great difficulty and intent, Juana manages to force out the words. "It didn't seem right to me that a head naked of knowledge should be dressed in hair. Knowledge is the more desirable adornment."

She lets that truth sit on them. They say nothing. Juana panics.

Did I share too much? Are they judging me? Do they think I'm vain? Full of pride?

Bridget shifts her weight. The desk creaks. But it holds. "I'm not much for books, but I like your spirit. The Madre Abadesa says this isn't your first convent . . ."

Paola's eyes widen. "Did you get kicked out?"

"No!" Juana feels like she's passed the first hurdle. "I joined the Carmelitas when I was seventeen, but I only stayed with them a few months. Too many rules. And not any that made sense."

Bridget laughs. "Hieronymite sisters are much more fun."

Paola makes herself comfortable on the bed. Juana restrains the urge to join her. Paola smiles provocatively. "We have rules, too."

Juana nods. "Yes. But you leave the cloister to do decent work. And, you have the locutorio room, where people from the outside may come to visit."

"Are you expecting visitors?" Tamzin's honest face reminds Juana of Leo.

"Not yet," Juana admits, blinking back tears. "But I like that leaving the material world for the spiritual one doesn't mean that I must give up talking about ideas. I hope to do so with interesting people."

~ 21 ~

HONEY

Chad doesn't like this 'new Honey.' Or at least that's what he says when he's not sulking.

"I don't understand why you're putting your health and safety at risk," he says. "If you're not going to worry about yourself, then I guess I have to."

She feels hot anger prickling up and down her neck. If the girls weren't in bed, she'd scream at him. Being forced to whisper-shout makes her even madder. "Why does anyone have to worry if I take a walk? It's a walk! Nothing bad happened!"

"Thank God. Promise me you won't do anything that stupid again."

Stupid?

Honey bites her lip. She tastes blood. "The only stupid thing I did was think you'd be proud of me."

"Look," he says in a gentle tone of voice that makes her want to smack him. "I'm all for you doing things that help you feel independent. But when you're only thinking of yourself, you're being selfish. Think about me and the girls. What would we do if something happened to you?"

She's so mad, her eyeballs hurt. The blood pounding behind them tinges the darkness a rosy hue.

Is this what they mean by 'seeing red'?

"You're talking as if I'm putting my life at risk. I walked home from the bus stop. Alone. Successfully! You don't understand, but this is important to me. I don't want to live the rest of my life as an invalid."

"You're not an invalid, you're a wife and mother. But you do have limitations, for chrissakes, you're blind."

"I had a life before I lost my eyesight. We used to do things before, and I don't see what's wrong with wanting to try—"

"I know."

She hates when he interrupts her. But before she can stop him, he adds, "I just want you to be safe."

"Who says I can't be safe?" She waits for him to reply. But he has nothing to say. "Why don't you trust me?"

"It's not that I don't trust you."

Something dark ripples under his words. She sucks in a breath and musters her courage. "Then what is it?"

Chad clears his throat. "I worry that . . ." He lets that thought die. He begins again, "Lately, you've been . . ."

She tries to be patient, but the anger pushes its way out again. "You think I'm crazy?"

"No, but . . ."

She can feel him trying to pick his words. The care he is taking inflames her. "No, but you think I'm *stupid*, you said—"

"That's not fair. You know how much we've all—"

"Yeah, you've all sacrificed a lot," Honey says, heading for the door. "I refuse to keep pretending like I can't do anything on my own. I'm not helpless. I'm working on getting stronger and being more than what I was. So, if you can't keep up, you need to get out of my way!"

She wants to slam the door, but the girls are sleeping. She doesn't want to wake them up two nights in a row. She takes the walking stick by the door and closes it gently. But she shoots one last, spiteful look at Chad that she hopes he sees.

May it burn him to the quick.

She shivers out on the porch. The temperature dropped a lot since the girls came home. This morning felt like fall. Now winter is on the wind.

Damn. I'm freezing.

The coat is hanging by the rack next to the door, but Honey refuses to go back in to get it. If she does, Chad might restrain her. The thought that he might come here to bring her back in drives her further from the door. She steps off the small porch and walks down the stairs to the left, meeting a low branch with her forehead. She winces and grabs it, using its heft to guide her safely out of its way.

She tries to remember what the path on this side of the house looks like.

A little bend past the laurel, right? And then a straight shot through the pine grove?

She stubs a toe before she remembers there is an old mill stone the previous owners left. Her knee catches the side of a bench she forgot is also in the yard. Angry and limping, she climbs up the path until her hands brush pine leaves.

Her heart leaps.

I made it!

She's reclaimed this little path from the darkness, too. She stops to celebrate.

Something crashes through the brush. Honey jumps. It sounds large. There's more than one.

Is it a bear? Wolves?

She tries to remember how to defend herself. Should she shout? Play dead? Run? They're headed straight towards her. She lifts the stick.

Wait. I can't do this. I can't fight.

A wild panic grips her. She turns, trips, and falls. The stick jumps out of her hand.

Oh no!

She searches the ground but can't find anything but dirt and leaves. The crackling, trampling sound is on top of her.

Get up! Run!

She scrambles up, palms bleeding. She runs as fast as she can towards the house. Feeling small and vulnerable, she scrambles up the short flight of stairs to the porch. She grasps the handle and thrusts the door open. Breathless, bleeding, relieved, and ashamed, Honey bolts it and slides to the ground.

"Jesus," Chad says.

"You're right." Honey weeps desperate tears and feels her heart break.

I am not strong. I am so stupid.

She is glad she cannot read his expression as she confesses, "You're right. You're right. You're right."

~ 22 ~

SEKHMET

She can't move her arms or legs. Her tongue is two sizes too big for her mouth.

But at least we're not still at sea.

Sekhmet looks at the smooth white walls that form a cell around her. She lays a hand against the surface. It looks like quartz, but it is not.

Cruel joke.

Everything around her here is also dead material, insulators rather than conductive. She leans her head back on what passes for a bed. It is a body-shaped indentation in the wall, not a suitable place to rest. She's too broken to climb into it, anyway. She's managed to crawl from where they threw her, but not far. The stone feels cool against the flayed skin of her back.

This is what passes for good these days.

Her neck hurts.

At least it's still attached to my shoulders.

She grins, cracking sores that live on the corners of her mouth. She laughs into the abyss.

At least I haven't lost my sense of humor.

They come every day. Maybe more than once a day. She doesn't know. She doesn't care.

This is a game of endurance.

When they strike her, she imagines she's a bolt of steel. She is something permanent, inflexible, unfeeling.

She remembers what she came here to do. She thinks of the Source. Of the One.

People who might die if she fails. This is bigger than her.

I do not matter.

When she volunteered for this mission, she felt like a champion.

Look at me now.

She doesn't have the energy to keep self-pity at bay. She lets it wash over her.

The only thing I'm a champion of now is punishment.

She'd cry. But everything in her body is dry. She's a husk in the fire.

I thought this mission would be so easy. What a fool I was.

The only thing she's proud of is that she shares nothing when tortured. She doesn't even moan. She goes to that cool metal place she keeps hidden deep inside. She lives there until the Brotherhood gives up or loses interest.

Only one thing still scares her.

I'm tough, but I'm not immortal.

Death has no power over her. But she doesn't want to give them the satisfaction of seeing her beaten. Of forcing her soul to be reborn before she's ready.

She laughs. She knows what her new mission is, though it feels absurd. She doesn't even know if it's possible.

My new mission: don't die.

She laughs herself to sleep.

~ 23 ~

FILOMÉLA

The monster kicks. It wants to be born. Wild claws of pain tear at Filoméla. She grits her teeth and refuses to let her awful shame see the light of this world.

It wants its freedom. But it will not have it.

The handmaiden looks at Filoméla with worried eyes. “You have to push.”

Filoméla shakes her head. Her body cramps her into a crescent.

Oh, gods, it burns.

When the pain recedes, she tries to stand. The women around her force her to the ground, back into a squat.

“You need to hurry up and let the child come.”

No, Filoméla thinks wildly. *This is my liberation night. I will not share it.*

The handmaiden slaps her face. “You have to push the baby out or it will kill you!” She looks over Filoméla’s head, beseeching.

Filoméla feels a cool hand on her back.

Prōknē. My sister, my savior.

Filoméla wants to smile, but another spasm of pain makes her mind go hot white, erasing everything else.

How has any woman ever survived this?

Filoméla hisses. For once, she is glad no one can hear her. Stopping on the road like this is dangerous, but at least she isn't drawing people to them with her screams.

Prōknē's breath is hot on her neck. "Sister, we won't be safe until we get you home. If the baby wants to come, let it come quickly. Being born doesn't mean it has to live."

Filoméla feels the monster snaking through her. The handmaiden pushes Filoméla's knees apart. The women hold them open. Filoméla tries to close them, but Prōknē's hand stops her.

"Dear sister, you're so close. We're almost home. Please."

Filoméla closes her eyes. She can't fight any longer. She thinks of her sister's promise. She tells the monster, *Being born doesn't mean you have to live.*

The monster answers with a flash of pain that rattles her teeth.

Pain like this might kill her. She can feel that now.

I don't want to die, not like this.

Filoméla surrenders. She leans back into the net of women's arms. Prōknē gently pushes her forward until her sweaty forehead kisses the handmaiden's dry one. The women's hands on her shoulders and legs root her to river rocks they've positioned under her feet.

Filoméla isn't sure where her body ends, and the women's begin. They feel like one large, hot, wet, beast, straining together. The handmaiden encourages her to push when the pain comes.

Her sister gives her the instruction, "Imagine shitting it out, and it will come faster."

Despite all the horror, all the exhaustion, Filoméla laughs and obeys.

The monster flies into the world on wings of pain.

The handmaiden tears the cord with her teeth.

Prōknē takes the beast by its bloody ankles and dips it in the river.

Filoméla's heart leaps, thinking Prōknē is already fulfilling her promise to drown it. But the handmaiden takes the babe from her mistress and wipes it clean. Then she offers the horrible thing to Filoméla.

Its little bird mouth cries out. In its wails Filoméla hears so much anger.

It's angry, too?

Something in her trembles in recognition. The monster isn't covered in hair or horned. It has fingers like hers, impossibly small. It is a girl.

Like me.

"For the love of the gods, feed it before they find us," the handmaiden hisses.

The women take the child and press it to Filoméla's breast. It wriggles and gums its way blindly across her chest until it finds a nipple to latch on to. The women lift her hands to support the small thing as it milks her.

Filoméla wonders at it. It is completely alien. And hers.

As the milk lets down, she is overwhelmed with feeling. There are so many emotions. Her body is not large enough to contain them all.

~ 24 ~

FORACH

Her head aches from drinking and her eyes are swollen from tears shed the night before. Forach enters her father's tent feeling fuzzy and weak the morning after Cian's burial.

She is startled to see Óengus's father, Nad Froich mac Cuirc. He isn't as powerful as the High King of Tara, but the people of these southern lands call him their king, all the same.

She pays her respects and takes a seat by the fire. She wants to ask her father what plot he is hatching, but she doesn't want to embarrass him in front of this king. A third man enters and sits beside her, bringing chilly air in with him. It is her uncle Óengus, the Dread Spear.

Like the red deer of the forest, her muscles seize, anticipating danger.

I do not like this.

She looks at Dread Spear.

Is he one of this confederacy?

His eyes betray no secrets.

Sickness churns her stomach. Forach forces her attention outside herself. She notes that the King of Munster bears more than a passing resemblance to his son. Thick neck, broad shoulders, and muscles that haven't sagged. She hasn't washed, so the smell of her

Óengus still hangs thickly on her. She wishes she were back on the cliff in his arms.

Anywhere but here.

King Nad Froich smiles at Forach. "I see why many men have died for your sake."

Dread Spear laughs.

Forach marvels at how casually cruel men can be. His comment wounds, but she manages to reply with a civil tongue. "That is why I long for peace."

The king nods. "Your father and I have been talking about how to make that happen."

She doesn't like the sound of that. She feels the sick lump in her stomach ice over with fear.

The king smiles. "My Óengus would have you to wed, and I'll not stand against it. Your father and I have talked terms. You've no rich dowry, but your people are honest and industrious. I gladly accept them as vassals. Their work will pay off your debt."

Another debt. Will they never be out of bondage for my sake?

Forach fights the urge to flee. She shoots a pleading glance at her father. But he is too busy clapping for wine to see it. Forach bows her head to the ground and says nothing. She chokes back her tears.

They're all so happy.

It's horrifying. Their plan is stupid and reckless.

But what can I say?

Her people are exiles because of *her*. They suffer and die for *her*.

Do I have the right to say no?

If she does, she'll prove an enemy to their happiness. She cannot bear bringing them more disappointment.

But if I say yes . . .

She wants to wed Óengus, bear his bairn, and live a long, sweet life in his arms. But that isn't what the fates have in store for her. She knows this, in her bones.

Life isn't a fairy tale. It's hard and ugly, and then you die.

Could they not see that her wedding to Óengus would bring the High King Cormac's wrath down on them all?

She looks at King Nad Froich. He doesn't look like an ambitious man, but she knows her looks aren't the only thing he finds attractive.

My bastard is the High King's only heir . . . marriage would give Óengus a claim to Tara . . .

All men have ambition. King Nad Froich's must be for his son to rule all of Eire's lands.

The Kingdom of Munster is strong, but not strong enough to defeat Tara. How can he not know this?

She looks at Dread Spear. A vein in his forehead throbs. Her heart flutters.

He knows this is bad. He knows this marriage will not bring peace, only war and more death.

She waits for Dread Spear to speak out, to protest. To point out the fatal flaw in their plan. She wants him to give voice to the doubts she's not allowed to voice.

They won't listen to a woman, but if you speak, they might hear!

But Dread Spear only bends his head in obedience, same as her, and holds his tongue.

~ 25 ~

JUANA

It isn't the condition of the patients at the Amor de Dios hospital that shocks Juana. It is the smell.

"Breathe through your mouth," Bridget advises. Even so, Juana still finds the stench overwhelming. Plus, it feels like she's eating the smells when they come into her mouth. Breathing through her nose makes her gag, but at least it doesn't give other people's evils a way to enter her body.

The hospital chaplain greets them with bed linens. He is a tall bespectacled man with a sharp face and thin strip of a beard down his chin. "Welcome sisters. We appreciate your help."

"And we are happy to give it, with God's love," Bridget replies. She takes the bedsheets from him and splits them with Juana. "We've got a recruit: Sor Juana. She's a writer, too."

The chaplain's pale blue eyes light up. "Aha, what do you write?"

Juana blushes. "Poetry. Some philosophy."

He smiles, and Juana thinks she sees little flecks of amber glinting against the ice chips of his eyes. *"In tlilli in tlapalli."*

Juana gasps in recognition of the Nahuatl words. Few people in Mexico speak the language of the Aztecs. She pulls a proper quotation from her studies of the native language. "I do think it's important to record our knowledge for the generations to come. *Ixtli, yollotli quitquitinemi.*"

The chaplain smiles. "Children *do* bear the seeds of our future. Long may they flower." He bows deeply. "It is an honor to meet you, sister. I am Don Carlos, at your service. Are you criollo?"

She nods. She suspects he is also native born. Most Spaniards look down upon those born in New Spain. But there is a fondness criollos have for each other. She confesses, "I wish I were Aztec, but alas, I've only studied their culture."

His smile tells her that she has found an ally. He extends a hand. "Your Nahuatl will come in handy here. We have quite a few patients who have resisted becoming proper vassals of New Spain."

Bridget interjects before Juana can respond. "I can send her to you later if you like, so you can keep flirting. But we should get to work. We'll start with changing the sheets."

Juana flushes.

Don Carlos laughs. "Don't worry sister. Sor Bridget loves to tease. I know your intentions are pure. You see, I'm a philosopher, too. I'm studying mathematics and science at the university. I would love to hear more about your work. Please come speak with me later. It's rare to find people who develop their minds and spirits, as we have done. I think it's one of the best ways to serve God."

Juana hesitates. His invitation feels too intimate.

Bridget leans towards Juana and whispers, "You'll be all right. He's not one of the men you must worry about. True, they kicked him out of the Jesuits, but he's chaste all the same. The only thing his heart burns with passion for is the exchange of ideas."

Juana examines Don Carlos's face and finds nothing but kindness, curiosity, and deep intelligence. She relaxes. This is the kind of opportunity and type of person her heart yearns to find.

She smiles, an invitation. "I look forward to it."

~ 26 ~

HONEY

Honey hears the house stirring, but she doesn't want to rise. She wants to hide. She begged Chad to take care of the girls this morning, and he'd obliged. Honey burrows deeper under the covers. She hides from the tempting smell of bacon and the warmth of her children's voices.

Amy pads in on stockinged feet. "Mommy, you want breakfast?"

"No."

"But you're walking us to school, right?"

Something sharp twists inside of Honey. The pride she took in walking the woods alone, despite her disability, shatters. She is thankful the covers hide her face. What she feels is too ugly to reveal to an innocent child.

"Mommy's not feeling well, baby. Your Daddy's going to take you and Emily to the bus stop."

Honey hopes that is enough to send the girl away. But Amy is not Emily. She is not thoughtful or obedient. Amy storms up and punches Honey's butt with an angry fist.

"I don't want Daddy to take us. I want you!"

Honey stifles the urge to laugh. It is such an outrageous gesture. But she is afraid if she opens her mouth, a sob will burst out.

Thankfully, Amy's outburst draws Chad away from the kitchen.

"Hey! Get back in here. Finish your breakfast and leave your mother alone. She's not feeling well."

Amy protests. "I don't want you to walk us to the bus stop. I want Mommy." Angry feet pound back toward the kitchen table.

Emily's sweet voice chirps, "I'm glad you want to walk us, Daddy."

Honey listens to the girls squabble until Chad hustles them out the door.

She sighs in relief to have them gone. She'll be alone for the next few hours.

Now I can lick my wounds in peace.

She doesn't want to get out of bed. She doesn't want to do anything. She lets the dishes stay on the table. She falls back asleep.

The wolves from the night before return to her dreams to hunt her. She keeps tripping and falling. She can feel their hot breath, the tug of their teeth on her shirt. She wakes up screaming.

She is still laying there when Chad lets the girls in that afternoon.

"I have to go back to work," he yells. "I'll be back at six-thirty. I found your stick in the backyard. If you want it, it's by the door."

"Okay." She is glad he didn't come in. Didn't see the breakfast dishes gathering dust, the dirty pans unwashed, and her still hiding.

The last thing I want to do is go outside. Can I stay here forever?

The girls run in.

Amy first: "Why are you still in bed?"

Emily next, always a step behind. "Mommy's sick, stupid." She climbs into the bed and wraps her arms around Honey. "Hi, Mommy."

Honey pulls Emily across her lap and kisses her. "Hi, baby. How was school?"

She can feel Amy holding back, suspicious. "Are we going to get sick if we touch you?"

"No," Honey says.

"Good!" A second later, Amy's tiny body barrels into them both, and all three fall back against the pillows, laughing.

“School was fine,” Emily says, nestling into Honey’s shoulder, hungry for cuddles.

“Fine and boring,” Amy adds, sitting up. She never snuggles long. “Can we play outside?”

Honey kisses her hand. “Sure.”

Amy pulls at her. “You come with us.”

“Oh, I don’t know. I’ve been in bed all day.”

Emily pulls at her other hand. “Fresh air makes you feel better, right?”

Honey chuckles. “Yes, I do say that.”

The girls keep pulling.

It might be what she needs. Honey relents. “Is it cold outside? Let me get a sweater and some pants on.”

The girls cheer and a little of the burden weighing on Honey’s heart lifts. For some reason, the house feels lighter with just the three of them in it.

That’s not fair to Chad, you’re just mad at him.

Was his being right enough to depress her? Or is she mad at herself for thinking she is more than what she is: a woman in her forties who can no longer see. Who lives in a world that will always be smaller than the one she remembers.

She doesn’t like thinking of herself as a cripple. She rages against that thought. But the terror of the night before hangs about her like a choker bead, pressed tight against her throat. She can’t deny it.

I have limits. They are hard limits. I need to learn to live between them, so I don’t hurt myself. So, I don’t hurt others who care about me.

“Are you coming?” Amy the impatient, the fearless, the prodding, the questing one calls from the open door. “Come *on!*“

Honey remembers what it was like to experience life as Amy does. She prays Amy won’t inherit the blindness from her. But she knows the gods are cruel. It is far more likely that adult-onset blindness or something like it will trim Amy’s wings one day.

Is everything wild destined to be broken and tamed?

The timid hearts like Emily and Chad never seem to suffer in the same way as the wild ones.

Would my life be any easier to bear if I'd been born tame like them? Or is suffering its own blessing?

"Oh, Emily, look! A bunny!" Honey hears Amy's feet pound across the deck and leap off the left side, running into the woods.

"Amy!" Honey calls. "Don't run!"

She knows it is pointless. She hears heavy footsteps crunching over leaves. Emily's cautious feet run to catch up to her sister. They are already past the grove of mountain laurel.

"Wait for me!" Honey calls after them. She grabs the stick. It jingles.

Bells? He put bells on my walking stick. What am I, a dog?

Honey tosses the stick away in disgust.

"Hurry up!" The girls laugh, but Honey's heart seizes in panic.

She doesn't know if she can do this again. Venture into the woods, alone. The woods no longer feel friendly or welcoming. She met the dark that lurks there last night. She doesn't want to meet it again.

But that's what her girls might do without her. They are running straight towards it.

I need to stop them. Protect them.

Honey plunges off the deck and runs through the laurel. She remembers the millstone and the bench this time, avoiding both. She clears the grove.

I can do this.

"Slow down! Wait for me!" Fear flaps behind her like a cape, but it does not slow her down.

Where'd they go?

She listens. There. Footsteps, headed toward the pine grove. Honey pushes her blind self forward, losing caution. She moves the branches away impatiently, trying to run faster. It's so hard to move uphill.

I should have brought that stupid stick. Damnit.

"Girls! Wait for me!"

There is a chill in the air. Honey hears the trees of the pine grove trembling. She passes them. Now she is at the clearing where her path meets the neighborhood trail. This is where she met the monsters last night. She stops.

The sound of her children's laughter filters through the leaves like sunlight. It sounds like they've gone to the right, up the mountain trail. She wants to follow, but the fear presses heavily against her throat.

"Girls!" She calls louder, begging them to come back. But they do not. She wants to turn around, run to the house, lock the door, and climb back under the covers.

This is too much. I'm not strong enough to do this.

A sharp inner voice chastises her, *You would let them face what you fear, alone?*

Honey knows she cannot.

She grits her teeth and turns to the right. She picks her way up the unfamiliar trail, yelling, "Where are you?"

She hears a noise. Sticks breaking underfoot.

Was that them?

She runs up a hill. She falls and bashes her knee against a root. She gets up and continues to run.

Blindly, her mind thinks wildly. *I'm running blind.*

Something about it strikes her as funny. But she's afraid if she starts to laugh she will not stop.

Don't get hysterical.

She forces herself to call out again. "Amy? Emily?"

It is difficult moving quickly because of the incline and uneven ground. She runs into a tree when the path takes a sharp turn to the right. But she thinks she can finally hear their footsteps again. She plunges ahead, so intent on finding and protecting them that she no longer fears for herself.

The footsteps turn off the path. Honey leaps over the edge after them. Something in the air ripples. It feels like she's pushing back a thin curtain as her feet turn downhill. She picks up speed. The frigid wind bites her cheeks, makes her eyes and nose water. But she is so close, she can feel the nearness of them. “Girls!”

The footsteps she’s been chasing stop. The wind dies. She smells something unlike pine and damp leaves. It is almost animal, musky. Could it be her children?

They must be sweaty. Maybe they found the rabbit?

“Girls, come to me.” She opens her arms, triumphant, relieved.

A woman laughs. It is an unfamiliar sound. Honey freezes like a deer in headlights.

The voice tells her, “I would not call us girls, but you must have called because we have come.”

The voice is deep and muscular, but still female. Honey’s spine stiffens.

How did I lose the girls? Who is this?

The voice is kind. “Do you know how you did this?”

How I did this? What does she mean?

Honey’s mouth opens, but no words come out. All the other homeowners here are older than her and Chad, and retired, so many of them hike.

I must have followed one by accident. Does she just want to talk? I don’t have time for this.

Impatience tugs at her.

Only the worst mom would lose her kids in the woods.

“I’m sorry,” Honey says, “this isn’t a good time.”

Though . . . if the woman can see?

“Wait. Have you seen my girls? They were chasing a rabbit and we got separated. Two little ones, about seven and nine? Red hair? Green eyes?”

Then Honey realizes she’s never seen Amy’s face. She lost her sight so soon after Emily’s birth. Amy was born during her time in darkness.

Does she look like me and Emily at all? Or does she have Chad’s coloring: violet eyes and black hair?

The voice sounds confused. "You called us. We came. We haven't seen them. Are you ready?"

"Ready for what?" Honey's neck and arms tingle.

We?

She forces herself to calm down and send feelers out.

Oh, no.

Honey senses multiple people standing nearby, people she hadn't noticed before. In addition to the one who spoke, she can feel two, maybe three more. "Who are you?"

"Why don't you see for yourself?"

The way the voice says that so casually angers Honey.

"That's not fair Sekhmet," a soft, lilting voice says. "You know her condition."

"Do you mean her blindness is self-imposed?" says a third with another accent Honey can't place. "Could she see us if she wanted?"

What does she mean, see them? "I'm blind," Honey says.

But even as she says it, she feels the fog in front of her eyes tremble. She has a flash of a memory: a veil lifting, gazing into a mirror, seeing faces.

That was a dream. Am I dreaming now?

Maybe she's fallen and hit her head. Maybe she's passed out on the path and Amy and Emily are trying to wake her.

Whether she is awake or not, the darkness before her eyes is beginning to lift. Rather than a velvet curtain drawn tight, it is a swirling mist. Honey prays to see the light. If she strains, she can make out four figures of different heights. They all appear to be female, but shadowy as they are, it's hard to tell.

Am I seeing? Is this real?

Honey tries to focus. It hurts her head. As soon as her eyes grip the edge of an image, it slips out of focus again. She shakes her head, but it does nothing to clear the darkness. It pulses, like something alive. It keeps sliding back against her attempts to clear it, like pudding resettling on the bottom of a bowl.

Keep back.

She pushes and gains more ground. It will not hold for long, but by concentrating, she does manage to keep a small window of sight open.

"Well look at that, Sekhmet," says the woman with the lilting accent. "It appears she can see if she wants. Was she spelled?"

"What the Brotherhood does isn't magic," Sekhmet says, bitterly. "It's about mind games and control."

Honey gasps and rubs her eyes.

Am I seeing her correctly? What's on her head. Is that a . . . ?

'Lion' is what Honey wants to say, but it's only Sekhmet's head that is distinctly leonine. Her body, though covered by fur, looks a woman's. A heavily muscled woman, but a woman, nonetheless. "What are you?"

Sekhmet doesn't appear to understand the question. "Your Soul Council."

Soul Council?

"What do you mean? I don't understand."

A young girl walks toward her. A thick web of scars crisscrosses her neck. Honey wants to flinch away, but she cannot. Their eyes meet. Honey sees so much pain there. A pain that she recognizes. And something else. The hairs along Honey's arm, neck, and back stand on end.

I must be dreaming.

This girl looks nothing like her. And yet, sadness is not the only thing they have in common.

She has my eyes.

Honey is unsure if she should run, scream for help, or wake up.

There is only one thing she knows for sure.

I saw this girl in the mirror. She is one of the faces I saw that night. But in the dream, she was the one without a mouth.

Honey stands rooted, firm as a tree battered by wind. She stares into the girl's green-gold eyes, and marvels. How can it be that her eyes are staring back at her from out of this stranger's face?

~ 27 ~

BOOK OF LYRAN, PART ONE: THE BEGINNING

In the beginning, there was only One.

Unity was the beginning and end, light and dark. It was the fullness of everything and nothing at all.

For a while, this Oneness existed, and that was enough.

But eventually, the One became aware of itself and sought to know: is this all there is? Is there nothing else?

Here I am, it thought. *Am I alone?*

In all its seeking, the One could not find anything that lived outside the borders of its own self. It was impossible to know anything but the unity of being One. As perfect as that was, it was not enough.

The One decided that it needed to become more than one thing. It was the only way for it to discover more, grow, know, and evolve.

After all, the One reasoned, *there must be more to existence than peace, grace, love, and truth. If I am to know all and love all, I must experience all that is.*

And so, the One divided itself into Aspects, and gave each Aspect a divine spark. Each divine spark then had a star seed that contained within it all the promise of unique talents and gifts. These talents and gifts would help each Aspect evolve, as it lived out as many lives as it needed to divine the Answer it was designed to seek. The star seed also connected each Aspect of the One to each other, and to an awareness that they had once been the One.

In this way, the One became the divine Source of all things.

And the Aspects reflected all that had once comprised the One—the light *and* the dark. These were brought into being along with Many Worlds to house them.

The Aspects of the One's Light became known as Lyrans. They settled among the Many Worlds on the planet of Vega, in the star system of Lyra. They lived in the light and sought to perfect themselves in search of the Answer. They sought harmony and peace with their neighbors. They allied themselves with the shaded Aspects that favored the light.

The Aspects of the One's Darkness became known as the Brotherhood of the Snake. They settled among the Many Worlds on the planet of Thuban, in the star system of Draco. They craved darkness and sought to obstruct and divide as they sought the Answer. They abhorred the Lyrans and those who honored the Source from which they'd come. They sought to conquer, enslave, and eliminate them.

Part Two

~ 28 ~

SEKHMET

Sekhmet dreams she stands in the shadow of a great stone energy dragon. The pyramid-shaped structure hums with Source. Its connection to the light shines over Earth and the Many Worlds. Pure, healing energy radiates from it to the crown of her head, filling her from toe to tip with its power.

The dragon provides her body with the energy it needs to knit itself back together. As it does, she connects to the other star seeds scattered among the Many Worlds. She tells them everything: her story, sorrow, and how she's failed them in this mission. They comfort and console her.

If you can reach us, they remind her, *all is not lost. Take as much time as you need. You have this lifetime and all the ones beyond. The wheel keeps turning, and the champions will keep fighting until we are One.*

Sekhmet laughs.

They tell me not to give up. That's all I want to do.

She hates this broken body, the humiliation of losing. She takes a deep breath.

The fight is not over yet.

She surrenders her bitterness to the dragon's light. She should not hold onto that kind of darkness in this holy place. She replaces the hurt with music. She selects a note from her heart's song, an aspect of her true nature, and lets it vibrate through her. She finds harmony, then concordance with the natural vibration of the dragon itself.

I am not home, but I am close enough for now.

The light intensifies until it mends everything broken and burns all sickness away.

Sekhmet wakes, feeling whole. She is on her back, gazing at a cloudless blue sky. She sees movement on her right. She leaps into a fighting stance to face the threat and marvels at her body's renewed ability.

It wasn't a dream. I am restored.

She wonders for a moment if she has died.

But if this is rebirth, I wouldn't remember Sekhmet's life. I am still she.

She can feel the Source rising through the soles of her feet. She is standing on top of a stone slab.

Conducive. Connected. Where am I?

Her memories are fuzzy, hidden behind a haze of pain.

They tortured and broke me. Did someone rescue me from them?

She expands her circle of awareness. She stands on a platform in the middle of a courtyard. Everything is arranged to amplify lines of power laid down by the Source.

I thought the Brotherhood destroyed all our dragons. But someone has built one in this space. Who?

As if in answer, a man appears. He holds up his hands to show he comes in peace.

Sekhmet does not strike. Nor does she drop her ready stance. If he is the one responsible for rescuing and healing her, she doesn't want to kill him. But it's too early to know yet what threat level he might pose. His hair is glossy black and looks clean. This is not a farmer or slave. His eyes are a violet shade that makes her think of precious jewels. Something trembles in the air between them.

So, he's more than human.

She senses Lyran blood, something that connects him to the Source. But the light energy emanating from him is not strong.

Maybe he's part human?

Her people have been known to intermix. It helps hide their offspring from the Brotherhood. The blood also provides a line of descent for future incarnations. She knows she eventually will need to breed this way to secure her own line of hosts for future soul journeys.

He claps his hands together and lays them over his heart. "Miracle of miracles. Your healing was wondrous to behold."

He prostrates himself before her.

Satisfied he poses no threat; she lifts him up.

He kisses her hand. "Together," he says, eyes shining, "we shall perform great work."

~ 29 ~

FILOMÉLA

The last mile to safety is the hardest to traverse. Filoméla can't count on her leg muscles. They are exhausted from squatting for the birth. She leans on the women beside her as they run. She hobbles them, but they do not complain.

The newborn creature is lashed to her chest. It lazily paws at her breast as they move through the darkness. Something about how casually the babe eats, how naturally it fits the curve of her chest, softens her hate.

The looming trees lining the road have shifted shades from black to bluish-gray. Where the rising sun touches them, leaves turn green.

Everything is fading away so fast. The women no longer look like fearsome maenads. Now, they resemble dirty children play-acting.

They reach the castle as the sun finally crests a hill. Prōknē's servants greet them with tubs of hot water and fresh linens.

Filoméla slips into a tub and gently unwinds the bandage around the babe. She cradles its sleeping form in-between her knees. She wonders at it as women's hands wash the stink of the forest off her skin.

Prōknē's words rattle around her skull: *it doesn't have to live.* Watching it sleep, with its tiny hands clasped under its dimpled chin, Filoméla is no longer sure what she wants. She takes a tiny hand in hers. Its nails are grizzled, like an old woman's.

How did its nails get so long?

She brings its fingers up to her mouth and clips the nails with her teeth. Tiny eyes blink open. For a moment, Filoméla thinks she sees a flicker of a smile cross its lips. Then, it wails. Filoméla tenses.

But they are no longer in the forest. Now they are in the queen's home, where babies are always around, invariably crying. The women stop to smile at the child's discomfort as if it's the sweetest thing in the world.

Prōknē smiles. "There's a lovely anger in that voice."

Filoméla nods.

That is something we share, outrage at being born.

Prōknē leans over the rim of her tub. "Do you still want me to drown it?"

Filoméla stiffens.

Do I?

She strokes the baby's wailing face. It responds to her touch, grasping her finger between its tiny hands and goes quiet.

She looks up at her sister and shakes her head.

Prōknē leans her head back and lets out a contented sigh. "Let me know if you change your mind. We can always kill it later."

~ 30 ~

FORACH

The sky's bright aspect grates on Forach's nerves. A thunderous storm would better match her current mood. She winces and shades her eyes as she exits her tent and heads toward the river. Aoife dances by her side.

She can feel the women's eyes on her, full of congratulations. Not one of them would turn down the chance to be queen one day. They envy her. That makes them foolish.

No one will enjoy my reign of death and ruin. For that's what will come for us on the High King's horse. Mark my words.

The men smile as she passes. She knows what they are thinking: her whoring might buy them a permanent home, after all.

Stupid. Stupid.

Aoife laughs and claps her hands. It reminds Forach of how her father clapped for the wine last night.

"Don't clap like that," she scolds the child, "people will think you're soft in the head."

She sets the basket down by the river and begins to wash.

A slippery voice startles her from her work. "Congratulations. I hear you're going to be married."

Forach's anger flares. "Ethnui, is there something you have against walking where a person can see you? Must you always be skulking and creeping? You nearly frightened me to death."

Ethnui doesn't snap back. "I come to help you sister." She plucks a soiled nappy from the basket, extending it to Forach like an olive branch.

Forach barks a laugh. "To be sure. You? Helping me? We're not sisters."

Ethnui shrugs her thin shoulders. "Maybe not in blood, but in essence."

Forach's eyes narrow. "Go on with you." She grabs the soiled cloth from Ethnui. She keeps one eye on her as she scrubs her child's mess off onto a river rock.

Ethnui smiles, exposing her wickedly pointed teeth. They flash like bone daggers in the sunlight. "Every woman's buzzing about the match made between you and the Munster king's Óengus. But I can't help noticing that you're not happy about it."

Her tone sets Forach's nerve on edge. "And why would I not be happy?"

Ethnui sits back on her haunches like a coiled snake. She looks for all the world like she's about to attack.

Forach's stomach lurches. She instinctively looks for Aoife. Satisfied the child is safe, she turns her attention back to the witchy beast. "Go on. Tell me. Why would I not be happy to marry my love?"

Ethnui lowers her voice. "You know as well as I that the moment you slip that ring on your finger, you sentence every man, woman, and child in this camp to death."

The sun burns no less hot, but a chill creeps over Forach. It seeps deep into her bones. She searches for a clever quip, something to deflect the truth of what Ethnui has said. She cannot find one. She is caught. But she is not ready to admit that Ethnui is right. She stubbornly sticks out her chin. "And what if that's true?"

"Then you know you cannot wed," Ethnui says, licking her lips.

"What do you think I should do, then?" Forach means to sound mocking, but her voice shakes.

Ethnui smiles. The bony daggers in her mouth make Forach want to scream. "Give him, to me."

Forach frowns. "Give who to you?"

"Óengus. Release him. Give him to me. I'll marry him in your place. My people can back his armies. And I've already forged an alliance with your father. If I marry Óengus, your people will have home. And the High King will not come for them. I'm as well-born as you. Better, even. He'll never miss you. So, give him to me."

The nerve!

Forach wants to laugh. But her anger chokes it at the source. "You want me to give you Óengus? A man's not for giving. A man chooses. He and his father chose *me.*"

Ethnui shrugs. "Then they can choose me just as easily once they realize I'm a better, and safer, match."

Forach shakes her head. "His father would never agree. Aoife is the reason why he wants me to wed. It gives Óengus a legitimate claim to the throne of Tara."

"And certain destruction should he try to grab it in this lifetime." Ethnui's violet eyes glitter with a dark cleverness. "But I can bring into the marriage tribes that control the land to the west and east of the High King's seat. When our children's children come for Tara, they'll win it, and they'll have the strength to keep it. Forever. Surely an ambitious man will see the advantage of that."

Forach's head swims. She grabs the wet things and puts them back in the basket. It is too soon, they'll molder, but she'll hang them on the line. She can't stay here any longer.

"Think about it," Ethnui hisses. "You know it's the only sensible thing to do."

Forach walk-runs up the hill back to camp. "Aoife!"

Ethnui calls after her. "Don't keep me waiting too long for your answer."

Forach shouts over her shoulder. "The answer is no."

Ethnui will not let her be. "Why can't you do anything the easy way?"

Forach ignores Ethnui and calls to her child.

Aoife, curls bouncing, runs to her. Forach drops the basket. She kneels to hold the child. She buries her head in her curls, breathing in the deep earthy scent of her child. She tries to banish all the dark thoughts from her head.

She's not wrong. I can't marry Óengus. But he loves me. He'd never agree to wed her if I'm here. And I can't stay here and see him marry her.

Forach pulls back to look at her child's sunny face, all red hair and freckles and green eyes and sunshine. A cloud passes overhead. In its shadow Forach sees the white mare and the red horse. She is standing on a cliff. But now both she and her lover are racing toward death.

Forach knows there is only one thing she can do.

I pray he forgives me.

~ 31 ~

JUANA

Juana weeds the garden. In her imagination, each invasive plant is a sin. She is clearing a path for God to bring forth new life.

Sor Tamzin calls out, "Sor Juana! You have a visitor. They're waiting in the locutorio!"

Juana drops her gloves and runs in. She arrives breathless. The long, pointed beard-face of Don Carlos greets her. Her face falls.

He chuckles. "Oh, you're disappointed to see me. You were expecting someone else?"

"No," she lies. "I just didn't expect to find you here."

Who did I expect? Leo is long dead.

She blushes at her own idiocy.

"Sor Bridget warned you I was enthusiastic about ideas, did she not? When I've met the most brilliant woman in Mexico City, how could I stay away?"

Juana stiffens. She did not come here to suffer the indignities of male attention. "Don Carlos, if you're going to talk to me in such a familiar way, I must ask you to leave. Please, never visit me again—"

His laughter cuts her off. "Oh sister, you are full of pride. Do you think your earthly body is worthy of my desire?"

She flushes, furious.

Am I wrong? I know men.

She juts out her chin. "I don't appreciate you flirting."

"Oh!" His eyes widen. He claps his hands in delight. "No, my dear, that was banter."

He shakes his head sadly. "I can see now that you've had only the dullest wits to practice yours on. And let me guess, the only appreciation they ever threw your way were proposals? To wed or . . .?" He wiggles his eyebrows instead of finishing the suggestive end of that thought. She hates the amber twinkle in his pale, blue eyes.

Before she knows how to respond, he holds up his hands and relents. "I see I've upset you. My apologies, Sor Juana. I have a habit of doing that. My mind moves faster than I can catch it, and it makes my tongue a reckless beast. I am just so excited to meet someone with a fine mind, noble sentiments, and a pure heart. You don't know how lonely it is . . ."

He reaches for her hand. She snatches it away. "Don Carlos! You upset me, tease me, then want to make love to me? This is too much. I am a bride of Christ. You disrespect our Lord and Savior when you mistreat me. You must leave."

"Make love? Oh no, no, no." He looks around the locutorio to confirm they are alone. He clears his throat. Tamzin abandons the curtain she is dusting and scuttles away.

He lowers his voice. "You've been to court, have you not?"

She doesn't know what he is hinting at. "I have."

"So, you've met men of all types."

"Of course."

"Surely you've met men who don't indulge in the pursuit of women?"

Juana does not hold high opinions of courtly men. In her experience they either want to enslave or impregnate her. Leo's wise instruction, and the odd dram of laudanum, helped her escape most hazards. The one she couldn't . . . well, she knows that could have ended worse. She only had to bear the burden for nine months rather than give up her life's ambition.

She looks at Carlos's trim, well-kept beard and considers his words.

Men who don't pursue women.

Now that she thinks of it, there were a few clever, witty men who never bothered her that way. She fancied one or two, because they were so good-looking. But they were never forward, never tried to kiss or fondle her when no one was looking. Leo sometimes let them sleep in her bed, and they lay there like chaste siblings or fallen angels all night. It took her longer than it should have to realize that was because they weren't interested in women. At all. They preferred the intimate company of men.

She looks warily at Don Carlos. "I have."

"And are they not the dearest and wittiest of our kind? The best friend to women?"

A smile tugs at the corner of her mouth. "They are." Anticipation begins to replace irritation. Not that she wants to soften so soon or warm so quickly to Don Carlos, but if he is what he promises . . . With a man who doesn't desire her, she can pour her thoughts out like wine into a crystal goblet without worry of taint. Their friendship could remain in the realm of ideas and thoughts. She'd never have to worry about it being dragged down by anything physical.

She checks to be sure Tamzin or Bridget aren't lurking behind a curtain, then speaks low. "Is that why you were kicked out of the Jesuits?"

Don Carlos throws his head back and howls with laughter. "Oh, oh, no. But close! I will tell you one day if we become friends. Do you think we can be?"

Sor Juana takes his hand in hers. "I would like that very much."

~ 32 ~

HONEY

Honey breathes hard, but no air reaches her lungs. She bends over to hold her knees, but nothing helps.

Oh God, am I dying? Am I going to die like this?

A hand touches her back. Honey jerks up and away, tripping over a fallen log, and landing in a pile of wet leaves.

The dark, muscular voice, Sekhmet's voice, laughs at her. "This is our champion?"

Honey glares at the lion-woman and realizes that Sekhmet, too, has green-gold eyes.

This can't be happening.

"Are you wearing a mask?" Honey's mind is reeling, trying to make sense of what she is seeing.

Wake up! Wake up!

Honey does not wake up. Sharp sticks prick the bottoms of her palms. But the ground beneath Sekhmet's feet is smooth and white, like marble.

"This isn't a mask. This is my true face."

"Are you going to kill me?"

"I'm not going to kill you."

"I want to wake up," Honey whimpers.

A small, dark woman in a nun's habit places a hand on Sekhmet's shoulder. "Maybe only one of us should have come. She's overwhelmed." Honey recognizes her voice as the other accent she couldn't place. "I imagine it must be a great shock finding out that the fate of the world is in your hands." She turns her tiny, birdlike head toward Honey.

Honey is no longer shocked to discover the color and shape of the nun's eyes is the same as the others.

The same as my eyes. "What do you mean?"

"Sekhmet makes light of it, but you are our champion," the nun says.

Honey laughs. "Of course, I am." She brushes wet leaves off her pants and stands up.

If I can't wake up, I might as well engage.

The fog keeps crossing in and out of view. It's hard to focus on them for long, but she can get a general impression of the four women. "And you're my Soul Council of advisors, right? My soul sisters?"

The nun is small and pale-skinned with reddish hair so dark, it's almost black. Her green-gold eyes sparkle with youthful curiosity, but Honey thinks they're probably close to the same age. The other foreign woman is tall and broad. Her face is freckled and ruddy. Her wild hair leaps like campfire flames about her head. She looks full of mischief. The sad, young one is dark as a nut, with coppery red hair and that angry web of pinkish scarred skin across her neck. Sekhmet looks like she could rip apart machinery with her bare hands.

And then there's me. A chubby, middle-aged blind woman.

Five vastly different women. Ten identical eyes.

What is this dream trying to tell me?

Honey laughs. "Some champion I am." She tugs her top down, wishing it covered her soft belly better. "What am I supposed to be the champion of? Bad decisions?"

Sekhmet frowns. "Maybe we've come too early. She may not be ready."

"But she called us, right?" The tall woman sounds annoyed. "Jeanne wasn't ready to go into battle when we first appeared. I'm sure they all need some training."

"Jeanne had potential you could see," Sekhmet shoots back. "Look at this one. Would you have leaped into the void for her?"

"Did you call us?" The nun cocks her head. "What is your name?"

"I'm Honey. I ran into the woods to find my girls. I was calling them, not you. This is the worst dream."

The nun looks at Sekhmet.

Reluctantly the lion-headed woman steps forward. "This is not a dream. We've been waiting for you. Somehow you did call us from the in-between. My name is Sekhmet, and I am the first of our Lyran line. We think you, Honey, are the last."

Sekhmet gestures behind her. "These other women are other incarnations of our soul's journey on Earth that I harvested to help us. Together, we form a Soul Council of sisters to help you win. For this turn of the wheel, you are our champion. We will help you battle the Brotherhood."

Honey feels herself on the edge of collapse. It's painful trying to make sense of this dream. She's exhausted. Keeping her lines of sight clear from the creeping darkness gives her a headache.

Wheel? Champion? She forces herself to nod. *Maybe if I give in, I can wake up.*

Sekhmet continues, "I was part of a group, the tzaddikim nistarim. We volunteered to come to Earth and battle the Brotherhood of the Snake."

Sekhmet gestures to her Soul Council. "Each of us, in our lifetimes, have battled the darkness in our own way, like how you struggle with your blindness. We failed. Miserably, brutally, painfully. But we have learned important lessons. Lessons we hope will help you, our champion, to win this time."

Honey waits, but Sekhmet doesn't continue. She musters up her courage and asks, "What happens if I don't win?"

Sekhmet shakes her head. "Losing is not an option."

~ 33 ~

SEKHMET

The man before her is tall, lithe, and well-muscled, but not excessively so. There is an easy grace to his movements and a promise in his smile. His skin is smooth and dark, like wood. His deep, violet eyes glitter like amethysts and his hair reminds her of a river stone.

She sniffs. He speaks about working but smells like leisure. This place is untouched by war. The resources needed to ensure that are considerable. "You don't strike me as a man accustomed to working. And you clearly don't fight. Who are you?"

"They call me lord of the two lands." He bows deeply. "But I serve the One, as you do."

Sekhmet sits back on the stone, enjoying how it hums at her touch. He hasn't taken precautions. That's reckless. If she needs to, she can harness the Source's power and weaponize it.

Is it because he's unused to being challenged?

In Kemet, it could mean he's one of two things. And he doesn't look like a priest. "You are a pharaoh?"

He nods.

"Then you serve many gods."

He wags a finger at her. "The Amun priesthood serves many gods. But even the Brotherhood knows there is only the One."

Sekhmet leans forward. He must know it's dangerous to talk like this.

How much power does he have? "The Brotherhood of the Snake would not like to hear that. They like their gods. And the money they generate from the people's worship of them."

He laughs. "Indeed. Did you know that you are one of them now?"

Sekhmet's brow furrows. "What do you mean?"

"I bought this in the marketplace this morning." He claps his hands, and a servant brings out a golden tray. On it stands a delicate figurine. He hands it to her. "I hear you killed ten guards at the dock, tore their limbs off, and threw them into the sea. Too many witnesses to hide it. The Brotherhood needed to explain what happened to the people somehow, so they made you a god."

"More like twenty men. Not that I keep track." She takes the slender clay statuette. It's a beautifully painted sculpture of a woman with a lion's head. "I make a very pretty god. What am I a god of?"

He smiles. "Oh, Sekhmet is a terrifying god of war. The Child of Ra himself, she has been sent here to punish people for being evil to each other. She destroys as fast as she creates."

"Oooh, this terrifying god of war . . . does she have a good side?"

He chuckles. "You also have the power to heal."

She turns over the clay piece and reads the legend, *Eye of Ra*. She throws it back to him. "They're not far off, pharaoh, but they got the name of my origin wrong. What do they call you? What are you a god of?"

"I am not a god," he says as if he means it. "I have no wish to be a god."

Sekhmet snorts. "I have yet to meet a king of men who does not fancy himself at least a child of god."

"That is because you have not yet met me." He draws himself to his full height.

She can see traces of Lyran bloodline in his face. Or, as the Children of the Garden call them: angels. Most of the royal families of Earth either bred with the snakes or Lyrans. Sometimes both.

He places a hand on his breast and bows his head to show respect. "I am Amenhotep, the fourth of his name. I've been waiting for you, child of Aten. I would like to assist you on your mission."

At the sound of that holy name for the One, Sekhmet stiffens. She sends a line through the stone to her people.

Is it possible? Is he to be trusted?

The answer comes as a chorus of voices humming down the dragon lines from the Many Worlds.

Yes. Yes. Yes.

~ 34 ~

FILOMÉLA

Filoméla tenses at the sound of feet pounding down the hallway. She cradles the child at her breast.

Are we discovered so soon?

Instead of guards, it is a red-haired child, her nephew Itys.

"Mama!" He throws both arms around Prōknē's legs. He's too small to hug any higher.

Filoméla watches her sister twirl Itys around. He shouts with glee. Prōknē pretends to nibble at his neck. "Nomnomnom nomnomnomnom. So tasty. I'm going to eat you up!"

"No! No!"

They wrestle for a bit, both howling with laughter.

Will my child and I play like this?

Prōknē looks up, and says with a wink, "They're always monsters until they're born."

Filoméla flinches. Her sister's comment cuts too close to her private thoughts. She looks at the dozing baby in her arms. Drunk on milk, it lazily pats her breast. As it purrs, something like a smile plays across its rosy lips. Filoméla realizes her fear has already transitioned from loathing. And even that is melting away.

Soon, I might begin to love you.

She doesn't know if that is a good thing. She is feathery with fear.

"Look, mama!" Itys holds a small ivory tooth aloft as if it were the head of a Gorgon.

Prōknē takes it from him. "Did this fall out of your mouth today?"

"It did! It did!"

"Well, I will put it to clever use, Itys. Thank you!" She kisses the boy's head. "Go with your nursemaid. She's going to take you on a little trip while I prepare a surprise for your father."

The son is whisked away from the world of women. Filoméla thinks of Tereus. She gestures, asking for a veil.

"To what? Disguise yourself?" Prōknē laughs dismissively. "You don't need to hide. My husband never steps foot in the kitchen. We can work undisturbed."

Prōknē summons her serving girls and gives them orders. The kitchen begins to hum with activity. Prōknē stands at its heart, conducting them all, giving them purpose, making things happen.

Filoméla marvels at her sister's brilliance. So calm, so sure, so unbroken. Next to Prōknē, Filoméla feels useless.

Prōknē turns to her and grins, dark eyes sparkling. "Do you still like to bake?"

~ 35 ~

FORACH

It will be a long, hard, dark night. Forach tightens the binding cloth that ties Aoife to her back. Thunder rumbles.

And a wet night, too.

"Remember," Forach whispers to the child, "not a peep. We'll see who can be quieter, yes?"

"Yes." Chubby hands squeeze Forach's neck. Wet lips kiss the back of her head.

I hope this will only be a game to her, nothing more, when she looks back on this night. That would be a blessing.

She regrets leaving her people. Leaving Óengus is even harder.

But there's no other way to keep them safe. One day, I hope they'll understand and forgive me.

She thinks of Ethnui.

She won't be the only one glad to see me go.

Forach picks her way carefully past the tents. An occasional half-asleep cry or drunken snore punctures the thick wooly silence. Otherwise, she and Aoife are quite, quietly alone.

At the edge of the camp, Forach enters the forest. The canopy of trees closes in, blotting out the stars. The darkness weighs heavily on her. It swirls in the mist between the trees, malignant and searching. Thunder threatens again, but still no rain.

A twig breaks, then two. Forach recognizes the sound of horses advancing through the woods. She reaches behind to grab Aoife's head, warning the girl to stay quiet rather than ask why they're stopping.

Forach steps backward. Her bare feet work to avoid cracking anything that might betray their position.

Lightning flashes, illuminating the sharp points of knocked arrows.

An army? Here?

Forach slips a hand over her own mouth to keep from screaming.

We're caught. I need to go back. Warn the Déisi.

She turns. Something fast whizzes by her nose. There is a thwacking sound as the arrow lands in the ash tree behind her. Forach whirls to face the archer.

Aoife's tiny body shakes, but bless her, she stays silent. Forach is shaking, too. She knows this assailant.

"Ethnui," Forach says. "I am leaving this place. We have no quarrel between us. Let me pass. I'll not stand between you and Óengus."

Ethnui's laugh sounds like dry leaves burning in a fire. "I know you won't. But I can't let you pass. You should have told me you changed your mind. You would have saved me a lot of trouble."

Forach is torn between running and fighting. If she turns her back, though, Aoife will be hit by the next arrow. Besides, the woods are full of men. Forach's hand travels to a blade concealed at her waist.

If I need to, I'll take as many as I can down with me.

A horse approaches on the left. The rider's voice is deep and familiar. "This is well done. You'll have the peace you sued for, Ethnui."

Forach feels the forest falling away at the sound of the High King's voice. It strips her naked and leaves her bare.

The sky trembles with angry thunder. The storm is closing in. A childhood rhyme jumps to mind.

Thundering Taranis wants sacrifice,
Shakes the sky, looking for vice.
Best be wise, better be good,
He'll strike you down inside the wood.

Aoife's hands squeeze so tight, Forach can feel the hairs on her head begin to snap. She grabs a chubby hand and kisses it. She lets the tears fall. No use in holding them back or pretending to be brave. They are caught.

In case I'm not able to say goodbye, please know I love you. Your mother loves you so much.

Lightening chases the thunderclap. Its light flashes across the High King's face. It pools in his empty eye socket and flares against the scar on his cheek.

Forach remembers the night Dread Spear gave him that memento.

He's come to collect the final payment on the debt he thinks I owe him.

Her gut turns.

Forach cannot see Ethnui's face, but she hears the smile in her voice. "You have Princess Forach, and the child, as I promised. You'll have no more trouble from the Déisi. Are all the terms met?"

Aoife remains silent. Forach feels her shaking like a sail in the wind.

He will take Aoife. He will take everything.

She wants to speak, but she can't get her tongue to make the sounds she needs to plead for their lives.

The High King fixes his good eye on Forach, but he addresses Ethnui. "If your people stay in Munster, you'll have nothing more to fear from Tara."

Those are words Forach has prayed long to hear. But this is not the price she wanted to pay.

Dread Ethnui will go down in history as the one who saved us all.

Trees become men. They lay hands on her, ripping Aoife from her back. The forest fills with an awful sound. It takes Forach a long time to realize she is the one who is screaming. The men are a wall of stink, restraining her. Aoife's face is purple in the moonlight, her mouth a sorrowful *O*. The distance between their arms grows, becoming a wide riverbed of sorrow.

Forach watches the High King seat Aoife on his horse and then he is gone. She cries out into the wilderness until she becomes something wild.

By the time they lash Forach to a tree on the cliff, she is beyond reach. The first drops of rain weep from the sky. But Lugh's tears are not enough to douse the flames that lick up the dry wood of her funeral pyre.

The first fingers of rosy dawn peak over the ocean's horizon. Forach focuses her attention away from the pain blossoming at her feet. She turns her mind to the promise, the promise, the promise of a new day.

~ 36 ~

JUANA

There is something about the company of friends that refreshes the soul. It doesn't matter how dull chores are, how monotonous the days. Sunday afternoons with Carlos shake the dust of Juana's cloistered life from her soul. They give her thoughts wings. She never tires of his company. Conversation with him elevates them both. She finds herself running to the locutorio after the afternoon prayers.

"Tell me again, how long it took you to learn Latin?" he asks, or "Do you know the original meaning of the word virgin?"

They discuss ideas, history, science, religion, and dreams. They would talk all night if the sisters didn't fetch Juana away for evening prayers.

One day, he says, "You know, the Nahuatl didn't only worship the big snake, Quetzalcoatl?"

Juana laughs. "Everyone knows that. The Aztec worshiped many gods."

Don Carlos nods impatiently. "Yes, but there is one lord with no cults, who still reigns supreme above them all."

Juana cocks her head. "Are you talking about Ometecuhtli, his father? Or I suppose I should say mother and father since they are a god of duality." Ometecuhtli sits so far up in the heavens, the

Aztecs don't believe the god cares about what happens on earth. Consequently, they don't worship it with the same fervor as the lesser gods who meddle in human affairs.

Don Carlos looks pleased. "Yes. Beneath all their pagan trappings, they worship the same god that we do, only they don't realize it."

Juana watches her friend's nervous fingers play upon his rosary beads. She smooths the rough nap of her habit. "So, you want to compare Aztec theology to our own. Quetzalcoatl was a serpent. A serpent tempted Eve with knowledge. Quetzalcoatl is a god of knowledge. Do you think the serpent Quetzalcoatl tempted the Nahuatl? And if so, how do you explain the bloody way they chose to worship him, if we worship the same god?"

Don Carlos's lips twist into a mischievous smile. "God, or gods, always sacrifice to keep us alive, do they not? And we make sacrifices to thank them for it. Let me ask you a question. How do the blood sacrifices of the Aztecs differ from the blood sacrifices made by the Hebrews?"

Juana laughs in shock. "Well, for one thing, the Jews held sacred the first commandment, thou shalt not kill. There's a substantial difference between a ram and a human child. One is murder, the other is expiation of sin."

"And yet, did not God ask his faithful to sacrifice children as a test of faith?"

"You're being wantonly provocative." Juana frowns. "You know he didn't ask for human sacrifices. God swapped out the ram for Isaac."

"After leading Abraham to believe that he would be sacrificing his only son."

Juana protests.

Carlos holds up a finger to silence her. "And what about Christ? Was he not called to sacrifice himself for our sake?"

"That's not the same thing."

"Isn't it? Is that not the greatest test of faith? Did he not make the greatest sacrifice? 'For God so loved the world, as to give his only begotten Son.' God makes sacrifices for us."

Juana shakes her head. She knows he will not budge on this line of argument, so she chooses a different thread to follow.

"About fathers and sons . . . we say we worship the one true god," Juana begins. "But does not the church truly worship three? The father, the son, and the Holy Spirit, whom we often entangle with the Virgin Mary? Is not the feathered snake of the Aztecs the son of their supreme God? If we are to continue to draw parallels, then we must admit that Quetzalcoatl is like Jesus. He symbolizes the battle between light and darkness. Unless the lesson we are to draw from this is that serpents are always bad."

Don Carlos smiles shyly into his hands. "Is it the serpent or what it stands for that is to blame? Maybe the snake is not bad at all, but only misunderstood. How often have you been told that it is unseemly for women to study? That your seeking after wisdom is a sin of pride?"

"Since I taught myself to read," Juana admits. "And regularly by every man I've outwitted since."

Don Carlos's ice-chip eyes glitter now. He loves teasing her. "Some people would say that is because the mind of a woman is incapable of fathoming the depths. That knowing too much will drive you insane."

Juana will cede him no ground here. This is something she cares passionately about. "Because I'm of the 'weaker sex'? Yes, I am familiar with that line of thinking. But as you can see, the study of biology failed to make me hysterical. I dare to look through a telescope and contemplate the mysteries of the universe. I haven't lost my mind yet."

"No," Don Carlos says, "Your goal is to know, to seek for knowledge's sake, and to serve the light, to bathe in God's love."

She isn't sure where he is going, but she is eager to follow. "Go on."

"Jesus was sent here to deliver God's message."

"Yes."

"But we've only read about how he was sent to the Hebrews." Don Carlos pauses before continuing.

She sucks in a breath. She hates his flair for the dramatic.

"What if, in México, God sent another son, Quetzalcoatl? Or, what if Quetzalcoatl was the name Jesus went by here?"

Juana leans forward. This is an interesting theory. "He was the father of the priests—"

"Like a rabbi—"

"And Quetzalcoatl was not successful, he was defeated and killed—"

"Driven out by the forces of black magic—"

"Darkness," Juana adds, "like the Roman Empire."

"And the Nahuatl expect him to return, like Jesus."

Juana smiles sadly. Montezuma believing Cortés was the reincarnation of Quetzalcoatl was a fatal mistake. He and so many of his people died after putting their faith in the wrong man. "It's an interesting line of thinking."

Don Carlos nods sadly. "In every culture, knowledge is demonized, and the seekers punished. But we do it anyway, despite the sacrifice."

"Life is a wheel that never stops turning," Juana muses. "They say Ometecuhtli released the souls of infants to prepare them for birth. After warriors die, the Nahuatl believe they are reincarnated as hummingbirds. The people of the East believe that the soul must be purified for many lifetimes before being reunited with God. Yet the Church believes we are granted only one life, and we cannot reap any rewards until we die. What are we to make of that?"

"I'll tell you what I make of it," Don Carlos says with a wicked grin. "When men make the rules, sometimes they get things wrong. And when they write history, they only share the perspective that proves they're right. But that doesn't mean we can't reconstruct the her-story of what really happened."

~ 37 ~

HONEY

Honey's head hurts. "What is it I need to win?"

The woman with the flaming hair smiles. "Oh you, know, just the battle between light and darkness. An ancient tale. Nothing you can't handle, champion."

Honey can place her accent now. Irish.

So, I have an imaginary friend who is Irish, one who is a lion-woman, a tiny foreign nun, and a mute girl. Nice set. "You're kidding right?"

The Irish one's smile continues to light up the forest, but the others look solemn.

The nun takes her hand. "You won't be alone. We are with you."

Sekhmet adds, "And others, like you, are beginning to wake up."

"You have the power to wake them," the Irish one says, "and gain their help."

This doesn't make any sense. "Wake them? How?"

The young one touches the scars on her neck and then holds up her hands.

Honey waits, but the woman-child makes no sound. "What happened to her? Why can't she talk?"

"Why can't you see when you're not with us?" Sekhmet says roughly.

A jet of rage flares up. "Because I lost my sight after I gave birth. Adult-onset blindness. It's a thing. And for the record, it's not easy seeing you now. It hurts."

The nun pats Honey's hand. "*Cálmate.*"

Now she recognizes the accent. It's Spanish.

Great. One of my imaginary friends is a Spanish nun. I'm more creative than I thought.

The nun continues, "Filoméla's tongue was cut out by her tormentor. It was restored to her after death, but she does not feel whole enough to speak yet."

Honey recoils. She doesn't like being reminded that these women might be dead. "How do I know that I'm not going insane? If I'm not sleeping, I could be hallucinating. Can you prove to me you really lived?"

"Look for Juana," the nun says, touching her breast. She gestures to the others. "And Forach, Sekhmet, and Filoméla. The Brotherhood has tried to erase us from history, but they can't, not completely. Search the margins."

Leaves crunch. A twig snaps.

Honey remembers the girls. "Emily? Amy! I'm over here!"

Sekhmet stiffens. "We've got to go."

"Wait, will my kids be able to see you?" *That would make me feel less insane.* "Please, don't go."

Juana squeezes her hand again. "Think about how we can spread our message of light to the world. Sekhmet says we need a lot of people to know the truth so we can open the portals and let our people in."

The sound of crunching leaves and laughing girls comes closer. Honey wants to call out again, but she needs to make sense of what Juana just said. "Let who in?"

"Those who have gotten stuck in-between worlds," Forach says. She follows Sekhmet under an arch of mountain laurel. Mist swirls about their feet. "I think it's something to do with the Source. Can you feel it?"

"Mommy!"

Honey's children sound scared. She wants to run to them, but her feet are still rooted.

Juana kisses Honey's hand. "Have faith that you are moving in the right direction. The Answer will find you."

"Wait!"

But Juana steps over the leaves until she stands on the smooth white floor with the others.

"What is the Source?" Honey feels panic licking her throat. "What happens if I can't open these portals?"

She can no longer see Forach, but the Irish woman's gay voice trills through the mist. "Then I guess we'll suffer through two thousand more years of darkness."

The line is tossed off like a joke, but it hits Honey in the gut.

It is getting hard to see again. The mist clots over her eyes, thickening into dark curtains. Filoméla and Juana are only shadows against an arch of blurry green.

Honey calls after them, "Why me?"

She hears Sekhmet's voice in her head: *It's the burden we were chosen to bear. We've carried it this far. Now, it's your turn.*

As her vision eclipses completely, Honey hears Juana say, "You'll find a way to bring us out of the darkness. I know you will."

As soon as the words are spoken, a bitter wind blows them away.

Honey shivers. She stands alone in the woods, blind, cold, confused, and scared.

She hears footsteps on the ridge above her.

She gasps. "Emily? Amy!"

Amy's shrill voice answers. "Mommy! What are you doing down there?"

Emily cautions her not to move. Someone is sliding down the hill, barreling toward her.

A warm, little body nearly knocks her over, hugging her around the thighs. "Mommy!"

Amy.

Honey exhales and holds her tight.

Amy cries. “Oh Mommy, I’m so sorry we ran off.”

Honey’s tears of relief flow over Amy’s wild hair. “I’m so glad you found me.”

Honey lets the girls push-pull her up the path to level ground and hugs them to her, once they’ve reached the top.

Something wriggles in Emily’s arms, poking Honey in the stomach.

Honey touches something impossibly soft and furry. “What is this?”

“The bunny!” Amy shouts triumphantly.

Honey opens her mouth to tell them to drop it, to let it go. She wants to tell the girls that this wild thing could be diseased, dangerous. That they can’t bring it into their house.

But Honey has met something wilder in the woods.

Is this sweet, innocent life really something to fear?

No.

She’s experienced fear. It’s nothing like this rabbit. She forces herself to smile. “You caught it?”

“It came to us!”

Amy and Emily tell her the whole, rambling epic of their bunny-hunting adventure. It ends with how it hopped right into their arms.

Honey surprises herself by saying, “Some wild things want to be found. If it chose you, it must be yours to care for now.”

~ 38 ~

SEKHMET

The Brotherhood of the Snake never show their true faces. They hide behind whatever veneer makes them look like a planet's dominant species.

This is a habit Sekhmet loathes. She especially hates wearing a mask of humanity, as they do. Not only does it make her feel like a hypocrite, but it also robs her of her ability to channel and shape the Source. She doesn't have access to her vast reserves of strength while in human form, either. But she's no longer free to be herself in public. Every stand in the marketplace sells statuettes of the lion-headed goddess Sekhmet.

What a clever idea. Now every man, woman, and child in Kemet knows what I look like. And if I'm spotted, news will travel fast. I can't be taken again.

"I hate it." Sekhmet prods the cheekbone of her new face. It's retained the structure of her leonine one, but she misses the warmth of fur, the wild plume of her mane. Her nose looks too narrow in the reflecting glass, her eyes too small. Her ears are ridiculously situated where she can't even see them. And don't even get her started on how useless these hands and limbs are. She hates how naked she feels in this skin.

The puny frame impedes her power, but thankfully not her senses. They remain keen.

She hears Amenhotep's bare feet on the tile and lays down the mirror. She is eager to talk but does not want him to think she is vain. She casually drapes herself over a long chair. She doesn't want him to think her too eager to see him, either.

He enters, admires her new form, and announces, "Behold, a beautiful woman has come!"

He always praises her. She does not need or appreciate it. But she does need his help. So, although she does not enjoy it, she lets him flatter her. He waits for an invitation to sit.

She enjoys his respect and encourages his deference. After all, she is an Aspect of the One. She extends her invitation.

He looks at her with a little too much heat. She doesn't like the way it prickles. His amethyst eyes make her feel naked. Then he smiles, and that soothes her discomfort. "What should we call you now?"

She raises her eyebrows. "You don't want to call me Sekhmet?"

He laughs. "With all of Kemet looking for the lion-headed goddess? In twenty years perhaps that will be a popular name, but the goddess was only just introduced a few weeks ago. No, it's too soon for you to have adopted it. You need another name. One that's more native to our people."

She thinks of his ridiculous, effusive praise, how over the top it is. How extravagant everything in Kemet is.

She laughs. "How about what you called me before?"

He looks at her curiously, begging for a hint.

She goads him. "What did you say when you saw me sitting here?"

"A beautiful woman has come?"

"Don't you think that should be my name? In the common tongue, it's Nefertiti?"

"Yes."

"Think of it. Every time they call me that name, they'll reinforce the idea that I'm human." She laughs and claps her hands.

"How clever you are." His laughter mingles with hers. "So, we're to call you Nefertiti?"

She rolls the name around her mouth. It's not as powerful as her true name. But there's something about it that fills her with delight. "Yes. Nefertiti."

"It suits you," he says. He moves from the chair to sit at her feet. He takes her hand. "My queen."

She does not pull away. His human blood has diluted the Lyran blood of their shared ancestors. But she feels power vibrate through him, and she wants it. His true name in the Ivrim tongue means "to draw out." And though he's unable to tap into the Source as she can, many things are drawn to him: wealth, power, luck, and people.

She, too, is drawn to him. She does not care for love, does not like the way it dulls other desires and sharpens longing into a stick. She'd rather be in the field, face to face with the enemy.

No one wins at love.

But he has convinced her that love is the way to beat the Brotherhood. That it is stronger than she thinks.

"After all," he murmurs between kisses, "what we do is for the people, out of love for them. If we can bring them closer to the Source, help them see the light, we may be able to win this war without further bloodshed."

It feels maniacally simple. Yet she has come to believe it is possible. After all, she's seen what happens when you simply attack.

Fire burns out without fuel. It leaves a trail of destruction and toxicity that poisons everything.

But the watery path of love . . . water's insistent, peaceful, relentless passage. Given enough time, it undermines the tallest structure and reshapes the roughest stone.

There's more than one way to be a warrior. More than one way to win a war.

"We will sweep over them like the Nile," he whispers as she arches in pleasure, "and cleanse this land of darkness. Together."

~ 39 ~

FILOMÉLA

Revenge is demanding work. There's a laundry-list of preparations. But prepping and baking the meal is the easy part. What Filoméla struggles with is hearing the women around her laughing. It's painful listening to them telling stories, swapping jokes, and being unable to join in. All she can do is smile and let the buzz of their conversation wrap her like a blanket.

It feels odd not to have any children around, but Prōknē sent them all away. "It's not safe," she insists. "Once we've scared him and reconciled, then they can return."

Filoméla rolls out the dough for top layer of crust for her meat pie. This will be the centerpiece of their revenge. It feels good to be elbow-deep in making. Transforming butter and meat into something magical is incredibly fulfilling.

She used to love baking in her father's house. At first, he discouraged her from dirtying her hands at the work. But her pies were better than what their kitchen slaves made. Eventually, he indulged her eccentric habit, even making requests on special occasions.

Prōknē stands over a bucket, washing blood off her hands.

What on Earth is she up to?

She holds up a set of Itys's clothes. "Props. I smeared them with lamb's blood." She dries her hands on her skirts and pokes a finger in the center of the pie's beef filling. Filoméla slaps her hand away, but Prōknē manages to get a taste in. Her eyes close in rapture. "Oh, sister, you make masterpieces."

Filoméla wishes she could do more than smile dumbly, but the reunion with her sister is its own kind of bliss.

Prōknē grins wickedly and holds up Itys's little tooth. She winks and drops it into the filling of the pie.

Filoméla tries to extract it, but Prōknē stops her, pushing it deeper. "Let Tereus think we're crazy enough to kill the child and serve his carcass to him. It will drive him mad with grief. We won't let him suffer long. But I want him to feel guilty and repent what he did to you."

Filoméla thinks of what Tereus did to her. Abduction, rape, mutilation.

I don't think a meat pie, even if he thinks it is filled with his dead son's meat, is punishment enough. My father would have castrated him, flayed his skin from his bones, and flown it as a flag upon our battlements.

Prōknē insists they not involve their father, though. Her marriage to Tereus ended a hundred-year war. "Do you want to start that nonsense again?"

No. But I wonder if you're still in love with him. Does he even feel guilty for what he did to me? We're letting him off easy.

Filoméla is almost disappointed that there will be no war to avenge her. A terribly delicious meat pie followed by atonement doesn't seem enough.

Prōknē pinches the crust closed and slips the pie into the oven. "This will do the trick. Trust me."

~ 40 ~

FORACH

The pain is an ocean, and she is drowning. Instead of cold darkness, though, she is illuminated. Forach sees nothing but the dawn and thinks of Aoife's smile.

Ethnui was right that I would die alone.

She was wrong about the ravens, though.

The flames will leave nothing for them to fight over.

She wants to close her eyes, but her eyelids have burned away. Tears turn to steam as soon as they're shed. She hears them mingle with raindrops, sizzling on the pyre.

I was the one racing to my death, only I was too proud to see it.

Aoife has been taken from her.

But the High King will make her his heir, she'll have a good life.

Óengus will think she left him.

You did. He's Ethnui's now. As you intended.

Her heart aches.

But not like this way . . .

Forach remembers her father. The pit of despair in her chest grows wider.

It's not fair to him, losing both children. We should have outlived him.

But there will be a peace. That will be better for the Déisi than exile.

Once the fire dies, will the Déisi know me? Or will my body lie here unclaimed?

The sea will take her bones. Its salt will scour away the char marks. One day, she'll wash up broken somewhere else, white and smooth as a shell. Scattered along the shores of the wide world beyond the one she knows.

Will anyone miss me? Will anyone remember me at all?

The trail of the Sionna River catches fire in the dawn's light. It snakes toward the sea. There, its white peaks become a mouth of pointed teeth.

No. I'll not have my dying thoughts be of her.

The sea loses its teeth. Forach stares into the sun. She wants to walk into its light and leave this accursed world behind.

And then she does.

Pain recedes like the tide. She's afraid to look back. She wants to see what's happening to her body. But she's scared that if she looks, she'll go mad. Or worse, get caught between the worlds.

Move on.

She expects Cian will meet her on the other side. But he's nowhere to be seen. Instead, two women greet her.

Or rather, they both have womanly bodies. One has the head of a beast. The other looks to be about Ethnui's age, small and somber.

The beastly woman is bigger than anyone Forach's ever seen, larger than Dread Spear, even. From the neck down she looks comely, but a head like a lynx or a giant cat sits where the woman's face should be.

But the cat-woman's eyes . . . there's something about them that draws Forach in. She moves closer to be sure she can trust what she's seeing.

Oh no. How can this be?

Forach recognizes those eyes: green-gold and burning. She should. They've looked back at her from every pool of water, every looking glass since the day she had eyes to see.

Forach turns to the woman-child. This one's hair is reddish-brown, with skin darker than any person Forach knows, but there's no mistaking it.

Both women have the same eyes.

My eyes.

"Who are you?"

Instead of answering, the cat-woman embraces her. Forach feels something powerful hum through them both.

The woman-child joins them.

Forach lets herself be held, lets herself be healed.

She feels like she's being made whole.

There is powerful magic here.

Perhaps the end, she thinks, *is not always the end.*

~ 41 ~

JUANA

She places the tub full of dishes by the sink. Sor Paola looks up and wipes a lock of hair from her forehead with a soapy wrist. "Is that all of them?"

"I think so." Juana grabs a towel and moves to the other side of the sink to help.

They work in silence for a while, Paola washing, Juana drying.

Juana doesn't know why she can never find words for Paola when they are alone. When Bridget and Tamzin are with them, conversation flows like water. For hours, the four of them find no end of things to explore, laugh, and exclaim at.

Juana sneaks a glance at Paola.

Is it me?

She wonders if Paola only tolerates her when the others are around. But then she remembers the night the trio first visited her chambers. The way Paola questioned her made Juana feel prickly.

There was something in that heat.

Paola hands her a cup. Their fingers brush. Juana's cheeks flush. She dries the cup a little longer than the others, almost afraid to grab another one.

Paola laughs, her voice raspy and teasing. "I think that one's dry enough. Are you ready for another?"

Juana forces herself to put it down and holds out her hand.

Instead of wet clay, a warm hand pulls Juana close. She looks up in surprise.

Paola furtively kisses Juana on the lips.

The kiss is so brief, Juana wonders if it has happened at all. Her fingers move to her lips, trying to decide if she's imagined how soft, sweet, and sudden it was.

Paola chuckles again and hands her a cup.

Madre Abadesa's voice intrudes upon them. "Sor Juana!"

Juana drops the cup. It shatters.

The two sisters whirl around and bow their heads to the abbess in respect.

Did the Madre see us? The thought sends a shiver of white fear up Juana's spine.

The Madre's face betrays nothing. "Sor Juana, come with me."

Juana is too terrified to look at Paola. Red-faced and ashamed, she follows Madre Abadesa out of the kitchen. They travel down the hall, up the stairs, and down another hall. She feels sweat trickling down her back. Her mind spins.

Is she going to throw me out? What will happen to Paola?

Madre Abadesa stops at her office door and gestures for Juana to follow. "Sit."

Juana does as she is told, eyes downcast.

Surely I'll be allowed to atone for this sin?

She makes a mental note to avoid Paola in the future. Or only see her if Bridget and Tamzin are with them.

Was it even an intentional kiss? It could have been an accident.

Juana remembers how her heart fluttered at Paola's touch. She flushes hotter.

Madre clears her throat.

Terrified, Juana raises her head to meet the older woman's gaze. She is surprised to find no malice. In fact, the Madre is looking kindly upon her.

"You know we will have a new Virrey soon," Madre begins.

Juana isn't sure where this is going. "Yes?"

"Whenever a new Virrey arrives from Spain, there is a celebration."

What does this have to do with kissing Paola?

Madre Abadesa sighs. "I don't know why they requested *you* but . . ."

Juana straightens.

Maybe I'm not in trouble? I've been requested. For what?

It would be rude to speak without permission. She waits for Madre to explain.

Finally, the older woman shrugs. "The city fathers desire a pair of triumphal arches to welcome the new Virrey to México-Tenochtitlán. Don Carlos is to design one."

Juana's heart leaps in excitement for her friend. She claps her hands in joy, forgetting how rude she is being. "What an honor for him!"

Madre frowns. She looks down her long nose at Juana and sighs. "And they requested that *you* design the other."

~ 42 ~

HONEY

Chad is not impressed. "I was about to call the police," he says. "I got home a half-hour ago. Where have you been? And Honey, you went without the stick?"

She mentally counts to ten to keep from exploding. *I can't even start with that now.*

Emily whimpers. Amy protests. Honey inserts herself between them and their father's disapproval. "We were playing in the woods."

"Clearly."

"We'll go wash up." She pushes the girls toward the stairs.

Chad's voice stops them. "You can't bring that thing upstairs!"

Uh-oh. The bunny.

Both girls squeal.

Honey places a hand on Chad's chest. "Can you find a cage or something they can keep it in?" She can feel him tense, knows he is about to erupt so she kisses his cheek and whispers, "Please?"

"Give me the rabbit." He doesn't sound happy. But he also doesn't say no. That is as good as it will get.

Honey follows the girls upstairs to draw a bath for them. Then, she comes down to shower. She hears Chad in the living room. "Did you find something for the bunny?"

"I found an egg crate we can tip upside down on a cookie sheet with newspaper for now. But honestly, what on Earth were you thinking?"

Honey shrugs. "You know Amy when she gets something stuck in her head. And it just came to them, jumped right into their arms. I couldn't say no. It seems tame."

She doesn't wait for him to argue. She sweeps into the bathroom, leaving him to mutter about wild things and the woods on his own.

The water takes a while to warm up. As it does, she goes over the conversation she had in the woods with the strange women. She has far more questions than answers. As soon as she's alone, she wants to look up the women's names and see what she can find.

She hears the girls giggling and splashing upstairs. Their bathroom is right above hers. "Try not to splash any water out of the tub," she calls up the pipes, their own private intercom system.

The girls giggle back, "Okay, Mommy!"

She leaves her clothes in a pile by the door, where they'll be easy to find and pick up later. She remembers what Sekhmet said about her disability and gets angry all over again.

I don't choose to be blind!

But she wasn't blind when she was with them.

Why is that?

She muses out loud, "Maybe I'm not using my eyes to see?"

Absurd. How else can you see?

"And they're all what . . . versions of me?"

A lion-headed woman, a mute girl, an Irish maiden, and a Spanish nun. It sounds like the beginning of a dirty joke. She washes her hair and laughs as her fingers pluck leaves and pine needles out of her curls. She can't imagine how crazy she must have looked to Chad.

Am I going crazy?

She doesn't feel like it.

If I am crazy, would I even know?

She chuckles. "I'm seeing things, and I'm blind. That's probably a tip-off that I'm going insane."

She rinses the dirt of the forest down the drain and steps out of the shower.

"Chad? Can you check on the girls and make sure they've rinsed the shampoo out of their hair?" They are old enough that she can leave them alone to get clean, but they are horrible at washing their hair. Or at least rinsing the half-bottle of shampoo they usually use out of it.

She pulls on a robe and tosses her dirty things into the wash basket. She feels around the counter and picks up her phone. She sits on the couch and speaks into it: "Siri, who is Sekhmet?"

"In Egyptian mythology, Sekhmet is the goddess of war and healing. Would you like me to read more?"

Bingo!

Honey shivers with anticipation.

Is it going to be this easy finding them all?

"Yes, please."

The faux-British voice continues. "Sekhmet is depicted as a lion-headed goddess. She was the protector of pharaohs and led them into battle. After death, she guided them to the afterlife. She is a sun deity said to be the daughter of Ra."

Lion-headed.

Check.

Goddess of war and healing?

Well, she was terrifying. Good to know she has a softer side.

Led them to the afterlife?

Is that where Honey met them? In the afterlife? That would make sense if they were all dead.

Let's see if Siri can tell me about the others.

"Siri, who was Forach?"

"Marco Anthony Archer, better known by his stage name Phora, is an American rapper from Anaheim, California. Would you like to hear more?"

Clearly not the person I'm looking for. "No, thank you."

"No problem." Siri sounds chipper, but Honey is disappointed.

Maybe I mispronounced her name? Or maybe I need an Irish accent?

She moves on. "Who is Juana?"

"I'm sorry, I can't complete your request. There is no Juana in your contacts."

Damnit.

She sighs. "Hey Siri, tell me about Philomela."

"I found this on the web."

Honey sits forward. *Thank God, I got another hit.* "What does the first article say?"

"Philomela is a minor character in Greek mythology that is often evoked in literature. After being raped and mutilated by her sister's husband Tereus, she obtained her revenge and was transformed into a nightingale."

Honey thinks of the thick scars on the dark girl's wrists and throat, how she refused to speak.

"Oh! She's in *The Metamorphosis*!" Honey studied Ovid's book in college.

Honey's professor made a big deal about how Philomela's tapestry told the truth of her trauma after her abuser thought he had silenced her. She insisted that proved "art had transformative power to overcome suffering."

Honey didn't agree.

All it proves is that men have always felt entitled to take what they want at a woman's expense.

It also didn't seem fair that everyone in the story—the abused and the abuser—all got turned into birds.

Why was he allowed to pursue them? Didn't the women suffer enough?

Honey sighs. It's too bad that Siri couldn't tell her about Juana or Forach. But she isn't completely empty-handed. "Two out of four's not bad."

“What are you talking about?” Chad’s voice startles her. His footsteps descend the stairs. “And why are you sitting around in your bathrobe? You should get some pajamas on, it’s cold.”

She rises, reluctantly. “I was researching something I heard earlier today. I don’t feel cold.”

“Honestly,” he says. She bets he is shaking his head as he does. “You’re as bad as the girls. I don’t know what you’d do without me.”

~ 43 ~

BOOK OF LYRAN, PART TWO: THE TURNING OF THE WHEEL

Soon after the One divided into its many Aspects and became the Source, back when the Aspects were new and nothing was known of Light and Dark, before even the creation of the Many Worlds, the Aspects gathered to understand their awareness of the Source and what it required of them now that the One had become many.

Nothing is required, the Source told them, *save to experience and learn. Each of you is uniquely positioned to discover an Answer. When you have discovered the Answer you were born to know, return here, to the Source, and we shall again become One.*

The Aspects asked the Source, *How long will it take us to discover our Answer?*

The Source replied, *That will depend on your soul's journey. It may pass through many lives, gathering what it needs to know, a piece at a time.*

The Aspects conferred among themselves and were troubled. They applied another question to the Source. *If we return at separate times, how is it we can unite into the One?*

The Source considered this. *I will set a great wheel to spin and track our time of searching. The wheel shall spin for one Great Year, or 25,776 revolutions. At the end of the Great Year, all Aspects shall return to me. During the year, you may live many lives, as long or short as needed. Bring your Answer with you to our reunion. There, the many shall become One, once more, united in love.*

Part Three

~ 44 ~

SEKHMET

Sekhmet gazes upon her husband. He stands tall and straight, like a reed from the bank of the Nile. The priests joke that the midwife plucked him from the mighty river instead of a woman's womb. He is so unlike the other pharaohs of Kemet. Like its wild waters, he gives life to this country and its people.

That's not the only way he differs from the pharaohs who came before him. Her husband is no shadow puppet of the Amun priests or the Brotherhood. In fact, he's shrugged off the name Amenhotep and taken a new one to proclaim his faith in the One, whom they call Aten. He tells the people of Kemet to eschew their many idols for the One. His new name, Akhenaten, cements monotheism in their mouths. As does the name of the city he builds: Akhetaten.

This new capital city is where they'll plant the Lyran seed and encourage faith in the One. From this seat of power, they will awaken their people to the Source. They will teach them to harness its light.

That is the "great work," Akhenaten seduced her with. They are five years into his plan, and it continues to bear fruit.

As do I.

It was never Sekhmet's intention to marry, but she needed to hide in plain sight. And better as Royal Wife Nefertiti than as the fugitive Lyran warrior Sekhmet. She rubs her swollen belly.

Two sisters already brought into this world. Soon there will be three.

She wants seven, in honor of her Lyran brethren from the Pleiades. Akhenaten insists they must have at least one son, to continue the royal line. She hasn't decided yet if she will grant his request. She dislikes this preference for the male. It smacks of the Brotherhood. But they can't flaunt all the rules. The Brotherhood and their lackeys, the priests, will wink at their eccentricities. If they don't disrupt the established system of power.

I will do what I must to keep the peace.

In the light of the fading sun, Sekhmet sees the faint outline of the first of two energy dragons. It is nearly complete.

They will connect us directly to the Source. Perhaps we'll be able to open the channel with the people's prayers.

The thought comforts Sekhmet. It's not even her turn of the wheel. If she can prepare the people of Kemet for the champion. They might be able to end the Great War in this lifetime if she can open the channel between the worlds.

If we're smart, who in Waset will even know what we're up to until the work is done?

Akhenaten catches her eye. He smiles and gestures toward the broad avenue he's constructed. "What do you think?"

Sekhmet frowns at the colossal statues guarding the road. They are massive and imposing. And look like they are trying to outdo the opulence preferred by the Amun priests.

They are supposed to be welcoming visitors. Sometimes I wonder if he understands what we're trying to do.

A red granite effigy of him is mirrored by a pure white quartz statue of her, as Nefertiti. They are terrifying.

She snorts. "It looks like you want our people to worship more than one god."

He laughs and takes her face in his hands. He kisses her cheeks. "They won't, my love. But if we want to remain in power long enough to complete our work, we need to inspire some fear. And it's important that people think of you as my equal. This work accomplishes both."

She teases, "Your equal?"

He places his hand over his heart. "They'll soon learn how much greater you are."

She kisses his lips and eyelids. She tries to pull him close, but he bumps against the swell of her belly.

So many seeds planted.

It's good they're not at war, that they chose this peaceful, more subtle path.

Children are a liability. A vulnerability.

True, they are a constant vexation. Yet, Sekhmet has discovered children inspire joy.

But is motherhood good for me? Am I losing my edge?

She has a tough time reconciling who Queen Nefertiti is with who Sekhmet was.

They both live inside of me. But who am I now?

The duality exists in the myths told about her, too. New ones have popped up to explain her disappearance. The Amun priesthood says that her father Ra transformed her into Hathor, a goddess of love. The Brotherhood of the Snake are more derisive. Sekhmet fell in love, they say. Now she's a domesticated cat goddess Bastet, a healer. No threat at all.

Wishful thinking. Still, it's not too far from the truth. I am domesticated. A mother is a neutralized threat, is she not?

She tries to imagine combat while pregnant.

I'm sure protectiveness would make me fiercer. But how would I maneuver with all this extra weight? And I'd have to recalibrate everything around this awkward center of gravity.

She decides, pregnant or not, she needs to resume her training. The breeze lifts her hair, displacing her unpleasant thoughts. It smells sweet.

It is so different here. So open and free, compared to the fetid squalor of Waset.

She closes her eyes and listens. The Earth hums beneath her. "The ground is so good. The Source sings from every corner of this city. You have chosen well Akhenaten."

Small hands tug at her skirts. Sekhmet bends down and lifts her daughters, careful not to fall over from the weight of the unborn child. She kisses their sticky cheeks until they squeal with delight. "What do you think of your new home?"

The eldest, Meritaten, crinkles her nose. She is so serious, so literal. The blue flecks in her large black eyes stand out like flower petals in a lagoon. She scans the landscape and her small forehead knots with concern. "Where is it?"

The youngest, Meketaten, is wild like a monkey. She points to the statue of her father and asks, "Why did they make your nose so big, Baba?"

Amenhotep takes Meketaten into his arms and whirls her around until she squeals. "To sniff out corruption, habibi."

The child kisses her father, points to Sekhmet and asks, "Why did they make Ommi so skinny?"

Meritaten defends her. "Ommi doesn't stay fat, stupid! She gets thin in-between babies."

"That's right," Amenhotep says, "but no matter what shape your mother is in, she's always beautiful, isn't she?" He winks.

Sekhmet shakes her head "For a pharaoh, you are a silly man."

He kisses her head and throws his free arm around her. For a while, the four of them stand watching the sun set over their future home.

Sekhmet shivers as darkness begins to lick at the feet of the mammoth idols.

Nothing good lasts.

Sekhmet throws an arm around Akhenaten's waist and pulls him tight. "The priests have indulged us so far. How long do you think they will let us do our work unmolested before they come for us?"

His voice does not shake, and he does not hesitate in his reply. "It does not matter. Let them try to stop us."

~ 45 ~

FILOMÉLA

Filoméla quivers like the golden-brown pie, but she is full of malice, not meat.

The smell makes Filoméla's mouth water. She isn't invited to dinner with Tereus. She will hide behind a curtain while Prōknē confronts her husband.

Prōknē takes the pie and reverently places it among grape leaves. "A masterpiece. Well done, sister." She hands the charger to a serving girl and squeezes Filoméla's arm. "It will work. Stand here until you're ready to come forth and be seen."

Filoméla nods and hides herself. She stands behind the thick woolen wall hanging. Behind her is a long, slender window. It overlooks the woods below. Beyond that, the sea hurls itself against the rocks, regathers its strength, and tries again.

I thought I was useless, like a sword broken in battle. But perhaps, I am more like those waves. I keep finding new ways to go on.

She cannot see her father's home. But it exists somewhere beyond the waves. In his castle, he'll be sitting down for dinner soon, too.

She hears the rustle of linen. The clank of serving ware signals the final preparations. Her heart flutters like a bird's. She imagines Tereus tearing his hair, beating his breast, and begging her forgiveness. Her hands dance around the space where she carried the monster. She remembers how tight it stretched during her captivity. Now, her belly feels slack and useless.

But it is arduous work making magic. And I have transformed something monstrous into a child.

Her breasts hurt. Now the front of her dress is damp with milk. She curses silently.

It's time to feed her.

She yearns to hold her baby again. She wants to feel its toothless mouth sucking and feel the little thrill run up her breast while it eats. She shakes with the revelation that she feels something for the child.

I suppose I'll have to give it a name.

The thought pleases her. She smiles into the dusty curtain separating her from future justice.

Tereus enters the room. She knows his step and smell. No amount of time will burn him out of her memory. Her wrists and throat itch as if the wounds have reopened. She wants to cry.

Don't be stupid. He doesn't deserve any more tears.

She takes a deep breath and banishes self-pity. She focuses instead on her hate. Now it is a psychic ember sharp enough to kill.

Tereus orders people about. He settles down for the meal. Prōknē serves him the pie. It pleases him. He speaks about how tasty it is. She serves him piece after piece, encouraging him to eat it all.

He discovers the clue Prōknē planted. Itys's tooth.

Filoméla peaks through an opening in the curtained wall. She wants to see the look of horror on his face.

Tereus looks confused, not terrified, as he examines it.

Filoméla swallows disappointment.

There's still time. Perhaps he doesn't realize what the tooth means. He will soon. Then, the idea that he ate his only child will consume him.

A domed dish is brought out. Prōknē smiles wickedly. "I hope you enjoyed your feast. There's one more course." She lifts the domed lid, exposing Filoméla's tapestry. "It's time for the truth."

Filoméla pushes her way out of hiding.

This is the moment for which I've been waiting.

She has so much to say to this man, and no way to say it.

What a cruel joke.

The tapestry he holds in his hand will have to be enough. She watches him make sense of the figures that lay his shame naked to the gods.

Tereus looks up at Prōknē.

She claps her hands to summon the servants. "I know everything that you did to my sister. You will pay for your sins." A basket of bloody clothes is brought in. They are thrown at his feet. "This is all that is left of our son."

"Itys?" He looks at again at the tooth.

"Did you like how he tasted?" Prōknē gestures to the empty pie dish. "We made your feast as monstrous as you are."

It's time.

Filoméla steps forward. Tereus sees her. He drops the tooth and yells for the boy. "Itys!"

For a long, dreadful moment, there is silence. He calls again. And again. And again.

Prōknē finally speaks. "He's dead, my lord. Because of your foul misdeeds."

He finally acknowledges Filoméla. "You."

Filoméla takes Prōknē's hand. She trembles but reminds herself that there is nothing that he can do to her anymore.

I am here, with Prōknē, surrounded with women who are on our side, not his.

Filoméla takes a deep breath and waits. This is the moment she's waited for. His expression is inscrutable.

Will he go mad? Rage at us? Throw himself upon me and beg forgiveness?

Instead, he throws his head back and laughs.

Prōknē's women exchange glances.

This isn't how it is supposed to go.

"Little lord Itys is dead, King Tereus," one of them says, as if to remind him that this is serious business.

He only laughs louder. "Oh, this is good. Exceptionally good." He fixes Filoméla with his terrible eyes. "And I suppose *you* killed our child?"

It takes her a moment to realize what he is asking.

He turns to Prōknē. "Or did you kill our son?"

Prōknē is so surprised by his reaction, she's unable to respond. When they rehearsed it, she was haughty, proud even.

Tereus roars. "Oh, you silly women."

Filoméla looks at her sister.

He's not repentant, horrified, or remorseful.

This all feels . . . dangerous somehow.

Have we played at power and lost?

Tereus no longer looks like himself. The thick beard is vanishing into his neck. Under the hair, something green and smooth closes over the skin. His head changes shape. The nose and chin blend together. His skin looks green and scaly.

Filoméla's heart leaps.

Maybe the gods are punishing him at last?

They have been known to transform mortals into cows, flies, and all manner of vegetation. Now they have transformed her tormentor into a giant snake. He stands upright like a man, with hands and feet, but there is nothing human about the way he looks now.

What's wrong with him? Isn't he scared?

Tereus's face betrays no fear. Instead, he smiles.

Something icy grips Filoméla between her shoulder blades. She wants to scream.

"Very good." The snake man claps those horrible hands together and walks toward them. "Well done."

Filoméla sees her fear reflected in Prōknē's eyes. She doesn't know what devil this man is and she doesn't want to stay to find out. She yanks at her sister's hand, whirling them both around.

"Wait," Tereus calls out mockingly. "Don't you want to stay and talk? It's been such a long time, Filoméla."

She's too frenzied to let his barb land.

We must get out of here.

Her eyes dart around the room. They catch on the window. She pulls Prōknē after her. They must get away from this thing.

Prōknē protests, but Filoméla jerks her roughly. He will kill them, or worse. Prōknē must see that.

He lunges for them, and Prōknē stops resisting. She turns and runs with Filoméla. They crash through the window together.

I'd rather die than stay and see how he wants to punish us.

But they do not fall to their deaths.

Something in the air holds them aloft. Filoméla's mouth works wordlessly.

The air before them trembles and opens. The hand of some fearsome god plucks them out of the sky, and Filoméla feels herself fill with trembling light.

~ 46 ~

FORACH

Forach remembers burning. Now she feels whole. "Am I dead?"

"What do you think?" The voice from the catlike one sounds harsh.

"I think you must be sidhe," Forach says, chin out. "Else why you be wearing that mask?"

The cat's mouth opens wide, giving Forach a glimpse of fangs Ethnui would have envied, and roars in anger. "I'm no cat. And no sidhe. They work with the Brotherhood. I am Sekhmet, of the Lion-Hearted Lyrans. This is my true face."

The child-woman says nothing.

Forach isn't sure what a lion is, but it must be a big cat. Not that she'd dare say something like that out loud again. Feeling awkward, she looks at the small, dark one. Staring into those green-gold eyes makes Forach uncomfortable. This child's refusal to speak makes it worse. She notices a thick web of scars crisscrossing the young one's neck. "What's wrong with her that she can't speak?"

"It's not that she can't speak. She won't. She's not ready yet."

Sekhmet pats the seat beside her. "You should make yourself comfortable. We're not in any hurry."

Forach pulls the chair back to what she feels is a safe distance and sits. "Sekhmet." The name feels odd in her mouth. It is heavy and full of power. "And the other? What's her name?"

"Filoméla," Sekhmet says.

Forach feels more settled now that things are named. But she still feels prickly with annoyance. "I thought I died. What fresh torment is this?"

Sekhmet laughs. "There's no torture here. We are here to learn."

"We?"

"You, me, Filoméla . . . We share the same mission, the same soul. I think you have discovered something important. We will talk about that. If you desire to pass on after we speak . . . you may. But I hope you join our Soul Council and help us."

Forach crosses her arms. "Help with what?"

Sekhmet brings her hands together and stretches them out as if playing a child's game with string. But instead of wool, she holds galaxies between her fingers.

Forach's breath catches in her throat. "This is powerful magic. Stop pulling my leg. What are you if you're no sidhe?"

"In the land of Eire, they called my people the Tuatha Dé Danann, but they had no idea how far we traveled to reach your shore."

Sekhmet blows the stars from her hands. They tumble toward the other women, filling the spaces between them.

Forach claps her hands in delight, leaping up, laughing like a child. *Oh, I wish Aoife could see this!*

As quickly as the thought comes, so does the awful, final understanding. It slaps Forach in the face and steals her joy.

Aoife will never see this. And I will never see my sweet child again.

A tide of sorrow washes over Forach, nearly breaking her.

Sekhmet's features soften in recognition. "I know. I had children, too. As did Filoméla. But if we don't leave them behind, they can't lay down the lines for us."

Forach's brow furrows. "The lines?"

"For us to return. It's important that the champions to come bear Lyran as well as human blood. We need that unity of spirit and flesh to defeat the Brotherhood of the Snake."

Sekhmet points to a cluster of stars Forach recognizes as the Harp. One glows brighter than the rest.

"This is our home, Vega. It was destroyed at the beginning of the Great War. That was when the Brotherhood declared their intention to extinguish every living Lyran. Those of us who escaped found shelter among the Many Worlds: on Pleiades, Sirius, and the worlds beyond. We brought the Children of the Garden with us to Earth. This is where we shall win. When we do, we will drive the darkness of the Brotherhood out of the world. That is why our children's children and their children's children house our souls when it's time to be reborn."

The light of a million stars, a thousand moons, a hundred suns ripple across Sekhmet's face. "The bodies we inhabit become less Lyran and more human over time.

"But our soul?

"Our soul is forever tethered to the stars."

~ 47 ~

HONEY

Amy bounces up and down, wet curls whipping water down the back of her nightgown. "I want to light the candles!"

Chad clears the dinner dishes from the table. "No playing with fire, thank you."

"It's Hanukkah," Honey protests. "Kids are supposed to help. Would you prefer I light them?" She means it to sound like a joke, but it comes out sharper.

He catches her annoyance and meets it with his own. "I'd prefer we didn't have open flames in the house at all. I don't know why you insist on lighting candles."

She doesn't want to fight but can't help pointing out the stupidity of his comment. "It wouldn't be much of a Festival of Lights without the lights."

"They have electric menorahs now; with bulbs you can just screw in each night. It's safer."

"Oh, come on."

He must still be pissed at me not being here when he got home.

She takes a deep breath and addresses him as sweetly as she can. "Chad, why don't you light the shamash, and then hand it to Amy and Emily so they can light the candle for the first night?"

She hears him grumble, then strike a match. She smiles in relief. She'll take any victory, no matter how small.

She asks the girls, "Do you remember why we call that candle the shamash?" She pauses to see if they remember. "Shamash means helper. It helps us light the other candles. Help me sing the blessings?"

The girls hesitantly stumble over the Hebrew as Honey sings the three blessings. The first over the candles. The second for the miracles performed for their ancestors. And the last to thank God for giving them life, sustaining them, and allowing them to live to see this season.

Chad moves her out of the way so he can help the girls with the candle. "You know Shamash isn't just a candle, it's a Babylonian sun-god."

"Hmm." She isn't sure why he is interrupting Hanukkah to talk about Babylonian sun gods.

Undeterred, Chad continues, "In the epic of Gilgamesh, Shamash basically just hangs around to help Gilgamesh and Enkidu."

She quips, "Must be nice to have your own personal god." She tells the girls, "Go pick out a present."

They run, shouting toward the corner where the presents are heaped under a Christmas tree. Of course, Chad set that up before Thanksgiving. Honey can hear them shaking the boxes, deciding which they want to open first. She sits beside them. "Do you remember why we light the candles for Hanukkah?"

Chad curses softly.

She knows what he is struggling with—they have the same problem with the menorah every year. "If you're having trouble getting the candle back in, melt some of the wax on the bottom. That will help it stay in the candle holder."

"I don't understand why the candles never fit."

She hears another match light.

"I swear next year, I'm going to get you a new one," he grumbles.

Her spine stiffens. "You can't get me a new one. It's the menorah I grew up with, my mother's. Candles have never fit it."

She can hear the frustration in his voice. "Then why use it?"

"That's part of the tradition." She can't see if Chad is enjoying her joke, but from the giggles at her elbow, she knows the girls are. "Do you know why we light the candles?"

Honey tells the girls the story of the Lion of Judah and the miracle that kept the eternal flame burning for a week longer than it should, a beacon of hope through the darkest nights. The girls rip open their packages, shouting enthusiastically. She hears Chad sit down across from them, observing but not participating. Casting a shadow over their happiness.

Chad supported me instructing the girls about their Jewish heritage. But the older they get, the more he seems to resent it. Is he offended in some way?

She tells him all the time to take the girls to church or teach them about Jesus if he wants. But he doesn't do it. She doesn't know what he wants. It is exhausting trying to figure out how to appease him, so she doesn't try.

The girls throw their arms around her. They burrow in that delicious way that means sleep is coming. She kisses the top of each freshly shampooed head. They smell like apples and cinnamon. "C'mon. Time for bed."

They grumble but take her hands and follow her to the stairs.

Honey gives them three quick squeezes, a silent *I love you*. She asks, "Did you like your presents? Cause, you'll get seven more."

They squeal in delight as Chad grumbles, "I hope you left something good for Christmas."

She ignores him, helping Amy and Emily into their room.

Emily grabs her arm as Honey tucks her into bed. "Mommy? How come Daddy's so grumpy?"

Honey pats her hand. "We scared him earlier. When he came home and we weren't here waiting for him, he didn't know if something bad had happened to us. When people get scared, sometimes it comes out in weird ways. He won't be so grumpy tomorrow."

Amy sounds half-asleep. "What's he so scared of? Doesn't he know that the animals in the woods love you?"

Honey laughs and tucks in her youngest. “They do?”

“They do.” Amy yawns. The words came slurring out. “I saw you running with them.”

The hairs on Honey’s arms stand on end as she remembers fleeing back to the house in terror.

Was that last night? The night before?

She clears her throat, almost afraid to ask Amy what she means. “Running with who?”

“The deer, Mommy.”

Deer? They were wolves. Weren’t they?

Could deer have scared me?

Emily turns over and sleepily adds, “The deer really liked you. You ran fast like them.”

~ 48 ~

SEKHMET

Sekhmet closes her eyes and inhales deeply. The night air is sweet with the scent of wild grasses. They remind her of the seaside reefs of her home on the other side of the world, the place where she began this mission.

Although, if she were being honest, no place on Earth is her true home.

She lets the veneer of Nefertiti's womanhood fall away. When she opens her eyes, they are in Sekhmet's face. She leans her head back, enjoying the feel of desert wind through her mane. It tickles the light fur springing up across her arms and chest.

She scans the sky. Sekhmet can feel the light of the motherly sun reflected off the cool fullness of the fatherly moon.

She turns back to her men. They are used to her transformations. The Ivrim are Lyran allies. They will tell no one what happens here. They work nightly until dawn.

Amenhotep doesn't understand why she reveals her true face to them.

"Building doesn't require beauty," she insists. But the truth is, in human form, she feels weak, vulnerable. She wants to reclaim the strength that Sekhmet has. If she must be Nefertiti during the day, at least she can be her true self at night.

Besides, the Ivrim and their Essene brethren aren't idol-worshipping fools. They can look on her true face without terror or awe. They know there is only one divine Source. Their people remember their own creation and embrace the One. They still sing songs and tell the story of the Garden. And although she must remind them she's no angel, they know she's an ally.

And more than that. A friend.

It's a comfort to have friends behind enemy lines. Especially when they are rebuilding what's been lost.

The battle that sank Lemuria and Atlantis also destroyed the energy dragon grid. But Sekhmet remembers when they girded the Earth. The dragons powered a pure Source-driven form of energy. That grid connected Earth to the Many Worlds. Now only a few of the pyramid-shaped structures exist, cut off and dead.

She and the Ivrim are building a second dragon in this new city. The lines are good. And once the stones are set, she should be able to bring the Lyran connection back online.

The thought fills her with keen longing. She hasn't spoken to her people since Akhenaten healed her in his courtyard.

I hope we will have enough time to finish our work.

Sekhmet nods to the men. They arrange themselves along the edge of the pit. They toil by moonlight to discourage spies. No one's worked the stones like this for thousands of years. It's not something the men of this world need to know how to do.

They must advance on their own. Otherwise, they won't appreciate what they have or learn the hard lessons.

If the Brotherhood agreed, there would have been no need to destroy the energy dragons. But the snakes wanted to speed up the Children of the Garden's evolution. So, they gave the men of Earth fire, iron, gunpowder, and many other cursed gifts.

Their only true gift is chaos.

The Brotherhood meddled with men. They gave them tools and technology instead of letting them evolve. That enabled bloody, stupid wars that brought out the worst in humanity. The Lyrans had to destroy the grid to keep the brotherhood from weaponizing it.

They ruin everything. Maybe the next champion will win and drive the darkness of the Brotherhood back forever.

Or maybe we'll lose.

Sekhmet bites the thought in two. No need in suffering twice worrying about the future. It will come soon enough. Besides, she's lost before. And she learned losing is not the end.

Sometimes you must lose to win. I lost brutally. But I gained much love and many blessings.

She thinks of Akhenaten and flushes, tasting his salt on her tongue. She likes the way his name feels in her mouth. She likes the way everything about him feels.

Maybe too much.

This fourth child wants to be born soon. It kicks, punches, and tries to beat its way out like a wild, little monster.

She pats the swell of her belly. *Not until I'm done with this dragon, child.*

She probes the edges of the stone with the steel flint of her mind. She finds comfort in breaking it free of the earth and lifting it to the surface. She takes pride in watching the Ivrim gently prod it into position on the dragon's north face.

Brick by brick, she builds the foundation.

Drip by drip, Akhenaten erodes the priests' hold on the people.

Step by step, they drag Kemet toward the light.

~ 49 ~

FILOMÉLA

Filoméla's stomach lurches as her body stops falling. The vertical drop becomes a horizontal slide. Her forehead bounces off a polished floor. The cave of the gods glows like fine marble. But the rock feels warm, like skin. It pulses like something alive.

Filoméla skids to a stop against Prōknē. She grips her sister and struggles to sit up. That's when she notices that Prōknē doesn't react to her touch.

Prōknē!

Filoméla shakes her. Prōknē's unblinking eyes stare without seeing. Filoméla drops her sister's body in shock.

"She's dead."

Filoméla whirls around to face the speaker.

Is this a goddess?

A wild, red-gold mane ripples behind the tall figure like sunrise. She is so bright and beautiful that it almost hurts Filoméla to look at her. Instead of a woman's face, the visage of a lion greets her.

The furry mouth opens. "For that matter, you also are dead." The goddess waves a hand and Prōknē's body disappears.

No!

Filoméla scrabbles over the hard floor, trying to pry it open.

"I can bring her back." The goddess shrugs. Prōknē's body reappears.

Filoméla throws herself on top of it, sobbing silently.

"She's not here. Not really." The goddess' presence is solid as a touch, even though she is the length of a man away. "I can bend the Source to create images in this place."

Filoméla flinches as the goddess approaches.

"I'm sorry I scared you." The goddess shrugs. "I thought this would be a better way for you to transition to the in-between. But I miscalculated."

Filoméla does not know what to make of her divine companion. There is no myth in which a god or goddess apologizes. Not to a mortal. They take what they want. And sometimes curse you for eternity after.

Maybe she's not a goddess? She's not Greek. At least, I don't think there are any with lion heads. Where is she from?

Something feels odd.

It takes Filoméla a minute to realize this odd sensation used to be a familiar one.

No . . .

It is impossible, but her tongue—*her tongue!*—presses against the back of her teeth as if Tereus never cut it out.

She opens her mouth and wiggles it to where she can see it. *How can this be?*

The goddess lowers her head, green-gold eyes filled with impatience. "Yes, yes, you're whole again. I wanted to erase the scars, too. But evidently, you're attached to them. They must be part of who you are now. Or essential to what you learned in this life."

The goddess waits. But Filoméla does not speak. She goes on. "It happens after death, after you leave the body. The soul is restored and that is reflected in how you appear in the in-between. For instance, I lost my head. It's back now. But, anyway, you are not the whole soul. You're an after-image, a fragment, like I am. We are both imprinted with the life we lived, and all its lessons learned. The rest of the soul is reborn into a new body, a new life, to collect new wisdom."

Filoméla stares at her, dumb-struck.

The goddess sighs. "I'm interested in what you discovered. It may help us in the battle to come. I harvested you and brought you here, to the in-between. This is where we will wait until it is our turn of the wheel."

A scowl mars her beautiful face. "Aren't you going to speak to me? Say something!"

Speak?

That's all Filoméla has wanted to do for months.

How I wanted to rage at the gods when I was in bondage.

How I yearned to talk with Prōknē.

How envious I was of the women laughing in the kitchen.

Moments ago, she imagined giving anything to sing to her baby one, loving song. But now, the idea of voicing her thoughts strikes her as odder than having a tongue back in her mouth.

The goddess waves a hand, and a table and chairs appear as Prōknē's body vanishes. "Sit."

Filoméla does as she is told. The goddess takes a chair, resting her chin in a furry hand tipped with terrifying-looking claws. She gazes deeply into Filoméla's eyes.

Into *her* eyes. Filoméla realizes with shock that she and the goddess have the same eyes.

"Yes," the goddess says, "in every lifetime we look different, but the eyes never change. They are unique to our star seed."

Our star seed?

The goddess touches her chest. "I am Sekhmet, first of our Lyran line. You, Filoméla, are not the second, but you are the first to discover something new, something we can use. That's why I'd like you to join me on this Soul Council for the champion to come."

Sekhmet leans forward, eyes burning with green-gold fire. "Tell me: how did you get the snake to reveal himself?"

~ 50 ~

FORACH

Forach touches the glimmering star Sekhmet called Vega.

This is my home?

As Forach's fingers touch the orb, a power flows through her. She pulls back in shock. "Is it voices I hear?"

Filoméla nods.

Forach touches Vega again. The voices run through her like honey, thick and sweet. But they do not talk of beautiful things. "They're in so much pain."

Sekhmet nods. "The channel collapsed when Vega was destroyed. Some of our people have been trapped in-between the Many Worlds. Not in comfort as we are. But stuck, suffering, and cut off from the ability to live and evolve for thousands of years."

Filoméla takes Forach's hand and presses it to one of the stars among the Seven Sisters.

"These people are stronger," Forach says. "Are they alive?"

Sekhmet nods. "They incarnate as we do on Earth. I don't know if there are any pure Lyrans left. We've been in exile so long. We had to intermarry and breed with our allies to continue the lines. Many of the strongest Aspects settled among the Pleiades. But Lyrans scattered throughout the Many Worlds. Only a few of us volunteered for this mission on Earth."

It's hard for Forach to read any emotion on Sekhmet's face, but she hears a note of something familiar. *Is it regret? Longing?* "Why did you come here?"

Sekhmet's face hardens. "I could have stayed relatively safe among the other Aspects. But I couldn't watch the Brotherhood destroy our lands and people and do nothing.

"That's why I volunteered for the Tzaddik Nistarim mission on Earth. Our job is to awaken the Children of the Garden, liberate the trapped, and banish the darkness. If we win the battle here, then we can stop the Great War everywhere. And usher in a new era of peace."

"Oh, simple. Women's work." Forach cackles. "We should have that done in a jiffy." She crosses her arms. "How is a lion-woman, a slip of a girl, and I to drive the snakes out of Eire's land, much less the entire world and those beyond?"

Sekhmet snorts. "You don't have to help. You can leave the in-between."

"What might happen to me, then?"

"What happens to all the soul fragments I don't harvest. You rejoin the greater soul attached to our star seed and become part of our next incarnation on Earth."

Forach considers this. "Will I remember Aoife?"

Sekhmet's eyes, *her own eyes,* settle on her sadly. "You will remember nothing of this or any other life you live."

Forach nods. "And if I stay with you?"

"You become part of the Soul Council I'm assembling. Every turn of the wheel, the Lyrans have a new champion and chance to win. Our turn hasn't come yet. But I'm gathering the fragments of soul that I think might give our champion the best chance to win. To act as advisors."

"Who is our champion?"

Sekhmet shrugs. "She, or he, has yet to be born."

Forach thinks of Aoife, Cian, her father, and sweet Óengus. "And if I stay here, I'll remember everything?"

"Yes."

Forach sucks in a quick breath. *Is it worth remembering my loves if I must remember Ethnui, Prince Conn, and the High King, too?*

Forach studies Filoméla. She bears her scars serenely.

Darkness marks us all. If I have an eternity, then I have plenty of time to make my peace with what happened.

Forach asks Sekhmet, "How long do we have to wait?"

"No way to tell."

Forach nods. She sits and gestures for the others to join her. "You said I discovered something important? Let's talk about that."

~ 51 ~

JUANA

There is a joy in pushing boundaries and discovering your creative capacity. Juana smiles at the design for the triumphal arch she's etched onto her scrap of parchment. It's not perfect, but it's done.

I hope it's not a sin to be proud of this work.

She's ready to share it with Carlos. She wipes charcoal dust off the tips of her fingers and calls out, "How are you doing?"

Don Carlos's skinny face shoots up, alarmed. "You're already done?"

She tries not to rub it in, but his defeated look makes her laugh. "I'm not completely done but I want to show you what I have. Are you ready to share? I want to get your feedback."

He frowns at his own drawing. "Okay." His hand darts out, adding a curve here, a line there. "But remember, mine isn't done yet."

"Of course." She leaps up and runs to his table.

Her enthusiasm amuses him. "This better be good."

"It's better than good." And she means it.

He tsks at her. "Modesty, sister. Isn't that one of your virtues?"

"Not my strongest one," Juana admits, laying her parchment down. "But I can pray for strength during vespers tonight."

She smooths the roll out so he can judge her work.

He leans forward. "Wow."

She waits for him to finish taking it in.

A smile creeps across his face. He touches a figure she's sketched at the top of the arch. "Is this Neptune?"

"Poseidon. I prefer the Greek gods to the Roman ones."

He raises an eyebrow.

She lifts a hand and puts the other on her heart. "Except when it comes to His Holiness and the Church."

"You better."

She smacks her lips at him. "I'm not going to be lectured about piety by a defrocked Jesuit."

He shrugs. "It's not my fault they go to bed so early. There's too much life on the streets to see. And I was what, twenty-three? I was too young to give up so much."

Juana crosses her arms, unimpressed. "I was nineteen when I took my vows and I've made it this far."

His eyes glitter with mischief. "Well, you're old and dried up already."

She grabs a book off the shelf and smacks the back of his head. "Are you going to behave?"

"Said the mad sister smacking me around?"

She shakes the book at him. "You'll keep getting smacks until you tell me what you think of my arch."

He tries to hold his laughter in. She narrows her eyes, waiting to see what he is plotting. It takes him a while but, finally, he manages to spit out, "I think it's very good work for a criollo bastard."

The laughter bursts out of him.

"*Marica.*" Juana shoves him off the bench.

He stretches his hands up to her, laughing still. "Help me up."

"No, what a wicked thing to say." Juana scowls at him. "I love you. But sometimes, you're too much."

"What does it matter now? You're a bride of Christ. Though I wonder . . ." He sits up.

She peers down her nose at him, suspicious. "You wonder what, you evil thing?"

He grabs her legs and pulls her toward him. "How you don't boil over with passion. Does your heavenly husband appreciate everything you give to him?"

She slaps his hands away. "As long as he can't get me with child, he's the best husband for me. And get off the floor, you flirt. Anyone hiding behind that curtain might think you're serious."

"I am serious," he says, looking wounded.

"You know what I mean." She doesn't know why he risks going out at night to meet with men. She can't believe he hasn't already been called up for Inquisition, but what he's doing is dangerous. She thinks about the sisters. Paola isn't the only one who prefers the same sex.

Surely some monks share this passion: to be with those of their own kind.

Juana asks, "Wouldn't it be safer for you to stay cloistered, with other men?"

He sighs and shakes his head. "Oh, Juana, sometimes I think you have no imagination."

He takes her parchment and smooths it open again before she can protest.

He smiles. "And then you bring me something like this, and I think how marvelous it is that someone like you exists in this world. And how lucky I am that I've found you."

She shakes her head. "Flattery won't get you anywhere."

"I'm serious." And he sounds like he means it.

She sneaks a look at him. He looks serious.

He examines her designs for the triumphal arch. "It's beautiful. Well done. Tell me: why Poseidon?"

"The new Virrey, his royal title is Marquess de la Laguna, of the lake."

He chuckles. "And you promoted him to god of the sea?"

"Yes." She can't help smiling at the joke.

Don Carlos narrows his eyes. "Poseidon's not the best tempered god."

"No," Juana admits. "He's warlike, selfish, moody, and vengeful. Just like Spain. And, knowing the other viceroys we've had, probably just like the new ruler they're sending us. I thought it a fitting tribute."

Don Carlos looks at her, incredulous. "You repay the great honor they've bestowed upon you with spite?"

Juana clenches her jaw and snatches back her roll of parchment. "I'm not being spiteful. I'm being honest. And I'm not rejecting the honor. You, yourself, said the work is good."

"It is good. But you're going to tell the royal envoy to New Spain that he serves a warlike, selfish, moody, and vengeful country? That he's probably a brutal pig, just like his government?"

Juana retreats to her desk. "Of course not. When I write my descriptive pamphlet about my victory arch, I'll extol the virtues of New Spain. I'll draw flattering parallels between the new Virrey and the old sea god. After all, without having the power of the sea behind them, Spain would be a paltry city-state of Europe. Instead, our empire expands beyond the horizon. Poseidon, it can be argued, was second only to Zeus. I respect the modesty of the Catholic church by not claiming that Spain is the best. Only blessed by the Lord our God to be one of the strongest, like Poseidon."

Don Carlos chuckles. "Good girl. That's much better."

Sor Juana glares at him. "I will not be won over by empty praise."

He opens his arms to her, beseechingly. "Am I wrong to look out for you? You're clever. But even the dullest wit knows when he's being abused. Your design is beautiful, your words appropriately deferential. I will keep the scorn they hide a secret. I'm sure the new Virrey and his court will see nothing but compliments in your tribute. But you shouldn't share your critiques with anyone else. They'll take them as proof that educating women only creates devils in skirts."

She narrows her eyes, hating that he is right. Her desire to know always creates challenges.

Still, I am thankful I am not ignorant. With time, maybe I can help people get over their prejudice against educating women. I'd like to help all women live a better life. They can't do that if they know nothing.

Juana juts out her chin. "What good is enlightenment if you can't enlighten others? What use is it to know the truth if you can't make others see it?"

"Are you serious?" When he sees she is, Carlos laughs at her. "Oh, I forgot, you're the little nun who's going to change the world and make it a better place."

She flushes. To cover her embarrassment, she asks, "Aren't you going to show me your design? Or are you too embarrassed because mine is so much better?"

"Oh ho! Challenge accepted." Don Carlos takes his parchment up. Before opening it, he warns, "Remember, it's just a rough sketch. I don't work as quickly as you."

"I know," she says, impatiently.

He unfurls the parchment.

Juana gasps. True, it is only a rudimentary design. But she can feel the power and promise the finished arch will convey.

"Oh, Carlos, this is phenomenal work." She traces the design with her fingers. Quetzalcoatl, the feathered serpent, encircles one pillar of the arch. Down the other winds Coatlicue, with her long skirt of snakes.

"I thought it fitting to welcome the Virrey with an arch celebrating the culture of his new subjects. I want to show him the beauty of Nahuatl art and Aztec culture. Coatlicue is a good fit with New Spain, being the goddess of warfare, architecture, and good governance. And of course, having Quetzalcoatl is key. As the god of intelligence, self-reflection, learning, and science, he represents cultural sophistication. The Aztec culture rivals the ancient Greeks."

She smiles. "This is important work. If the Virrey can respect our native peoples, maybe he will provide them some relief. They suffer so much under our rule."

He frowns. "What do you mean?"

"You see the poverty, the abject conditions the Nahuatl live under here. The descendants of the Aztecs are treated like animals. They deserve better."

"They get exactly what they deserve," Carlos says. "The Nahuatl have as much in common with pre-colonial Aztec culture as you do with the Blessed Virgin Mary."

Juana leans forward. "You don't think it's hypocritical to praise the grandfather and treat his grandson like a donkey?"

"Not if it's true. Look at the filth we have in this city." Carlos looks out the window and snarls. "If you're not careful, they'll pick your pocket. Or worse if they catch you after dark."

"Because they're starving to death." Juana can't believe her friend is capable of such cruel bigotry. "And it's our fault. They didn't ask us to come here, steal their land, and take their gold."

Carlos scoffs, but Juana will not be silenced. "It is our fault, Carlos. A hundred years ago, Cortés arrived, and they welcomed him with open arms. They thought he was their sun god returning home. And how did Cortés repay their hospitality? By slaughtering them. They've suffered under Spain's boot ever since."

"We liberated them from superstition and brought them civilization and enlightenment. Not to mention, the true word of God."

"Some enlightenment. We've slaughtered, raped, and exploited them. And what do they get in return? We forced them to leave their homes, pay taxes, and work in the mines. I'd be ready to riot, too, if a Spanish boot were always on my neck. They say the Hopi in the north are threatening to secede. Revolution will come to our city, too."

"And if the savages rebel against New Spain, you'd support the uprising?"

"You think slaughter and oppression are what God wants?"

Carlos rolls his parchment up and shoots Juana a warning look. "What God wants is reflected by the people he puts in power. If God wanted the Aztecs to survive, he would have dashed Cortés's boat against the rocks."

He crosses his arms. "But he did not. Cortés's conquest and the glory of New Spain is God's will. That is why we're here, and you would do well to remember that."

~ 52 ~

HONEY

By the time Honey loads the last dish in the washer, Chad is gurgling away like a chainsaw. She dries her hands on the towel beside the sink and sighs.

No use in trying to sleep now.

She makes a cup of tea and settles down on her couch. She thinks about her night of terror and defeat. How the wolves frightened her. How foolish she'd felt for enjoying the tiny scraps of freedom she'd wrested from the darkness. How she wanted to give in and give up, with no struggle at all.

Is it true that was just my imagination? Emily and Amy both saw deer running beside me. Not wolves.

The tight band of shame around Honey's heart loses its grip. She giggles. The terror of that night loses its teeth.

Honey sips her tea and considers the potential threats she might face.

There's nothing out there that can harm me.

Honey lets that thought echo.

Nothing out there can harm me.

She brings it into her mouth so she can hear and feel it. "There's nothing out there that can harm me."

The phrase tastes sweet, like freedom.

The neighbors once agonized over a rabid raccoon and a three-legged fox. The girls worry over a goose by the lake with a broken foot. Bears live in the woods, but aren't they hibernating now, sleeping under a blanket of autumn leaves? There might be bobcats, but they don't bother people. The howling of wolves always sounds so far away. The neighborhood is full of deer. Snakes? She knows they are all over. In the summertime, the copperheads and king snakes like to warm their bellies on the trail near the creek. But they'd be sleeping now, too, wouldn't they?

She sets her tea aside and heads for the door. She reaches for the stick out of habit, remembers the bells, and stops.

I don't need that either.

She dons a coat and hat, checks her pocket for gloves, and steps out onto the half-deck outside. She can't see the moon or stars but feels them watching her. She imagines them cheering her on as she steps into the woods.

Her feet find the trail easily, as if she blazed it herself. She avoids the branches and the bench that tripped her up before. She trusts her body to guide her, now. She knows her feet will keep her from falling.

At the clearing of the pine trees, she turns right and begins picking her way up the mountain. She is unaware of what, exactly, she is looking for until she comes to the sharp fork. There is the tree she hit when chasing Amy and Emily. She gives it a pat.

There, there, old friend.

The woods have lost their teeth. They embrace her again, as a friend. She thinks of what Chad would say if he woke and found her wandering blind through the woods. She discovers she feels nothing but a blazing defiance.

Let him rage. He can't harm me either.

She hesitates. She meant 'stop' not 'harm.' Chad isn't capable of harming anyone. He is such a gentle man, such a worrier. She feels guilty for thinking ill of him.

He's doing his best. I'm not easy to live with. I must be driving him crazy.

She is grateful for her life. "I'm lucky he stayed. Few men would do that. Or let me have a second child, blind."

"Please, stop," says a voice.

Honey stiffens. "Who's there?"

"Who do you think?" Sekhmet steps out of the mist. The brilliance of her being drives the shadows from Honey's eyes.

Honey blinks and gapes in the unfamiliar light of the moon. The goddess is magnificent.

Sekhmet crosses her arms and nods. "You found your way back. I heard you call. Those are both good signs."

~ 53 ~

SEKHMET

Akhenaten looks every inch the son of a god. Sekhmet thinks he makes an even better priest. She's surprised he's able to convert the Source channeled by the dragon into healing energy. But he must have a purer line of Lyran blood than she imagined. Their six daughters, too, can pull and guide the Source through the dragon's stones. Only their son has no appetite for the great work.

But he will be pharaoh one day. His sisters can take over the priesthood.

Sekhmet smiles. She likes the idea of a holy sisterhood displacing the men of the Amun priesthood.

It's been ten years since Akhenaten healed her and she first took him to bed. The way he wraps around her like a blanket still lights her up inside. Even after all these years, his ability to quake her, stir love from her depths is undiminished. She is grateful to experience this side of the divine Oneness with him.

Even if it can't last.

That bitter knowledge makes their joy sweeter.

She's even learned to love the fruit of their union. She knows she shouldn't be surprised. After all, she is a cousin of the Great Creators. But she never expected to love these children the way she does. They, as much as the dragons she and the Ivrim have erected, are her works of art.

Some of their children are already stumbling toward adulthood. She regrets not bearing seven sisters. But her husband requested one son. After all they've been through, she couldn't deny him that one indulgence.

Besides, I may be able to bring one more soul into this world. If it wants to be born.

The first Amun priests arrived in the city this year. They've begun erecting one of their temples across from the largest of her energy dragons. Their artless shrine fills her with loathing.

But our people will see it for what it is: a den of snakes and lies. A pit of shame and darkness.

She smiles. "Our people." Those words leave a sweet taste in her mouth.

The people of Kemet have embraced worship of the One faster than she'd hoped. It helps that Aten is a god of joy. One who shows compassion and love. A deity who inspires unity rather than division. The many gods of Kemet trade in intrigue, hatred, and vengeance.

Who wouldn't choose divine love over punishment? Besides, once you've danced in the light how could you be happy worshipping in darkness?

The way of the Brotherhood is pinched, oppressive. She neither has seen nor felt their presence in this new city. But she knows they're here, somewhere, hidden behind the robes of the Amun priesthood.

Cowards.

Drumbeats echo down the corridor from the heart of the dragon, which is their place of worship. Sekhmet feels her feet lifting in joyous anticipation of becoming one with others. She tears her eyes from the cursed temple of Amun and looks toward the circle of dancers. She watches how they twirl around the energy dragon's sacred chamber. The open ceiling showers them with Aten's light, driving all the shadows away.

Whirling, laughing, singing. She enters the knot of people worshiping and cleansing their spirits. They dance as one body with many arms and legs. In their ecstasy, they give thanks for all.

What a miracle it is that we have lived to see this day.

Sekhmet's man stands in the center, high above the circle of worshippers, on the dais. He raises his arms, bathing in the light of the sun. The light that brings Aten's love and blessings to all of them. Bathing them in the Source. Bringing them all closer to the One. Unifying them in love.

She feels the ground shake beneath her dancing feet. She doesn't need eyes to know where everyone is. She feels them, their beating hearts and shining faces. Beyond them, she touches her people connecting to the Source all over the world. Exiles, like her, have erected new dragons. The Tzaddik Nistarim are introducing new generations to the ancient ways. She can even communicate with the Lyran exiles among the Many Worlds at night. She lays her hands upon the stones, when she's alone, and joins them in song.

Lyran resistance to the Brotherhood continues to grow. The connection to the stars has been reestablished. The stones are in place. The star seeds are warming down the lines for the champion to come. The next turn of the wheel must be soon upon them.

But Sekhmet is no dreamer. She knows it may not be enough.

Maybe it will never be enough. But we will never give up. We will never give in.

She will give it all she has until there is none of her left to give, to ensure they win.

~ 54 ~

FILOMÉLA

Filoméla stares dumbly at the goddess. This is not the way the day should have gone.

Today, we were going to triumph over tyranny. Instead . . .

She looks over her shoulder, but Prōknē no longer lays stiff on the cave floor. The marble walls pulse with a soft white light. It is celestial and awe-inspiring.

Am I in the realm of the gods?

Sekhmet sighs.

Filoméla feels her disappointment, heavy and sad.

"What am I going to do with you if you won't speak to me?" Sekhmet beckons. "Come."

Filoméla follows.

Sekhmet places her hand on the pulsing wall. It reflects her light, a moon to her sun. "Now you."

Filoméla hears the stone singing even before she touches it. When she does, the current is so strong, she pulls her hand away.

The scowl on Sekhmet's face convinces her to try again.

Filoméla lays her hand on the stone and feels the jolt travel up her arm again. It is, she imagines, like being struck by a bolt of Zeus's lightning.

But the current doesn't char or tear her. It fills her up until she overflows with light. It is pleasant.

Sekhmet grabs her wrist and suddenly Filoméla feels the edges of her body blur. She's no longer sure she knows where she ends, and the goddess begins. All is pulsating warmth. She feels light and whole and happy as a child. The stone sings to her and she drinks in its secrets.

Then the song changes. It is still beautiful, but sad. Filoméla feels her heart breaking from the suffering, the pain in the song. It is hers and not hers. Totally strange and yet remembered. These people know her and what she's suffered. Their pain is hers and what is hers is theirs, and they are all One.

For the first time since leaving her father's house, Filoméla doesn't feel alone. These are her people.

She looks again at the goddess, and now she understands the goddess is just a girl.

Like me, Filoméla thinks before realizing that of course they are alike.

We have shared this Source since the beginning. And we will be united, although unique, until the end of time.

Or until we win . . .

Filoméla understands the importance of this mission. The impossible odds the others have faced. The times they thought they might win only to suffer a brutal defeat. It is not yet their time, and yet . . .

Sekhmet turns those green-gold eyes her way and asks, "Will you help?"

Filoméla does not need to deliberate.

She nods.

~ 55 ~

FORACH

Sekhmet's muscles ripple under the fur of her skin like water. Forach knows if the big woman willed it, her head would be severed from her neck before she had time to mourn its loss. In another place and time, Forach might have trembled in the face of such awesome power. But she no longer has the capacity to feel fear.

Hasn't the fire taken everything from me already? I've nothing to lose.

If this is a test, she's ready for it. She knows the fairy stories. There are three possible explanations for this place: dreams, the Otherword, or the crossroads of the dead.

If she's dreaming, she'll wake from this nightmare and deal with Ethnui, that snake, before she has time to strike.

If she's dead, the sidhe could have brought her here, to the Otherworld. If so, there are worse things than to be than young and deathless forever.

If she's dead and not chosen by the sidhe, then this must be the crossroads before her soul is reborn. Like Sekhmet said earlier, she'll remember none of this life if she's reincarnated.

No need to suffer twice by worrying now. I'll know the truth of my situation soon enough.

Sekhmet sits. Filoméla follows her lead.

Forach places her hands on the table and feels the strange power pulsing through it. "What is this?"

"A current of the Source," Sekhmet says. "It's our connection to home. It runs through everything, on all the Many Worlds, but only those who have awakened can tap into it."

Forach remembers standing on the cliff after Cian's burial. "It reminds me of the sea."

"It flows through the sea, the wind, and the Earth itself." Sekhmet turns her palms up and a little spark shoots from the center of one, igniting a flame above her hand. "Metal, wood, and certain stones, these all can be used as channels to the Source. They can renew us, give us strength. The Source allows us to communicate with our kind across the light years. We can even weaponize it, if we must, as a last resort."

Forach turns her hands over. With one eye on Sekhmet's flame, she tries to recreate the magic. She can feel the power from the table flow into her hand, but she's not sure what to do with it.

Sekhmet lends Forach a spark. It ignites a cool flame that does not burn above her palm. Now Forach can feel what's above and below and how they connect. It's a single, unbroken line. It takes effort to bring it into being. But now that she's found the connection, it could run through her perpetually.

The more I give, the more I have.

Forach grins, eyes wide. "It's like a well that never runs dry."

Sekhmet smiles. "You were remarkably close to awakening. That's why agents of the Brotherhood took you when you were so young. They did the same to Filoméla. But they couldn't darken your spirit, the way they did hers. I'd like to know how you resisted. How did you overcome your rage?"

Forach laughs. The flame in her hand dances with the joy of it. "Oh, I'm plenty angry. Sometimes my blood boils with the injustice of life. But what good is rage, impotent as it is? What good is vengeance? All it harvests is buckets of blood. And I'll not contribute to more waste, more destruction."

She juggles the flame between her hands. "I'd rather create, as poor as my contributions may be, and choose to see what's good rather than let what's bad overwhelm me. It's much harder to build things up. Far more difficult to love, and keep loving, knowing nothing will last."

Forach claps her hands and extinguishes the flame. "And isn't that the glory of it? We're all fools marching toward our death. And if that's not funny, nothing is."

~ 56 ~

JUANA

Juana jerks awake. She clutches at the thin wool coverlet and pulls it up to her neck. She is back with Leo, in the small room off her lady's chamber.

She hears a footstep and stiffens.

Is it the Duke again?

This time, she vows, he will not take her. He stole her maidenhead as casually as he might pluck a grape from a tray. And gave it as much thought afterward. This time, she will mark him. Trade her pain for his.

"Leo?" Maybe if she can wake his wife, he'll retreat.

A voice answers, but it isn't the Duke. "It's not Leo. It's Paola. Are you disappointed?"

Paola?

Juana sits bolt-upright and tears off the illusion that clings to her. She isn't in Leo's chambers.

I was dreaming.

She wakes in her sparse convent room. Her hands fly to her stomach. It is not full. But the sad little pouch that once held a child still hangs on the bottom of it. "Paola?" Half-awake as she is, the name doesn't yet hold any meaning for Juana.

A door opens. Feet pad toward her. "I couldn't sleep. Did I wake you?"

"Yes," Juana says, "but it's fine. What's the matter?"

"Nothing."

Juana turns her attention to the lonely figure illuminated by moonlight. And she remembers her.

Paola. Juana's cheeks flush remembering the stolen, soapy kiss they shared in the kitchen.

Paola stands stiff as a rod. Hair unbound; muslin shift untied around her neck. She hesitates, as if deciding whether to run away or fling herself forward.

The moon slides over the plains of Paola's broad cheeks. It glints off her teeth and catches upon the soft pillow of her parted lips.

Juana feels a sharp pang of desire. She wishes to be that moonbeam, sliding between those teeth. She imagines catching Paola's tongue in her mouth. She knows she will not be happy until she can feel that body against her own.

"Then why are you here?" Even to her own ears, Juana's voice sounds weak and afraid.

Paola approaches slowly, as if Juana might bite.

Juana wants to attack her, tear off her shift, hold her down, and grind her into dust. But she's afraid if she moves, Paola might bolt away. The hunger has moved from her stomach to the deepest heart of her. It throbs between her legs, demanding to be fed.

Juana clears her throat. Her voice is deeper now, pleading. "Paola?"

Paola answers her by kneeling alongside Juana's bed. There is a question in her eyes. Juana wants to scream the answer, but she's afraid of breaking something fragile and precious.

Instead, Juana looks at the moon for courage. Her heart beats its frenzied wings against the cage of her chest. She turns back and is caught by the longing in Paola's gaze.

A tiny thrill runs through Juana. She has agonized over the nature of sin. But when something so divine calls you, there is no shame in it.

There can't be. The true sin would be to turn away love so purely given. To deny one's own nature. After all, if there is a Divine Spark in all of us, then what can we do that is not God's will?

Juana reaches out a hand to touch Paola's face. Paola curls into her palm like a cat. She kisses Juana's wrist, raising her eyes to see what effect she's had.

Juana brings her hand back so she can untie the knot at her own throat and lets her shift slide off her shoulders. It sighs onto the bed.

Paola stands, letting her own fall away.

Juana catches Paola's hands and pulls her down. She smooths her body down against the rough sheets.

Paola is a new book she is eager to read, but she will not tear through it.

She will savor each page.

~ 57 ~

HONEY

"How come I can see when I'm with you?"

Honey's question hangs in the space between them. Sekhmet considers it for a long time before answering. "How come you're blind when you're not?"

Honey's temper lashes out. "Do you think I fake it?"

"I'm not saying it's fake," Sekhmet says in a measured tone. "It could be part of the binding. A curse of the Brotherhood."

That doesn't sound good. "What do you mean by binding? Who is the Brotherhood?"

Sekhmet narrows her eyes. "How much of your life do you let this Chad dictate? Is he your master?"

"Excuse me?" Four years of liberal arts education and nearly fifty years of life chafes at Honey. "I don't have a master. It's not 1860. Chad is my husband. And we're equals, thank you very much."

"Then why does his approval drive you?"

Honey knows Sekhmet isn't speaking to hurt her, but the words still wound.

Honey tries to explain. "He's my husband, the father of my children, my caretaker. Ever since I lost my sight . . ."

"Hmm." Sekhmet looks over her shoulder, deep in thought.

Honey realizes they are not standing ankle-deep in leaves anymore. They are in that strange cavelike place. "Where are we?"

The walls glow from within. Smooth as marble, they pulse with light in a way that makes them almost seem alive.

"The in-between," Sekhmet says by way of explanation. "Do you want to meet them?"

"Meet who?" Honey hates Sekhmet's habit of dropping info bombs and shifting to new topics. It gives her mental whiplash.

Sekhmet must hear Honey's irritation. Her demeanor changes. All the maternal warmth, patience, and care drains out of her face.

"Can you even tap into the Source? I wonder if that veil will keep you from it. You have so much work to do."

~ 58 ~

SEKHMET

No old order will ever cede ground to a new one without a fight. Fifteen years have passed since Akhenaten made monotheism the national religion. He remains in power. But there's a new battle with the priests every day. They've coexisted in the capital city for the past five years. They allow the priests to tutor their son, the future Pharoah Tutankhaten, but even that happens under Akhenaten's supervision.

Angry voices draw Sekhmet to the throne room. She enters under the guise of Nefertiti. Akhenaten looks relieved to see her.

She smiles at her love. *Here I am.*

The high priest of Amun acknowledges her. His eyes slide over her body briefly, as if that is all her worth seeing.

Sekhmet hides her disgust. He is a lackey of the Brotherhood, but no threat in himself. This one tutors her son Tutankhaten, her little Tutaki. And if she can trust the accounts of the child, he is a dull-witted fool.

We may live to see another day. Maybe another year.

The priest looks questioningly at the Pharaoh and gestures to her.

Akhenaten is impatient. "Anything you say to me can be said in front of my wife."

This does not please the priest. The Brotherhood and their agents prefer women to stay domestic, out of the world and affairs of men. It is not the Lyran way. And she is thankful her husband agrees to equity. The priests must think Akhenaten indulges her out of love. Not because he is sympathetic to the Lyrans.

If they did, they would have come after you already.

She scoffs at the idea. Being Nefertiti is the perfect disguise. Marrying this eccentric pharaoh, the best cover. The Brotherhood see them as inconveniences, not true threats.

Yet.

The priest looks at her sourly before addressing her husband. He sounds tired. "Surely, you can see the wisdom of my council?"

Akhenaten bristles.

Sekhmet is relieved to hear the same old argument. The priest will beg, *Restore the old gods, discard the worship of the One.* Afterwards, Pharaoh Akhenaten will patiently explain to him that the people of Kemet will not go back to the darkness.

Who could, after embracing the light?

Sekhmet relaxes. She was half-afraid, from the tone of their voices, that there was a new complaint. She's always on the alert for anything that might prove dangerous and unexpected. But that doesn't appear to be the case.

In his exasperation, the high priest looks to her for help. "Surely, the Great Mother can attest to how much better life was before this monotheistic folly?" He takes several steps toward her.

Akhenaten thrusts his rod between them, as if warning the priest to stay away.

A flicker of something ugly crosses the priest's face. He touches the Pharaoh's staff. It begins to wriggle with angry life.

The staff becomes a serpent in Akhenaten's hands, the ankh end growing long teeth, dripping with venom. Before it has a chance to drive its poison into Akhenaten's arm, she transforms it back to wood.

The priest's eyes flicker, surprised at her power. She is frozen, in awe of his.

If he's just a lackey, he couldn't have done that. This is no agent or ally of the Brotherhood. He must be one of them.

Sekhmet's heart sinks. She has revealed herself.

The priest simply says, "I see." He turns and strides quickly out of the throne room.

Akhenaten smiles, turning to her triumphantly. He tries to embrace her.

"No," Sekhmet gasps. "This is bad. We must leave."

"Why? You displayed your power and he left."

She takes his face in her hands. "He knows who I am. That was no illusion. He transmuted the wood. If I were simply a woman, you would be dead. I saved you from the snake. But there is only one of me. I cannot protect us all if they attack. We must leave. Now. Before they return. Meet me at the back gate."

She remembers their seven jewels. "I have to gather the children!" She kisses him roughly and leaves him there.

He calls after her, but she is already running toward the royal chambers.

She meets one of her women in the hall. "Grab only what we can carry—blankets, water, food, anyone else you can find—and meet us at the back gate. Our enemies are coming. Tell the others."

Sekhmet skitters around the corner, calling: "Meritaten! Meketaten! Grab your sisters. I'll get Tutaki."

The girls pop their heads out, looking confused.

"Now!" Sekhmet roars. "Meet your father at the back gate. They're coming for us!"

The girls grab their rods to round up the younger ones.

Sekhmet heads toward her baby's room. Although Tutankhaten, at eleven, is almost a man, the boy will always be her baby. She finds him in the doorway. He stands oddly, with one hand behind his back, as if hiding a gift.

"Come," she says, extending a hand. "We need to leave. The Brotherhood is coming."

Tutankhaten does not take her hand. Sekhmet's face creases in concern.

He knows who the Brotherhood is. I've drilled them since infancy. So, when the day came, they'd be ready. The time has come.

Thinking he doesn't understand, she repeats, "We need to go. The serpents are coming for us. Now."

"The serpents, as you call us, are already here," a voice says.

The hair on the back of Sekhmet's neck stands up. There shouldn't be anyone else in Tutaki's room.

The high priest smiles and lays a hand on her son's shoulder. "I know who you are. We've been looking for you. Why don't you come out of hiding, Sekhmet?"

She cannot fight him in her human form. But she hesitates to shift into her Lyran shape. She's never shown her children her true face.

The priest's eyes glint yellow in the dim light. They suck all the air out of the room.

She waits for him to transform. If he shows his face first, Tutaki will recognize the snake's evil and run from him.

If she shifts first, she can fight the snake and win, but that might terrify her son.

Is it worth it?

The snake refuses to shed his humanity. Sekhmet can wait no longer, or she'll lose what little advantage they have.

Scaring the child is better than all of us dying.

Sekhmet looks apologetically at her son and then lets her human form fall away.

Nefertiti's reddish-gold hair transforms into Sekhmet's wild mane. Her features broaden. Her slender frame grows muscular and sprouts hair.

Sekhmet, Lion-Hearted Lyran, sent to Earth to punish those who do evil to others, stands tall. She glares at the snake. “Here I am. Now show me your face.”

Tutaki whimpers. His face contorts in horror.

For an instant, Sekhmet forgets her enemy and only wants to comfort her son.

But the snake does not forget her. He whispers to Tutaki, “I told you she was a monster. One of the great devils.”

Tutaki moves away from her, as if she’s the evil one.

“No!” *He’s infected with the Brotherhood’s poison. How can this be?*

An angry voice chides her, *You should not have born a male. You should have insisted on seven sisters, and told Akhenaten no.*

She shakes that thought from her head. She assumes Nefertiti’s face and form. She doesn’t care if it makes her vulnerable. She pleads. “I’m not a monster. I’m your mother.”

It’s not too late. We can fight this snake together.

“Now, Tutankhamun!” the priest yells.

Sekhmet’s thoughts are disordered. Her focus, divided. She looks at the snake and thinks wildly, *That is not Tutaki’s name. The god we worship is Aten, not Amun.*

She looks to her son for an answer. He reveals the hidden arm. He grasps something ugly and leaden.

Instead of an explanation, Sekhmet receives a bloody blow from her son’s axe. It enters her temple, cleaving her face in two.

Her human body cracks under the strain. She falls, broken to the floor. Sekhmet tries to mouth Tutankhaten’s name, but she no longer has lips to form the words or breath to speak.

Darkness laps at her, eroding her edges, and erasing her from this world.

~ 59 ~

FILOMÉLA

Filoméla studies Forach. Eyes aside, they look nothing alike. Forach is as tall, broad, and pale as Filoméla is short, thin, and dark. Even the hair on their heads occupies vastly different reddish tones.

Psychically, too, they are night and day.

She knows the pain of being stolen from herself. Only, it didn't curdle her.

Filoméla and Sekhmet have watched countless generations of their soul's journey. Forach is the first one who has managed to calm the rage that they all inherit from Sekhmet.

That feels like a victory.

Filoméla knows that certain traits follow the soul, even though no memories from the past survive. Lifetime after lifetime, anger derailed the incarnations of their line. Sometimes they self-destructed without any intervention from the Brotherhood.

Wasn't rage my defining feature?

She's been dead a thousand years and still longs for vengeance.

But from this vantage point, even she can see rage is not a gift. It robs the soul of sense, narrows its vision. And until the line of Sekhmet can evolve its crippling anger, they have no hope of winning this war.

You can't defeat monsters when you're acting monstrous.

Memories may not survive incarnations, but trauma does. That's one of the advantages the Brotherhood has. The pain and despair they inflict takes lifetimes to shake.

What cripples them?

Filoméla wishes she knew. She wants to hurt, wound, and traumatize the snakes. But she can't spot any weakness in the Brotherhood's confederacy.

The Brotherhood of the Snake's tentacles run deep. Their agents are present in every government, every religion. Their blood runs in the lines of every royal family. They control money, militaries, and the minds of millions.

The Lyran blood runs through these networks, too. But children of the Lyran blood are peacemakers. In contrast, the offspring of the Brotherhood are aggressive. As soon as one Lyran star seed begins to awaken, the Brotherhood rears its ugly head to thwart their development or cut them down.

That's what makes Forach so remarkable.

She sits before them, arms crossed like a clan chief. She controls the conversation, making Sekhmet come to her. Despite everything the Brotherhood took from her, Forach remained filled with light. She remains capable of love, and full of laughter.

Filoméla marvels at Forach's self-possession, her calm aspect. She suffered indignities and died in the most hideous way imaginable. Still, she pushes back, unafraid to take ground and hold her own.

And yet, Filoméla senses no anger, no corrupting rage.

Perhaps it's finally burned away?

It gives her hope.

We're evolving.

And if they can evolve . . .

~ 60 ~

FORACH

Sekhmet's brow creases as she extinguishes the flame. Forach marvels at how human her expressions are. She reaches out a hand to touch the fur along Sekhmet's cheek.

Sekhmet growls and slaps her hand away. "What are you doing?"

Forach smiles despite the sting. She giggles. "Seeing what your mask is made of."

Sekhmet lowers her head and snarls, "It's my true face."

"Oh?" Forach looks to Filoméla, who confirms it with a nod.

"Oh. Do all the Lyrans look the same as you?"

"If they are Lion-Hearted Aspects, they do. Others reflect strengths you might see in eagles, water buffalo, wolves, and so on."

Forach knows she's angered Sekhmet. But she's dealt with warriors before. If you take enough piss out of them, all that's left is vinegar. But she's not sure it's best to keep poking the bear. Not if she wants serious answers. That's not a fair trade. She takes a deep breath. "You wanted to know how I kept myself whole while Conn and Cormac and the lot tried to grind me to dust?"

Filoméla nods. Sekhmet leans in.

Forach's smile twists. "They only had my body. But I am more than that lump of clay. My spirit is in the bird's song. It's dust dancing in a sunbeam, the sound of rain pounding the earth, the river beating stones smooth as all."

She lifts her head, eyes wet and defiant. “Whatever I could think of, wherever I could bury myself, that was who I was, and I could be everything and nothing. They could bind me, but they never could catch me. That’s how I kept myself whole. By slipping out of myself. That’s how I stepped out of the flames to you.”

~ 61 ~

JUANA

The moon is setting. Juana watches it slip over the edge of the world from her window. The dark bruise of night fades into gray. The sun waits to be born anew. She cannot see it, but she can feel its impatience. It will rise soon.

She whispers through Paola's hair: "You should be going."

"Not yet." Kisses gentle as butterfly wings pepper Juana's neck.

Juana doesn't want this to end, but the sisters will be up soon. She remains firm. "You don't want to be seen leaving my room."

"Why not?" Paola's laughter is larksong.

"What would you say if you were caught?"

"That I was in your room praying," Paola says. "And it's not far from the truth." She takes one of Juana's nipples in her teeth.

Juana closes her eyes and lets her body bloom under Paola's soft hands. As she surrenders to the joy, she thinks, *This is the closest we can ever get to knowing God.*

~ 62 ~

HONEY

The mist swirls around their feet. Honey panics.

Our time together can't be over yet. I haven't learned anything!

She reaches out to stop Sekhmet. "Wait! Don't go!"

Sekhmet snorts. "I can't control this. It's up to you."

Honey lurches after her. The curtains closing over her eyes make it difficult for her to see. "Take me with you!"

"I'm sorry, I can't."

The veil between the woods and Sekhmet's glowing world begins to close.

Honey can't puncture it. "No!"

She takes another step forward, leaves crunching underfoot. She cries out into the wilderness: "Who are the others? Do you mean the women I saw last time?"

Or are there others she wants me to meet?

Honey's eyes cloud. She's not ready to lose her sight again. Then, she remembers what Sekhmet said.

Is this a choice? To be blind? Could I see if I wanted?

It feels ridiculous, but Honey tries to will the fog away from her vision. She imagines pulling it back like a curtain.

For a moment, the darkness flickers.

But it happens so quickly, she can't be sure if she saw anything.

Maybe it was only wishful thinking?

Honey turns her face up to where the moon should be. She can't see it, but she feels it watching her. "I wonder what time it is?"

A man's voice answers. "Late."

Startled, Honey nearly trips and falls. "Who's there?"

"Your husband," Chad says, angrily. "What the hell are you doing out here?"

"I . . ." Her mind races, trying to find words that won't make her sound like a total lunatic, and fails.

"Come on." He grabs her arm and roughly pulls her up the hill.

She stumbles behind him. Her feet snag every root on the way up. "Slow down."

His voice comes out terse and biting. "No one's with the girls and they're sleeping, we must get back. What are you trying to do, kill yourself?"

"No."

He jerks her roughly around a corner and her hip connects with a tree.

"Ow!"

"Sorry." But he doesn't slow his pace. They are headed downhill now. Her foot slips on a clump of leaves and she almost loses her balance.

He jerks his hand up to keep her from falling and nearly pulls her arm out of its socket.

"Can you slow down please? You're hurting me!"

Chad stops. She can hear his breath coming hard and rough. Anger radiates off him. For a moment she fears he might strike her.

But that's ridiculous. He would never. Would he?

Ragged breath catches in his chest and sputters out like something wet.

"Chad?"

He doesn't answer.

She rubs her arm. "You hurt me. I'm going to have a bruise."

She waits for him to apologize. He doesn't. It no longer sounds like he is breathing. It sounds like he is choking.

No. Not choking.

She takes a step toward him, forgetting the pain he's caused her. "Chad, are you crying?"

What is he wrestling with? Can I help?

He shoves her off, not wanting to be held. Finally, after a long time, he takes her arm again. He pulls her off the neighborhood trail and through the pine grove, into their backyard. He drags her up the steps, onto the porch, and into the house.

As he climbs into bed, he says by way of an excuse, "I'm afraid I'm losing you."

Honey resists the urge to comfort him. She doesn't like how he dragged her back, as if she were a dog that deserved punishment. She turns over and fumes. It takes a long time for sleep to dull her rage.

~ 63 ~

BOOK OF LYRAN, PART THREE: THE CREATION OF THE MANY WORLDS

Being no longer unified as part of the One, many of its Aspects felt lost.

They felt alone and unmoored. They cried out, *To whom do we belong?*

All the love they carried with them from the Source had no outlet.

All the truth they inherited from the One had nowhere to be applied.

All the grace they felt flowing between them seemed without purpose.

Knowing they had an eternity to search for the Answer they were born to know did not comfort them.

One group of Aspects fought their despair, and in so doing, they became Great Creators. Just as the One created the Aspects, these Aspects created the Many Worlds. And because these Many Worlds were still united by the Source, the Great Creators called their work the Universe, in honor of the One from whom they had all come.

When the other Aspects saw the Universe, they confronted the Great Creators and demanded to know, *What is it that you have done?*

They replied, *We are shaping various places for us to live and explore. We are developing different forms of life to keep us company on these worlds, beings to care for and challenge us.*

The other Aspects protested.

And so, the Great Creators asked, *Are we not here to experience life to discover the Answer we were born to know? If we return again and again and nothing has changed, what can we learn? We have made the Many Worlds, each as unique from each other as we are from one another. We have brought life into being and given it many forms. But like us, our creations are united by the Source of the Light of the One.*

Can we not learn much by living our many lives among these Many Worlds? By engaging with these various beings.

And the other Aspects surveyed the creations and saw that the Great Creators were right, and that their work was good.

And thus began the diaspora, as Aspects left the Source and began to settle among the stars and planets the Great Creators had made. They gathered in like groups, their soul families, and learned to love all the beings that lived and breathed among the Many Worlds.

In time, each Aspect acquired a physicality that reflected their chosen world and family. And they learned much: from the world around them, from caring for others, and being loved and challenged by them.

Part Four

~ 64 ~

SEKHMET

The pain of dying is nothing compared to the shame Sekhmet feels.

My son. An agent of the Brotherhood.

She should have known better. If she'd stuck to her plan to bear only girls, the Brotherhood would not have turned a child of hers so easily.

Should have, would have, could have.

There is no time to dwell on what went wrong or who's to blame. She needs to exit this body before her soul gets stuck in the channel tied to this Earth.

It is hard to concentrate. But she must if she's to find the passage to the in-between.

Her broken skull is leaking all over the floor, turning the sunbaked bricks into mud. The hallways are filled with shouts and pounding feet.

The Brotherhood must be ransacking the palace compound.

She wants to find Akhenaten and the girls, and make sure they're safe.

But this first.

Sekhmet focuses on finding the line. The royal house sits on top of a channel of the Source that feeds the pyramid-shaped energy dragons. It flows like a river over everything, gathering its strength in the temples to Aten.

The blood in her ears becomes the ocean. She dives in-between its waves. She holds onto the line to the Source. It yanks her up and out of her human body with a swooping rush.

Sekhmet looks down upon the sad wreck of Nefertiti, Great Mother and trusting fool.

Then, she snaps the cord anchoring her to the human world. Her soul rushes down the channel toward the great stone dragons at the edge of town.

She flies past the back gate. It is worse than she dreamed.

The battle is not raging. It is already over.

The survivors stand in chains. The Brotherhood is already setting fire to the city. They will burn what she and Akhenaten built to the ground. They will march the Ivrim and Essene allies to Waset, the old capital, and sell them off as slaves.

It will be as if our reign, and our religion, never existed.

At least Akhenaten is not among them. Nor her daughters.

They've escaped? Where are they?

Sekhmet rises above the walls to seek Akhenaten's light. She hears him calling out to God from the great temple of Aten.

She flows toward him. The shores of the river are clogged with corpses. The waters of the Iteru shine sunset red. The fish will choke on the blood. Nothing here will survive this plague. At least the bodies of her loved ones are not among the fallen.

Akhenaten is praying in the temple, arms outstretched. Meritaten is with him, her sisters encircling them. They all pray to Aten, asking for help.

She knows what they cannot—that the One answers no one, only waits, and watches. She slips down a sunbeam to shower her family with love.

They cannot see her face, but she can make herself heard.

"This place is dead to you now," she tells them. "Go east. Follow the sun. Find friends across the sea."

~ 65 ~

FILOMÉLA

The veil between worlds is thinning. When it does, portions of the Earth and its people appear through windows in the in-between. Filoméla enjoys watching them. She never knows when the window will open, but it's happening now.

Water sounds echo through the space around her. The wall ripples, revealing a river full of leaping fish. Beyond it, on the muddy shore, a young woman weaves a basket of reeds.

Filoméla wants to join the woman, feel the river, and help.

I don't know how. But I'll figure it out.

Sekhmet grasps her wrist, holding her back. "I don't think we should interfere. She's of our kind, but not our line. She has her own watcher to mind her. It must be a new turn of the wheel. She is the next champion."

Filoméla meets Sekhmet's gaze. In the millennia they've spent together they've developed a kind of telepathy. After all, they are very much alike. Soul sisters. She raises her eyebrows. They've watched many champions come and go.

Sekhmet answers the question in Filoméla's eyes. "I hope we win this time. But it's uncertain whether we can."

By the time Filoméla looks back, the window has closed. The river, woman, and fish are all gone, replaced by the smooth white wall of the in-between.

If I'd jumped, could I have returned? Sekhmet found her way back when she left me here alone.

Filoméla imagines being on her own. It makes her feel empty and cold.

I don't have the courage.

She grasps Sekhmet's hand. A unifying power pulses through her grip. Filoméla finds comfort there.

Sekhmet smiles sadly. "Forty-five of us volunteered for this mission. Every time a champion fails, we lose another Tzadik Nistar. We are down to thirty-eight. Those are all the turns we have left."

~ 66 ~

FORACH

Forach has spent so much time alone that being among these women deeply unsettles her. She doesn't like their twin eyes. She hates how she must concentrate on breathing differently. If she doesn't, she falls into their rhythm. It makes her want to run screaming through the wall, back into the fire.

She finally breaks the silence. "How is it we can speak to each other? If we're the same person?"

Sekhmet shrugs. "We are, and we are not."

Forach snorts. "That's not much of an answer, you great cat."

Sekhmet scowls. Forach wonders if she's gone too far, been too flip. But Sekhmet tries again, "When you look at the sun and close your eyes, what do you see?"

"A big purple dot."

"Yes. Where the sun used to be. It's not the sun but it's also not the memory of it. It exists because the sun existed, in front of you to see. When you close your eyes, the sun doesn't stop being, but it moves on from that place. And you carry with you the imprint of its light, its after-image."

She gestures to Filoméla. "Filoméla is the after-image of my soul's light, as it passed through her during her lifetime. My soul has already passed through you and into another body, waiting to be born. But here you sit as its vestige, another echo of my soul's journey. We are connected, yet we are not the same. We are different iterations of the same soul. The sum of our individual experiences, which have taught us different lessons."

Forach shakes her head. It is full of thoughts, and none of them are useful. "I don't know if I understand."

Sekhmet extends her dangerous-looking paw. "Take my hand and close your eyes."

Forach obeys. Filoméla grabs Forach's other hand. As soon as the circle is complete, Forach feels the current of the Source. Only instead of the gentle pulse she gets from the wall, it's a raging torrent. She pulls back, not wanting to be swept away.

"Relax," Sekhmet says. "Don't fight it. It can't hurt you. This is our direct line to the Source and each other. It's not something to fear. It's a way to unify our power, consolidate it, as we connect with each other."

Forach takes a deep breath and closes her eyes again. Immediately, the wall of leaping energy comes for her.

She tenses. Then she remembers: *this cannot hurt me.* She steps into the center and lets the current sweep her down. She is part of the flow of energy running through the channel, down, down, down . . .

And then she is somewhere.

Forach opens her eyes, but it's not Sekhmet or Filoméla she sees. A face that she does not know looks out at her from a reflecting glass. The hair is tightly plaited and piled on top of the woman's head. The dress is the color of a berry and drawn tight around her chest, like a binding cloth. Forach can't draw a full breath in it.

I'm in her? I'm in this woman?

There is a pale, sickly look about the face. Forach doesn't need to look to know what color the stranger's eyes are. Of course, they are green-gold—eyes that Forach's grown to recognize as her own and not hers at all.

Who are you? Do you even know I'm here?

Then there is a tug, like a rope yanking her backward. And Forach jerks roughly back up the channel. The tightness in her chest falls away. She feels the seat beneath her. She opens her eyes and glares at Sekhmet and Filoméla.

"Why didn't you tell me we could do that?" Forach feels shame and anger rising like bile at the back of her throat. She pulls back her hands and demands to know, "Did you enter me? Watch me that way?"

Filoméla nods.

"You know . . . everything? Already?"

They saw me with Conn. And Óengus?

Forach feels naked and exposed.

"No," Sekhmet says. "We can tap into the soul journey whenever we want, but there's no reason to stay and watch your intimate moments."

Forach isn't convinced.

Sekhmet sighs. "Honestly, you're not that interesting. It's not worth it—none of them are."

Forach frowns. "That wasn't a babe, or a child, she was full grown. How much time has passed since I died in the fire? Was that the woman who came after me?"

Sekhmet shakes her head. "There were three before her."

Forach's jaw drops. "Three of us have died since me? Shouldn't you have been harvesting?"

"No. They've all been . . . unremarkable." Sekhmet sounds weary. "I see them all. I feel them all. But not all of them are worth talking to . . . after."

"Why?" Forach looks at Filoméla, who cannot answer.

Sekhmet sighs. "Every time we incarnate, the trauma of birth wipes our slate clean. We enter without memories of who we are or were. We've spent countless lifetimes making the same mistakes, learning nothing, and never waking up. If a life adds nothing to the work we're here to do, there's no point in harvesting the soul afterwards. It's rare that a life is worth noticing. You and Filoméla were special. Not everyone is Soul Council material."

"And if I don't want to help, I can pass on," Forach muses. "If I did now, would anyone remember me?"

"You've already been forgotten." Sekhmet laughs. "No one who knew you lives anymore. We are the only ones who care that you were ever born."

"I don't care to be remembered," Forach says. "But I'd not give up who I was or loved. If I need to live with my memories, I choose to remember it all, as it happened. Good and bad and everything in-between. I accept your invitation. I will sit on your council."

~ 67 ~

JUANA

Juana has the unpleasant urge to sneeze from all the sawdust and oil paint. But there's nowhere else she'd rather be. It's not every day that you get to see your dreams become solid and real.

Don Carlos takes Juana's hand, and she beams at him. His pale aquamarine, gold-flecked eyes sparkle with excitement.

She squeezes his hand. "I can't believe they're done."

"I can't believe it's taken so long," he says. "Are you ready?"

She nods.

He signals to the workmen perched high on ladders. Canvas tarps fall to the ground. Juana shivers at the sound. It reminds her of Leo's silk robe slipping off her shoulders and Paola's rough garb pooling at her feet. She is no less excited to see their triumphal arches revealed.

Juana is overwhelmed. But she forces herself to gaze at the arches, first hers and then Carlos's. "They are magnificent!"

A smile creases Carlos's handsome face. "They're perfect."

Juana crosses herself and thanks God that skilled men like this exist in the world. "Thank you for coaxing our dreams out of wood."

The foreman nods and blushes. "It is a great honor to work on a tribute for the Virrey."

Carlos clasps his shoulder. "May it bring you and your family many blessings and much prosperity."

Juana runs to the base of her ivory-white arch and dances in its shadow. She touches the wood. The carved waves pulse under her hands, almost liquid, humming faintly.

Or is that my imagination?

Gazing up into the face of Poseidon, she is filled with awe and a twinge of guilt.

Am I too prideful? Should I have made this tribute in the image of the one true God?

She shakes her head. There is no disgrace in honoring the past.

Besides, of the One, we can make no carven idols.

"It is fine work," says a voice.

Juana has forgotten she and Carlos are not alone. She smiles and nods at the Madre Abadesa. But it is not her approval she seeks. She cannot give away her love. She forces herself to smile at everyone else first.

She laughs at Bridget's wild cheering, and waves back at Tamzin's shy show of support. Finally, she looks for Paola. She finds her standing off to the side, half-hidden behind two rows of sisters.

Paola.

The last one she seeks, but the one she wants most. Their eyes meet. Paola nods, almost imperceptibly. Juana's heart flutters, triumphant.

She turns back to the arches. The ancient Aztec snake gods curve along Carlos's arch. They are regal, imposing, sly, and dangerous. It is, she feels, an apt metaphor for the incoming ruler of New Spain. Her archway strikes a nice contrast to his. Where Carlos's Aztec imagery is all sharp lines, the undulating sea dominates her classical archway—a softer, but no less important, power.

Carlos's face lights up at the sight of a handsome young man with startling violet eyes and glossy black hair.

"Ah! You came!" Carlos says, grasping the stranger's elbow.

"Very impressive work." Something about Carlos's friend reminds Juana of Old Spain.

She waits to be introduced. Instead, Carlos leaps about the man like a spaniel, lapping up his compliments. Finally, the stranger turns his penetrating eyes to Juana. "I suppose you had to help her, as well?"

"No, no, no, Bishop," Carlos says, flushing. He catches Juana's look of annoyance. "Here, let me introduce you to our Mexican Athena. Don Manuel Fernández de Santa Cruz, Bishop of Puebla, meet Sor Juana Inés de la Cruz, the most brilliant woman in New Spain. She is an artist, poet, musician, philosopher, scientist—"

Don Manuel cuts him off. "My, my, Sor Juana, with all of that activity, when do you have time for your prayers?"

She feels an icy rage inch up her spine as he takes her hand and bends to kiss it. His amethyst eyes fail to leave her face, so she is forced to dissemble. It is challenging to look placid while flame engulfs her insides.

Here is a man to be wary of, she thinks, *he means to look inside my very soul.*

"God is in everything we do," she says evenly. "Every action I make is a prayer, thanks be to His glory."

"Indeed." The Bishop straightens, but he does not release her hand. His eyes take her in from tip to toe. "You're too good looking to be a nun. Why didn't you marry?"

It's none of his business, but to tell the Bishop so would be imprudent. Instead, she simply says, "I was born out of wedlock to a criollo." Being a low-caste woman is a common enough excuse for taking up the cross and becoming a bride of Christ.

The Bishop nods, flicking his eyes once more over her shrouded body. "Pity. You'd make pretty children. But just as well you took your vows. The last thing New Spain needs is more bastards. And with a face like that . . ."

He lets the thought trail off and turns back to Carlos. "Did you hear about Santa Fe?"

The Bishop pulls her friend away. She watches them go with clenched fists.

~ 68 ~

HONEY

"I have a lot of work to do." Honey says the words out loud and tries to make sense of them.

What did Sekhmet mean?

Chad sets a cup of coffee down in front of her and places her hand on its handle. "*I've* got a lot of work to do. *You* get to sit around here all day."

Honey's stomach tightens. "Right, eating bonbons while the dishes and clothes wash themselves. There's a reason why they call it house*work*." She leaves the coffee there and calls up the stairs, "Girls? You almost ready?"

"I'll go get them," Chad mutters. And the way he says it—as if he is doing her a favor by checking on their children—makes her want to scream.

She takes two bowls from the pantry and carefully spoons oatmeal from the hot pot into each. She counts the steps to Emily's place, then lays a bowl at Amy's.

She goes over how much she does while Chad is at work. By the time she's cleaned and straightened up, made herself lunch, and done a little exercise, school is over. It isn't like she has gobs of time to laze around. She doesn't binge-watch shows. If it weren't for the National Federation for the Blind NewsLine, she'd have no idea what was going on in the outside world.

Although, as crappy as the news has been, she often thinks of giving up listening to it. It is too depressing.

The pandemic has become endemic. Each new Covid variation makes her anxious, even though it doesn't feel as serious or threatening as it used to. There's one overseas that people are talking about now. There might be a new wave of restrictions. She never wants to go back to a hard lockdown again. The time she spent with the girls and Chad underfoot, all working remotely, was a nightmare.

This house is her haven, and she finds it hard to breathe when they're all on top of each other. Especially with Chad's new political obsessions, which brand everything she cares about 'socialist' or 'depraved.'

Since when did having compassion for others become a crime?

Chad descends the stairs.

Honey asks, "How are they doing?"

"They're up," he assures her.

Honey tries to sound casual. "Hey, are they talking about closing up your office again?"

"Why, because of the plandemic?"

She flinches at his choice of words. Everyone has developed unpleasant habits during the lockdown.

Why couldn't his vice be sourdough bread or growing a silly beard?

Instead, Chad abandoned the 'lamestream' media in favor of 'truth' he could only find on YouTube. Now they can't discuss anything without fighting because she's not 'informed.'

It's like arguing with a child.

"It's not just happening here, Chad, they're locking down Europe and Canada again. Even Israel—"

"Right, where they're on their millionth booster shot. I told you, it's all a scam."

She lets it drop. She doesn't have the energy to argue with him. She hates that caring for herself and others has become a political statement. His attitude was so noxious that she had to get vaccinated in secret. She enlisted a neighbor's help to go on three 'grocery trips' while Chad was working. She got her two shots and booster while picking up 'emergency' milk and eggs.

Why do I have to lie to my husband about doing the right thing?

He didn't always used to be this way. She remembers at the beginning he was caring, warm, and gracious.

When did he get so bitter and angry?

He's not alone. Angry people are rising up everywhere: school board meetings, political rallies, neighborhood socials. All this division is making the longest, most boring Apocalypse increasingly worse.

Dummies.

Little feet run down the stairs. Honey smiles, grateful for the distraction. "Hey, eat up before your oatmeal gets cold."

"Too late," Amy says grumpily.

"It's not too bad," Emily counters.

"Thank you, Emily." Honey sips her coffee. "Amy, if you want warm oatmeal, try getting up and ready for school faster. It was hot a moment ago."

Honey realizes Chad hasn't joined them. "Chad? Aren't you going to eat?"

"Not hungry. But hurry up girls, I'll drive you to the bus stop."

Amy groans.

"If you're in a hurry, go to work. I'll walk the girls to the bus stop."

He laughs sharply. "I don't think that's a good idea. I'll drive them."

Amy slams her spoon down. "I don't want you to drive us. I want Mommy."

"Mommy's not feeling well," Chad says.

"Excuse me?" Honey's blood pressure surges. "I feel fine. And I will walk the girls."

She can't see his face, but she can feel an aggressive wave coming off him.

He has no right to be mad at her. Isn't he the one who just called her sick?

Fuck him.

"Go to work. I'll walk the girls."

He doesn't respond immediately. When he does, it is with a single word. "Fine."

Amy and Emily cheer, which Honey is sure enrages him.

They chirp, "Bye, Daddy! Have a good day at work!"

But he is already gone. Honey hears his angry feet moving downstairs towards the garage.

"What about the bunny?" Amy's question fills Honey with panic.

I forgot about the bunny! Shoot. Did Chad feed it?

Honey tries to sound casual. "Daddy said he was making a home for it in the garage. If we hurry, we can catch him before he leaves."

The girls fling open the door and shout after their father. She retrieves a carrot from the fridge and carefully descends the stairs.

The sound of sobs arrests her. It's not just one, but both girls are hysterical. "What's wrong?"

Amy is the first to choke out the sad news. "Daddy. Let. The. Bunny. Go!"

~ 69 ~

SEKHMET

The journey home should be easy enough now that she's shed her body. Sekhmet feels the tug of the stars, her connection to the Source.

I could leave this cursed place. Follow the channel to reunite with my people in another world, one where the Brotherhood isn't so strong.

But that would mean giving up.

She would have to leave her family and admit the Brotherhood has a hold on Earth that she and her kind will never break.

Earth is where the last battle will be fought. Am I so ready to give up and admit defeat?

Even without a body, her essence bristles at the thought.

If I leave now, there will be no rebirth. No line of Sekhmet, No future champion. No turn of the wheel to show what I'm capable of, only an endless longing for what might have been if I'd stayed. And waiting . . . endless waiting to see if others can do what I could not.

If she stays, she might be able to look after Akhenaten and her children for a little while. Or she might overstay her welcome in this formless state. What might happen to her essence if she exists too long without a body?

Will I lose myself? Is there a time limit to be reborn?

In this state, she has no physical power. But she can manipulate the currents, ride the waves of the Source, and become visible to those who know how to see. It takes so much energy to manifest, though. Sekhmet finds herself drifting, often.

It would be so easy to let go.

But, when she looks upon the faces of her children, who carry a fragment of her star seed, she knows she is bound to Earth.

I will stay and see how this ends.

Sekhmet does not have the atmospheric gifts of some other Lyran Aspects. Still, the droplets of water in the air possess their own positive and negative charge. The sunlight, too, contains energy.

And are we not all connected in the Source?

Sekhmet sends feelers through the space around her. She finds enough matter to help her manifest as an orb, which attracts her family's attention. Akhenaten and their six daughters—*there should have been seven*—trail her like shadows. Without a body, she can't do much. She lights their way through the dark night, leads them to water, and helps them find shelter before dawn.

It must be enough.

It's too dangerous to travel during the day. And besides, Akhenaten and her daughters would be unable to see her then. She'd have to appear darker, like smoke, and it takes more energy to burn than glow.

She tries not to dwell on the past, though from time to time, as she leads them across the sand, she thinks of her lost son.

I can't believe we're in retreat. Is he Pharaoh now? Erasing all the progress we made?

Her son's betrayal stings worse than any torture.

He sits upon a stolen throne, sucking up to serpents, wearing a name that denies the One. How did that creature issue from my womb?

If she had teeth to grit, she would.

How smug and foolish I was. I thought we were so safe, so protected. That's what you get for becoming too soft, too human. Now everyone suffers.

Her soul rebels at the thought of the beautiful city they built reduced to ashes.

Our temples to Oneness lay defiled, the river chokes on corpses, and our friends bear the lash. But we will return to free them, she tells herself before correcting the thought. *Akhenaten will return to free our people from slavery.*

She has no voice with which to speak to Akhenaten while he is awake, but she finds herself slipping into his dreams. She sends him visions of how he will return to Kemet.

You must face the Brotherhood and succeed in setting our people free.

To convince the Amun Priesthood, he will need a considerable show of strength: both of men and magic.

Convince the Pharaoh that keeping the children of Israel under his thumb is too much trouble.

She thanks the One that she's not the only Lyran on this mission. She hopes they have found their own allies as she has found hers.

May the other Tzaddikim be more successful than I was.

There is one advantage to being in this deathless state. From this vantage point, she knows where the other Tzaddikim are. She doesn't just feel the lines tethering her to them. She can follow the Source and discover them.

But are they sleeping or awake? Are they aware of their purpose? Are they agents, as I was, or champions?

Those are things she cannot know.

One thing she is sure of, however, is there's another Lyran close by, a day's journey from where Akhenaten sleeps. Something else waits for them. Something powerful waits for them in the yard of another Lyran star seed.

We shall know soon. That must be enough to keep going.

So, she drags them across the sand, as luminescent as a second moon hanging low in the sky.

~ 70 ~

FILOMÉLA

The hardest thing isn't losing. It's watching the toll losing takes on the world.

Two thousand years between my time and Forach's.

From the in-between, it feels like an eye-blink.

We lived so many lives, learning nothing.

And in the interval between the spins of the wheel, so much changed.

And more that failed to evolve.

Every time the Lyrans fail to win, the Brotherhood solidifies its advantage. They never seem to start over from zero, the way the Lyrans do.

Are they even reborn? Or are they deathless, Filoméla wonders.

One thing is clear: the women of Sekhmet's line have increasing difficulty waking up to their purpose. Sometimes the Brotherhood succeed in mowing them down before they can awaken. Other times they simply succumb to the flaws in their own nature and self-destruct.

It took her a while, but now Filoméla understands why she's the first fragment Sekhmet harvested. And why it took so long for a second to become worthy. Despite the generations of experience, the line of Sekhmet learns slowly.

Will it be different if Lyrans win next time? Will that allow Lyrans to stay in control? Will that force the Brotherhood to be reborn without advantage?

If only we could remember what we've learned, then we could grow and expand as they have done. The Brotherhood's string of victories—is that why the darkness of the snakes never seems to retreat? Is that why the Lyran message of light and love keeps going out like a damp candlewick?

Sekhmet is restless. She always is when the veil thins, and they have another champion at the wheel. "We need light, love, and unity to spread, to open the channel between the Many Worlds."

Filoméla has seen the spark of unity and love kindle repeatedly. But it never catches fire or spreads over more than the smallest portion of the Earth's population. And even when Lyran thought gains ground, it's never long before the darkness beats it back.

We'll never be able to get enough people to believe.

How can they? The Brotherhood controls all the royal families. They write the laws. They own the churches, mosques, synagogues, and temples. The Brotherhood dictates who enjoy power, property, and rights. And which classes and categories of people will be denied rights that are granted to others.

But despite having their fingers on all the scales, there's one thing the Brotherhood can't resist. They love to rub their victory in the faces of the vanquished.

That is an ugly habit.

Could it give us an advantage? Tereus showed his true face to me when I tried to exact my revenge. If the right people could bear witness to that could we exploit that vulnerability? Is that why I'm here?

Sekhmet frowns. "What we need is some kind of mass awakening."

Filoméla agrees, but she's not sure how to make that happen. The Lyran message of love, light, and unity appeals more to the women of Earth than the men. But generation after generation, women are the ones the snakes guard most closely. They are constantly enacting new rules to keep the boot on womens' necks.

That must be by design.

Filoméla remembers how she was forced to live. In her time, women possessed no home of their own. They moved from father to husband to son's house, always under the man's roof and control. Not much has changed in two thousand years.

With women cloistered like this, how will our message ever reach the masses? Do we have to rely on a man to act as our voice?

She's seen many men with Lyran attributes. But Filoméla doubts they are any better protected from the Brotherhood.

Everyone is oppressed in their own way.

She thinks of her captivity. Of her desperation.

Despite it all, I still found a way to smuggle out news of my plight. It can be done.

But the path she took was through women's work: long, arduous, and costly. Not something easily taught or reproduced.

We need to build another web of communication. One that spans the globe, like how the energy dragons spread connection to the Source.

Filoméla touches the wall and feels its gentle pulse beneath her fingers. She looks at Sekhmet. Filoméla gestures to the wall and then spreads her hands.

Can we spread the Source to the world? Find a way to help everyone feel it?

Sekhmet shakes her head. "Each generation gets further from the Source, less Lyran and more human. Maybe if the energy dragons still existed to connect and amplify it . . . but there's no way to rebuild the dragons now. That knowledge is lost to time. I don't know how we can wake people up without creating a movement."

There must be another way. The dragons are gone, but the Source lines still gird the Earth. The other righteous ones keep getting born. There must be a chance for us to win. Otherwise, why keep going?

Sekhmet hasn't given up. That alone gives Filoméla hope. They are here to discover an Answer, Sekhmet says. Maybe they're asking the wrong question.

What if this battle isn't about light beating darkness?

Filoméla sighs. She looks at her hands. She remembers how long she worked to get her truth out into the world. She thinks of the thousands of times Sekhmet had to be reborn to reach Filoméla's lifetime.

It took more than ten thousand years for our line to learn how to transmute pain into something productive. We don't learn quickly. We need all these lives to help us accumulate wisdom. They move us closer to the Answer, one small truth at a time.

But will we have enough time?

~ 71 ~

FORACH

"Here." Sekhmet beckons.

Forach heeds, amused. Sekhmet doesn't often emerge from her corner of the in-between to converse. And Filoméla doesn't speak at all. It's been a long, boring slog since she arrived.

Sekhmet nods toward a section of the wall. "The veil is thinning. That means it's another turn of the wheel. Another chance for a champion to win."

Forach peers at the wall. The solid white is translucent in spots. "When it thins, we can make contact? With the incarnations on Earth?"

"Yes. Our line and other Lyrans."

Forach touches a faded patch. Her hand floats through the normally solid space. "And champions?"

Sekhmet's brow wrinkles. "We are able to contact them, too."

"Can we save them?" Forach travels the channel down the line of Sekhmet often. She enjoys looking through the eyes of their incarnations. She watches their lives spool out, trying her damnedest to help, to keep them from harm.

And it never works. It's like watching Ethnui win over and over again.

Sekhmet's expression is hard to read. "Can we save anyone?"

Forach feels a fire ignite, tight and hot, in her chest. "Then what's the point? Why are we here? What good are we if all we can do is watch?"

Sekhmet is faster than a cat. Her fist closes around Forach's neck, lifting her into the air. Deathless as she is, there is still a shock that courses through Forach.

"Patience," Sekhmet hisses through clenched teeth. "We do more than watch. We learn."

The pressure around Forach's neck disappears and she collapses at Sekhmet's feet. She can feel residual Source energy pulsing through her neck.

You'll do more learning by doing than watching, she thinks. But she does not want to provoke Sekhmet's temper again.

The white of the wall disappears completely, revealing a young woman plowing a field. She is strong. Her jaw clenches with effort.

This is not one to shirk arduous work. She looks promising

With difficulty, Forach asks: "Is she of our line?"

Sekhmet shakes her head. "Not ours."

"How can you tell?"

Sekhmet points out how the air around the young woman shimmers. "When you see our star seed, you'll know. This one is Lyran but not of our line. We might see the first of her line come through the veil soon."

"She's a potential champion?"

"Yes."

That's the only answer Forach needs.

This is a chance to beat back the darkness!

Forach leaps up, runs past Sekhmet, and hurtles through the tear in the wall.

Without a body to anchor her to the Earth, Forach floats high above the girl without falling. She turns and sees the wall knitting itself back together. It closes over Sekhmet's horrified face.

Forach is feeling so pleased with herself it takes a moment to realize she is not alone. Two other entities have leapt through holes in the veil.

The woman has skin that shines as black and holy as a river stone. Her well-muscled body and wide neck lead to a bovine head. Two curved horns wing over each ear like a mat of bony hair. Her dark eyes crackle with blue lightning. She carries a short, flinty blade that reflects the light of the sky. She is painful to look at and even harder to look away from. She is regal and awe-inspiring.

The man, if you could call him that, is borne aloft by two wings sprouting from his shoulder blades. He sports the head of a great red eagle with blue eyes that are nearly translucent, save for flecks of gold. In his right hand, he holds a flaming sword. The feathers leap from his head, like flames.

Like the hair of a Déisi.

If any blood still coursed through Forach's veins, the sight of this pair would have stopped her heart.

These two must be Lyran star seed, like Sekhmet. I was a fool to think I can help. What powers do I have, pitiful woman that I am?

The man smiles. It is like the sun emerging after a storm. Forach feels all her fear and apprehension melt away.

He greets the strange woman, "It is good to see you again, Oya." Then he reaches out a hand to Forach.

Forach grabs hold of him and feels the light of the Source, clear and strong, filling her spirit. "Who are you?"

"I'm Mikha'el," he says. "Thank you for coming to help my champion."

~ 72 ~

JUANA

Juana is restless as a child. The other nuns have been congratulating her all day, but she only wants to talk about the arches with Carlos.

He is more than a friend: he is her joy, her escape, her playmate. He lets her feel proud of her accomplishments, without shaming her.

Around everyone else, Juana keeps her guard up. With Carlos, she can be herself.

It is the best kind of freedom.

Even when she was in Leo's court, surrounded by women, Juana did not have this. The other ladies always viewed her as a curiosity. Something wild that Leo kept as a pet. Then after Leo's husband . . .

I'm sure they never missed me. They were probably relieved to see me go.

Leo made sure they all went away before anyone could guess Juana's secret. When they returned five months later from their grand tour, it was Leo who held a squealing baby.

I wonder where she is now. My daughter?

Juana feels a twinge of guilt.

I could have stayed and raised her.

She knows that's not true. Leo's body was barely in the ground before her husband proposed. Juana could have accepted. Pretended to step-mother her own child.

She trembles. "I am not a liar. I could not live that lie."

No. But, was it better to run away?

"If I stayed, I would have died."

The thought makes her laugh sadly.

Who else but you would die of a broken heart from being separated from books instead of your child? Or forced to embroider silks rather than conduct scientific experiments? Or converse about the weather rather than whether we have free will?

"I love books, science, and ideas more than anything made of flesh and blood," Juana whispers to herself.

That is what's true.

There is nothing more important than knowledge and seeking answers. Just as nothing is more fun than talking about ideas with brilliant people like Carlos.

But when she arrives at the locutorio, breathless from her short run, Carlos is not the person she sees. She freezes, a deer caught in the doorway.

It is the Bishop, looking oily and pleased with himself, like a cat about to pounce. Juana imagines malice sparkling in his violet eyes.

Don Manuel laughs. "You are a spirited nun. Do you run everywhere you go?"

Juana flushes. She darts a look around the locutorio. She spots Don Carlos. But her friend isn't looking at her. Carlos's face is shining, tilted toward Don Manuel. Her heart sinks. Carlos is a flower drinking up sunlight, and Manuel is the center of his universe.

He'll be no help at all, she thinks sourly.

Manuel smiles. "Carlos told me how brilliant you were. But I'll admit, I thought him a fool, a lovesick fool, until I saw your work yesterday. I must confess, I am impressed. You possess much talent, Sor Juana."

She marvels at how, the nicer he is to her, the more frightened she feels. "Thank you, Don Manuel."

"Although I don't know why I was surprised. I did hear of your triumph at the court of Don Antonio."

Manuel's smile does not change. But now Juana senses something dangerous ignite beneath it.

Carlos is insensible to any threat. "Oh?" Reluctantly, he pulls his eyes from Manuel and finally gazes upon her. "What triumph is this? You haven't spoken to me of it."

Before Juana can explain, Manuel speaks for her. She clenches her jaw and waits him out. He smiles. "You remember the late Doña Eleonora?"

Carlos nods. "Leo and Juana were great friends."

"Indeed." Manuel looks at Juana and arranges his features to express concern. "My condolences."

Juana swallows the anger boiling up from her body and nods serenely.

"Well, Doña Eleonora couldn't stop raving to her husband about how brilliant this young lady was. Don Antonio didn't believe her, of course. I mean, how many women do you know who can read?"

Carlos laughs with Manuel. "Not many, to be sure." Juana forces herself to not throw her shoe at him.

Manuel shoots a quick glance to make sure she's still listening before he goes on.

Juana lowers her eyes in what she hopes he interprets as an act of modesty.

God give me strength.

Manuel continues. She doesn't have to raise her eyes to know he's smiling. She can hear the mocking tone in his voice. "So, Don Antonio invites his friends over for an exhibition. 'Come see this learned woman my wife has found,' he told them. And they came—great professors from the universities, theologians, noblemen . . ."

Carlos is rapt. "And what happened?"

Juana stiffens, remembering the exhibition and examination Don Antonio put her through. She had no trouble debating that boorish brotherhood of priests, philosophers, and professors. They thought their questions were so clever. They were incredulous that she could have a single original thought in her head. Her ability to respond in an intelligent and logical way shocked them. She'd shredded their arguments like ribbons. And skewered them with her wit, without trying hard at all.

"They asked me questions and I answered them," she says simply.

Manuel chuckles and the sound sends a shiver up Juana's spine. "You did more than that." He turns to Carlos. "A seventeen-year-old girl bested the greatest minds of New Spain. She humiliated them."

Juana flushes. "Forgive me Don Manuel, but all I did was answer the questions they put to me."

"She humiliated them," he repeats. "I don't think they ever recovered. An educated woman is like keeping a snake in the house of God. Dangerous, indeed."

~ 73 ~

HONEY

The squeal of brakes, a belch of exhaust, two soggy hugs, and the girls are gone, whisked away by the school bus. Honey takes a moment to collect herself. Getting to the stop took all the energy she had. The girls cried about the bunny the whole way there.

I wonder when they'll stop crying.

"What's wrong with him? He could have explained why they couldn't keep it."

Did he think they'd never find out that he let their bunny go? That's so weird.

She shakes the thought loose.

There will be plenty of time to argue about it tonight.

She turns to walk home. Then she realizes that's the last place she wants to be. She wants to keep walking. But in her anger and haste, she left the stick home. Getting to the stop, she had the girls to guide her.

I know the way back well enough. But should I walk an unfamiliar path without my stick?

It's unseasonably warm, almost springlike, even though it's December. The gentle breeze feels gorgeous on her cheeks and the birdsong makes her want to dance. There will be plenty of harsh weather during the next few months.

Who cares. I don't want to be cooped up. I can do this.

It is a crazy thought. One that makes her giggle. She hasn't walked the lake trail since Emily was a baby.

But I used to do it every day. Let's see if I still can.

Honey rolls the thought around and it makes her feel almost naughty. "Okay, let's go."

Instead of turning left down the path home, she goes right. She carefully feels her way to the edge of the street. Her toe catches on a speed bump and she remembers Chad cursing after the workers put it in last year. She doesn't mind it, if it keeps the girls safe, but he complained for weeks about the inconvenience.

I wish he hadn't put those damn bells on my stick. I could use one now.

There's no sound of approaching cars. Honey moves across the bump to the other side, feeling like a tightrope walker.

It isn't until her foot lands on grass that she exhales. She laughs, surprised. She didn't know she was holding her breath.

But crossing the street, navigating new obstacles, and unable to see cars? Yeah, that is scary. "Good on you, Honey."

That makes her laugh again. What a weird thing to say to herself.

I must look crazy, laughing and muttering with no one around.

She defiantly tilts her chin up and says into the wind, "Good for anyone watching."

Although, since it isn't even seven in the morning, she doubts anyone is.

Better yet.

She takes a step. Her foot doesn't land right. Her ankle wobbles, and she falls forward.

"Oh, shit."

She remembers too late that on this side of the trail there is a little drainage ditch. Luckily, it hasn't rained in the past week, so she doesn't get wet. But from how her cheeks burn, she knows she's more than a little red with embarrassment.

As she scrabbles around, trying to stand, her right hand lands on a fallen branch, about an inch or so around. It feels strong and good, useful.

Hmm.

She brings the stick up with her, touching its far end to the ground. She delights in finding it reaches to her shoulders. She puts some weight on it, tentatively, and it holds.

Nice. Now I've got a walking stick that doesn't jingle!

Sure, it feels caked with a thick layer of dirt, but she can wash it off later. She thinks of Chad and his humiliating bells.

I'm not your pet, like some stray cat you need to keep tabs on.

No. I'm a wayward girl.

She smiles at the thought. It makes her feel wicked.

That's so much better.

She uses the rod to feel the ground ahead of her, looking for rocks and roots. But the path here (now that she's passed the ditch) is as flat as she remembers. The wind rustles the leaves overhead. She feels strong and sure, like she can walk forever.

Let's see if you can make it ten feet without falling first.

If she remembers correctly, the path will fork in about a quarter of a mile. If she goes to the left, it will be another half-mile straight before the trail takes her into a bog. That section has a series of bridges over creeks that feed the lake. She feels confident, but even that seems a little too much to handle on her first attempt.

She chooses a safer, more paved route.

If I'm to be a champion, I've got to build up my skills first.

~ 74 ~

SEKHMET

In the valley of the Madyan people, Akhenaton falls upon his face. "I can travel no more."

Sekhmet watches from above and notes his proximity to a well. *At least they will be provided for here.*

Her daughters form a barrier between Akhenaton and the punishing wind. They lost their sandals to the desert days ago. Now the soles of their feet shine like polished stones in the moonlight. They wash their father's face with their tears.

Sekhmet knows they are not the only ones who suffer. If the Brotherhood remains in control, suffering will be as common as clay.

Our misery is a drop of rain in the ocean during an endless storm.

She is tired. The Source tugs at her constantly. She cannot be reborn if she does not follow it.

This is all taking too long. I am running out of time.

She knows what she must do. Sekhmet latches on to the night breeze and sends a message to her family. "Stay by the well. I will find an ally and return."

There is a shepherd in the desert. She has seen his star seed shining like a beacon in the night. She flows to him and enters his tent.

She finds him, head bent over the ten strings of his kinnor. The music of the lyre plucks at her soul. The voice of her people flows from his tongue. He sings of their shared dream of peace.

She feels a deep and burning shame next to the singer's purity of expression. *This is a man who remembers who he is.*

She takes refuge in the flame of his oil lamp and speaks to him. "Aron."

He stops to investigate her light. "Hineni."

Here I am.

He rests his hand on the stone beneath the flame, in the old manner of speaking.

She flows into it, through his arm, up his neck, and into his thoughts. She rings them like a bell. "Your brother awaits you. He is lost in the wilderness."

Aron does not hesitate. He straps the kinnor to his back, grabs a skin of water, and follows her to the well.

Akhenaton sleeps beside it. His six daughters rest beside him like puppies warming themselves against the night. Their snores rumble like thunder. They are beyond exhausted.

Sekhmet wishes she could stay with them forever. But every moment there is less of her and more reason to leave. She cannot be replaced, and if she fails to go . . . she cannot put the mission in jeopardy. She's brought them an ally. There's one more connection to make. Then they must go it alone.

Aron tunes his kinnor. His Lyran songs invoke the rosy fingers of dawn. Orange beams creep over Mount Horeb. The Source ripples through the air.

That is not all Aron's song calls.

A young woman appears as if summoned. She wants to draw water from the well for her flock. But where light comes, darkness is soon to follow.

Sekhmet is the first to see the snakes. She cries out a warning. But no one can hear her. She is a ghost, a memory.

Aron strikes out with the only thing he has. The lyre shatters against a scaly back. Splinters of hardwood shower Sekhmet's daughters. They wake, confronted by a horrible mass of vipers streaming toward them across the sand.

Meritaten grabs a shard of lyre wood and strikes out at the snake nearest her. She pins it to the well. Blue sparks glint from the dark pools of her eyes as she feels the thrill of conquest. The split snake shrivels. The venom it spits corrodes the stones.

These are no ordinary snakes. Sekhmet wonders if they are members of the Brotherhood in alien form. *Or some variation?*

Meritaten and Meketaten beat at the river of snakes. But the serpentine ring closes in on the sisters.

There are so many of them. They will be massacred.

The young woman at the well is shrieking. The basket's rope is a snake encircling her wrists, threatening to pull her into its dark maw.

Akhenaten is on his feet. His staff swings at the head of the snake. It explodes, poisoning the water of the well.

Sekhmet watches the struggle, knowing she cannot help.

This is my fault for lingering too long, for trying to cheat fate. And what good did I do? Will I have to watch the Brotherhood slaughter my family ?

The serpents ensnare her youngest daughter, Setempre. They pull her underneath the sand. One by one, the curls of Setempre's hair disappear. The snakes erase her from the world as if she'd never been.

Another daughter, Nefernye, tears at the ground until her fingers bleed. The snakes take her, too.

Not even her strong, brave Meketaten can save them. Sekhmet's favorite daughter's lips turn blue as she chokes on her own tongue. Then she, too, is gone, dragged into a sandy crypt beneath the dunes.

I had six daughters. Now, there are only three?

Akhenaten is wild with grief. He pounds his staff on the ground. Sparks shoot from the fine quartz sand.

Sparks? Hope flickers. *His staff conducts energy.* Now Sekhmet knows how to help. She focuses the light of the sun through the rod, driving it down into the quartz fragments beneath his feet. She uses its vibratory nature to pierce the deep light and heat dwelling at the Earth's core.

The air around Akhenaten trembles. The stone beneath him splits, sending a geyser of water high into the sky. The snakes flee from the boiling stream. But it rains down on them. Any serpents who linger, boil. The water does not harm Sekhmet's small family and their allies.

Akhenaten is breathless from drawing the soul of the Earth out of the rock. His violet eyes glow with an unearthly light. He stands there, gasping, staring at his staff.

Then he looks up, for her. He knows this is Sekhmet's work.

She longs for him, too. *I wish I could kiss you, my love.*

The young woman of the well kneels before Akhenaten. She weeps thanks and promises fidelity. Her flock drinks from the boiling spring and remain unharmed by its waters.

That bodes well.

She tells them her name is Zipporah. Akhenaten hesitates to share his pharaonic name, so he tells her his true one. It is an apt description of the power he displayed.

"I am he who draws out—Moses," he tells her.

Sekhmet etches the words of power upon his staff so he will not forget them after she is gone. He will need to remember how this day felt. If he needs to bring this power into being again, he can. He'll need it if he is to lead their people to safety across the desert.

Zipporah insists on taking them to her father's house. With relief, Sekhmet realizes that is the other light she saw. Zipporah is taking them to the teacher, the light bringer who lives in the shadow of the twin mountain.

The Madyan high priest, Yitro Reuel Shu'ayb, is her father.

~ 75 ~

FILOMÉLA

Time is slippery in the in-between. Filoméla can't tell when or where they are. The only thing she knows for sure is that from time to time the veil thins and a portal opens. That allows them to look onto the field of battle, see a champion and, sometimes, learn how they lose.

Why do we never win? Is darkness so much stronger than light?

Some veil thinnings last seconds, and some stay open for weeks. There's no pattern she can discern.

Since that first glimpse of the woman at the river, Filoméla has resisted the temptation to leap into the void. But she's the only one.

Sekhmet tried to help a champion and failed. Brave Forach, of course, would not listen to Sekhmet's council. She had to see for herself.

Sekhmet and Forach's efforts gave birth to heroes. But who are heroes?

Only brave people who meet tragic ends.

So many times, the Lyrans appeared to win. The champion's death had meaning. Lyran ideas spread. People unified. They believed in the One. They awoke to the Source. They loved and cared for one another. They recognized their shared divinity. They felt their connection to everything around them.

But it was never enough. It never lasted long enough to hold.

Like clockwork, the Brotherhood would find a way to influence the next generation. They use fear and anger to manipulate the baser human instincts for self-preservation. They galvanize reactionaries to roll back any progress. They persecute all who protest or exhibit Lyran sympathies. Within two generations all progress is lost.

The worst thing is how they pervert the truth to win.

The accounts recorded in the histories, news, and religious texts seem true. But the Brotherhood's heavy varnish obscures the original Lyran intent.

If only we could turn back the half-truths. It is for the best that I never tried to make a difference. If our champions and stronger Lyrans like Sekhmet couldn't change the outcome, what impact could I have?

The Brotherhood is like oil on water. Everything underneath remains pure, but nothing can penetrate the layer of corrupting muck smothering it.

This place is smothering me.

Filoméla misses her sister Prōknē. She knows Elysium doesn't exist. If she'd chosen to move on instead of help, they would not have been reunited.

But if she's been reborn, could we meet again?

Filoméla runs her fingers along the raised scars encircling her neck. She can't shake her rage. But it no longer drives her.

I made the right choice to stay. No one should have to suffer the way I did.

Once we win, no one will ever suffer that way again.

Forach and their new soul sister, Juana, spend their days in conversation. They have enough words for a small army of women. Sekhmet often begs them for quiet so she can think. If she has a plan, it must constantly shift with each turn of the wheel.

Otherwise, she'd share with us. Hopefully, she will soon.

No one asks Filoméla to speak anymore. Instead, she waits, and watches.

That is why, when the window opens five hundred years after Juana's harvest, Filoméla is the first to see it.

When the veil thins, Filoméla moves towards the gap. She stops when she hears something crunch. Leaves litter the floor beneath her feet. Birdsong filters through the wall. She panics and looks back, afraid that she's leapt into the void without meaning to. She is relieved to see Forach and Juana. Leaves settle at their feet, interrupting their conversation.

Juana twirls one in her hand. "Is this normal?"

Forach shakes her head. Sekhmet emerges from her chambers. Above them, the whiteness of the in-between has become a canopy of treetops.

We have not stepped into the void. The veil has swallowed us.

"I think we are being summoned," Sekhmet says. "We go as one. This may be our turn of the wheel."

Before any of them can respond, a human woman crashes through the grove of trees, into their circle. She is of middle age. Her thick muscles are turning to fat. Her hair is more gray than red, and a cloudy layer of milky corruption occludes each eyeball.

The woman is gasping for air, panicked and scared. But there is a fierce beauty in her face, a natural strength and grace in her movements.

Filoméla recognizes something in this woman. She is not alone. Forach, Juana and Sekhmet also are drawn to her.

She has our eyes.

"This is our champion," Sekhmet says. "She's able to pierce the veil. She must have called us."

Our champion? Then this is the end of our line? What happens if we lose?

Filoméla realizes she's lost time. Sekhmet and the others have been talking to the woman. Filoméla tries to focus on what they're saying. But it's so hard. She has so many questions.

Sekhmet waves a hand in front of the woman. Filoméla watches the milky layer of filth disappear from the champion's eyes. Now the woman can see. That terrifies her.

Filoméla reaches for the woman, to comfort and welcome her. The woman recoils and falls back into a pile of wet leaves.

Sekhmet scowls. "*This* is our champion?"

~ 76 ~

FORACH

Forach takes Mikha'el's hand and reaches out to Oya. The power shoots through them, lighting up the sky. Forach vibrates, a plucked string in the hands of something glorious.

"Jeanne," Mikha'el says. His voice echoes as if he spoke into a cave. But there is nothing before them, except a poor man's garden ringed by trees. "Jeanne, Jeanne."

The girl turns her face toward them and shields her eyes from their light. "Who calls me?"

"Mikha'el," he replies.

The change in her aspect is immediate. She falls to her knees. "Saint Michel, l'archange!"

Archangel? Forach didn't grow up with saints and angels. Her people had no such kind helpers hanging over them. But she knows those words and what they represent. Ethnui used to prate on and on about them to Forach's father. But the chieftain had no desire to throw over the old gods of Eire for her new one. Ethnui remained the only Christian in their camp.

If she took credit for the peace with Cormac, did that change? Not that it matters now.

Forach can barely make out the lines of Mikha'el's face through the heated light they're generating. But he looks like a god. And the child knows his name. How can that be?

Maybe, like Sekhmet, he was a god, once?

Mikha'el's voice ripples through the trembling air to the child. She lays prostrate, face-down on the loamy black earth. "Jeanne, France is depending on you. You are the only one who can liberate them from oppression."

The child lifts her tear-stained face. Jeanne looks like she's staring into a campfire. "I am only a girl. What can I do?"

"You are not alone. We will help you."

Forach doesn't want to doubt Mikha'el, but she can't help wondering, *How? She is even younger than Filoméla.*

Mikha'el squeezes Forach's hand before continuing. She gasps as a surge of golden energy courses through her. This taste of Source differs from when she connects with Filoméla or Sekhmet. In the in-between, she and her soul sisters come together as three halves of a whole.

In this triad with Mikha'el and Oya, Forach feels amplified. Like the Sionna River flows into a great sea that bands the world. The power and potential are limitless.

"We are here to guide you," Mikha'el tells the child. "Listen to us and heed our advice. Believe that you are the one whom God has chosen for this mission. Believe that together, we will be victorious."

~ 77 ~

JUANA

Paola runs her hands along the spines of the books on the shelf. Juana reddens, remembering the feel of Paola's hands on her own bindings.

And she unravels me.

Paola glances over her shoulder. Mischievous blue fire glints from the dark pools of her eyes. "Impressive collection. I can't believe it's all yours."

Juana smiles. "Collecting them has been my life's work. They are my greatest treasures."

She ignores the derisive way Manuel snorts. She plays with a small crystal prism. But the beautiful colors it extracts from the sunlight's beams can't distract her. His oppressive presence still looms.

Why does he keep coming here? Is it only to torment me?

It was bad enough when he spoiled the arch unveiling. But he's become a constant gadfly since. Even visiting on days that Carlos does not. She wishes he would go away, but he's the Bishop. This is a convent in his diocese. Why would he not be welcome here?

It is dangerous to disrespect him, Juana reminds herself.

"Do you read, Sor Paola?" Manuel asks.

Paola's cheeks flush. "I am sorry to say I do not, Don Manuel."

"Don't apologize for being a credit to your sex," he says, causing Juana to bristle. "It's best not to distract your better impulses with the temptations you might find in books."

Juana feels irritation prickling up and down her spine. "I don't read to learn more or delve into salacious material. I read so that I might become less ignorant. God loves knowledge, does he not? I seek to know the truth. That is all."

"That is all?" Manuel laughs, and it is a sick, choking kind of sound. "To know the truth is something that even the most learned of men may not achieve in a lifetime."

Carlos finally comes to her defense. "Juana possesses an intellect that surpasses most men. If I were not a faithful Christian, I would believe she is Athena incarnate. The Athena of New Spain!"

Manuel looks vexed, and Juana is tired of this refrain. But Paola looks pleased. She turns her attention to Carlos. "You're the chair of Mathematics and Astronomy at the University, are you not?"

Don Carlos grins, puffing with pride. "I am. Although I'm prouder of the mathematics part. Astronomy is a diabolical invention alien to science, method, principle, and truth."

Manuel clears his throat. "If you're so in love with science, method, principle, and truth, then why are you so keen on the Nahuatl?"

Carlos sits bolt upright. "The inventiveness of the Aztecs is unparalleled in the modern world. There is every indication that their great pyramids even predate those of Egypt. We should all be in love with the Indigenous culture and achievements."

Manuel leans forward. "Then you approve of the Santa Fe slaughter?"

Carlos looks stricken. "Of course not, don't be ridiculous."

Juana hasn't heard of this. But anytime slaughter is mentioned, her heart sinks. She hopes the native peoples were not involved. "What slaughter in Santa Fe?"

"Oh, my dear child," Carlos answers, gripping her hand. "Savages in Santa Fe rebelled against Spain. All the tribes banded together and in a single day undid everything we've worked so hard to establish. They murdered our compatriots. Killed all the priests. There are hardly any survivors."

"That's horrible," Juana says. "They killed the padres?" She doesn't agree with the oppressive way Spain governs its colonies. But to kill men dedicated to God?

Who would do such a thing?

"It is horrible," Manuel says in a discordantly gleeful tone. "What a mess for the new Virrey to inherit." He turns to gloat at Carlos. "But you haven't answered me. How do you square that barbarism with the native 'culture' and 'achievements' you love so much?"

Carlos frowns and adjusts his glasses. "First of all, let me point out that the Hopi are not the Aztec. We're talking about different tribes. They have completely different mythologies, culture, and systems of government. Secondly, my admiration is for pre-colonial culture. Anyone would be hard-pressed to find anything admirable in today's native peoples. For example, I have great admiration for Aztec leaders of the past. But if Spain were to retreat from México-Tenochtitlán, it would be a grave error to let the Nahuatl rule themselves."

"Oh ho?" Manuel's leer reminds Juana of a fox stalking chickens, about to pounce. "And if Spain were to retreat, who should rule?"

"The criollos," Don Carlos says, without hesitation. "We have the benefit of the learning and faith of Spain. But being born here, we understand, better than anyone, how to protect and care for this land."

Manuel laughs. "So, Paola and I would not be welcome here anymore? You and Juana should rule in our stead?"

"He didn't say that," Juana says, fed up with Manuel's baiting. "But you're welcome to leave, if you find our company no longer to your fine taste."

Manuel rises, adjusts his fine robes, and bows. “I would not stay where I am not wanted.”

“Stay, please.” Carlos grabs at his sleeve. “She is sharpening her wit against your patience. She didn’t mean for you to take her seriously.”

Manuel pats his hand and smiles. “Oh no. I know when I am being a nuisance. I do not want to try our sister’s patience any further.”

The way he milks his hurt makes Juana’s hand itch. She really wants to break a chair over his head.

The Bishop smiles sadly, as if he’s Christ forgiving all their sins. “I know when it’s time to make an exit.”

Carlos scowls and wags a finger at Juana as he would at a disobedient child. “You shouldn’t have done that. He could be an immensely powerful enemy.”

But Juana does not want to apologize. “What was he even doing here?”

“Humoring me!” Carlos nearly spits at her. “Do you know how long I had to work on him before he agreed to come?”

Juana knows Carlos wants her to apologize. Instead, she asks, “Why did you bother?”

Carlos sighs. “Because of you, you brilliant idiot. I can’t believe how little of this world you understand. You can’t retire from the world. You still must live in it. And to live in it well, you need the right kind of people.”

“For what?” Juana is so angry that she can barely see. “To flatter? Indulge?”

“No.” Carlos’s clear, amber-flecked eyes fill with tears. “You need the right kind of people to protect you.”

~ 78 ~

HONEY

Honey manages to get halfway around the lake before she stumbles at all.

My muscles must remember the trail.

She feels strong enough to complete the loop through the bog, bridges, and all. After the horse barn, the trail gets rougher. It is slow going, picking her way through the narrowed opening in the trees. More than once, she catches a sleeve on a prickly vine.

She is thankful to have the staff. With it, she can easily disentangle herself from the hitchhiker plants. It helps her pick her way across the rough terrain.

She forgets about a wild rose vine that arches over the river bridge, though. She hits her head on it so hard she sees stars. Once her ears stop ringing, she ducks under it and starts across the bridge. The roar of the river stops her.

She stands motionless. The water is so powerful. It rushes past, shaking the boards beneath her feet. As the bridge vibrates, Honey feels its energy arc through her in the most exciting way. There is a current connecting her to the trees, the river, the rocks, and the wood of the bridge. It's as if she's plugged into some incredible life source.

Above the rushing of the water, there are other sounds. Frogs, bugs, and birds sing together. Squirrels rustle in search of nuts under the fallen leaves. Woodpeckers beat an incessant rhythm against dead trees.

The blood racing in Honey's ears echoes the wild chorus. The wind rips through the leaves, and she hears the ocean. Honey feels so small, yet so connected to everything around her. She throws up her hands and lets the sun hit her cheeks.

Here I am.

She basks in the warmth of the sun's rays.

How lucky I am to experience this moment. Despite everything that is ugly and hateful, life goes on. And it's beautiful.

Her heart is full. She struggles to remember a Rumi quote.

How does it go? We are not a drop of the ocean, but the ocean is a drop within us?

She's not sure, but she takes a mental snapshot of this moment so she can remember it forever. She wants to have this peace and unity to keep in a safe place, to remind her, when she's sad, of what's possible.

All these things—living and breathing, singing and flowing through the woods—we are all One.

The sphere of energy around Honey expands. The top of her head tingles. She is a radio antenna. She inhales and exhales, pushing the ball of energy around her outward. Now she sways with the trees. She strains her roots and waves bare branches against the sky. Honey inhales again, blowing the sphere further out with each exhale. She intends to keep going up and out until she touches heaven.

A panicked voice pierces Honey's bubble. "Don't move!"

Honey turns toward the far bank of the river, where the voice came from.

Before Honey could ask why, the woman exclaims, "Snakes!"

Snakes?

Honey's blood turns to ice. She can handle roaches, spiders, silverfish, even mice. But she's always feared snakes. Once, on a camping trip, a snake sunbathing on a rock trapped her in her sleeping bag. She refused to come out until her companions had chased it off.

She tries to locate the snake the way she did the river and the trees with her sphere of energy. But with the woman leaping and yelling and shaking the bridge, she can't. Her sphere has shrunk and withered to nothing.

"There! On your left!"

Without thinking, Honey whirls, scraping her staff against the bridge. It hooks on something. She roars and shakes the staff over the edge of the bridge. There is a splash. Terrified, she gasps, "Did I get it?"

A peal of laughter answers her. "I think you hurled it all the way into the horse pasture."

"Are there any more near me?"

"No."

Honey sighs with relief. "What kind of snake was it?"

"Snakes," the woman says, emphasizing the plural. "Copperheads. I don't know what they're doing out, they should be hibernating. But it has been warm. Maybe they think it's spring already?"

Honey feels sick. "How many snakes were there?"

"About ten. A dozen?"

Honey wants to crawl out of her skin. She's glad she couldn't see them.

The woman prattles on. "You know those cartoons where the Indian man plays a pipe, and a snake rises from a basket? It was like that. They all danced toward you like you were a snake charmer. I managed to scare most of them off by stomping, except for that last one. Nice shot."

"Thank you." Honey hustles to get off the bridge. The woman backs up to let her pass.

Honey hears the woman behind her.

"What were you doing?"

Honey stops. "It sounds stupid, but I had to stop and listen to the river."

The woman chuckles. “It doesn’t sound stupid. Connecting to nature is the only thing that’s helped me through the pandemic. Do you walk often? I haven’t seen you before.”

“No,” Honey says. “This is my first time since . . .”

What could she say? *Since I went blind?*

Why not?

“. . . since I lost my sight.”

“No way! You’re blind?”

Honey feels the woman standing in front of her. She flinches backward.

“Sorry. I know I should keep my distance. Your eyes do look a little cloudy. Is it glaucoma?”

“No,” Honey says. “The doctors don’t really know what caused it. My vision started getting cloudy about fifteen years ago, just after I got married. After the birth of my first child, I lost my sight completely.”

“Wow! And you’re out here walking? That’s incredible! You’re badass.”

Honey blushes. It *is* an accomplishment getting all this way by herself. She is glad someone beside Chad is here to witness it. “This was my first attempt. It’s a good thing you scared the snakes away or it might have been my last.”

“I walk this trail every morning. It’s kept me from going stir crazy. I’d be happy to be your eyes if you want to get out more.”

Honey leaps at the offer. “I’d like that. What’s your name? I’m Honey.”

“Regina,” the woman says. “And we can bump elbows instead of shake hands.”

Honey tentatively holds her elbow out, and Regina bumps it. Honey stumbles back a little. Her hand tingles.

Wow. She’s strong.

Regina asks, “Where do you pick up the trail?”

“I drop my girls Monday through Friday at the back gate to catch the school bus. It’s usually there by seven.”

"Perfect. I live just up the road. It'll be nice to have a friend to walk with."

Honey laughs. She tries not to sound pitiful when she replies, "It'll be nice to have a friend."

~ 79 ~

BOOK OF LYRAN, PART FOUR: THE GREAT WAR

Among the Aspects arose two great powers: the Lyrans and the Brotherhood of the Snake. And even though they were united in the Source, they could not live in peace. For one held fast to the light of the Source while the other preferred the dark places divorced from it, and neither could find a place in which to meet.

For many generations, the allies of the Brotherhood of the Snake and the allies of the Lyrans lived far apart from each other. And all was well during this time of the Great Peace.

During the Great Peace, Aspects lived among those like them and shunned the society of the Aspects they could not understand. Thus, Brotherhood clan lived with Brotherhood clan and Lyran sought out Lyran soul families.

Just as the Great Creators fashioned the Many Worlds, they created creatures great and small to fill them with. The Lyrans favored the warm-blooded animals and birds. They modeled the ruler of this kingdom after the Lion-Hearted Lyran soul family. The Brotherhood of the Snake preferred the cold-blooded animals, insects, and fish. They created many places of darkness in which their creatures might hide and thrive. The deadliest of these were named in homage of the Brotherhood's true face.

Like the era of Oneness, the Great Peace also was not meant to last.

One day, Aspects of the Brotherhood questioned, *What good is peace? Why do we only live in this small corner of the Many Worlds? Why do we avoid those who irritate us? Why not punish them instead? Do we not have sufficient strength to conquer and triumph?*

And so, the Brotherhood of the Snake began The Great War.

They destroyed the planet of Vega, in the star system of Lyra, forcing the Lyrans, their children, and their creations to find new homes among the Many Worlds.

Some of the Lyrans, unable to leave before the great destruction, were trapped in the channel between the worlds. There, they would remain stuck, unable to be reborn or reunite with the Source, until a reopening of the channel, or until the final turn of the wheel, when all would return to the One.

The Great War did not end with the destruction of Vega. The Brotherhood continued to hunt the Aspects of the Lyrans, wherever they appeared among the Many Worlds. For this reason, the Lyrans began to marry their creations, to obscure the lines of their descendants from the hunt.

Yet their blood cannot be destroyed, as that Divine Spark, the star seed, remains, no matter how many bodies the Aspect travels through. For any child of the line may awaken, connect to the Source, and reopen the channel to the One.

With every turn of the wheel, there is an opportunity for light to conquer darkness, for the Lyrans to overthrow the Brotherhood. Many Lyran Aspects have volunteered for this mission. These warrior Aspects are known as the Tzadikim Nistarim. When the wheel begins a new rotation, a champion is chosen from among these Lyran warriors. If the Lyran champion wins, the channels will reopen, the Aspects will return to the One, and peace will be restored. If victory goes to the Brotherhood, however, then the war will continue, discord and division will spread, and the Lyran champion's Aspect will go dark, forgetting itself until the last turn of the wheel.

Part Five

~ 80 ~

SEKHMET

She is a shadow among shadows, trailing her loved ones as they once followed her. From time to time, Akhenaten looks over his shoulder seeking her. Sekhmet lacks the energy to apparate, even as smoke.

She knows they have arrived before Zipporah announces it. Who else would live in the shadow of the twin peaks of the holy mountain? The sun is setting over Mt. Horeb as its sister Mt. Sinai greets the moonrise. The ragged band of refugees enter the Yitro's yard.

The door to the mud-brick home opens. Sekhmet sees the flame from the hearth flicker behind the high priest. She reflects its light, illuminating the congregation before him.

Yitro Reuel does not shrink from her. His pale eyes contain their own amber sparks. His hair lifts in the breeze like a pillar of fire. "Who comes hither?"

Aron answers for them. "Travelers seeking shelter from the darkness, your excellency."

Zipporah kneels in supplication. "I owe them my life, father."

Yitro Reuel looks at them for a long time without speaking. He steps to one side. The light from his hearth streams past him into the yard. It illuminates a rod plunged into the ground before them. It sparkles like a cloudless sky. "I knew you would come," the holy man says.

Sekhmet feels the sapphire rod vibrating. She recognizes its power.

The Source! This must be a relic of the Great Creators, something made before the destruction of Vega.

Yitro Reuel points to the staff and addresses Aron. "Do you know this power? Would you own it? Call it by its name. If it heeds you, it is yours."

Aron begins to sing. There is no mistaking who he is.

Our champion.

Sekhmet hears voices on the wind, singing back to him. She cannot tell if Aron hears the voices or not. But he heeds them, approaching the trembling instrument.

As Aron lays his hands upon the rod, the earth quakes. He sings out the name of the One. A bolt of lightning shoots from his hands to the sky. The ground beneath the staff cracks, opening a new channel of power.

Aron extracts the rod and holds it high above his head.

"Hineni!" *'Here I am.'*

Yes, Aron. Here you are. How I wish I could stay with you and fight. But I am fading from this world.

Akhenaten needs the Madyan people's aid to liberate their enslaved allies in Kemet. In the home of Yithro, Aron gives Sekhmet's daughters new names, ones that will make sense to the Madyan people. He transforms her wise, dark-eyed Meritaten into Miriam. She is no longer Akhenaton's child, but his sister. This will afford her greater protection. Ankesenpaaten, who is still an androgynous child, becomes Miriam's 'son' Hur. The beautiful, patient Neferneferuaten takes the name Elisheva. Sekhmet can already tell Aron favors her.

Not that it matters. I don't get to see how this story ends. Besides, Aron is the champion of this age, not me.

Aron senses her reluctance to let go.

"You must," he insists. "If I fail, you need to be reborn to fight on."

She hesitates.

"Trust me," Aron whispers. His dove gray eyes with their blue clouds make a promise to her.

I do.

As he sings to his staff, Sekhmet once again hears the voices of her people. They are calling to her.

All of them.

Not only the ones across the sea, but also the ones living among the Many Worlds, and the ones trapped in the channel in-between the worlds.

We are all connected.

Despite all the bloodshed and trauma, she finds a kind of peace in that.

I am ready.

The moon is high and full. She refracts its light so she can dance once more across Akhenaten's lips and kiss her daughters goodbye.

There is a sigh in the air. It shivers as she lets go.

As her loves slumber, Sekhmet slips between the veil of this world and into the in-between.

~ 81 ~

FILOMÉLA

Filoméla knows the stories about past champions, their triumphs, and struggles. From Filoméla's vantage point, being a champion is a suicide mission. One that ends badly for everyone involved. Meeting Honey hasn't made her feel any better.

No matter how strong, they all succumb. And what strength does Honey have?

To the tales of past battles, Filoméla adds her own observations. Her conclusion: Lyrans have discovered thousands of ways not to win.

According to Sekhmet, Aron believed faith was key to defeating the Brotherhood.

But his allies wavered in theirs. They never knew the promised land in their lifetime. All these generations later, the Brotherhood continues to persecute the lions of Judah.

Sekhmet leaped through the veil to help a champion named Yeshua. He reminded her of the selfless Christos Templar allies she fought beside. Yeshua believed compassion offered the best path to Lyran victory. He healed the sick, performed miracles, and inspired hope for peace on Earth.

Then, the Brotherhood crucified him. Called him Christ in mockery of the wars they would wage in his name. They continue to twist his teachings. They encourage 'true believers' to persecute anyone who aligns with Yeshua's values of radical inclusion, justice, and equity. They deny the existence of natural human instincts. That forces many into a life of shame and hypocrisy. Then they channel this anger to create even more destruction and division.

Forach's chosen champion, Jeanne, fought valiantly. She inspired her followers to overthrow the oppressive regime of the Brotherhood. Her error was believing nothing more than courage was required.

And what happened to her? Burnt at the stake before reaching adulthood. The Brotherhood revised her story. Now the people know her as a madwoman's saint. But she was a brilliant strategist and tactician, a great leader of men. How horrified she'd be to see bad people claiming to be like her when they seek to overturn governments.

Champions have been poets, warriors, imams, reverends, revolutionaries, lawyers, nuns, teachers, nurses, and more. They came from every race, creed, gender, and class. They chose diverse ways to amass huge followings, enlighten others, and inspire change.

And yet, the result always is the same. They lose. They always lose.

Filoméla's stomach knots in despair.

If this is our star seed's turn to lead the charge, this is our last chance.

She hasn't felt this panicky since Tereus abducted her. On board his ship, she knew things were bad, but was unable to tell how much worse they would become. Not knowing leaves too much space for her imagination. She knows a million ways Honey could lose.

How can we succeed where everyone else has failed?

She considers the previous battles.

What do they all have in common?

The Lyran side always represents a new order or way of being. They always challenge the established Brotherhood dogma. The champion's strategy is always the same: amass an army and pitch battle—either with weapons, ideas, or unarmed resistance.

But why must we always amass an army?

Filoméla knows what Sekhmet would say: "A tremendous amount of energy is required to open the channel and free those trapped by the destruction of Vega. To generate that, we need a mass awakening."

It's a simple strategy. Easy to follow. But it never works. Why?

Filoméla considers Honey. She lives within the cloistered, claustrophobic, domestic sphere of home and family, not much different from how women lived in Filoméla's day.

She may be even more isolated due to her blindness. How on Earth will she amass a following and influence others to join her?

Filoméla stops that line of thought.

Wait. Is that really what we need her to do?

If they never win that way . . .

Will we keep losing until we try something different?

What did all the other champions do?

Convince others to follow them. Challenge the Brotherhood's authority. Teach others the importance of love, unity, compassion, and fidelity to the One.

What haven't they tried?

To go it alone. Avoid confronting the Brotherhood. Open the channel to the Source first.

Filoméla's hands flutter to her mouth. She is smiling.

Wouldn't the Source then flow through us all of us at once? If it's open, and we're all connected, then do we need a mass anything? The Source would create that mass awakening, wouldn't it?

Filoméla looks to see if any of her soul sisters are around.

Is it crazy to think this way?

She's never seen anyone try to open the channel first. Certainly not on their own.

An unfamiliar emotion surges over her. It takes her a while to identify and name it. But it doesn't weigh her down. It buoys her spirit.

You don't need an army to open a door. You only need a key.

We have one key.

The champion.

Honey is the key.

For the first time in millennia, Filoméla begins to hope.

~ 82 ~

FORACH

The plan is to take their time and train the child, wait until Jeanne matures. But Forach knows time is something they don't have.

"We're fading," she tells Mikha'el. "Either we started too late, or we came too early, but the girl has to make her move, or we'll be of no help to her."

Gazing upon Mikha'el's face is like looking into the sun. He blazes with such beauty, Forach has trouble focusing on him. Oya gives Forach a different feeling altogether. She reflects light, she is the cool moon, a dark pool in which Forach could gaze forever.

She wonders how she appears to them. Then she remembers that she is more human than Lyran. Pure Lyran spirits appear like gods, with their own powers and gifts.

Do I reflect any of Sekhmet's light at all? Can they see her power in me? Or am I too far removed?

Oya and Mikha'el think Sekhmet's Soul Council strategy is interesting, but they don't understand it. They see no value in harvesting soul fragments from their line. They watch and divine what they think they ought to learn from their lives on Earth. But they don't want to converse with their own incarnations.

Forach can't imagine what this after-life would have been like without her soul sisters. She asked them once, "Don't you get lonely, watching from your place in the in-between, with no one to keep you company?"

Oya laughed and Mikha'el looked surprised. "With each incarnation on Earth," he explained, "there is less and less of the Lyran blood in our line. What could we learn that we don't already know?"

Forach hopes they value her contributions, as poor as they are.

"I'm fading," she says. "How strong do you feel?"

Oya and Mikha'el exchange glances.

Forach shakes her head. "If we wait for Jeanne to grow into a woman, I may not be able to help."

Oya frowns, and her dark thoughts gather storm clouds around her. Her gift alters the weather. It's a handy talent. But when she does it without thinking, it terrifies Forach. The blue sparks of Oya's eyes mirror the bolts of lightning flickering across the sky.

Having come to some agreement with herself, Oya nods. "Mikha'el, she is right. I cannot access the Source in this place. I cannot replenish myself. With every day, I become less and less. I will have to leave soon, too. I fear, if I do not, I will not have enough strength left for my own champion."

Flames shoot from Mikha'el's eyes. When he needs to summon it, that element is always at his disposal. "I never called you. You willingly came."

"And we willingly offer our help. We are tired of losing, too." Oya's words are a watery balm that extinguishes his anger. "We regret nothing. Only we ask: can this be the time we begin the arduous work? If it is, let us make the most of it and mobilize. If it is not, then Forach and I cannot stay with you until the end. Is this something you want to do alone?"

Mikha'el bends his head in thought. He draws his sword and tests its weight. Placing both hands on the hilt, he drives the blade into the earth. Flames shoot forth, licking their way up the steel length of it. He gazes first at Oya, then at Forach. He stares deeply into the flames, his avian face looking troubled.

Of course, Mikha'el could train and lead Jeanne to victory without them. In the early days of the Great War on Earth, he single-handedly drove the leader of the snakes into hiding.

He remembers both Sekhmet and Oya from Vega before its destruction. He has even told Forach about the aspect she possesses that Sekhmet does not.

Mikha'el reminds Forach so much of her brother Cian that she is loath to leave him. She does not want to say goodbye to another loved on. But she's here to learn, not to risk her own chance of winning by overstaying her welcome.

Finally, Mikha'el looks up and draws his sword from the earth.

"It appears the time has made itself," he says. "Let us prepare the child."

~ 83 ~

JUANA

Flowers litter the street. It seems a shame to crush them underfoot, but Juana can see no other way to get to the plaza for the Virrey's welcome. And they don't have long before the presentation of the victory arches. She sighs and gathers up her long skirts. She wants to cry as she hears petals squish beneath her slippers.

Why is so much beauty wasted? Whose idea was it to pluck these flowers so that we might crush them into the mud with our unworthy feet?

Juana whispers a little prayer to the Virgin. Carlos chuckles at her, but she does not feel foolish.

"Everything possesses a spark of the divine," she reminds him, "and so, is worthy of our deference and respect."

A soldier approaches, peaked hat glinting in the sun. But instead of the heavy steel armor customary of the conquistador, he's wearing a leather version. It's an Aztec design.

Juana sneaks a sly glance at Carlos. "Is that your idea?"

Carlos flushes and grins. "I might have suggested it. I want our new leader to know he is welcome. But I also want him to admire the inventiveness of the people under his command. Besides, it will be good for him to understand how we have benefitted from the native peoples as much as they have benefited from our rule."

Juana isn't sure the Nahuatl would agree about the benefits of being an occupied nation, but she holds her tongue.

Tomorrow, in the locutorio, I'll debate and dissect his arguments. Today is a day for celebration.

The soldier reaches them. He bows so low, Juana wonders how his heavy hat manages to stay on. "Sor Juana and Don Carlos, your litter awaits. My men and I are honored to convey you to the plaza."

Juana laughs. The idea of a nun and a man of faith riding on the backs of other men is ridiculous. "Oh no, my legs work just—Ow!" She looks sharply at her friend, who is removing his elbow from her ribs.

Don Carlos bows low to the soldier. "I think what the kind sister meant to say is: we'd be delighted to accept."

The soldier pivots away. Don Carlos pinches her.

"Hey!" Juana rubs her arm, shocked. "What did you do that for?"

His pale blue eyes flame with amber fire. "Because you're acting like a child. I didn't get you this commission so you could waste every advantage it affords you. You are a titan of intellect who, among the dirt of this city, shines like a pearl. Why do you insist on refusing all the credit and glory that is your due?"

Juana shakes her head. His passion embarrasses her. She did not ask for this magnitude of attention. "I don't want glory. I do my work for the love of doing it. I would rather destroy vanity in my life rather than let vanity destroy my life. What will people think if I let men carry me into the plaza like I am a princess?"

"Well, I guess you'll find out," Carlos says, climbing onto the craft and extending a hand to help her up.

Sor Juana hesitates, horrified. This is no carriage with doors or curtains she can hide behind. It's not even a canopied litter.

This is a parade paso, open and exposed. Everyone will see me. There'll be no mistaking who I am!

The paso is gorgeous, to be sure. Its elaborately carved mahogany base displays flowery vines. Statues of Jésus and the Verge de Guadeloupe stand sentinel on its back corners. In the center stands two throne-like chairs: one for her and the other for Carlos. He is already waving at the peasants below.

Blood rises to her cheeks.

There's nowhere to hide!

"Carlos, this feels wrong." She imagines the disapproving eyes of Madre Abadesa on her. She knows what people will think if she gets on this paso.

They will think I am too full of myself. That I think myself better than them.

Juana begs Carlos with wet eyes. "Please, I can't."

The soldier is behind her. "Excuse us, sister, but we need to be going." Strong hands lift her. She suppresses the urge to kick free. The soldiers deposit her on the top step of the paso.

She considers jumping.

Suicide is a deadly sin. But is it worse than pride?

Carlos beckons. "If you don't want to be thrown off, I suggest you sit down. We have an important date with the new Virrey. You don't want to keep him waiting do you?"

Forty soldiers bend to the ground to grasp the long poles attached to the base of the paso. Juana scrambles to her seat a millisecond before the men hoist the paso to their shoulders.

God, forgive me.

The paso lurches forward. Juana's shoulder bounces painfully off the side of her wooden throne. Her right hand reaches for the rosary at her waist. While Carlos smiles and waves, she fights back nausea and whispers the Nuestra Padre.

Forgive me.

~ 84 ~

HONEY

A key turns in the lock, drawing back the bolt. It startles Honey. She drops her phone. She hears it skitter across the floor, under the coffee table.

"What are you doing home?" Honey tries to sound casual, but she curses inwardly. If she knew Chad was going to pop in, she would have put headphones on.

Instead, the sound of the Vice President is clearly audible from an area of the room much closer to where he stands. She refuses to run after the phone like a child caught doing something naughty. But she dreads what his reaction will be when he realizes she's tuned into the broadcast.

"I forgot something I wanted to give to Dave," Chad says, grunting as he bends to pick up the phone. "Here, you dropped this."

"Thanks." Honey lowers the volume. She moves toward the bedroom so she can still hear what is being said about the insurrection.

Chad follows her. "Why are you listening to that?"

"It's a message from the President and the Vice President of the United States. Why wouldn't I?"

"Because it's political theater." He listens for a moment. "Ugh, that woman's voice gives me the creeps."

Honey stops. "It's not political theater. It's a reminder not to forget that there was an attempted coup to overthrow democracy."

"Bullshit. It was a bunch of patriots angry that Biden stole the election. ."

Honey takes a deep breath. She avoids talking politics as much as possible. She doesn't want to get into a pissing match with him. But avoiding conflict is no less exhausting than engaging in it. She's tired of hiding her thoughts. She doesn't want to become complicit by remaining silent. She wants to push back against his ugliness and push back hard.

She holds up her phone, letting the voice of the legitimately elected President speak for her.

"My fellow Americans in life, there's truth. And tragically, there are lies. Lies conceived and spread for profit and power. We must be clear about what is true and what is a lie. And here's the truth—"

Chad knocks the phone out of her hand. It crashes into the kitchen island and goes silent.

Honey's hand hurts. But not as much as her disappointment with him. She cradles her hand and says, "Get out."

"As soon as I get what I came for, I'm leaving."

"No. You have to go." Honey can't believe what is coming out of her mouth, but she can't stop it, doesn't want to stop it. It feels too right, too true. "Don't come back."

"Don't be stupid."

She balls up her fists. "I'm not stupid."

"You know what I mean. You can't get around without me. Who's going to protect you?"

"Protect me?" Honey hears her voice break, and she wills the tears to dry up. "You think the people who stormed the capitol are patriots! Some of them were waving Confederate flags and wearing 'Six Million Were Not Enough' T-shirts. They hate people like me. How are you going to protect me from them when *you're on their side*?"

"Don't—"

"No," she cuts him off. "Haven't you ever studied history? It repeats. Did you know, about every eighty years someone tries to exterminate the Jews? I'm Jewish. It's been eighty years since the Holocaust. Now, in America, we have a bunch of racist, misogynistic, fascist yahoos trying to overthrow democracy. And you support them! I. Don't. Want. You. In. This. House."

Chad speaks softly. "Honey."

The thought of him touching her makes her want to scream. "No. Get out! Leave me alone!"

"You don't know what you're saying. You need me."

Do I?

Honey trembles, suddenly unsure. After fifteen years together does she really want him to go? Does she want to grow old alone?

Then, she asks herself: *do you really want to grow old with this man?*

A swelling tide of resentment unearths fifteen years of disappointments and dumps them at her feet. She examines all those horrible, hurtful memories. At the time, the incidents seemed so minor, she brushed them off. But lumped together, they create a picture of a man who's grown small-minded, fearful, bitter, and cruel. And not even in a direct way, but in an insidious passive-aggressive way that's made her feel like it's all been her fault.

What happened to the generous, funny man I fell in love with?

He used to be her biggest fan, a source of support, and a friend. The Chad she lives with now sneers at things she cares about. He questions her judgment when she disagrees with him. He makes fun of her spiritual beliefs. He opposes any progress she makes towards independence.

Why can't he be proud of me?

She knows the answer and it makes her heart ache.

Because he doesn't want me to evolve. He's stuck. He wants me to stay stuck with him.

Honey thinks about Amy and Emily. What would happen if they spent a lifetime listening to his little jabs and critiques? What would they believe is right, hearing his cautions and crazy conspiracy theories? What would they learn by watching Chad prevent her from growing and becoming who she is meant to be? What would they think, watching him belittle and discourage her? Would they think that's an acceptable way for a man to treat his wife? Would they choose to marry a man like him? Would they one day suffer like her?

That's not the life or love she wants for them.

I can't let him stay here and do that to me. I can't do that to them. I'd rather die.

Honey finds her voice and it no longer trembles. She speaks firmly, hoping he can hear her. "I don't need you anymore."

"Honey." Even now, his voice drips with annoyance, like this is a little fit of hers that will blow away.

"Why aren't you listening to me?" She pounds the floor with her feet to make him shut up. The rage travels from her belly to her mouth so fast, she isn't sure of what she's saying until she does. "I want a divorce!"

It feels so good that she says it again. "I want a divorce!"

A feeling of relief, a rebellious thirst for freedom fills her. She says for a third time, like a magic spell: "I want a divorce!"

Everything stops. Honey catches her breath, waiting to see what he will say next.

But the cat has his tongue.

Her invocation drives him away and out the door.

~ 85 ~

FILOMÉLA

The idea of being inside another person's head appalls Filoméla. Juana and Forach take trips down the channel all the time, and always seem to enjoy it. She doesn't think Sekhmet does, but she checks in on Honey often enough.

Filoméla desires to see through Honey's eyes, as well. That is why, for the first time in centuries, Filoméla descends the channel to visit an incarnation.

The soul path stretches farther than she remembers. Coming into the body is unpleasant. The field of darkness ahead puzzles her. She wonders if Honey is asleep. Then, she remembers this woman is blind.

Or not.

Filoméla wonders if Sekhmet is right.

If her blindness is self-imposed, what does Honey not want to see? If it's because of the Brotherhood, how do we break that spell?

She can't wonder for long. An overwhelming feeling of upset and unhappiness washes over her.

It must be Honey. Something's wrong.

Filoméla finds it hard to breathe. Every shuddering heartbeat threatens to leap from her chest. She can feel Honey's nails digging into the palms of her hands.

Filoméla recognizes this feeling. It's what she felt every time she heard Tereus's footsteps.

She's preparing to defend herself. Is she in danger?

Filoméla hears a man's voice. "Who's going to protect you?"

Not him, Filoméla begs Honey. If she's this upset, this is not a good situation. Filoméla does not know this man, but she recognizes his tone. The way this man speaks to Honey is rough and haughty. This, too, reminds her of Tereus.

You do not need him.

Honey's voice rises precariously. What she says, Filoméla has trouble following. But there was one thing she hears clearly: this man is no longer welcome in this house.

It takes strength to say, and Filoméla is proud of Honey for doing so.

But this is not a man who gives up easily.

He is not leaving. He does not take her seriously. Does he not believe her?

The air is thick and heavy between them. It pulses with something dangerous.

Filoméla is glad that she can't see the expression on the man's face. Honey's heart is racing. They tremble together. She fears something bad is going to happen.

Filoméla cannot tell where her fear ends, and Honey's begins. But when the man takes a step toward them, they shout in unison.

"No. Get out! Leave me alone!"

The man hesitates. Filoméla senses something like a tentacle of energy, extend from him toward them. He tries a different, gentler tactic.

Filoméla shudders in disgust, as she feels Honey's resolve weaken. She hears Honey ask herself, *Do I really want to grow old alone?*

Enraged, Filoméla shoots back, *Do you really want to grow old with this man?*

Something within Honey breaks open, flooding them with memories. A hundred moments flow out of the vault. Times when Honey chose not to stand up for herself when she was hurt. Or explained away damaging behavior. Or ignored something ugly and cruel. They come bubbling up like vomit. They ruin every good thing, reopening old wounds and refreshing old doubts.

Filoméla is impressed by how thorough this man's cruelty has been. He's never physically harmed Honey, but he's left massive scars on her psyche.

If they were visible from outside, they would be just as ugly and obvious as the ones around my neck.

Filoméla is convinced Honey's blindness is tied to this man. There's so much she's buried and doesn't want to see. But now it's in the open. She can start to examine it. That will help her heal and regain control of what she sees.

You can't let him stay here and do that to you anymore, she tells Honey.

She is thrilled to hear Honey agree, echo her, and think, *I'd rather die.*

Make him listen, Filoméla urges. *Make sure he knows he cannot stay.*

Honey sweeps the painful images away to make room for herself. She taps into a deep reservoir of strength and speaks her will into being.

The words she speaks hold so much power, they silence the man, driving him from the room.

The heavy feeling in the air around them dissipates. Honey exhales.

Filoméla feels relief. Still, something malevolent lingers.

Salt. We need salt.

Honey's body moves in response to Filoméla's urging. Holding the salt cellar, Honey pauses and wonders what she is doing.

Filoméla advises, *Sprinkle a little salt in each corner. Draw a line outside your doors to keep the good things in and drive the evil out. Then we'll sweep it up and throw it away.*

Honey enjoys that thought, embraces it as her own, and does as she is told. Filoméla stays with her as she wanders from room to room.

Honey climbs a set of stairs and for a moment, Filoméla sees a flicker of light.

Can this be undone?

She pokes around the edges of the gap and tugs.

Honey stops moving and gasps, nearly dropping the salt as she brings her other hand up.

Filoméla is triumphant. She flies back up the channel and emerges at the in-between.

Six pairs of eyes and three mouths greet her with impatience. “Where have you been?”

Filoméla ignores their impatience.

She speaks. “Hear me.”

Three mouths gape open.

Filoméla continues, as if she hasn’t been silent for hundreds of years.

She claps her hands and shouts, “Our champion . . . she’s free!”

~ 86 ~

FORACH

The sun rises from its bed. It pushes itself off the sleepy green hills. Rosy fingers of dawn slide past the rough gate, up the side of the stone house, and through the open window. They bend to stroke the face of the sleeping maiden, champion of this turn of the wheel.

"Jeanne," Mikha'el whispers. "Rise and go forth. It is time."

The girl wakes with a smile.

The girl dons her cloak and retrieves the bag of radishes and potatoes she's hidden in the hay. Forach is filled with inexpressible sadness. She remembers being under siege. Nothing but blood and famine await this sweet child.

Jeanne knows nothing of war. She is ignorant of love, too, except what she expresses to God and the three of them. Only she doesn't call them Mikha'el, Oya, and Forach. The child calls them by the names of saints and angels: Michel, Catherine, and Marina.

Forach remembers being sixteen, or near enough.

Was I ever that innocent?

Her sixteenth year was one lost in captivity, to the lust of Prince Conn. His father burnt her to dust seven years later.

If I'd known what was waiting for me, would I have bathed in the Sionna that day?

Conn's abduction set so many things in motion. The exile of the Déisi. Aiofe's birth. Cian's death.

So many suffered because of me. We all died anyway. Was it worth it? To live such a short, brutal life?

Then she remembers how it felt to be held by Aoife's chubby hands.

A love I almost forgot to remember.

Forach breathes in the fresh dirt and spring flower scent of her baby. She remembers how it felt to hold and to be held.

Yes, it is enough to live, to find one good thing we can love. To know what we stand for, would die for, and must protect.

~ 87 ~

JUANA

There is a sliver of moonlight dancing down the curve of Paola's neck. Juana follows it with her tongue, harvesting the salt buried there.

Paola giggles and pulls Juana's head back by the hair. "You didn't answer my question."

Juana will not be deterred. If she cannot lick her way to safety, she will try burrowing.

But Paola feels Juana's hand seeking her lower lips and traps it between her thighs. Her dark eyes flash with blue fire. "Not until you answer my question!"

Juana's eyes twinkle. She tries to bite a nipple, but Paola pushes her off and rolls on top, pinning Juana's shoulders with her knees. "Why didn't you wave to me?"

Juana sighs and knocks her head against the straw mattress in frustration. "*Mi corazon*, I told you! I didn't wave to anyone. I wasn't looking for friends in the crowd. I was praying the earth would split open and swallow me up, paso and all. I was so embarrassed!"

Paola pouts. Her finger traces the soft curve of Juana's breast. "You didn't look embarrassed. You looked like a queen."

Soft ripples of pleasure expand from Juana's chest to cover the rest of her body. "You are my queen."

Juana cranes upward, hungry for Paola's mouth. But a sharp pain in her breast drives her back. "Ow!"

"I'm your queen?" Paola's fingers tighten over Juana's nipple. "Then why didn't you look at me? I noticed you looking at the new Virrena!"

Juana swallows the urge to laugh. "The Virrena? How could I not look at her? I had to welcome her. It was part of the ceremony."

Paola's breath catches, a half sob. "Do you love me?"

Juana reaches for Paola. She wants to pull her close and hug all the sadness away. "Mi vida! There's no one I love more!"

Paola pulls back, uncertain. "Do you?"

"Yes," Juana lifts Paola's face to hers and kisses the tears off her cheeks. "Yes."

Paola pouts again and Juana runs to the desk. "Look, I even wrote you a poem."

"You did?" Paola sits up in the narrow bed, smearing tears away.

Juana's breath catches at the sight of Paola in the moonlight. Where the light hits her dark skin, it shines silver. "Has there ever been a woman in the world more beautiful than you?"

Paola smiles shyly, then with a toss of her head says, "Shut up and read me my poem."

Juana laughs and clears her throat. "It's my first attempt. So please don't blame me if it's clumsy and bad. I'll fix it. I promise"

Paola leans back, liberating her lower body from the blanket. "You better."

Juana drinks in the blessing waiting for her, gives thanks to God, and begins to read:

How easy it is to worship our Father, who art in Heaven.
His light shines like the sun, they say,
visible to all who have eyes to see.
But what about the Mother of God?
Is she not even greater
to have brought such life into this world?
Is not her power more constant in its love,
like the sun itself?
Perhaps it is the Mother who is the forever present sun,
who gives all that we may live
and showers us with love.
And it is the Father who is the changeable moon,
showing us the way through the dark night,
influencing us and the tides,
even when absent.
Who really is the Great Creator?
The one who plants the seed,
or the one who bears the fruit?
The Mother of God smiles and holds a finger to her lips.
We know the truth.
Let them think our Mother only reflects the light.
We know which One is the true Source.

Paola gasps.

Juana lowers the paper, hurt. "I know it's clumsy, but you inspired it, and . . ."

"No," Paola is off the bed and at her side in an eye-blink. "Look!"

Juana follows her gaze out the window and forgets everything else.

Blazing across the night sky is a ball of fire, hanging suspended like a flame in a chandelier. Behind it, a long tail of light stretches toward the heavens. It is gorgeous and terrifying.

Long after she closes her eyes, Juana sees the comet burn against the night sky.

How can anyone sleep when such marvels exist in the world?

She endures breakfast and morning vespers and runs to the locutorio as soon as she's free. She's desperate to discuss the sight with her friends. As soon as she sees Carlos, she blurts out, "Did you see the flame in the sky?"

"You mean the comet?" Carlos adjusts his spectacles. "It's visible now."

"It is?" Juana runs to the window, ignoring his laughter. "It's magnificent!"

Don Carlos shrugs. "It's a comet."

"What do you think it means?"

His laughter comes out a bark. "It's an astrological phenomenon, it doesn't mean anything."

A man's voice tsks.

Juana's heart sinks. She should have known Manuel was here, too.

Manuel adjusts his heavy silver cufflinks. "Everyone knows comets are a sign of God's displeasure. I'm sure it signals a harsh winter, challenging times, or great hardships ahead."

"I don't know," Juana muses. "They say a comet heralded the birth of Our Savior. Maybe a special child is being born somewhere in this New World?"

"To do what?" Don Carlos asks. "Give power to the criollos? Send all the Europeans back home? We should be so lucky."

"Careful, Don Carlos," Manuel warns him. "I know you're joking. But one day someone will take you seriously and believe that you don't care for our esteemed leaders. You don't want anyone to believe you're disloyal to our fatherland, do you?"

"I love Spain," Carlos protests. "I just don't care for authority."

Manuel sniffs. "That's an unfortunate trait for a man of God."

Juana defends her friend. "It's an unfortunate trait for a man of God to lack a sense of humor, too, is it not?"

The Bishop laughs and wags a finger at her. "Careful, little sister. The Inquisition takes an interest in the impious, even when they live in the new, rather than old, world."

Juana's cheeks flare. "Are you suggesting I'm impious?"

"Not at all. Everyone could see your piety radiating from your throne on that paso."

It would be wonderful to break Manuel's nose. Juana restrains herself by digging her nails into her palms.

Manuel takes a seat in the chair closest to her and smooths out his robes. "But that's old news. Now the comet . . . I was just discussing that with Father Kino. He sees great portent in its passage across the sky. You know, it followed him from Spain all the way across the sea here?"

Carlos scowls. When Manuel compliments anyone, male or female, his temper flares. "There's nothing divine about a comet. It's a natural phenomenon."

Manuel chuckles. He turns to Juana. "I read something recently and thought of you." He extracts a pamphlet from his vest pocket and hands it to her.

The typeface is bold and gothic. She reads the author's name with curiosity. "António Vieyra?"

"Have you heard of him?"

Juana nods. "Who hasn't heard of the famous padre in Brasília?" She squints at the date on the pamphlet. "But this is such an old sermon. He gave this forty years ago?"

Manuel shrugs. "A colleague of mine brought it to my attention and I thought you would find it interesting. You write so much about God's love in your poetry—*divine love* as you put it? I thought you'd enjoy reading the padre's thoughts on what Christ's most profound expression of love is."

"Thank you." She doubts his intentions but can find no obvious malice in the gesture. She leaves Carlos and Manuel to banter and curls up in her favorite chair to read.

Juana barely makes it through the introductory argument before she gasps. As she gets deeper into the work, she can't hold back her vocal disapproval of the padre's thoughts.

Manuel arches an eyebrow.

Carlos breaks off mid-sentence to ask, "What on Earth is the matter with you?"

Juana shakes the pamphlet and laughs. "The hubris of Padre Vieyra! I'm shocked!"

Manuel's glittering violet eyes light on her. "Do tell. What do you find so offensive?"

Juana blushes. "I don't know if it's offensive. Everyone has a right to their opinion. But I've never seen someone go so far out of their way to argue with the orthodoxy of the Church! It's bold."

Manuel smiles. "I didn't realize you were in favor of orthodoxy. You ignore Saint Paul's dictum that women do not teach."

"That's untrue!" Juana protests. "I follow that prescription. I don't teach."

Carlos teases her. "You've taught me much."

"Not intentionally," Juana says. "We discuss ideas, things we have learned. And I learn only so that I might become less ignorant. I don't learn to teach other people what to think. That would be prideful!"

"Okay little fox," Manuel says in a tone that sets Juana's teeth on edge. "What faith in the orthodoxy is Padre Vieyra breaking?"

Juana laughs and flicks the pamphlet in her hands. "He cites San Agustín, San Aquino, and San Crisóstomo and then says he knows better than all of those esteemed saints!"

Manuel leans forward, cupping his chin in his hands, "Does he?"

"Of course not! Listen to this."

Juana flips to the meat of the argument. "What is the greatest demonstration of Christ's love for us?"

Juana looks up to see if they can guess, but they remain silent.

"According to San Augustín, it's that Christ was willing to die for us. San Aquino says Christ's spirit remains with us even though his physical body had to depart. San Chrisóstomo says the greatest demonstration of Christ's love was washing his disciples' feet."

Manuel's tongue wets his lips. "And our esteemed Padre's position?"

Juana is swept up by the power of the ideas she wants to express. She can feel the words coming hard and fast, like reckless horses. But she gives them free reign rather than holding them back.

"He ascribes human feelings to Christ, as if God is totally involved. As if God cares about everything we do."

She laughs. "God displays love for us by leaving us alone most of the time. I mean listen to this: Christ's greatest sacrifice was leaving us because he didn't want to. Was it punishing God in some way? And that's why we have sacraments? That's Vieyra's proof that Christ wanted to stick around on Earth? It's absurd!"

Juana is on her feet now. The ridiculousness of Vieyra's assumptions is a personal affront to correct. "Christ didn't invent the sacraments. Men did. And men are fallible."

She laughs. "And Christ didn't leave us. All that is divine, is around us, all the time. Christ's death encourages us to see the divine in every living thing. He certainly did."

"And yet," Manuel's amethyst eyes shine bright now, "you say God does not care about us?"

"No, that's not what I said," Juana says, cheeks flushing. "The fact that God does so little for us is proof of his love! God is not selfless and disinterested. On the contrary, God demands correspondence from us!"

Manuel's laugh comes sharp and hard, as if she's punched him with her words. "And what kind of correspondence does God require?"

"Love!" Juana says, letting the word land on them. There is a movement by the entrance. Paola is there, eavesdropping. Juana smiles at her. In Paola's expression, Juana feels her lover's tenderness as strongly as a caress.

Juana returns to the men. “God exists,” she tells them, gesturing to the light streaming in through the window. “That is all the benefit we need. God exists. That fact alone should be enough to inspire love and goodwill toward each other. That’s the correspondence God requires. He wants us to demonstrate our gratitude for living by expressing love to one another. We need to show that we can rise above our petty squabbles to see, acknowledge, and respect the divine in each other. To love each other instead of letting our differences tear us apart. That is what God requires of us as payment. As gratitude for the blessing of living to see this day.”

“You should write that down,” Carlos says, face glowing. “Thoughts that bold could change the world.”

Juana laughs and retreats to the safety of her chair. “There’s no reason for me to write my thoughts down. That would be presumptuous of me. My thoughts are not so noble that they deserve the ink it would cost to preserve them.”

Manuel shakes his head. “Don’t be so modest. You’ve managed to infuse the dogma of the faith with a strain of philosophy all your own. It’s quite unexpected for a woman to have such insights. I’m sure many people would be interested to see what becomes of educating the weaker sex.”

Carlos clasps her hands and pulls them to his chest, drawing her to him before she can cut Manuel dead. “For me, my Athena? Will you write your thoughts for me?”

She blushes. “Why would you need them written down? We can talk whenever you like.”

He looks at her with shining eyes. “I’d like to study them. Burn them upon my heart. Keep them with me forever.”

“Oh Carlos.” Juana cups his birdlike face in her hands. “Anything for you, Carlos.”

~ 88 ~

HONEY

The funny thing about a rupture is that long after the cut is made, you expect nothing will change. Honey realizes she's being ridiculous, but she maintains the pattern she's used to. That means long after the bus comes and goes, Honey waits by the neighborhood's back gate. Even though the school confirmed Chad picked Emily and Amy up, Honey hopes he'll drop them here for her. It isn't until a well-meaning neighbor informs her it is getting dark that she goes home. Even then, she expects the girls will run to greet her when she opens the door.

The silence of the house oppresses her.

It is too lonely here. There are no chubby feet running up and down the stairs. No one complains about their bedtime, so she can't fall asleep. Without children fighting over breakfast, she has no appetite. The house hangs about her, haunted and sad.

At six-thirty in the morning, she stumbles down to the bus stop as usual. She doesn't know where Chad and the girls spent the night, but she is hoping she'll see them here.

She doesn't know where else to go or what else to do.

It's not like anyone would take the girls from him. I'm blind. He's their dad.

She waits until she hears the bus's air brakes hiss and pop. The door opens with a whoosh.

"Hey," the bus driver calls, "are your girls on their way?"

She chokes on the sad realization. "No. No, they're not."

Honey wants to tell the bus driver that the girls aren't coming, she's made a stupid mistake, and everything she loves is lost forever. But the doors of the bus sigh shut as if they, too, are disappointed in her. The bus roars off.

Honey stands there, listening to the stream of cars whizzing by. For a wild moment, she considers throwing herself in front of them.

Cautious footsteps disturb the gravel behind her. Honey jumps even before Regina calls her name.

Oh no. I forgot she was meeting me here.

Regina is at her elbow. "Hey, are you okay?"

Honey turns her face away.

What a stupid question.

Honey doesn't know how to answer. The words refuse to rise and be spoken.

Regina moves in front of her to get a better look and gasps. "Oh, Honey, what happened?"

Suddenly, soft arms embrace her.

Honey collapses, sobbing into Regina's shoulder. "He took them."

"Who? Who'd he take?"

Honey lifts her head, struggling to choke out the words between sobs. "My girls. My husband took them."

"He can't do that!"

He can't?

Honey feels a surge of hope. "Really?"

"No! He can't. What happened? You threw him out or something?"

Honey nods. She needs a tissue. She pulls her head up to wipe her nose on her sleeve instead of Regina's soft shoulder.

"Well, he can't just take the kids. Did you call the police?"

"No, I didn't think . . . "

"My dirtbag ex-brother-in-law tried the same thing when my sister kicked him out." Regina takes her hand and marches her back into the neighborhood. "Don't you worry. We'll get them back. I know just what to do. Up the hill is the office for the neighborhood maintenance crew. My cell reception is spotty here, but I'm sure they have a phone. Let's call from there. The head of maintenance is a friend of mine."

Honey clings gratefully to Regina's hand. They crest a hill and Regina calls out, "Hey James! Can we use your phone?"

"Sure," says a person Honey assumes is James. He sounds chipper. Honey hesitates.

Regina pulls her over the threshold. There is a series of little clicks. "Is that a rotary phone?" Honey asks.

"If it ain't broke, don't fix it," James says with a laugh. "You a friend of Regina's?"

"Yes, I'm Honey."

"James."

The silence that follows is awkward. She can sense James is close by, but she has no idea what is happening. Not knowing the layout of this room, she's afraid to move, not wanting to stumble or fall over anything.

"James," Regina calls out, "Stop trying to shake her hand! She's blind. Besides, no one wants to shake hands these days."

"I'm double vaxxed and boosted," he protests. "Sorry, I didn't see your eyes, I didn't realize you're blind. I'm James Madison."

Without thinking, Honey asks, "Like the president?"

"Yeah, like the president." He laughs again.

"You laugh a lot."

Regina shushes them. "Hi, yes, I'd like to initiate an Amber alert."

Honey tries to stop her. "Oh, I don't know if that's—"

"Holy shit!" James says, "Someone took a kid? You saw it?"

"Her dirtbag husband took her girls." Regina says knowingly. "They're probably in Tennessee by now."

"Actually," Honey interrupts, "they're at school. I think?"

The mood in the room shifts. Honey's neck itches with embarrassment.

"What do you mean, they're at school?" Regina asks.

Honey flushes. "Well, it's a school day, and I'm sure Chad had to go to work, so he probably dropped them off at school?"

Regina tells the police to hold on and speaks to Honey. "I thought you said that your husband took your girls?"

The tears have dried up, but Honey's nose continues to drip. Now, she feels sweat on her face, too. "He did. They didn't come home last night, and I don't know where they're staying, and he's not answering his phone . . . "

Honey hears the click of the receiver.

"Okay," Regina says. "New plan."

~ 89 ~

SEKHMET

Sekhmet watches Forach arc out of reach, into the void, and curses.

Why are we so stubborn? Do we never learn?

Of course, Forach would be tempted to try and help a champion.

I told her it doesn't work. I should have kept the story to myself.

A rip appears in the air across the way. Sekhmet watches a sword of fire come through it. She takes a shattered breath in recognition.

Mikha'el?

The wall knits together, separating Sekhmet and Filoméla from the world of the Lyran champion. But Sekhmet's mind is no longer here in the in-between.

She has fallen through time, to the where and when she last saw that Aspect's human face.

Mikha'el. My brother. My comrade.

How haggard he looks in the lamplight of the past, speaking in hushed tones so as not to wake the others. His pale, amber-flecked eyes flame as wild as his red hair.

Even in human casing, Mikha'el burns.

That is his gift. Only, in the lifetime Sekhmet remembers now, he is not Mikha'el. In this incarnation he is known as Yehuda Es-Kariot. And Yeshua is not a champion of either of their lines. Yet, both felt compelled to join him.

When she stepped through the veil to help, she took the name her daughter Meritaten took to liberate their people. It felt right to be another Miriam helping the children of Israel. In the local dialect, her name is Maryam of Migdal.

Mikha'el.

She closes her eyes and feels Yeshua's hand on her shoulder. He has surprised them in the tent. She turns to gaze upon the champion, their golden promise, the man of peace. He puts one arm around her and the other around Mikha'el and presses his cheeks to theirs.

Yeshua whispers, "It is time. You know what needs to be done."

Mikha'el protests, but Yeshua shakes his head and looks toward the pile of sleeping apostles. "Do not wake Kepha."

Let him sleep like a stone, Sekhmet thinks. *If he wakes, all he'll do is whine that Yeshua shouldn't be wasting secrets on me.*

Of all the idiots they've attracted, Kepha is the worst. He understands nothing Yeshua's taught him.

Mikha'el swallows and nods, red curls bouncing. He kisses Yeshua goodbye, bows before him, and runs from the tent. The champion has charged Mikha'el with the worst job. But they know the best way to give the champion's ideas eternal life is to end his mortal one.

She throws her arms around Yeshua, unwilling to leave him, but knowing the end is near. This is all part of his plan. The people's hearts have been stirred, the teachings distributed, the miracles performed. This is the only part of the plan they have not yet fulfilled.

Her eyes are stinging. There is salt in her mouth. She doesn't know if it's from sweat or sorrow.

Sekhmet blinks and feels history wrinkle. She is here, with Yeshua the champion. She is also hundreds of years from here, with a shadow of herself in the in-between, watching another champion be born.

The wheel turns and turns. And nothing changes.

We were so sure. And his ideas survived after him, as we planned. They spread over the old and new worlds.

But the portals didn't open. There was no mass awakening.

We failed. We still fight.

What's worse is that Sekhmet has lived long enough to see the Brotherhood hijack sweet Yeshua's teachings. In the Brotherhood's Church, the focus is not on the divine spark of the One in every living being that unites us. They emphasize self-denial in this life to achieve an eternal reward. They encourage competition among the righteous,

They turned his path to liberation into one of constriction and condemnation. Yeshua's sweet words of love are used to create all sorts of divisions.

Sekhmet lays a hand on the smooth wall to feel the Source. She throws her head back and roars in frustration.

Did we change anything, Mikha'el?

Will Forach be able to help you?

~ 90 ~

FILOMÉLA

The Hibernian woman is so brave and fearless.

Filoméla watches Forach leap into the void and longs to follow. But Sekhmet is closest, and not even she has time to grab the rough cloth of Forach's dress before the veil closes.

For a while, Sekhmet and Filoméla stand there in shock, looking at the newly solid wall of the in-between. Then Sekhmet leans her head back and roars.

Her cry is full of anger, frustration, impotence—and Filoméla thinks—grief.

Sekhmet turns. "You'd never do anything so stupid, would you?"

Filoméla shakes her head. But she wonders, *Could I?* She envies Forach's courage, Sekhmet's strength. Not for the first time, she wonders, *Why am I here?*

Sekhmet folds up into herself, deep in thought. Filoméla goes to her, touches her shoulder and feels the connection hum between them. Sekhmet places a hand over hers and they sit in silence, in contemplation of the Source. It feels fainter than it had when Sekhmet first brought her to this place.

How much time do we have left?

There is so much she does not know.

Sekhmet raises her head, and Filoméla notices something different in her expression. "I can feel her. Can you?"

Filoméla closes her eyes and imagines Forach. She focuses on the Source and nods. Between Filoméla and the Source, Sekhmet pulses like the sun. She shoots off energy that runs through Filoméla and past her to the other incarnations.

Filoméla turns away from Sekhmet's burning presence. She focuses on the fainter traces that flow out of the center of her own being to the other end of the line, which has no end.

Out there, somewhere beyond the wall, there is a glowing star of energy. Filoméla's heart leaps in recognition.

Forach!

~ 91 ~

FORACH

The sun hides behind plumes of smoke. English corpses hang from the battlements. Grass gives way to rivers of bloody mud. The only thing clearly visible in the chaos is Jeanne's standard—a white banner attached to a sapphire rod. A flag of surrender answers it from the Orléans tower.

Forach clasps Oya's hand. "We've won?"

Oya nods, blue sparks glinting off the ebony chips of her eyes. "The girl is a marvel."

Forach remembers the pitiful arrows and swords her people used in battle.

What could the Déisi have done with Jeanne's cannons?

She knows what she would have done—torn down the walls of Tara.

Mikha'el touches her shoulder. The fires raging on the battlefield are reflected in his pale eyes. "This is the first of many conflicts. But if we can drive the English out of France . . . That might be enough to awaken the people to our cause."

Oya snaps her fingers. Rain falls from the sky. It washes both the fields and the dead clean.

Forach enjoys Oya and Mikha'el's company. She may not have their elemental powers, but she's learning the value of strategy and tactics. This is her talent.

"Strategy without tactics is the slowest way to victory." Mikha'el likes to quote one of his incarnations. "Tactics without strategy is the noise before defeat." Forach helps Jeanne apply both.

After the first victory in Orléans, Jeanne sends riders to all the besieged cities of France. "Leave the continent," her messengers boldly tell the English generals. "The maid of Orléans will kill anyone who stays."

"Capitulate or be massacred!" This is the declaration Jeanne makes in each new city. The British soon learn that the French maid does not make empty threats. French forces slaughter 3,500 English troops in the first few months.

With Forach's help, Jeanne always knows where to dig the trenches and place the cannons. And that's how the battles are won.

Not that she's without heavenly assistance. Mikha'el's flaming sword helps them cut down walls. Oya's fire burns the besieged cities to ashes. Jeanne calls them her avenging angels.

Jargeau, Meung, Beaugency, Troyes, and Saint-Pierre-le Moûtier all fall. Under Jeanne's banner, French troops rout the English at Patay, Montépilloy, and Lagny.

No one laughs at the virgin with the white banner anymore. The sight of her standard strikes fear into the hearts of anyone who opposes her. Thirty cities surrender without a fight.

The seeds of decay lie in the fruits of pleasure, however.

Once Jeanne's precious Dauphin is crowned King of France, he loses his stomach for battle. He tells Jeanne and her troops to stand down.

Jeanne and her angels discuss the royal command. Jeanne rages. "It's too early! Our work's not yet done."

Mikha'el is conflicted. "There's more than one way to win a battle," he advises.

"Nonsense!" Storm clouds gather around Oya, reflecting her dark mood. "The Brotherhood must be tempting him. Why else would he quit now?"

"Fie on the Brotherhood and all their agents," Forach says. Our army is strong. I say no rest until the snakes of England are driven out!"

Mikha'el loses that vote.

If there's more than one way to win a battle, there must be a hundred ways to lose. They soon learn that disobeying the King's orders is one of the fastest. Supplies are cut off, gunpowder runs out, and troops are ordered home.

Yet Jeanne soldiers on, with a small band of fervent men. She knows—they all know—the King is sabotaging the war effort.

He's going to get Jeanne killed.

At Compiègne, the Brotherhood finally comes for her. Forced to retreat across the Oise River, Jeanne lingers to guard the evacuation. Her horse stumbles, throwing Jeanne into the river. Forach watches helplessly as vipers rise out of the Oise and grab hold of Jeanne's armor.

Jeanne's angels struggle to keep her head above the water. Without corporeal form, there's a limit to physical items they can affect. They save her from drowning, but they cannot keep her from being captured. British soldiers pull her out of the river and place her under guard.

Forach wants to raid the prison and free Jeanne. But the veil lifts. Forach sees Sekhmet's face shining through it.

My time is up. If I don't return now . . .

"Let go of this world," Sekhmet tells her, extending a hand. "This is not the end."

With some relief, and tremendous sorrow, Forach returns to the in-between.

~ 92 ~

JUANA

The first jacaranda blossoms signal the end of winter. Juana smiles at them through the kitchen window. "Spring is finally here." She lets the tip of her finger slide close to Paola's on the rim of the sink. "God is gracious indeed to bless us with such beauty." Her eyes are on the trees, but her heart is with the dark-eyed woman washing dishes beside her.

Madre Abadesa interrupts. "Sor Juana, if you please?"

Juana reluctantly answers. "Madre?"

Madre lowers her head and gestures toward the hallway. "This is a private matter. Follow me to my chambers."

Are we found out?

Icy fear scrambles across Juana's spine and shivers down into her stomach to hide. She and Paola exchange a panicked look.

What else could she want to discuss in private?

It's a short walk to Madre's chambers. Juana walks with caution past the heavy wooden door. She sits in a stiff, upright chair. A crucifix hangs on the wall behind Madre. Jésus Christos looks down from it, his face pained. Below him, Madre looks just as exasperated.

Juana wants to bolt before judgment can be levied. But she forces herself to be patient.

Whatever it is, I can manage it.

If she needs to, she will leave the convent so that Paola can remain.

I will take the blame for our indiscretions.

Fear—not content to hide—burrows its way out of her stomach and crawls over the rest of her body. Gooseflesh breaks out along Juana's arms. Sweat beads on her upper lip. She knows her imagination is making the situation worse, but she can't stop herself. Paola is too important to her.

Finally, Madre sighs, and extracts a thin pamphlet from a drawer. She looks at the cover, shakes her head, and pushes it across the desk to Juana. "I thought you should see this."

"What is it?" Juana's mind spins. *Did someone write something about me?* She reads the cover, translating it from Latin. "A letter worthy of Athena?"

She looks at Madre Abadesa, not comprehending.

Carlos calls me that . . . What is this?

"Did you write this?" Madre's expression is inscrutable. She taps the script under the title.

Juana shakes her head. "That is my name on the cover, but I've not published any of my letters."

A letter . . .

She takes the pamphlet. "I've only written and sent letters to friends. Privately."

Did Carlos publish the letter I wrote about Vieyra last fall?

Her hands shake as she opens the pamphlet and reads. She recognizes the words on the page. Blood freezes in her veins.

Why would Carlos do this to me?

This is obviously her critique of Father António Vieyra's sermon.

But why would he print my thoughts without my permission?

Madre clears her throat. "Do you know this Sor Filotéa de la Cruz?"

Juana stares at her blankly. "Like Filotéa from the Greek myths? The one with no tongue?"

"No, a sister, here in the city." Madre taps the pamphlet. "They printed Sor Filotéa's response to your letter at the end of yours."

Juana's brow furrows. As far as she's aware, she's one of the few women in the Church who reads. She knows she's the only nun in México-Tenochtitlán who commits her thoughts to paper. "There's another sister who writes?"

Madre looks exasperated. "I can't believe there would be more, but here she is. Read for yourself."

Juana does. Sor Filotéa uses very pretty words, which she uses to artfully obscure the poison of her pen.

This is not Carlos's work. This is someone who hates me. Someone clever.

Carlos could be cutting, but no one would call him sly. If he had malicious intent, it would be more obvious than this 'response.'

Manuel. Did Carlos secure my letter for him? Or was he unwillingly duped into handing it over?

Juana thinks of the two of them in the locutorio. She sees Carlos's head tilt, like a sunflower, to receive the nourishing rays of Manuel's attention.

Instead, Manuel filled my friend with the dark sludge of his venomous thoughts, polluting both their souls.

Madre looks at Juana expectantly.

Juana manages to sputter out, "The good sister speaks prettily, but not well of me." Hot shame burns her cheeks. She's positive Manuel is 'Sor Filotéa.' He's insulted not only her learning, but also questions educating women at all. He's making an example of her to punish all women.

I am the worst nun.

Tears come fast but offer no relief. "I suppose I should write a response. They make serious claims about my character and impugn our entire sex."

"I'd advise against that," Madre says.

Juana's neck burns. She knows better than to argue with Madre Abadesa, but she can't let the 'good sister's' insults go unanswered.

If it were only personal, Juana could let it lie. But Manuel is aiming for a bigger goal: to deprive all women of education. And if he cannot, then force them to be silent or risk ridicule and persecution by the ignorant.

Someone needs to defend our sex. Someone needs to point out the error of his logic. And demonstrate why it's better to educate and liberate women.

Madre gives Juana a handkerchief to dry her eyes. "I am glad to see you take no pride in this. The Bishop visited to advise me this morning. If you are ready to hear it, I have your prescription for atonement."

Juana tries to focus. "Prescription?"

Madre folds her hands. "The Bishop and I agree that you must abandon your intellectual pursuits, for the good of your soul. You need to set a better example for your sisters."

Abandon my studies? I cannot . . .

"The Bishop is packing away your books and scientific instruments as we speak. Their sale will benefit the convent. He's also appointed you a special confessor. You will meet with him daily, starting today, to confess all your sinful thoughts."

My books, my scientific instruments, even my thoughts . . . will they leave me nothing?

The walls of the little room close in on Juana. "My paper? My pen? Might I keep those?"

Madre laughs. "Of course not. They're what got you into trouble in the first place. You are here to serve God. You have no right to speak of matters that are not pertinent to your faith. That would be vanity."

"It is not vanity to seek the truth," Juana whispers. Her face and hands itch from the salty tears. "God takes pleasure in our pursuit of knowledge. I do not know who published my private thoughts. And those were *my private thoughts*, Madre. I do not know who did this. But they did so to ruin me. Please don't let them. If I cannot learn, I will die."

"Sor Juana." The Madre smiles sadly. "Your private thoughts belong to the Church. Your body belongs to God. In resisting that, you have ruined yourself. But do not weep. We are all sinners. You can redeem yourself with penance and prayer. And isn't it better to die, if you must, without the sin of pride still burning in your heart?"

~ 93 ~

HONEY

It is strange to have a man in her house who is not her husband, but Honey is stuck with jolly James Madison. At least until Regina finishes her 'reconnaissance mission.'

Regina had told James to keep an eye on Honey before she left. He's taking that job seriously. He's underfoot. It's making Honey crazy.

Honey starts the coffee maker and reaches for the mugs. "Would you like something to drink?"

"No, thank you." His heavy work boots thump in the direction of her bookshelves. Honey imagines clumps of dried mud trail him. He touches her things, then asks, "What's this?"

She sighs. "Can you describe it or bring it here? I can't see what you mean."

"Oh, of course." His boots clomp toward her. "I found this behind the bookcase."

She holds out her hands and he places the questionable item in it. She feels along its length and edges. Dirt is flaking off it, too. "That's my walking stick."

"Really?" He takes it back. "Do you mind?"

Honey resists the urge to moan. Her not being able to see hasn't sunk in yet. "Do I mind what?"

"If I clean it off?"

"Sure, knock yourself out. It's just an old stick I found." She tries to ignore the weirdness of his request.

Who washes a tree branch?

She takes a deep breath.

He's Regina's friend. If she trusts him, I should try and do the same. Even if he is annoying.

From the sink he calls out, "Do you have some old rags? Something you don't mind getting muddy?"

God, give me strength.

This time Honey lets herself sigh because if she doesn't, she might scream. She retrieves a couple of rags from her laundry room and throws them in his direction. "How long do you think Regina will be gone?"

The coffee smells ready. She makes her way toward the pot.

"No telling," James replies, voice bouncing as he scrubs. "Once that woman gets something in her head, she's like a terrier."

"Do you think she'll find out where they went?" Honey pours coffee into the two mugs and places one by his elbow. She knows he said no, but if it's there, she's sure he'll pick it up.

He does. "If I know Regina, she'll find out where your husband's hiding, the last thing he ate, and what kind of underwear he has on." He chuckles at his own joke.

She does not laugh. She sips her coffee and swallows bitter thoughts she does not want to say aloud.

James works in silence for a long time before speaking again. "This is interesting."

Honey moves toward him. "What?"

"This isn't wood." He taps her stick against the sink. It rings.

"I thought it was a branch."

He chuckles. "Looked that way with all the mud. I managed to scour away a little bit. Here, feel this." He takes her hand and places it near an area he's cleaned.

She feels where the dirt thins and runs her fingers along the narrow channel James has created. It's too smooth to be wood. She washes the residue off and touches it again. She feels a shock. The stick vibrates.

Is it . . . humming?

The water on her hands is cold, but the rod beneath her fingers is warm, like skin. It feels smooth, like glass.

And it's moving, like it's alive

"Can you tell me what it looks like?" she asks.

"You want my honest opinion?"

"No, lie to me," she says with exasperation. "Of course, I want your honest opinion."

James chuckles. "I think it looks like some kind of jeweled rod."

~ 94 ~

SEKHMET

The Source still hums through her. Her ability to channel it is undiminished. But Sekhmet's strength is fading.

What a cruel joke to feel weak now. When it's our turn of the wheel.

She's felt it slipping away for some time. She has not told the others because she does not want to alarm them.

They need me to lead. Who else will defend them?

When she lingered to help Akhenaten and her daughters, her energy faded. The longer she stayed with Yeshua, the more her spirits flagged. But, both times, the in-between reinvigorated her. Her strength returned unabated.

Now it's the in-between that's draining it from her.

What is happening to me?

Her strength saves and provides. It protects and guides her, and the ones she loves. Imprisonment could not weaken it; starvation could not deprive her of it. Not even torture could drive it from her body.

But now . . .

Being powerless scares her more than the prospect of losing to the Brotherhood.

Is it because this is my champion's turn of the wheel? Is it because, if this woman loses, we will cease to be? Did Mikha'el weaken like this? Did Aron?

Forach and Juana laugh, heads bent together over some mischief.

Or is it because I had the hubris to harvest other parts of my self? Should I have left things alone? Done this on my own?

There is no way to know.

For what did I bring them here?

Filoméla watches and waits all day, while Forach and Juana do nothing but talk. About what, she has no idea.

Have I prepared them properly?

The thought is ridiculous.

For what is there to prepare? It's not like we have a manual.

Or a plan.

Not that she hasn't been thinking constantly about the battle ahead. She's been unable to formulate a plan because she's not sure what she can do that others haven't.

Aron and Moses established a new nation. Jeanne overthrew an empire. Yeshua's teachings changed the world.

All brilliant plans. Made worse after defeat.

For every liberated nation, the Brotherhood enslaved five. For every minority population empowered, the Brotherhood disenfranchised ten. Nothing defeats the Brotherhood—not native uprisings, intellectual renaissances, social movements, or technological advances. No matter how many people the Lyrans reach, it is never enough to open the channel.

People have grown so fragmented. How will we ever communicate our message in a way that can reach them all?

Sekhmet clenches her fists. She wants to pound the pristine whiteness of the in-between. She yearns to beat the walls until she's hurt them, or herself, in some unfixable way.

Although I'm already broken.

She places a hand on the wall.

How can I win? What am I to do?

Her heart cries out to the Source.

Give me a sign!

A voice rings out. It is rough and ragged.

Sekhmet turns to see who has invaded their space and is confounded by a miracle.

It is Filoméla. Speaking.

The young woman spreads her arms and tells them, "Our champion . . . she is free."

"What do you mean, free?" Sekhmet runs to her.

Forach gasps, "So Sekhmet was right. You can speak? You naughty girl." She shakes her soul sister by the shoulders.

"Shh, Forach," Juana says, pulling her off Filoméla. "Tell us more."

Filoméla's hands rise to her throat in shock.

Did she not realize she spoke to us?

Sekhmet remembers their first meeting, how surprised Filoméla was to discover her tongue back in place.

"Keep talking," Sekhmet coaxes. "Please. What did you see?"

The women gather around her. Filoméla's words croak out as if she's crossed a desert without water. "The man. She's driven the man out of her home."

Forach barks a laugh. "About time. I didn't like how he babied her."

Juana holds up a slender hand and Forach bites her tongue.

Filoméla clears her throat. "But there's more . . . I saw through her eyes."

The other women wait.

Forach is the first to lose patience. "Go on!"

Filoméla repeats, "I saw through her eyes. I shouldn't be able to do that if she's blind."

"No, you shouldn't." Sekhmet paces, trying to puzzle it out. "Did she see?"

"A flash, I think." Filoméla bites her lip. "I rushed back to tell you."

"What does that mean?" Forach asks.

Juana takes Filoméla's hand. "It means whatever hold the man had over her is lifting."

Forach's brow crinkles in confusion. "Are you saying her husband's some kind of wizard?"

"No," Sekhmet says. "Not a wizard. An agent of the Brotherhood. If Honey is free of him, then our work can begin."

~ 95 ~

FILOMÉLA

Juana speaks first. "What work?"

"Opening the portals." Sekhmet's hands probe the wall.

Thoughts cramp and scrape Filoméla's mouth, begging to be spoken. "What are you looking for?" She's held her tongue so tightly, for so long, that talking makes her feel loose and dangerous. "What portals?" The words are pouring out. "Where are they?" Filoméla fastens her hands to her mouth to keep the words in and waits for someone else to speak.

Forach asks, "What's the plan?"

Sekhmet lowers her hands. "I'm not sure."

Juana and Forach exchange a glance. Juana's sharp eyes glitter like a bird's. "What do you mean, you don't have a plan?"

"There's no guidebook." Sekhmet faces the others. "I was hoping that in gathering you to me, that would give me a better idea. But you're no closer to finding the Answer than I am."

Juana crosses her arms. "What do you mean: the Answer?"

Sekhmet sits. "The *Book of Lyran* says that each Aspect of the One incarnates among the Many Worlds for a reason. And that is to discover their unique Answer. Until we learn our Answer, we can't return to the Source. Although if we can't open the portals, it won't matter anyway, because we'll cease to be."

Filoméla kneels by Sekhmet, gravel in her throat. "We can help." She doesn't like seeing their leader like this.

Forach nods. "We can collaborate on a strategy."

Juana asks, "Where is this book you mentioned?"

Sekhmet looks confused.

Juana sighs. "You said we had no guidebook. Then you mentioned a *Book of Lyran*? Give it to me. I can find the Answer in there. Didn't you harvest me because I'm the smart one?"

Sekhmet shakes her head. "I've looked. I don't think you'll find anything I haven't."

Juana's face hardens. "Before you tell me what I can't do, let me do what I *can*. Let me look." She snaps her fingers and holds out a hand.

Sekhmet shrugs, reaches under the communal table, and extracts a scroll. She tosses it to Juana, who disappears into an alcove.

Forach shakes her head. "Are we going to wait for her? Or start to plan? I can't believe you waited this long. I just assumed . . ."

"Shh!" Filoméla feels something, but it is so small . . . *Was I imagining it?* She closes her eyes to concentrate.

"What?" Forach sounds impatient.

Sekhmet places a hand over hers. "I feel it too." They start for the wall.

"Feel what?" Forach follows them in irritation. "Where are you going?

Filoméla presses Forach's hand to the wall. The Source beats through it like something alive. "Feel that?"

Forach's eyes widen. "What is it?"

The wall shivers once, twice, three times.

Then it is gone.

Forach, Sekhmet, and Filoméla step through the veil into the void.

They find themselves in a space filled with wood and short walls. They hear running water.

Filoméla recognizes Honey but not the man with her. He is tall and broad. His red hair dances about his head like flames. He scrubs at something in his hands. Something that Honey touches. It vibrates violently.

Did she call us here?

Honey's eyes lift and meet Filoméla's.

Filoméla speaks. The words come easier now, although they still tweak her tongue. "Honey, can you see me?"

Honey jerks away from them, slamming into the counter behind her.

No, not yet.

"It's Filoméla, Sekhmet, and Forach." Filoméla steps closer. "You called us. Can you hear me?"

"Yes," Honey looks panicked.

Filoméla wants to comfort her, but the man is between them, staff raised high. "Who are you?" he says. "Where'd you come from?"

Filoméla's eyes widen. "You can see us?"

"Of course, he can," Sekhmet says, laying a hand on Filoméla's shoulder. "He's one of us."

~ 96 ~

FORACH

The first thought Forach has is: *he has hair like a Déisi.*

The second is: *he looks familiar.*

But it's not until Sekhmet confirms he's Lyran that she understands why. Beneath that flaming plume of hair his blue eyes gaze out at her, pale as ice, flecked with amber flames.

Everything stops as Forach realizes she's looking into the eyes of her brother Cian.

Why did I not see it?

Her heart is in her mouth.

They are Mikha'el's eyes, too.

"All the lines must be entwined with our own." Forach tells Sekhmet. "The wheel isn't the only thing turning. These people we know in each life . . . we wheel around each other, too. Same lines, same allies, time after time, facing the darkness together. Like a soul family."

The man raises the rod to strike. "I'm warning you . . ."

Honey touches his shoulder. "It's all right. I know them."

Forach nods. "You've nothing to fear from us, Mikha'el. We're old friends."

His brow creases in confusion but he lowers the staff. "I don't know you."

Forach nods. "Not in this life, perhaps, but—"

Sekhmet cuts her off. “How is this possible? The Tzaddik Nistar disappear from Earth when their champion loses.”

“Maybe they don’t disappear completely,” Forach says. “They only forget who they are? He’s clearly an incarnation of Mikha’el’s line.”

“What are you talking about?”

“It will be easier to show than tell you.” Sekhmet holds out her furred hand. “May I see that?”

The man eyes her claws, lowering the rod into it slowly. He releases it quickly and draws back. He asks Honey a question. Forach cannot hear, but she sees the answer is no.

Sekhmet lifts the rod to her face. She rotates it slowly. When she reaches the place without dirt, she blows on it.

The staff trembles.

Sekhmet taps it once against the countertop, and the dirt leaps off, revealing a shaft of deep ocean blue.

Forach gasps.

This is no muddy stick. Is it . . . sapphire?

Forach remembers where she’s seen this rod before. She calls to Mikha’el, “Do you recognize this? It is the base of your champion Jeanne’s standard!”

The angel still does not know himself. He shakes his head.

Sekhmet turns to her. “You know the rod of Aron?”

“Yes, though not by that name.” Forach doesn’t need a second look. There’s no mistaking it. “Jeanne had a sword, but she didn’t like to use it in battel. She preferred waving her white standard attached to this blue rod. Where did it come from?

Honey clears her throat. “I tripped over it, walking around the lake.”

Forach laughs. “Of course, you did.”

“Jeanne wasn’t the only champion who wielded it,” Sekhmet tells them. “In Kemet, Aron used it to liberate my people. Yeshua used this as his walking stick.”

"Maybe every champion uses it?" Forach looks back at Honey. She still has a tough time seeing a champion in this soft woman.

Sekhmet weighs the rod between her hands. "Or it comes to them when it's time?" She addresses Mikha'el, "Did you feel anything touching this?"

"I'm sorry," he says. "But before I can answer that, I must ask: what are you? Honey says that's not a mask. So, what is it?"

"My true face," Sekhmet says. "Many who walk upon the Earth resemble what you call animals more than human beings."

"Act like them, too," Forach quips, drawing an angry glance from Sekhmet. She buttons her lip. "Sorry. Couldn't resist."

Sekhmet turns back to Mikha'el. "We are all Aspects of the One. We needed no body until we chose to settle among the Many Worlds and incarnate. Then, based on our new homes, we chose diverse ways to manifest our spirit in the flesh. The Lion-Hearted Lyrans appear as I do. We are the primary settlers of Earth. The Lyrans of Sirius have wings, as you do, and the gift of flight. Earth's eagles resemble them. The Lyrans who settled among the Pleiades resemble oxen and water buffalo. Over time, as our races mixed with the local creatures, our offspring began to look more like them. Our bodies change with every incarnation. But no matter how many soul journeys we take, our eyes remain the same."

Sekhmet holds the sapphire rod in front of her. "I can feel the Source in this. I wonder: can we tap into a larger channel here?"

"The strength of the Source increases when we work together, right?" Before Sekhmet can answer, Forach grips the staff.

Oh, my.

It is more than a current, it is an ocean hungry to sweep her away. "Filoméla. Grab this."

Filoméla reaches around Sekhmet to lay her hand on the rod. The power intensifies.

Oh.

The Source flowing through them is stronger than Forach's ever felt. It rouses her, recharges her. She feels connected to everything that is. She gasps.

Maybe it can wake Mikha'el up?

Forach beckons to him and Honey. "Now, you two. Grab hold of the rod."

The man shakes his head. "Nuh-uh."

Honey clucks. "Will you at least walk me to it? I can't see what she's talking about."

He obeys, guiding Honey to the staff.

Once in range, Forach guides Honey's hand. Then she grabs Mikha'el's and forces it down.

Twin surges of Source run through Forach.

Ecstasy.

She wants to sing.

Is it working? Is Mikha'el awake?

She peers into his eyes but cannot tell.

Filoméla cries out and directs Forach's attention to Honey.

Forach draws in a sharp breath.

The milky veils over Honey's eyes are flapping like curtains in the wind.

~ 97 ~

JUANA

Juana examines the scroll's cover. Etchings decorate its surface.

So, this is the Book of Lyran.

A small light races along the grooves of the design, following the same path repeatedly. Juana places her finger in its way. It passes through her as if she is nothing. But when it does, she feels a jolt.

It is shocking and delightful. She smiles.

The best science is like magic.

She tests different areas of the design with comparable results.

If this is only the wrapper, what treasures will I find within?

She separates the cover from the scroll and places it to the side. She runs her fingers along the surface of the book.

The fabric of the scroll looks like lambskin. Unlike lambskin t, however, it vibrates and exudes heat.

The Source courses through this entire work. It hums through me.

Juana has always found comfort and nourishment from ideas found in books. This is the first time a book has let her return the favor. It's intoxicating.

She examines the handles, around which the text is bound. They look like carved ivory. But she doubts any cruel acts created this work of art.

It is breathtaking. Beautiful. And full of love.

I can feel it.

Unspooling the book thrills her. The pages, like the cover, feature a light that pulses through the words, illuminating them.

It's been so long since Juana has opened a new text. She's overwhelmed by the promise of learning something new. The joy of the moment evokes a bitter memory. It cuts through her like a toothache.

Juana's eyes burn. She has spent centuries not remembering. But this book has triggered the memory of her last shameful days on Earth.

Manuel, not I, was the clever one. He separated me from what I loved most of all—my books, instruments, and freedom. Not even my thoughts escaped policing. Who could live like that?

Isolated from the magical world of learning, she wasted away.

I lost my appetite for everything.

Even Paola, she thinks with a twinge of guilt.

It wasn't long before she became sick. Her poor body, pushed to the limit, did not have the strength to recover from infection.

How I resented Carlos. But I was the fool who put my thoughts on paper. It wasn't his fault. I was too proud. He didn't make me publish my reply. Madre was right. I ruined myself.

The day he stripped her of her possessions, Manuel's violet eyes shone with malevolence. "Turn your mind to God," he said. "It's wicked and dangerous for a woman to turn her mind to anything else."

Juana no longer burns with shame.

He was an instrument of the Brotherhood. But I no longer face the darkness alone. We will triumph this time.

"I am turning my mind to God, the holy One," she tells his ghost. "I will show you how wicked and dangerous a woman can be, you evil man."

Her hand is wet, and she realizes she's been crying. Juana rubs the tears away and takes a deep breath.

Nothing is a failure if you learn from it. And I should thank him for what he taught me about myself. Now, it is time to get to work.

Juana kisses the scroll's wrapper to banish the bitterness of the past.

She presses the scroll to her forehead to burn Manuel's memory from her mind.

Thank you God, for giving me these gifts and the opportunity to put them to beneficial use.

The language of *Book of Lyran* is unfamiliar. But as her eyes move over the shining, unfamiliar shapes, she realizes it is one known to her heart. The words reverberate around her skull, like music. She begins to hum them. In the rhythm and shapes of the song, she discovers deep meaning.

The *Book of Lyran* is the shortest text she's ever read. She sings it over and over until it makes sense. She puzzles over its sections one at a time.

In the beginning, there was only the One.

Sekhmet told them about the One. Juana has felt the Source and knows how it connects all things. But she thought Sekhmet, Oya and Mikha'el were children of the One. She realizes now that is not so.

They are parts of the divine One. Separate elements, like water, air, earth, and fire.

Juana thinks about the line of Sekhmet and its star seed.

Sekhmet is an Aspect. Mikha'el and Oya each are Aspects. And all Aspects may be of the light or darkness, or somewhere in-between.

She remembers the glass prism she kept in the locutorio. When she held it to the light, it split the white beam into many colors.

It follows then, once united, Aspects will cease to be diverse. Whether light or dark, they will become indistinguishable from the One.

She continues to the second part of the book:

> The Aspects asked the Source, *How long will it take us to discover this Answer?*
>
> The Source replied, *I have no way of knowing. That will depend on your soul's journey.*
>
> The Aspects conferred among themselves and were troubled. They applied another question to the Source, *How will we reunite as the One if we return at various times?*
>
> The Source considered this and finally replied, *I will set a great wheel to spin and track our time of searching. Take as many lives as you need to find your Answer, but you will all return at the same time.*

Juana chews her lip and muses over what she has read.

What is the Answer our line journeyed here to discover? Sekhmet, Filoméla, Forach, Honey, and myself . . . what do we have in common?

If all the Aspects go back at the same time, what about the Tzaddikim Nistarim who lost their battles? Will they return somehow?

She reads on:

> In time, each Aspect acquired a physicality that reflected their chosen world and family. And they learned much: from the world around them, from caring for others, and being loved and challenged by them.

Juana thinks the time of the Great Peace sounds idyllic. But, of course, it could not last.

Nothing good ever does.

> One day, Aspects of the Brotherhood questioned, *What good is peace? Why do we only live in this small corner of the Many Worlds? Why do we avoid those who irritate us? Why not punish them instead? After all, do we not have sufficient strength to conquer and triumph?*
>
> And so, the Brotherhood of the Snake began The Great War.

Juana thinks of how much pleasure Manuel took in destroying everything she'd built. Forach had her own Manuel in Ethnui. Filoméla, Sekhmet, and even this Honey had their own tormentors. *Snakes are everywhere.*

> The Great War did not end with the destruction of Vega. The Brotherhood continued to hunt the Aspects of the Lyrans, wherever they appeared among the Many Worlds. For this reason, the Lyrans began to marry their creations, to obscure the lines of their descendants from the hunt.

Juana despairs at how familiar the Great War sounds.

Why do small-minded people always persecute those who only want to love, live, know, and unite? And why does their might always trump our rights?

Juana's eye catches on a phrase near the end and her breathing slows.

> If the Lyran champion wins, the channels will reopen, the Aspects will return to the One, and peace

> will be restored. If victory goes to the Brotherhood; however, then the war will continue, discord and division will spread, and the Lyran champion's Aspect will go dark, forgetting itself until the last turn of the wheel.

In the last part of the book, she notes:

> With one turn of the wheel, a Lyran champion might yet defeat the Brotherhood.

Juana turns that phrase over and over.

Does that mean the Lyrans need only win once? Maybe all our past defeats, private and public, were by design.

She finishes the book:

> At this time, love will transform hatred, light will consume darkness, and all those who seek the truth shall be reborn.
>
> In this era of New Peace, all the Aspects will return to the Source, and from the many, they will reunite and become One.

She leans back and sighs. "Love and light and rebirth."

Juana lets her head fall into her hands.

If we only need to win once, then we don't need to lose faith because of past events. But how do we win? What can we do differently this time?

Then, she has it.

"Of course."

She grabs the scroll and runs into the main chamber of the in-between. Only there's a vast, gaping hole in the white walls. Through it, she can see her soul sisters.

She leaps into the void and emerges in this new dimension, waving the scroll over her head. "I've found it. I've found the Answer."

~ 98 ~

HONEY

When she was twelve, Honey lost a piece of bread in the toaster. Unwilling to wake her mom, she fished for it with a fork.

The shock she feels now, touching this rod, is nearly as painful. It holds her in its thrall, and she is unable to let go.

She feels the veil of blindness turning to tatters. She's caught half-in, half-out, and can't break free of the current.

Is this the Source Sekhmet told me about?

She tries to pull away. Something jerks her back.

Stop fighting, the Source tells her. *Lean in.*

Honey tries to pull away again. She ricochets back twice as hard and thinks wildly, *Let me go!*

The Source replies, *Not until you give in. Surrender.*

Honey's heart flutters in terror.

I can't.

She's afraid giving in will kill her.

I'll blow apart. Or something horrible will happen.

She can't surrender to this power.

Why not? The voice is sure of itself in a way Honey has forgotten how to be. *There's nowhere else you need to be. There's nothing else you can do. I will not release you. What other choice do you have other than give in?*

Honey concedes that the Source has a point. Straining against causes every fiber of her being to ache. She's not making any headway. In fact, pulling away is painful.

Honey knows the definition of insanity. She can't keep doing what she's doing, so she chooses something different. She leans into the Source.

As she does, the current sweeps her up and knocks her over its edge.

Her breath catches.

She waits for the worst.

But the light swallowing her is not interested in punishments or petty things.

It does not beat or tear her apart.

It does not want to break her down.

It exists to build her up.

The Source consumes her fear and transforms it.

It fills her limbs with light until her heart wants to burst.

Honey opens her eyes, full of song. She is close to being whole. She feels the other women so close now, they almost breathe as one.

Oh, how I love them.

Oh, how I love!

Even James Madison, who she wanted to throw in the trash earlier. Even he, with his heavy boots tracking mud all over her floor, is deserving of her love and admiration.

A voice cries out, "I've found it. I've found the Answer!"

Juana?

Honey feels the women's attention shift in a tidal pool toward the speaker.

They do not hear what she does.

A key is turning in the lock.

A barrier is falling away.

A door is opening.

~ 99 ~

SEKHMET

Sekhmet is rooted in the present, focused on their future when her past crashes through the door.

She curses. The first thing she should have done was secure the perimeter. She wants to blame the presence of Mikha'el and the rod for distracting her.

But the truth is, you're slipping. You've waited millennia for your chance to win. And now, you're going to blow it. Some leader.

Rage at her own shortcomings blinds her. She reaches for the rod, wanting to crush her self-doubt by subduing their opponent. But Honey will not let go.

I can't even pull it from her grasp.

That makes her angrier.

Fine. I'll do this alone. Without any help.

Sekhmet releases the staff. She vaults over the counter and places herself between the intruder and the others.

Claws extended, ready to strike, Sekhmet meets the violet eyes of the enemy.

She hesitates.

Violet eyes?

Sekhmet feels sick. She recognizes these eyes.

No.

Eyes that belonged to someone she loved.

It can't be.

Eyes she mourned and missed.

What trick is this?

She cannot hurt this man. She still loves him.

But maybe he's not what he seems. "Who are you?"

The man smiles. "You know me Sekhmet. Or should I call you by our pet name, Nefertiti? I've missed you."

Akhenaten? How can this be?

In his left hand, he holds a dark woman down. She struggles to free herself. Her angry black eyes reflect a stormy sky, disturbed by blue bolts of lightning. He throws her from him. She skids across the floor, smacking her head against the base of the kitchen island's low wall.

Honey cries out, "Regina!"

Filoméla yells, "Prōknē!"

But Sekhmet does not turn her eyes from the man who stands in front of her. She is afraid to look away.

This must be a trick. "Reveal yourself."

"Haven't I already, my love?" He places a hand on his chest and bows to her in a mocking way. He peers through inky black strands of hair, eyes sparkling like amethysts. "I have to say, you haven't aged well."

Sekhmet stiffens. She does not want to admit that he could be who he's implying he is. She holds firm. "I don't know what to call you, since you won't show your true face."

"Come now," he says. "You have seen all my faces. And I have seen all of yours. Every lifetime we dance this dance. Love me or hate me, I always win. What makes you think this turn of the wheel will be any different?"

"Akhenaten fought alongside me," Sekhmet says. "The Brotherhood caused our people to suffer. They destroyed our energy dragons. They killed our daughters. If you, my love, were part of the Brotherhood, did you want all those things to happen? That doesn't make any sense."

He laughs. "Oh, Sekhmet, what doesn't make sense is how you arrived at my palace from your prison cell. You poor child of light. How innocent you are. You see the good in everyone, don't you? They wouldn't have let you walk away. I asked for you. They gave you to me to play with. You were my special project. Torture couldn't break you. I wanted to try a unique way. A gentler, kinder way."

If he were of the Brotherhood, he would rejoice at anything that breaks my heart.

The thought pains her.

Did I unwittingly help the Brotherhood? No. Akhenaten loved me. I loved him. What he says cannot be true.

The man frowns at her stubborn silence. He calls over her shoulder to the others. "Forach, Juana, Filoméla, and sweet Honey: you know me, do you not?"

Yes, yes they do. She sees it in their faces.

The women of Sekhmet's line name the many forms his darkness has appeared in their lifetimes: *Tereus, Ethnui, Manuel, and Chad.*

But my Akhenaten?

Sekhmet struggles to make sense of who this man is.

"I know you," she admits. "But my story is not like the others. We were allies. You didn't torment me."

"I didn't torment you?" He laughs. "I took to bed Sekhmet, the Goddess of War, and turned you into Bastet, the Goddess of Domesticity. I tamed you, cut your claws, turned your son against you, had you killed, stole your daughters . . . and still you trailed after me like a dog."

He laughs. "Was that loyalty, Sekhmet? Stupidity? Or pride?" He shakes his head. "You never learn. None of you ever learn. It is so easy to defeat you. You think you are all good and we are all bad. The truth lies in-between. Light comes from darkness. Not the other way around. We were here first, and we'll always be stronger. Or are you too blinded by your own pride to see that you're as bad as I am?"

Sekhmet does not know how to respond. Claws retracted; she trembles on the edge of a horrible self-awareness.

The last shred of strength she has dissolves in despair.

She wants to lay down and die.

~ 100 ~

FILOMÉLA

The man is huge and full of hate, but Filoméla cares not. For he holds in his hand the most precious treasure in the world. When he flings her loose, she belongs to Filoméla once more.

"Prōknē!"

Filoméla falls to her knees and lifts her sister's head. The face is unfamiliar, but the eyes . . . she recognizes the icy blue fire that burns behind those dark spheres, a twin flame to her own.

Filoméla grips her sister's shoulders, hoping that her touch will awaken something.

Her sister blinks once, twice, three times.

"Do you know me?"

For a terrible moment, Filoméla fears the answer will be no, that the Brotherhood has managed to sever their connection for good.

But there is something electric that passes between them, forcing doors open.

Then the dark woman raises her hand to Filoméla's throat. Wet eyes shining, her fingers trace the scars meant to silence Filoméla forever.

Prōknē is awake.

She remembers.

"You're speaking, sister. How can that be?"

All the tears Filoméla refused to shed over the millennia crest the dam of her heart and drench them both.

~ 101 ~

FORACH

The big man's boasts do not shake Forach.

Every dog is bold in his own doorway. He barks loud. But if he were going to strike, he would have by now.

Besides, Sekhmet has leaped into the fray. She's the strongest of them all and will buy them time.

Forach reaches again for the staff. The comforting hum of the Source beneath her fingers helps her think.

Ethnui couldn't win by force, only trickery. And trickery takes time.

Forach watches Filoméla tend to the dark woman. Under Filoméla's touch, the woman awakens. She becomes more than Honey's friend. She's a lost sister. Forach's heart lifts.

If a sister can be reclaimed, can a brother?

The touch of the staff alone failed to wake Mikha'el, but maybe something in her touch will help, if she wills it . . .

Forach turns to Mikha'el and grabs his head between both hands. She feels his connection to the Source. It is as powerful as her own, but a shade different, like looking at the sun through a colored pane of glass.

"Come back to me," she cries.

His brow creases, but he does not pull away.

She moves her hands to his shoulders and feels the current move between them. "Do you remember who you are?"

"James," he says, uncertainly.

She forces his pale blue and amber eyes to meet her green and gold ones. "Are you now? What do you see, James?"

He blinks. Something ripples over the surface of his eyes.

Whatever enchantment he's under is weakening.

The words stutter out of him, "Do I know you from Orléans?"

She wants to kiss him, so she does. "Yes. I fought by your side." She touches her chest. "I am Forach, of Sekhmet's line. What else do you remember?"

"I am Mikha'el?" Amazement and relief flicker across his face. "I remember who I am. I am Mikha'el, first of his line."

He touches Forach's face. "And your brother Cian." He looks past her towards Filoméla. "I was the messenger boy who took the tapestry to your sister."

"Who were you to me?" Juana asks.

Tears well up in his eyes. "You were my Athena."

Forach shifts in her boots with impatience. "We don't have time for this." She wraps an arm around Mikha'el and jerks her head toward the big man. "Do you recognize that Snake?"

Mikha'el nods. "We've met in many lives."

"Do you think we can beat him?"

Mikha'el's eyes settle on the dark woman. "You, me, and Oya tried once already. We failed."

"Oya?" Forach looks at the woman in Filoméla's arms. For the first time she notices her eyes: razor-slashes of blue against the blackest sky.

There's no one else that could be. How did I not notice before?

Her heart swells with hope.

Oya stands. "Your line knew me as Prōknē, Dread Spear, Meritaten, and Paola. I am here to help however you need me. I know who I am now." She casts a guilty look at Juana. "I wish I'd been enough to keep your heart from breaking."

Juana's mouth tightens. "We cannot dwell on that. Sekhmet needs our help."

Forach gasps. Sekhmet lies at the big man's feet. "What's wrong with her? Why is Sekhmet down?" She calls for her to rise, but Sekhmet remains at the feet of the awful snake.

Behind her, she hears Honey say, "No."

Honey stands, staff in hand, bathed in its indigo glow.

"No," Honey repeats. She opens her eyes.

Forach gasps.

The Source has transformed her.

The veil has parted from her eyes and left its mark. A white X blazes across each of Honey's eyes.

Now this is our champion.

Honey fixes her spooky orbs on the big man.

"No," she says for a third time, pounding the sapphire staff against the ground. "This time, Snake, *you will lose.*"

~ 102 ~

JUANA

Juana recognizes the crosses over Honey's eyes. It is a powerful sign. As is the return of her sight.

This is our champion and I have the Answer.

"It is not enough to touch the Source," Juana says, "or try to awaken the masses. We must become One. That will open the channel."

Juana doesn't realize she's spoken out loud until she feels the others' eyes on her.

She continues, "The Brotherhood divides. We unite. We need to do that."

Forach looks at her incredulously. "What do you think we have been doing?"

Mikha'el sighs heavily. "I united a people and could not win."

Oya adds, "Our champions have broken the backs of empires and still lost."

"We do not need to lead an army," Filoméla says. "We only need one key . . . "

Juana's eyes sparkle.

Thank God someone else understands.

Juana smiles. "Yes! We must become One. All of us."

Mikha'el and Oya exchange a glance. "We're not . . . "

Juana waves the *Book of Lyran* at them. “We are all Aspects of the One. All of us. Like pieces of a shattered vase. Our line of Sekhmet makes us one piece. Mikha’el is another, and Oya yet another. But when we unite with the Source . . . ”

Honey finishes her thought. “We become One.”

“But we cannot be One without the other Aspects,” Oya says. “And so many have been lost to time.”

“You weren’t,” Forach points out. “Maybe they’re still with us, in the Source.”

“You all have to return at the same time,” Juana says. “The *Book of Lyran* says so. The others must still be here, within reach.”

Filoméla smiles. “If we tap into the Source and find them, find our connection to them . . . could we awaken the others?”

Oya frowns. “You make it sound easy, but nothing good ever is.”

Forach says, “We need Sekhmet. We can’t do this without her, can we?”

Juana hopes her voice is enough to break the spell. “Sekhmet!”

Sekhmet turns, red-rimmed eyes brimming with sorrow.

“Sekhmet,” Juana calls again. “Come back.”

Sekhmet shakes her head. “I . . . can’t.”

“Oh, isn’t that sad?” The Snake smiles, revealing a mouth of pointed teeth. “I guess you’ll have to carry on alone.”

~ 103 ~

HONEY

The enemy at their gates has entered the house. Honey knows she should be afraid, but she cannot feel anything that is not of the light of the One.

The Source prickles through the staff into Honey's hands. It surges up her arms, blasting a solid column of light from the base of her neck through the crown of her head.

Honey feels the light course through her body, burning away anything that she no longer needs. The pain is intense, like flaming needles, but she welcomes the cleansing.

Free me of this contamination. Burn away the darkness so I can see.

Someone tugs at the staff, but Honey will not relinquish it.

Not yet.

Fifteen years of suffering in silence warped her soul. She spent so much time hiding her true self so she could be loved and accepted by someone who did not have her best interests at heart. The Source has much poison to burn out. The lies she swallowed need to be purged. She must be a clean vessel before the magnificent work begins.

Honey closes her eyes tight and leans further into the Source. It's like sticking her head into a furnace. She feels the veil over her eyes burst into flame. She inhales the pain and, to keep from screaming, exhales it into the staff.

Then, Chad's voice hits her square in the chest. "You never learn. None of you ever learn. It is so easy to beat you."

Honey feels a great surge. Something rises from deep within herself.

Rage?

No, it's too calm.

Sorrow?

No, there's too much love in it.

Love for him?

No, not for him, never for him. For my sisters, only.

Wait, that is not the way. It is Filoméla's voice she hears, but Honey recognizes that it also lives inside of her. *If we act monstrous, we become monsters.*

The others live within her, too.

If we let ourselves hate, then we will never win, Forach tells her.

The light and the darkness, whispers Juana, *are all part of the One.*

Sekhmet's voice adds, *Marry your darkness to the light. Accept and unify. Love and transform.*

Honey has found her voice, and it belongs to everything and everyone.

The Source asks, *Will the Brotherhood beat us this time?*

Honey simply says, "No."

Because we know the Answer. The Answer our Aspect seeks: the way to heal the world.

The others focus their attention on her. She welcomes their strengths. The sisters of her Soul Council are all so unique, beautiful, and strong. She holds the staff over her head, summoning them.

"No." She denies the Snake a second time. She feels the Source take one last cleansing sweep. When she opens her eyes, the others gasp.

At last. I can see.

Chad the man falls away. Traces of his real face lurk under the skin cloak he wears, scaly and green.

I see him for who he is.

And I can still love him.

Not despite his darkness, but because of it.

I can love all.

"No," Honey says for a third time, pounding the sapphire staff against the ground. "This time, *you will lose.*"

Sekhmet is a rag doll at his feet.

Juana cries, "Sekhmet! Sekhmet, come back."

Sekhmet looks at them from a bottomless pit of sorrow. Barely any sparks of light gleam behind her eyes.

Sekhmet shakes her head, "I . . . can't."

"Oh, isn't that sad?" Chad smiles, revealing a mouth of pointed teeth. "I guess you'll have to carry on alone."

Honey holds the Answer in her mouth. But before she can voice it, Mikha'el rushes into battle.

Mikha'el's flaming sword cuts through the air with righteous fury. But the Snake siphons his anger like soda through a straw. The fearsome blade breaks against the Snake's chest. With a laugh, the Snake hurls Mikha'el against the wall. The house shudders around them.

"Next?" The Snake is full of pride. He is so sure of himself and the Brotherhood's capacity to win.

Oya holds a lightning bolt sharpened by her rage. She flings it toward the Snake. He catches it in his mouth. For a dreadful moment he smiles again, and Honey can feel Snakes everywhere smiling. She knows what they're thinking: *Look at the pitiful ways these Lyrans fight. They never learn.*

Honey investigates the Source. It knew all the Lyran champions. Honey can see them breaking themselves against the cliffs of darkness, repeatedly. Ignoring the strength that light gives them.

"That is not the way!" Honey cries. She focuses on the staff and its connection to the Source.

This battle happening now, is not only here, in this house. It reverberates throughout the Many Worlds. She travels inwards and sends a message down the channel to the other Aspects battling other snakes.

Do not attack with hate, she warns them. *Do not attack at all. If you want to win embrace and absorb the Brotherhood's darkness.*

The Snake in Honey's house spits Oya's lightning bolt back at her, amplified with his own hatred. It impales her on the wall above Mikha'el.

As they struggle to recover, the Snake grabs Sekhmet's majestic mane. She does not struggle. He holds her to him like a lover and locks his jaws around her neck.

She does not whimper, not even when he punctures her throat and injects his venom.

Honey hears her soul sisters cry out. No one moves. They are rooted in their fear. They do not know what Honey does. He deals in illusions.

I will awaken them to the truth.

The Snake tosses Sekhmet's limp body at Honey's feet. He wipes his mouth in an obscene imitation of earthly satisfaction.

The others move now. They cluster around Sekhmet, who is devoid of light. Honey feels their grief.

This is not the way, either. Grieve not. He is not of this Earth. And neither are we. These rules don't apply to us.

Filoméla is on her knees, face buried in Sekhmet's hair, weeping. Forach is beside her, beginning to keen. Juana holds them both, to comfort them.

"No," Honey says. "The end is not the end. We don't have to play by these rules."

She calls to Mikha'el and Oya. "Let me show you the way."

She holds out the staff, vertically, to connect heaven to Earth. "We are enough. Through us, all things are connected."

She lowers it. "Lay your hands on the staff. Lean into the Source with me."

The others grab hold. They feel how the Source licks at them.

"Lean in," Honey says and closes her eyes.

It is a whirlpool, a waterslide, a riptide, a tsunami, a hurricane. It sweeps them up and whirls them together. The line of Sekhmet, the line of Mikha'el, and the line of Oya. Beyond them, among the Many Worlds, the Source flows into the other Aspects. The connection grows. The portals are opening.

Almost.

It is a mudslide, an earthquake, a volcanic eruption. It erases their edges and draws new borders. Around the universe, everything lost is falling back into place.

Hold tight.

It is a strong gale, a dust storm, a tornado, eroding any differences, and smashing them into bits. Like parts of a puzzle, the Aspects begin to fit together. Across the miles, the light years, the eras, the Many Worlds, they are all on the way to becoming whole.

We are so close.

It is a bolt of lightning, a wildfire, burning down the old growth to make room for new life. The cracks fill with gold. The broken parts knit together. Now everything is made whole, stronger and more beautiful than before.

Now!

All hands move with one mind. They drive the staff into the body of the first of the line of Sekhmet. As they do, her blood rushes up the staff, infusing it with new strength.

Sekhmet is with us now.

And beyond this world, the other Aspects are on their way.

"Lean in," Honey cries. "Stay together! Let us welcome the others in!"

They do.

The Source trembles as it expands.

Honey does not know where she ends, and the others begin.

There is no end and no beginning.

They are beyond the beginning and at the end.

They are past the end and at the beginning again.

Everything is turning, blending, and becoming whole.

We are becoming everything and nothing.

They open their eyes and behold. They know themselves. Across the Many Worlds, they connect and merge.

Here I am. We are the One.

With one final thrust, they raise the staff and bring it down once more. It sounds like a bell as it shatters.

The shards of a million pieces pierce the Snake. Through him, the light pierces through all Aspects of the Brotherhood. There is no corner of the Many Worlds the Lyrans do not pierce with their light. Where it shines, darkness shrinks.

It is no use trying to patch the holes, they are infinite in number. Yet in his shame, the Snake tries to hold his darkness in. It leaks through his hands, running oily and thick across the wooden floorboards.

They approach him and he cowers. But they gather him up in their strong arms. Whether he likes it or not, the light is coming in.

We love you.

He struggles against them, but they will not let go. They squeeze the darkness from his limbs. Where the light shines in, his shame, fear, and anger dissolve.

We accept you.

He bites and kicks. They hold him tighter and love him more. They suck the poison from his mind and lips. They accept and absorb it until it becomes a part of themselves.

They know that darkness can be useful. It can be beautiful. All this time they ran from it. Now they embrace it. Understanding it is essential to grasping the Answer.

We know you. You are one of us. We are part of you.

The Snake screams. He claws at them with his last shred of strength. They drink his anger up and turn it to honey. They rock him until he understands that there is nothing that is not meant to be. Nothing that cannot be of use, even the darkness he nursed and the division he sowed. He has lost his appetite. Why would he fight to keep to that thorny path when this one is so much sweeter?

Around the Universe, dark Aspects emerge. They shrink from the feeling of light on their cheeks. But they are caught. They can no longer turn away. The light cleanses and expands them. They come to know the power of the One. It no longer scares them. They recognize it in themselves. For the first time since the One became the many, all Aspects know love.

And that is the Answer.

There is a great sigh that sweeps the Many Worlds clean.

Everything is One.

The Lyrans and the Brotherhood unite.

The Snake in Honey's house is no longer what he was. Or rather, he's what he always was. But now, there's a chance for him to grow and evolve, for all of them to do better. To do things differently. Not as Lyran against Brotherhood, but as One, united, across the Many Worlds.

The Source shimmers over the small cabin in the woods. It is a beacon, signaling a time of New Peace. It is one of many lights burning in triumph across the Universe.

By the time Amy and Emily jump off the school bus, a victorious champion waits for them.

When they see Honey, they squeal in delight.

"Oh, we've missed you!" Emily gushes, throwing her arms around Honey's waist.

"Mommy!" Amy says, burying her head in Honey's skirts. "It's so good to see you."

Honey laughs. "It's only been a day. But I missed you, too." She embraces her flame-haired children. "I love you so much."

Emily reaches up a hand in surprise. "Oh, Mommy, your eyes!"

Honey lets Emily's hand land on her cheek. "Yes, my eyes . . . they've cleared."

"Can you see me?" Amy cries, bouncing up and down, anxious to be seen.

"Yes, darling," Honey kneels and cups her face with one hand. The other cradles something precious on her hip. "And you're even more beautiful than I imagined." She turns to Emily. "You have grown up so well and strong."

"How?" A little line forms between Emily's eyebrows. "How can you see now?"

"I'll tell you everything you need to know when we get home," Honey says. "There are so many mysteries to discuss, we should do it in front of a warm fire, not out here in the cold."

Amy claps her hands. She loves fireside cuddles. "Will there be hot cocoa?"

"Of course." Honey says. "And I have one more surprise."

Emily's eyes widen. "What is it?"

"A friend of mine has a treasure they cannot keep. They asked me if we might be able to help." Honey brings her little bundle forward. She delicately unwraps the blanket so the girls can see the baby's sleeping face. "Do you think we can welcome this little boy into our family and help him grow into a good man?"

"A baby?" The little girls reach for him. "He's ours to keep?" Amy said.

"Well, it's more complicated than that." Honey chuckles. "But I would like to adopt him and raise him as your brother. Would you like that?"

Emily claps. "Yes!"

Amy frowns. "Will your friend come back and take him away again?"

Honey shakes her head. "No. Not if we accept the responsibility of giving him a home." Honey lets them coo over him. They examine his perfect toes, wonder over his violet eyes, and pat his thick thatch of black hair. "We must take care of him and make sure he knows how loved he is. Do you think we can do that?"

"Oh, yes!" Emily gently touches the baby's cheek. "I've always wanted a brother!"

"He's so perfect." Amy kisses the baby's nose, and the faint glimmer of a smile crosses its lips.

"Oh!" Amy clasps her hands at her heart. "I love him already."

~ 104 ~

BOOK OF LYRAN, PART FIVE: THE CHILDREN OF THE GARDEN

The Great Creators did not stop with the Many Worlds. They brought into being a variety of life forms and creatures great and small. These they distributed among the Many Worlds, to populate them.

After this period of activity, the Aspects enjoyed a period of Great Peace. Connected as all things were to the Source, they lived in harmony.

The Aspects embraced the circle of life, death, and rebirth. However, they found their journey toward the Answer slow. Attracted to those Aspects with similar interests, they found their conversations lacked substance. They grew restless, fearing they would never discover the Answer if they were to continue in this way.

The Great Creators were thus the first to ask, *What if we fashioned creatures in our own image? Ones who had our power to reason and learn? Who could make their own discoveries and decisions, and act without us telling them what to do? Who might bear within them all possibilities rather than a single Aspect of the One? Would this not help us know more? If we were to engage in conversation with those unlike us, would we not be able to discover more quickly? Perhaps we could learn much by watching those who differ from us experience life in their own way.*

And the other Aspects of Light met in council and decided, *Yes: this would be good.*

And so, the Great Creators brought forth the first human beings, whom they raised up in Vega's garden city of Eden. They gave them diverse ways to gather knowledge. They had feelings and senses, reasoning and logic, heart and soul.

The Great Creators let these young beings develop without interference. They trusted that if their connection to the Source remained strong, they would need no other guidance. Throughout the Many Worlds, these beings became known as Children of the Garden.

During the Great Peace, humans flourished and multiplied. They acknowledged the divinity of their Lyran kin, calling them angels and gods. And Lyrans encouraged their human cousins to see the spark of the divine One in themselves.

And there was much love, joy, and unity between them.

The children born of unions between the Lyrans and the humans, carried with them a deep connection to the star seed that made them. They became known as the Ones of Love, or the Seraphim. Once their life was spent, they could choose to die the final death or be reborn a descendant of their Aspect's line.

The Brotherhood of the Snake also knew the Children of the Garden. They first encountered them on Vega in the days before the Great War. The offspring of these unions bore the serpentine look of their fathers and became known as the Nephilim. They also bore a deep connection to the star seed that made them. They were likewise given a choice after death to die or be reborn a descendant of their Aspect's line.

There were two lines of thought about how to treat the Children of the Garden. The Lyrans believed the children needed to develop at their own pace, in isolation. The Brotherhood did not agree. They introduced the Children of the Garden to fire and other inventions to speed up human evolution. The Brotherhood encouraged them to destroy as well as create, fight as well as love, and divide as well as unite.

Some of the Children of the Garden, disturbed by the violence and chaos sown by the Brotherhood, alerted the Great Creators that all was not right. When the Lyrans discovered what the Brotherhood had done, they felt a great heaviness in their hearts. They had believed that the human beings' connection to the Source would keep them pure. But it was not able to keep the Children of the Garden from embracing and doing evil.

When Vega was destroyed, some of the Lyrans escaped to the garden planet of Earth. They resettled the Children of the Garden there. The Brotherhood followed. And the battle continues there, as it does among the Many Worlds.

With one turn of the wheel, a Lyran champion might yet defeat the Brotherhood, awaken the Children to their divine connection to the Source, and open the channel that frees every Aspect still caught in-between the Many Worlds.

At this time, love will transform hatred, light will consume darkness, and all those who seek the truth shall be reborn. The hearts of the Children of the Garden will turn away from learned evils and embrace light once more.

In this era of New Peace, all the Aspects will return to the Source, and from the many, they will reunite and become One.

Guided by the light of the One, the Children of the Garden will be left alone in the Universe, to govern the Many Worlds with love and wisdom.

So may it be, so it ever was.

All is One.

L'dor v'dor, l'olam v'ed.

Epilogue

~ 105 ~

HONEY

The girls nuzzle around the baby like puppies. They haven't stopped mourning the loss of their father. But this small child reminds them of him, so they pour the love they bore their father into this baby. Honey reminds them not to smother him with it.

"He can't stay with you all night," Honey warns. "I'll have to put him in his crib eventually."

Amy's little face crinkles. "Why?"

"Because I don't want you to roll over and squish him in the middle of the night."

Emily cups the baby's bald head. "I won't squish him! I'll make sure Amy won't either."

Honey chuckles. "I'm sure he appreciates that, but he must learn to sleep alone. We don't always have the luxury of having love and warmth around us. Nights get lonely if don't know how to soothe yourself. That's why Amy's getting in her bed, too, as soon as story time's over."

Amy pouts.

"Do you want me to read you a book?" Honey enjoys the novelty of seeing the words and pictures.

"No," Amy says. "Tell us the story about Daddy again."

"Again?"

Emily claps her hands. "Oh, yes. Please! I miss him so much."

"Okay." Honey stretches out beside them and takes a moment to admire the way their faces shine in the dim light.

How lucky we all are. How blessed.

"Where is he now?" Emily asks. "In Heaven?"

Honey nods. It's easier to say that than explain what really happened.

"But he's not really gone," she says. "Every time we think of him, he's with us. Every time you recall a fun time with Daddy, remember that he's here, standing by your side. His memory will be a blessing. Hold that love you have for him in your heart and know he loves you very much. And he'll never stop loving you."

Amy whispers to the ceiling. "I love you Daddy. I miss you."

"I miss you, too, Daddy." Emily whispers. Then she asks, "Will we get to see him again?"

"In a way," Honey says. "We might see him reflected in your little brother."

Amy's face lights up. "Oh, Cian, did you hear that?"

Emily crooks a pudgy finger under his soft chin. "You're going to grow up big and strong."

"And good, like Daddy," Amy adds. "You're going to be a good man."

Honey swallows hard. It is a relief not to have Chad in the house. They all feel it. She wishes that he were as good as they remember him being. But he'll have the chance to be a better man this time around. Not that she'll ever burden Cian with the knowledge of who he was before.

But will he sense it? Will he remember parts of his life from before this?

That's something she'll have to wait and see about.

She pulls a book from the shelf and begins to read, mouthing the words while her mind wanders.

She thinks of all the other snakes overthrown during her turn of the wheel.

Are they all starting over like Cian? Under the care of Lyran descendants like me?

It's hard to know. The only people of the line she knows of are Regina and James, and they've only the one baby between them.

Emily begins to purr as she drifts off to sleep. Amy's nodding off, too.

Honey puts the book back on the shelf. She lifts Cian first, then Amy, balancing a child on each hip as she stumbles to Amy's room.

With the children tucked in, Honey can slip down the stairs and rejoin the adults in the living room.

Regina looks up as Honey crosses to her bedroom. "Are they asleep?"

"Yes."

James hands her a glass of wine. "How are you doing?"

Honey curls up on the couch, cupping her glass. "Good. Still adjusting." She laughs. "It's hard to believe what happened here. Now we do . . . what?"

"Live our lives," Regina says with a laugh.

James smiles at Honey, "Do you miss them?"

"My soul sisters? Yes. I know they're gone, but I feel like I still hear them. They'll always be part of me."

Regina sighs. "It's odd. Until you woke me up, I would have thought all those memories from my past lives were dreams or stories. Now that I know who I was . . . it's hard to reconcile Oya's line with who I know I am."

"Right." James laughs. "But even though you can't throw lightning bolts anymore, I still think you're badass."

Regina shakes her head. "I only got to taste that divinity for a moment, but what I wouldn't give to be able to do that again. It was awesome."

"Yeah," James says, a wistful note creeping into his voice, "I wouldn't mind being able to fly around the neighborhood. It'd make my job a lot easier."

Honey runs a finger along the edge of her glass. "Where do you think they are now? All the Lyran star seeds?"

"Home," James says.

Regina nods. "All part of the One."

A little crease forms between Honey's brows. "Do you still feel it? Your connection to the Source?"

James and Regina nod.

"Thank God. I thought I was going crazy."

"You're not crazy." Regina scootches closer on the couch to hug her tight. "You're one of the heroes who won the Great War."

"Welcome to the New Age of Peace." James smiles. "We turned the tide. And we will raise a million more heroes before we're done."

Regina glances up toward the bedroom where Cian lies slumbering. "I wonder how many snake babies there are in this generation?"

"There may be babies," Honey says. "But they're no longer snakes. The Brotherhood and the Lyrans are both gone."

"So, balance has been restored," James says. "Does that mean the darkness is gone for good?"

Honey shakes her head. "No. You can't get rid of darkness. That's what we kept getting wrong. The only way you can win the battle and shake its death grip is to accept it, love it, and acknowledge that darkness is just the other side of the coin. It's the other half, the missing piece that completes everything that we know to be of the light."

A thoughtful silence settles over them. Through the window, the Pleiades shine brightly against the night sky.

Regina is the first to speak. "It's hard to believe that the Lyrans and Brotherhood were simply various Aspects of the One. They fought each other for so long, so bitterly."

James shrugs. "It's easy to hate what's different if we don't understand it. Or ourselves."

Honey lets that thought hang there. She is grateful that she and Regina and James have found each other. Their Lyran Aspects have left them alone on Earth. But they still share a spark of the divine.

Honey sips her wine and enjoys the company of her soul family. The ones she's connected to on Earth and beyond.

She lays a head on Regina's shoulder. "How do we get the world to see it? The connection we all share?"

James thinks for a moment before speaking. "Love."

Regina nods. "Love. It's the only way to heal the world."

INSIGHTS, AUTHOR NOTES, AND MORE

DEAR READER

Thank you for the gift of your time and attention. If you enjoyed Song of Lyran, please tell others about it. Leaving a positive review on Amazon, Goodreads, Barnes & Noble, or wherever you purchased this edition is one of the best ways to support independent authors like myself. If you'd like to help spread the word further, recommending this book to others, or purchasing copies as gifts for individuals, libraries, or institutions helps so much. Song of Lyran can also be purchased for reading groups and book clubs.

If you'd like to stay in touch, I do love writing letters! You can send me one c/o PO Box 746, Sautee Nacoochee, GA 30571.

If you'd like to read more of my stories and thoughts, follow and engage with me @trulykristi on TikTok, YouTube, Instagram, Twitter, or Facebook. You can sign up for my Find Inspiration. Get Unstuck. Truly Kristi newsletter at www.kristicasey.com.

Thank you, God bless, and may you have an amazing journey.

Kristi Leigh Casey
Long Beach Island Township, New Jersey
June 4, 2022

PRONOUNCIATIONS

How you want to say the names in your head could be the right way. But if you're a stickler for accuracy, here's a pronunciation guide. The syllable in all caps is where the emphasis is.

- Sekhmet [sek-MET]
- Filoméla [fill-o-MAY-la]
- Forach [fur-ACH or fur-AH if you can't make the guttural CH sound]
- Juana [WAN-a]
- Honey [HUN-nee]
- Prōknē [PROHK-nee]
- Óengus [AN-gus]
- Ethnui [Ed-NA]
- Mikha'el [mick-a-AIL]
- Oya [OH-ya]
- Jeanne [ZHAN]
- Sidhe [SHE]
- Déisi [DAY-see]

HISTORICAL AND CREATIVE NOTES

Much of the symbolism in this book is inspired by or borrowed from Judaism and Jewish mysticism. Since the Hebrews were the OGs of monotheism, it seemed a fitting tribute to include them in a book celebrating the concept. Also, because the other two major religions, Christianity and Islam, are based on Jewish texts and ideas, doing so also opened the door to a space where the Brotherhood of this book might be able to manipulate meaning, exploit intent, and otherwise mislead good people attracted to the concepts but unfamiliar with the source context or culture.

You may have noticed that some of the names of groups differ from what you learned in history class. For example, instead of Egypt, I call the land Kemet and use older names for the capital cities, because those are the names the Egyptians used. The Jewish tribes appear as Ivrim, which is what the Egyptians called them during that time. Similarly, the names of the women of Sekhmet's line and the people in their lives—all of whom are inspired by figures from history or myth—are spelled as they would have been known in those times. That is why Forach is not spelled Foreach and Filoméla does not appear as the more familiar Philomela.

One of the fascinating elements of Judaism is the value of each letter of the Hebrew alphabet, which give each word a deeper meaning than when it is spoken aloud or translated. For example, the letters het and yud in the word chai (חי), which means life, have a value of eighteen when added to together. Because of this, it's customary for those of the Jewish faith to give gifts in increments of eighteen to symbolically bless the recipient with the gift of a good, long life.

In the faux-religious book within this book, it is mentioned that the Aspects will be called back when the last turn of the wheel is completed. The value of that epoch is given as 25,776 years. People familiar with astronomy might wonder why I set it there rather than at 25,772 or 36,000 years. Those numbers are generally thought of as being the Great Year or Platonic Year, which is the time it takes the Earth equinoxes to complete one turn around the ecliptic, or for the sun, moon, and planets to travel to the same place you see them in now, respectively. It's because I wanted the number to be divisible by eighteen.

The choice of women of Sekhmet's line was a combination of art and science. When I was 19 years old, I had a vision, much like the one described in the first Honey chapter, during which I saw the faces of all the people I'd ever been, including one who had the head of a lion. They were all so different, but the one thing that bound us all was that we all possessed the same eyes.

A conversation with my friend Randall Harr, decades later, inspired me to take that vision and turn it into a longer narrative. If you enjoyed this story, you should thank Randall for putting the idea into my head that this was a story worth telling.

When I sat down to draft this book, I made a grid of all the women I remembered seeing along with potential birthplaces, cultures, and other half-remembered clues from that vision. I then chose a handful that I felt the strongest connection to, anchored them to real or mythic women who had similar enough facts to tie them to the story I wanted to tell and began to weave this narrative together.

The Brotherhood of the Snake was inspired by some of the QAnon conspiracy stories I heard second-hand during the pandemic. *What if the truly evil people were the ones who accused the innocent of what they, themselves, were guilty of?* So I played with this idea of misdirection and the concept of history vs. 'her-story' spiraled out from there.

If you are curious to learn more about the women featured in this story, search for Sekhmet and Nefertiti, Philomela and Ovid, Foreach and the exile of the Déisi people in Ireland, Sor Juana Ines de la Cruz and her friendship with Carlos de Siguenza, and talk to any unhappily married woman in present-day America. You might discover interesting similarities and more than a few creative departures to the characters who appear on these pages. After all, this is a fictional work of my imagination.

What I did not invent or elaborate on can be found via Google or Wikipedia search (Author's plea: Please donate to Wikipedia!). If you're curious to see more notes and source material I used for this book, visit kristicasey.com.

Although this is a creative work, I do think it is worthy to reexamine what we've inherited and assumed is a fact. After all, we know that the victors wrote history. Even religious texts have socio-political reasons for being. What, then, is the truth? We may never know. All we can do is hope to find the Answer we're looking for in this life. Stay curious and have fun exploring!

READING GROUP GUIDE

1. *Song of Lyran* is told from the perspective of five women—Sekhmet, Filoméla, Forach, Juana, and Honey. Whose story did you find most compelling, and why?
2. Each of the women represents a new incarnation of the same Aspect of the One. How did the soul of Sekhmet's line evolve as it moved from Sekhmet to Honey? What is one lesson each woman learned during her lifetime?
3. Kristi Casey draws inspiration from history and terrestrial/extraterrestrial mythologies. Were you familiar with any of these elements before reading *Song of Lyran*? If so, which elements? Which elements were new to you? What did you learn? Which elements do you want to investigate further?
4. In this novel, the Brotherhood of the Snake edits and promotes one-sided versions of the truth. Can you name a historical or religious story that might have a different 'her-story?' How would the 'her-story' version differ from the traditional story?
5. The women of Sekhmet's line live in different eras. What are some ways in which their lives were similar? What are some of the differences? How did the role of women evolve during the line's evolution to present day? Do women have more freedoms now than they did in other eras? Why/why not?
6. Why do you think this book is called *Song of Lyran*? Elements of music include rhythm, vocalization, patterns, repetition, and vibration. What are some of the ways Casey used these elements throughout this novel?

7. Casey created a faux-religious text—*Book of Lyran*—for this novel. The contents of this 'scroll' are distributed throughout the book. What did you discover about the line of Sekhmet, their mission, and the Lyran people from reading it? What would have happened to those discoveries if you read it all at the beginning or end of the novel?
8. Why do you think the Brotherhood of the Snake was so difficult to defeat? Chad says that everything comes from darkness, which is why they're stronger than the light. Would you agree with this statement? Why or why not?
9. Sekhmet possessed tremendous strength and the ability to channel energy. Mikha'el had the gift of flight and a flaming sword. Oya could control the weather and fashion bolts of lightning. Which two gifts would you like to have, if you were an Aspect of the One? What would you like your mission in life to be? If your life were to end tomorrow, what would the Answer you've discovered be?
10. Song of Lyran told the story of one Aspect's line. If we followed Mikha'el or Oya's line, which historical figures could have been their incarnations? Who might have been in the line of Aron or Yeshua?

ACKNOWLEDGMENTS

This book would never have existed if it were not for the Akimbo Writing in Community (WIC3) workshop. By the time I enrolled in October 2021, I was used to writing every day—I'd been doing it consistently for nearly five years—but I'd never experienced the power of writing with other people. What a difference, committing to showing up for 220+ days, posting, reading, supporting others, and finding support with hundreds of writers all running the same marathon as me!

Prior to joining the workshop, writing was something I did after my child was asleep, work ended, and no one else needed me. I stole the time to write from the margins of my life. In contrast, the WIC3 community gave me permission to make my writing a priority. They connected me to people I could discuss writing with every day. Having their support and feedback with every new post gave me the courage to make my writing central to my way of life.

From my original assigned @eastern4 cohort, I expanded the community of people I read, engaged with, and received feedback from every day. These generous writers included the lyrical poets and writers of @Nightingale, the publishing-minded @Woodchuck group, the spiritual duality of the @SnowLion/@SnowMonkey seekers, and the sci-fi/fantasy writers of @RedSquirrel. Within these groups, there are special people I need to mention as they became core pillars of support. Scott Lowe, Abbey Spiro, Stacey Mayo, and Heather Button were the people I relied on most to be there for me every day, and whose posts I never missed. Other writers I adored for the support, comments, and inspiration they gave me include my "love bug" Russell John, Melissa Kalinowski, Mars Jonez, Cindy Villanueva, Frauke Kasper, Paula Kusinska, Benjamin Boekweg, Mark Brement, Annette Mason, Salman Ansari, Suzyn Gonzalez, Annie Keeling, Micheleina Charles Hazelle, Angus Lockyer, Richard Stegman, Julie Hughes, Ross Shults, Iczel Katz, Debbie Mourey, Karen Collins, Shannon Turner, Lyn Garcia, Andi Hall, Jane Hardjono, Leah Caplan, Katy Dalgleish, Sarah Bronson, Carol Arcus, Mark Brement, Trent Selbrede, and Jay Juhl. If I missed you, blame my memory, not my lack of love. I really appreciated your feedback, encouragement, and support. Especially when I hit a wall, it was invaluable to have such a wealth of voices cheering me on for the 220+ days we worked side by side.

Thank you Seth Godin and Kristin Hatcher, for creating the Akimbo WIC3 workshop space where I could show up, create, connect, and commit to ship my first novel. I appreciate you and, especially Kristin, for making Writing in Community happen. Showing up, every day, and putting in the work is a discipline I encourage every writer to adapt. Community is the secret sauce to making magic happen.

Once the challenging work of laying down the notes of this song was done, the agonizing process of editing and pre-production began. Fellow Akimbo writers Dr. James Jap, David Berry, and Joann Malone reviewed the outline of this novel and asked great questions that helped me tighten up its structure. My intrepid beta readers Dr. Joy Berry, Stephanie Horlock, Phoebe Tam, Jennifer Lightbody, Sue Pidgeon, and Diane Casey read my first draft and gave me feedback and suggestions on how to make it better. If the cover influenced you at all to buy this book, then you (like me) must thank Jenny Schisler Hinely (a.k.a., Mighty 44) for the concept and my child Lex Sanders for creating the cover art. Additional thanks are due to my editor Zena Shapter, who helps me discover the best ways to shape the stories I want to tell. And Danger Amy Andrews—thank you for suggesting that Honey have a physical challenge. I can't imagine what this story would have been like without her blindness.

The final push to get this book published came while on a thirty-day RV odyssey with my parents. In the middle of a Casey family reunion, I uploaded and proofread the copy surrounded by one of the world's greatest families. Thanks Caseys for always being open to adventure and welcoming people in. "Inappropriate humor for the win!" RIP Uncle Gene: I'm glad you were first on the boat, in the best way.

Since this book is about love, I've saved the best and most heartfelt thanks for last. My Grandpa Joe and Grandma Bunny Shore taught me that there is always money for books, and they supported my reading habit generously for many happy years. My Mom and Dad—Diane and Tom Casey—allowed that escapist love to grow and always supported and believed in me, even when I didn't believe in myself. And, Diane Casey is a phenomenal proofreader. Great teachers I had, like Robin McConnell, Winnifred Thomas, Eugene Attaway, Phil Campbell, Bud Beyer, and Paul Edwards taught me how to express myself and find greater meaning in text. If you enjoy how I tell stories, thank them.

John Adams, thank you for making me laugh and letting me share my visions with you as they tumbled out of me onto the page. I really appreciate you taking care of and fixing the physical world around me so I could focus on creating this imaginary one. I treasure your generosity.

Writing is a solitary art, but I did have two constant companions. Our late, great family dog, Charlie Tango introduced me to the magic of strolls in dark woods. His insistence on regular walks helped engrave many of Honey's experiences on my heart and inspired the idea of falling into an in-between world, which I often felt was happening as we rambled. His successor, Bubs (a.k.a. our sausage dog of love) was my main snuggle buddy. The first drafts of many of these chapters were typed while he snored in my lap.

I owe many thanks to my Stxrlight child, Lex Sanders, who sets the world on fire every day with her brilliance. Lex: my love for you has no beginning or end. You will always be the best thing I've ever done. You are a constant source of inspiration. Thank you for choosing me to be your Mom. And for understanding when I need to write (even when you don't want to). I love you, baby.

Last, but not least, thank you, Dear Reader, for picking up this book and taking the time to read it! May you find the place and space in your life to shine the way you were meant to, love and be loved in the way you deserve, and find joy in the practice of living, forever and ever. Amen.

KRISTI CASEY delights in creating communities, telling tales, making art, dancing all night, wandering through the woods, and singing her heart out. SONG OF LYRAN is her first published work of fiction, but she's written thousands of print and digital articles for business, travel, and arts publications over the years. She's also the author of the official history of Atlanta's Fox Theatre, THE FOX THEATRE: ATLANTA, GEORGIA: THE MEMORY MAKER.

In a former life, she traveled the world performing as an actress and an improviser. One of the more prestigious gigs she had involved working with Boom Chicago in Amsterdam during its golden age, alongside future stars like Seth Meyers and Jordan Peele, and *Ted Lasso* creators Brendan Hunt and Joe Kelly. The women were as brilliant, you just don't know their names yet. One day, perhaps, you will care more about them and what they've created, because Nicole Parker, Becky Drysdale, and Lauren Dowden are superstars. For that matter, so are Amy Andrews, Adrianne Frost, and Suz Stone, with whom Kristi had the great honor of playing with at comedy festivals in the U.S. and New Zealand as part of the legendary all-female improv group GOGA. A graduate of Northwestern University, she's living proof that it doesn't matter what your degree is, if you follow your curiosity, trust your gut, and work hard, you'll find a way to make an honest living that won't shrink your soul.

A Georgia girl born and bred, Kristi now calls the North Georgia mountains her home. There, she gives birth to new worlds and mischief. She also dispenses advice on how to get unstuck through Truly Kristi. To sign up for her newsletter visit getunstuck.kristicasey.com. You can learn more about the author, this book, and other projects she's working on at kristicasey.com.

Kristi Casey is on Twitter, Facebook, TikTok, Instagram and YouTube as @trulykristi.

Remember: not all readers are leaders, but all leaders are readers. You got this.